"The ship was alive with the lives of those beings who trod her decks."

Aaron Peyser: "spineless" son-in-law of a rich merchant, suddenly called upon to lead the passengers.

Rabbi Einhorn: committed to the faith in life his religion decrees, yet beginning to lose faith in himself.

Carl Bender: Berlin psychiatrist who has detached himself from human involvement, especially from his Aryan wife, JULIA.

They are trapped with a thousand others in the floating prison the *Franz Joseph* has become—awaiting the decisions of others far away, making agonizing decisions of their own as suspense grows and despair alternates with hope. The weak tremble, the daring devise desperate plans, the hopeless contemplate suicide, and many discover within themselves identities from which there is no flight. . . .

THE VOYAGE OF THE FRANZ JOSEPH was originally published by G. P. Putnam's Sons.

Other books by James Yaffe

Poor Cousin Evelyn and Other Stories
The Good-for-Nothing
What's the Big Hurry?
Nothing but the Night
Mister Margolies
Nobody Does You Any Favors
The American Jews

James Yaffe

•

THE VOYAGE
of the
FRANZ JOSEPH

PUBLISHED BY POCKET BOOKS NEW YORK

THE VOYAGE OF THE FRANZ JOSEPH

G. P. Putnam edition published June, 1970
Pocket Book edition published July, 1971

This *Pocket Book* edition includes every word
contained in the original, higher-priced edition. It is printed
from brand-new plates made from completely reset, clear, easy-to-read
type. *Pocket Book* editions are published by Pocket Books, a division
of Simon & Schuster, Inc., 630 Fifth Avenue, New York, N.Y. 10020.
Trademarks registered in the United States and other countries.

To I. G.
In friendship

. . . the ship, a fragment detached from the earth, went on lonely and swift like a small planet. . . . She had her own future; she was alive with the lives of those beings who trod her decks; like that earth which had given her up to the sea, she had an intolerable load of regrets and hopes . . . like the earth, she was unconscious, fair to see—and condemned by men to an ignoble fate. The august loneliness of her path lent dignity to the sordid inspiration of her pilgrimage.

JOSEPH CONRAD
The Nigger of the Narcissus

NOTE

In the spring of 1939 the German liner *St. Louis* sailed from Hamburg with nearly one thousand Jewish refugees aboard. During the weeks that followed, these people searched desperately for some free nation willing to give them a haven. The central action of this novel was suggested by that search.

This is entirely a work of fiction, however. I have not felt myself bound to reproduce either the details or the outcome of the actual voyage. I have not hesitated to invent incidents that never occurred. None of my characters is knowingly based on any of the passengers or crew who sailed on the *St. Louis*—or, with one exception, on any of the people in the outside world who became involved in its fate.

THE VOYAGE
of the
FRANZ JOSEPH

ONE

IN the early summer of 1939 the American Jewish Defense
Agency—known as AJDA—celebrated its fortieth anniversary. A gala dinner was held in the second-floor banquet
room of the Plaza Hotel. A hundred and fifty specially invited guests, each of whom had paid a hundred dollars
per plate, sat at the round tables that filled the room. At the
long table in front were the guests of honor, the speakers,
and other important people.

The master of ceremonies for this occasion was the president of AJDA, former United States Senator Samuel L.
Friedkin. Among those who sat with him at the table of
honor were Judge Simeon Goodfreund of the state appellate
court, a stern patriarchal figure, very active in Jewish causes
and famous for his inexhaustible stock of dialect jokes;
Benjamin Zuckerman, the chairman (and also the only
Jewish member) of the board of the Continental Radio
Network; Rabbi H. Louis Littauer, spiritual leader of the
largest and wealthiest Reform congregation in New York;
Mrs. Sylvia Fingerhood, the department store owner's widow,
an indefatigable fund raiser, not only for AJDA but for
a dozen other Jewish groups; and, in a place of special
honor, the retired nose-and-throat specialist Dr. Jacob Meier,
who would soon be ninety-two years old and was all that
remained of AJDA's original founders.

Among those who did not sit at the table of honor were
most of the people—bright young sociologists, political
scientists, statisticians, and trained welfare workers—who
set the policies, made the decisions, and did the work that
kept AJDA going. These included Dan Wechsler, the executive director, an administrative genius who earned every
penny of his twenty thousand a year; Al Margolinski, once
head of the division investigating anti-Semitic propaganda,
now chief of the new Department of Refugee Affairs; and

1

his two assistants, Bernard Kramer and Morris Feldman. These men and other staff members of equal responsibility sat at one table in the back of the room, where the speakers' voices barely carried and the waiters made infrequent appearances.

After a while Morrie Feldman stopped straining his ears to hear the speakers. He already knew pretty much what they had to say; he himself had supplied most of their facts and figures. He gave himself up to the familiar nagging thoughts he had been having lately about his relationship with this organization.

Morrie was twenty-nine years old, and he had been brought up in a section of Brooklyn where there wasn't much money but plenty of the old-fashioned Jewish virtues. He had been taught to love his family, study hard at school, stay out of fights, and feel an obligation to those less fortunate than himself. And he had continued to feel that obligation even after he grew up. He graduated from CCNY, got his master's degree from the Columbia University School of Social Work, and went straight to AJDA.

Nothing could have pleased him more, because in his eyes AJDA stood for everything he most fervently believed in. It had been founded in 1899 by a dozen pillars of New York City's old established German Jewish community. Their purpose was to bring relief and hope to the increasingly large numbers of immigrants from East Europe who were fleeing starvation and pogroms and pouring into the United States. To carry out this purpose AJDA advanced money for boat passages, set up soup kitchens, distributed free clothing, sponsored English-language classes, established settlement houses in the slums. In the early nineteen twenties, when East European immigration was cut off by act of Congress, AJDA turned its attention to other, equally worthy causes— fighting anti-Semitism through delicate behind-the-scenes appeals to influential people; promoting better understanding with the Christian world by sponsoring dinners at which the guest speakers were prominent Catholic or Protestant clergymen; publishing its great series of sociological studies and statistical surveys of American Jewish attitudes. And in the early thirties, with the advent of Hitler and his persecution of Germany's Jews, AJDA became deeply involved in the refugee problem. It established its Department of Refugee Affairs, whose function was not only to provide for Hitler's

2

victims once they entered the United States but to bring in more of them by offering them financial aid, vouching for them on quota applications, and petitioning the United States government to liberalize its immigration policies.

In short, there was no organization—so Morrie told himself when he got the job—which could offer better opportunities to somebody with his ideals and ambitions.

In his first three years with AJDA he had been made to grind away at bread-and-butter duties. He had realized that they were necessary, and he had never complained, but he hadn't got much satisfaction out of them. Then, two years ago, the Department of Refugee Affairs was formed, and Morrie was immediately filled with the desire to become a part of it. He didn't know Al Margolinski too well, but he went to him anyway and pleaded for the chance to work under him. When Al agreed to take him on, Morrie walked on air for weeks. At last he would be doing what he had wanted to do all along—he would be dealing directly with people who neded help.

It wasn't long, though, before he was back on solid earth again. His duties with the new department turned out to be not much different from what his old duties had been. They consisted mainly in digging up statistics and interpolating them into reports; then Al would turn those reports into hard-hitting rhetoric and hand them out to the press, or get them printed in elegant brochures for distribution to the members, or stuff them into the mouths of the distinguished speakers whom Al referred to as "our stable of fan dancers." Morrie's hopes for his new job had been high, but here he was, two years later, sitting at another banquet, eating overdone steak, listening to speeches he had heard a thousand times before—and reflecting on the discouraging fact that after all this time with the Department of Refugee Affairs, he still hadn't set eyes on a real live refugee.

In the middle of Judge Goodfreund's speech—the main speech of the evening, and it seemed to go on forever—a waiter came up and told Al that he was wanted on the telephone. Al left the table and didn't come back until the judge had finished and Senator Friedkin was paying a tribute to old Dr. Meier.

Al whispered in Dan Wechsler's ear, and Dan's solemn expression showed Morrie that something important was up. Then Al took his seat again and said to Morrie, "There's an

3

emergency. We'll have to go to the office after this is over tonight."

"Tonight." Ruth would be upset, Morrie thought. He had been working late an awful lot in the last few weeks. Ruth never accused him, as her mother did, of getting "too emotionally involved" in his job, of forgetting his obligations to his wife and his children; she always told him how proud she was to have a husband who wanted more out of life than just piling up money, who wanted to "make a contribution." But still, he knew it wasn't much fun for her when she had to spend her nights alone.

"What's it all about?" Morrie said. "Can't it wait till tomorrow?"

"If it could, it would." Al turned to Bernie Kramer. "We'll need you, too."

"Al, I have to get back to Mount Vernon tonight." Bernie was in his fifties and had been with AJDA for a long time. He did a lot of complaining—though Morrie had never heard him complain about working under a man ten years his junior.

"Call Millie and tell her you're staying in town. I'll put you up on the sofa in my place." Al's divorce had come through a few months ago; he had a lot of room in his apartment.

"Have a heart, will you. Tomorrow's my day to fix breakfast so that Millie can sleep late."

"Tell Millie it's for humanity. She'll be happy to give up sleep for such a worthy cause."

Bernie shook his head a while longer, then he gave a sigh and said, "All right, I'll be there. The sacrifices I make—"

Rabbi Littauer rose to his feet to deliver the benediction. Everybody else got up, too. Heads were bowed, piously or awkwardly. As usual, Morrie wasn't quite sure what to do with his hands.

"Grant us peace, Thy most precious gift, Thou eternal source of peace—"

It was a beautiful prayer, but the rabbi couldn't leave it alone. When he got to where it should have ended, he kept adding names for the Lord to bless. Our beloved United States of America. Our fellow Jews in Germany enduring their martyrdom in silent dignity. Our sorely tried leader, President Franklin D. Roosevelt . . .

Morrie let his mind wander. Was Ruth's mother right

about him? *Was* he too emotionally involved in his job? Whenever she said this, he dismissed the idea with a shrug. But wasn't this pretty much what Al was always saying to him, too? Whenever Morrie got indignant at some instance of hardship or injustice, Al would give one of his laughs that was hardly more than a grunt. "Okay, okay," he would say, "there are nasty wicked people in the world, and you'd like to wave your magic wand and make them all see the light. You're an optimist. You've got the all-men-are-basically-good disease—the most pernicious piece of mythology ever invented. It leads to brotherly love, and brotherly love leads to—a knife in the back. So don't bring your bleeding heart around *this* office. We can't use it. It just gets in the way."

It was hard for Morrie to believe that Al really felt the same about working for AJDA as he would have felt about working for some business organization. And yet—maybe Al was absolutely right. Maybe all that "emotional involvement" was nothing but kid stuff, and you have to be uninvolved, objective, even cold if you want to do the job efficiently.

"Amen," said Rabbi Littauer.

"Amen," said the crowd. Then chairs were pushed back, voices were raised, people headed for the doors.

Morrie called Ruth from a phone booth in the lobby. He apologized for not coming home, and of course she didn't say one word of reproach—which made it worse. He hung up the phone and followed Al and Bernie out to the front of the hotel.

It was raining, one of those vicious, slashing New York rains that seems to have a personal grudge against the city. The streets were streaked and dirty, windshield wipers flapped madly, people huddled under their dripping umbrellas. Like a damp preview of hell, Morrie thought. The civilized world was falling to pieces—Spain, Austria, Czechoslovakia, piece by piece it was crumbling away. If the moment of horror ever came to New York, surely it would be on a rainy night like this. Yes, he could imagine the scene—the Storm Troopers marching up Fifth Avenue, goose-stepping past the Plaza fountain and Bergdorf Goodman, while the rain beat down on the silent faces of the crowd lining the street.

A cab pulled up to the hotel. Morrie, Al, and Bernie rode down to their office building in the east forties. This time of night the building was deserted. They had to run the elevator themselves up to the tenth floor, which was occupied solely by AJDA offices. With nobody there but the three of them, the place semed strange to Morrie, kind of unearthly. No typewriters clacking, no voices shouting, no feet pounding along the corridors. It was like a graveyard, and the black cover on the receptionist's typewriter was like a shroud.

My God, this was really his night to be morbid! He couldn't understand why. Was it that anniversary dinner? Had he finally heard one boring speech too many and decided that humanity was doomed?

They went to Al's private office. Al settled into the chair behind the desk, leaned back, and clasped his hands behind his head. He looked relaxed, sloppy, indolent, as he often did. In reality, Morrie thought, he was about as indolent as a tiger waiting in ambush.

"Okay, let's get down to it," Al said.

* * *

The *Franz Joseph* was a German cruise ship owned and operated by the Hamburg Line. It was built in the early years of this century, at a time when friendship with Austria was a cornerstone of German diplomatic policy. With much fanfare the ship was named after the Kaiser's royal Hapsburg ally, who returned the compliment by calling one of his racehorses Wilhelm Hohenzollern.

In the twenties the *Franz Joseph* was one of several ships used by the Hamburg Line for luxury cruises to New York and then to ports in the Caribbean. But after Hitler came to power, the bottom dropped out of the German cruise business. Anti-Nazi feeling hadn't crystallized yet in America, but it existed as a kind of subliminal uneasiness. People who wanted a good time on a cruise somehow felt, without thinking it through, that they'd rather not take a German ship.

In 1934, therefore, the Hamburg Line found it necessary to take on a new type of cargo—refugees. By special arrangement with the Nazi government, it sold passages on several of its luxury ships, including the *Franz Joseph*, to German Jews who wanted to get out of the country and had entry visas to foreign ports. This turned out to be a lucrative business, even with the government taking its percentage. Naturally passengers of this type could be made to pay a great deal more than ordinary holidaygoers.

This trade flourished from 1934 to 1938, with the *Franz*

6

Joseph making twelve trips to New York and certain Latin American ports. Then Hitler put a stop to it, declaring that it was contrary to the interests of the Reich for any more Jews to leave the country; the interests of the Reich, he said, must come before private interests. Not surprisingly, the Hamburg Line was displeased at this decision. It had some powerful men behind it and applied considerable pressure on the government, but Hitler held firm. As Al said, "Even his worst enemies have to admit that he's a man of principle."

Early in April, 1939, however, Hitler reversed himself. He agreed to let the Hamburg Line carry another load of Jews, one thousand of them, as long as they could find some foreign country to give them visas on short notice. There was much speculation as to why Hitler had changed his mind. The most plausible theory, in the light of later events, suggested that he was getting ready to launch some large-scale military action that could have international repercussions. It was important to him that the men behind the Hamburg Line should give him their full cooperation when the crisis came.

Now that Hitler's permission was secured, the Hamburg Line made discreet inquiries at various embassies in an effort to find a country that would take in those thousand Jews. This wasn't an easy task, for most of the countries of Europe, South America, and North America had stringent immigration laws which they weren't eager to relax; there were too many refugees floating around the world already. Eventually, however, the Hamburg Line got an affirmative response from the Republic of Cuba. Its administration was more flexible than that of older, more established states; it agreed to issue visas to a thousand people, at the equivalent of one hundred and fifty dollars each, provided that these people could guarantee they wouldn't stay in Cuba longer than one year. Nobody could qualify for such a visa, in short, unless he had already applied for immigration to some other country and had received a quota number which was scheduled to come up before the middle of 1940.

There were many such people in Germany, many more than a thousand. Most of them had United States quota numbers, though by May, 1939, they had long given up any hope of being allowed to leave the country. It is just possible to imagine their feelings when they read their letters from

7

the Hamburg Line inviting them to apply for passage on the *Franz Joseph*. Within a week, however, the list had been narrowed down to a thousand. Most of the names were eliminated by one simple circumstance. After six years of Nazism, the resources of the German Jews were exhausted. In big cities they were crowded into ghettos and forced to pay exorbitant rents; in small towns they were ostracized by their neighbors, their stores boycotted, their professional services rejected. Few of them were permitted to earn salaries, few of them had property not yet confiscated by the government, few of them had any savings left. It was impossible for most of them to raise the money necessary for visas and passage—approximately five hundred dollars. That a thousand of them did manage to do the impossible—through hidden hoards, contributions smuggled in from relatives outside the country, and in a few cases help from non-Jewish friends within the country—must be considered a kind of miracle.

Then followed a period of dreadful anxiety. Every day the status of the *Franz Joseph* seemed to change. The sailing was off again, on again, off again; but finally the last piece of red tape was cut. Near the end of June the word came officially: In twenty-four hours the *Franz Joseph* would definitely set sail. This was the news which Al had received by phone—through certain private sources in the Hamburg Line's New York office—during AJDA's anniversary dinner.

"And now, gentlemen," Al said, leaning forward in his chair, "let's see how AJDA and our department come into this situation. Up to now, both the Cuban government and the Nazis have kept the voyage of the *Franz Joseph* under wraps. The Cubans because whoever stands to rake in the profits from the sale of those visas doesn't want to go shares with too many of his fellow public servants. The Nazis because Hitler is anxious right now to keep his image untarnished; nobody should say that his holy war against the Jews can be subverted by money. So no public announcements of the sailing have been made. As far as I know, AJDA is the only American Jewish organization that's got the information.

"Now, that means we've got to act fast. Just as soon as that ship docks in Havana, those people will need help and need it badly. The Nazis are letting them out with one suitcase and five German marks apiece. They'll have no place to sleep, hardly any changes of clothing, not even the price of their first three meals. I don't have to tell you what a mess it'll be if some organization isn't on the spot to help them—prepared, if necessary, to keep them alive until their U.S. quota numbers come up. And it's obvious that AJDA has to do that job. First thing tomorrow we'll contact some other Jewish groups, and they'll cooperate all they can, but let's face it, the big Jewish money in this country is still the old German money—nobody except AJDA can mount an expensive operation like this one."

Al paused, then gave a grunt. "Incidentally, I don't mind admitting that this could be vital to the future of our department. As you may or may not realize, we're under a lot of pressure these days. At the board meeting last week Ben Zuckerman and some of the other diehards were asking how we could justify such a big budget for refugee affairs when the number of refugees is dropping. Dan put up a fight for us, naturally, and that kept the majority in line, but who knows what could happen the next time? Our best insurance is to do a damn good job with the *Franz Joseph* business!"

Then Al reached into a drawer of his desk and brought out a thick white envelope. "Now here's something else I got from my private sources. This came in a couple of days ago, but I didn't know till tonight just when I'd be using it."

From the envelope he pulled several sheets of folded paper. "This is a list of passengers who'll be sailing on the *Franz Joseph,* along with their quota numbers and the names and addresses of the people who are sponsoring their entry into this country—mostly relatives and business connections. Your job, Bernie, is to get in touch with these sponsors and find out how much they can do in the way of providing money, clothing, and so on for the refugees. That'll give us some idea what's left for *us* to do. Now, while you're working on that, Dan and the Senator and I will be meeting with some of our big contributors, getting provisional pledges to underwrite the project—"

"A thousand people," Bernie said, shaking his head over the list of names. "I'll tell you honestly, I don't know how long it'll take—"

"The *Franz Joseph* docks at Havana on Wednesday morning, so you'll have to finish that list by Monday."

"That would mean working night and day! Millie made

me go for a checkup last month, and the doctor told me I should get my full allowance of rest—"

"When this job is over, you can go to bed for a week."

"Maybe I could give Bernie a hand," Morrie said. "If we divided the list in half—"

"You won't be around," Al said. "You'll be in Cuba." He gave one of his sour grins. "Close your mouth, I'm not your dentist. *Somebody* has to go down there and set things up—find out what facilities are available, buy supplies, make arrangements with the authorities. Everything has to be ready by the time the ship comes in—that's your responsibility. Draw some money from the emergency fund tomorrow morning, and we'll get you on a plane tomorrow afternoon. We've got a good contact down there, by the way, an expert who can be very helpful to you. She'll meet your plane—"

"It's pretty short notice, Al," Morrie said, thinking how upset Ruth was going to be.

"Short notice! My God, you ought to be jumping for joy. Isn't this what you've been kvetching about for the last two years? You're finally going to see some refugees."

*　　*　　*

At three in the morning they left the AJDA offices. For three hours Al had gone over the Cuban plans in detail, and another session was scheduled for ten o'clock.

The rain had stopped. The streets were wet and sleek, empty of cars and people. A cool breeze stirred the air. Morrie decided to walk home; it was only ten blocks, and his head needed clearing. He wouldn't get much sleep tonight, anyway; he had too many things to think about. So he left Al and Bernie in front of the building waiting for a stray cab to wander by.

As he walked, he started thinking about Ruth again. When she heard about Cuba, she would be in a terrible state. She might even end up sobbing a little—in the dark, of course, hoping he wouldn't hear. Ordinarily there was nothing he wouldn't do for her when she turned on the tears.

But he wouldn't call off this trip. No matter how miserable it made her, he wouldn't give up this chance. He would be sorry to see her unhappy, but not sorry enough to lose this excitement, this exultation, almost, which had been growing in him for the last few hours. When the moment a man's been waiting for all his life finally comes to him, he can't pay much attention to a crying woman.

Al was all wrong, he told himself. There *were* such things as magic wands; brotherly love *didn't* always lead to a knife in the back. People could be helped, could be changed—the world could be made better.

He came to his building. In a few minutes the ordeal with Ruth would begin. So he stopped under the awning, shut his eyes, and gave himself up for a moment to visualizing the *Franz Joseph* and all those people moving up its gangway, moving up to a new life, leaving the horror behind them forever. And he was going to be part of that. He was going to *do* something at last.

TWO

THE ship tied to the pier on that beautiful June day looked like an illustration in a children's storybook. Silver water sparkled all around it. Its twin smokestacks, gleaming with new coats of white paint, rose gracefully against a blue and cloudless sky. Strings of pennants, red and yellow and green, fluttered in the breeze. And crowning it all, higher than anything else on the ship, the swastika gaily danced.

The members of the ship's band—eleven men and a lady harpist—were gathered on the shady part of the quarterdeck, seated on folding chairs. Their leader, bandmaster Edelmann, stood in front of them, tall and impressive, with his great black mustache and his military bearing. He kept an eye on the gangway down below. As soon as the first passenger set foot on that gangway, Edelmann lifted his stick, and the band launched into its rousing arrangement of "Vienna, City of my Dreams."

As he moved his stick up and down in time to the music, Edelmann looked almost like a drill sergeant putting his platoon through a dress parade. Even the grin on his face—the same affable grin that he conscientiously assumed every night when the nightclub was full of dancers—couldn't make him look one bit less military. And like everything else he conducted, including the lastest rhumbas and tangos, "Vienna, City of my Dreams" came out sounding something like a march.

Heinrich Muller, the ship's first officer, stood at the railing on the bridge looking down at the festive scene. Sometimes he stole a glance at the window several feet above him which formed one wall of the captain's office. Muller was very conscious of the stiff, motionless figure standing behind that window. For a long time now the captain had been watching what Muller was watching. With a smile on his face, no doubt, that peculiar, inward-turning smile whose precise meaning no member of his crew had ever been able to read.

Muller certainly wasn't smiling. Everything he saw down there on the gangway, every detail that caught his eye in every direction, reminded him of the folly—the madness—which had taken over this ship today. For example, the uniforms on the men in the band—white duck trousers, blue blazers with gold buttons, smart yachting caps—as if this were a holiday cruise! Days ago, when he had heard about these plans, Muller had made his protest. But the captain had simply given his mysterious smile and said, "This is the way we will do it."

Muller had asked himself many times what in the name of God was going on in the captain's head. It defied one's imagination. At one moment he seemed to be merely a fool, his brains hopelessly scrambled with hysterical emotions. Guilt? Vanity? Perhaps even "Christian" love? But at another moment Muller had the uneasy suspicion that the captain was far wiser than he appeared, that he might even be playing some deep game with the sanction of the highest authorities back home.

Muller was also in touch with the authorities back home. He couldn't be sure, however, if *his* authorities were, in fact, the "highest." When he filed his report on the captain's behavior, ought his tone be disapproving or laudatory, or merely noncommittal? It was useless to debate this with himself. As yet he could come to no definite decision. He must simply keep his eyes open.

"You notice their little suitcases?" said young Dietrich, the second officer, who stood next to Muller by the railing. "All they possess in the world, poor devils."

"They're getting away with their lives," Muller said. "Should we also let them take what they've stolen from us?"

"Of course you're right, Heinrich—but you know, there are old people there. Look, that old lady must be over seventy. How are people like that going to live?"

"They all have rich relatives in America. Don't waste your pity on them. You can depend on them to take care of their own."

Muller's mind wasn't really on this conversation. He found that he had become intensely interested in the people moving up the gangway far below. What an ugly, shabby bunch, straggling up one or two at a time, each one carrying his piece of luggage—only necessities; no valuables allowed. Everybody moved just a little bit too slowly or a little bit too quickly. Many were staring around, turning their heads here and there. Though he couldn't see their faces too well, he could imagine the eyes blinking, the mouths working, as if they were waking up from a sleep and still didn't have their bearings.

It made him a little sick just to look at them. Even at this distance he could almost smell their putrid Jewish smell. But still he couldn't take his eyes off them. He had never seen so many of them before all together in one place. Soft, cowardly, an inferior breed, as the Führer said. Yet he had this peculiar feeling as he watched them trudging up the gangway. A feeling almost of—

He shook his head quickly. Even to *think* such a thing was shameful! He was twenty-eight years old, and he had belonged to the party since he was quite young—earlier than anyone on his first three ships, long before it was fashionable to join. He had done well for himself and would do better, and this wasn't because he made a habit of giving in to foolish fears. Since his childhood he had worked hard, and he had known what bad times are—unlike foolish, pampered Dietrich, the rich man's son.

And yet he went on staring down at the gangway. One after another they emerged from the darkness of the dock shed, moved through the bright afternoon sunlight, disappeared into the side of the ship. They kept on coming; there was no end to them. And it was impossible to know what they were thinking, what feelings were secretly smoldering in them. That one there, in the center of the gangway now— that man in the gray overcoat holding a woman by the arm and talking over his shoulder to a boy of maybe twelve. With his graying hair, his round shoulders, obviously he was as weak and flabby as all the rest of them. But for just a moment, when he lifted his head and blinked through his glasses into the sun, Muller could have sworn that he was staring at *him*. And on his face (though this was nonsense, because from this distance it was impossible to see his face) was a look of such anger, a look so full of hatred—

In that instant Muller understood something. We will have to kill them someday, he thought. Forcing them out of the country won't be enough. The camps and prisons won't be

14

enough. Sooner or later each one of them must be killed, or none of us will ever be safe again.

"There's a child," Dietrich cried. "She couldn't be more than two years old. She can hardly walk up the gangway by herself."

Muller tightened his grip on the railing. Sentimentality! The curse of our people. If anything brings us down to defeat again, it will be our sentimentality.

Curtly he ordered Dietrich to go down to the engine room and make sure that everything was in order. His eyes lifted again, and for one long moment he stared at that stiff figure behind the window. Then he turned back to the strange procession which was winding its way into the ship.

* * *

As he herded his family up the gangway, Aaron Peyser tried to keep from thinking about the music. It was too strange, that music, after everything that had gone before, after these last six years—and just an hour ago the policemen on the dock dumping suitcases open, ripping out the linings of dresses as they made their "customs inspection." And now, all of a sudden, came this happy, carefree music. He had a feeling that he ought to be frightened by it; he ought to be experiencing some sort of sadistic trick. Maybe they had no intention of letting this ship leave the dock, after all.

That was a terrible thought, a terrifying thought. Yet somehow it wasn't making his stomach throb with pain, as terrifying thoughts usually did. The music seemed to have pushed him beyond terror; it had overwhelmed him with the most peculiar, the most disconcerting sensation of unreality, as if the world were dissolving around him, as if he were standing outside himself watching things happen to him, the way he sometimes did in dreams.

"You recognize it, Aaron?" Sophie was giving his arm a squeeze. " 'Vienna, City of my Dreams.' The restaurant with the garden—the night of my thirtieth birthday?" She began to hum along with the music.

She had done this sort of thing many times in the past. Sweet little Sophie—incurably romantic, like so many shy girls. Usually, when she hummed in this way, her eyes would shine, and she would smile the "little girl" smile which he had

15

so often teased her about. But he could see that she wasn't smiling now, and there was no brightness in her eyes, and her voice was shaking a little. She was feeling the terror that his good sense told him *he* ought to be feeling, and she was trying to hide it from him, from herself, by making a stab at "nostalgia." She couldn't fool him for a moment, though. Almost from the first day he had known her—they had met in the lecture hall at the university, medieval history—he had been able to see exactly what feelings were inside her.

"Of course I remember," he said. "How could I forget such an important matter?"

He put on his teasing tone because this would make her think that he took her "nostalgia" at face value, that he didn't suspect her of being afraid—and therefore that he had no fears himself. That was the important thing right now, he knew—to calm Sophie down, to give her and the boys and even Sophie's parents as much reassurance as possible.

"Why are they playing that music?" His mother-in-law spoke up in her shrill quavery voice. As long as Aaron had known her, she had always sounded as if she were complaining about something, even when she made perfectly ordinary remarks. "I don't like them playing that music. Bruno, it makes me nervous."

"What *doesn't* make you nervous?" said old Schwarzkopf, Aaron's father-in-law. "That's my fate in life—I'm surrounded by a family of jellyfish." And the old man made a point of turning his head and giving a wink at Aaron.

After all these years Sophie's father still talked to him like that. But Aaron had long since got over resenting it. He knew that old Schwarzkopf didn't mean to be unkind. It was simply his way.

They were off the gangway now. On the deck, with people pushing all around them, Aaron made a count of heads and suitcases and checked his tickets again for the numbers of their cabins. This was the seventh time he had checked them in the last half hour. "B deck," he said. "We go down, I think."

They followed the crowd through glass doors and down red-carpeted stairs. Red carpets—crystal chandeliers—gold-framed mirrors lining the walls. The feeling of unreality grew in Aaron. And it *wasn't* just the ship, he realized. He had been feeling this for six or seven weeks now, ever since the letter had come from the Hamburg Line. Everyone else was

16

so full of hope. Visas, boat tickets, exit permits—out of a sheer blue sky—when for months everyone had thought it was too late. And all the time Aaron had been going through the motions like a sleepwalker, wondering when he would wake up.

Yet nobody had ever suspected how he felt. He had kept it all to himself because he didn't want to upset Sophie and the boys. And maybe also because he knew how the old man would have laughed at him, would have made remarks about people who are too timid and cautious to get out of bed in the morning—

They left the stairs at B deck and found their cabins, two next to each other for the boys and for Sophie and him, one across the passageway for the Schwarzkopfs. Aaron remembered how it always used to be at the resort hotels in the old days—Sophie's mother complaining after five minutes that the bed was too hard or the bathroom too small, and they simply had to find another room for her. She wasn't likely to do much complaining this time, Aaron thought.

He shut the door of his cabin. That music was finally out of hearing. And the cabin was rather nice. Not very large, but it seemed to be comfortable enough, even clean. Yes, there were clean towels on the bathroom rack.

Why clean towels? Somebody had to clean them, somebody had to fold them and hang them up so neatly. Somebody had taken trouble to do these things. Who was going to take such trouble for *them?* No, it simply wasn't real—

David and Joshua came in. Joshua's face was flushed, and he was excited and bewildered. "Do you know what, Papa? There are buttons on the wall, next to the bed! And the sign says to push them if you want the steward! Do you think— if we pushed a button—somebody would really come?"

"It's possible," Aaron said. Yes, it must be a novelty for Joshua, he thought. The last time there were servants to do things for him, he wasn't much more than a baby.

"And there's a sign on the door," Joshua said, "it says we should go to the dining room and make reservations for a table. Do you want me to do that, Papa?"

"I don't want him going off by himself," Sophie said quickly. "Not till we're out on the ocean."

"You go with him to the dining room, David," Aaron said. "Reserve a table for six people. And hurry back."

17

"Yes, Papa," David said. "And afterwards could I talk to you about something? It's important."

"Certainly you can talk to me."

David turned away, and Joshua followed him out the door shaking his head, still marveling over the buttons, Aaron supposed. He wasn't worried about Joshua, though. Somehow he knew that Joshua, though he was only twelve, would be all right.

Was he worried about David, then? He was nineteen, a very difficult age, and he was more complicated, more sensitive than his younger brother. And his face just now had been so serious, so troubled. In fact, he had been looking that way for weeks. Aaron had noticed it, but he simply hadn't had a chance to take the boy aside and talk to him. There had been so much tension, so many things to do—scraping together the money, waiting in endless lines, swallowing his pride with the nasty little officials who had to take their last kicks at the departing Jewboys. Though one ought to be used to that sort of thing by now—Still, it wasn't like Aaron to turn his back on his son. There was no point to a man's life if he wasn't ready at all times to give comfort and help and advice to his family. You can compromise about many things in this world, as long as you don't compromise about *that*.

Sophie and he unpacked in silence for a while. Then she said, "If you need some more room for your things, I've only used two of these drawers—"

Her voice trailed off, and he said, "No, thank you, it's all right." He knew what she was thinking. She was remembering how it used to be in the old days whenever they stayed at a hotel. Her things always filled up every drawer on her dresser and overflowed into his, and he used to laugh at her and say, "We'll be away for only one week. You've brought enough for a lifetime." Not such a funny remark anymore, he thought.

Suddenly she ran up to him and put her arms around him. He could feel her sobbing into his chest. He knew what was expected of him. He patted her shoulder and murmured into her ear, "It's going to be fine, everything's going to be fine. The worst is over now."

There was a knock on the door, then old Schwarzkopf stuck his head in. "So, so? You're not ready yet, you're still hanging up your clothes?"

It was amazing. The old man was as full of confidence as

18

if nothing in his life had changed, as if he were still a big man in the business world. And yet he was sixty-three years old, and his future in America depended entirely on the generosity of a few American manufacturers, Jews, who had once had dealings with the department store. They weren't even Schwarzkopf's contacts, in fact—it was Aaron who had done business with them, and it was Aaron who had persuaded them a couple of years ago to sign the family's immigration applications. Kindhearted as they were, the most these men could be expected to do was to give Aaron and the old man unimportant positions for a year or two until they could open some little dry goods store of their own.

How did the old man manage to act as if he didn't know all this?

Later the boys returned from the dining room. They brought the news that all the tables were for eight people; the family would have to share its meals with two strangers. "That sort of thing wouldn't have happened on this ship in the old days," Schwarzkopf said.

Years ago he had taken this ship on a business trip to New York. All the way in the train this morning, all during that hot crowded ride, with everyone's heart missing a few beats whenever there was a stop, he had kept on talking about "the old *Franz Joseph*."

"When is the ship supposed to leave?" Sophie asked. "Doesn't it say three o'clock on the tickets? It's almost four thirty now!"

"Ships never leave on time," Aaron said, seeing the look on her face. "We'll be off eventually. They didn't go to all this trouble, with a band playing and clean towels, just so we could sit at the dock."

Schwarzkopf suggested they all take a tour of the ship. "I'll show you the points of interest. I remember it like it was yesterday. There's a smoking room off the main lounge where I used to beat poor old Zimmerman at pinochle every night."

"I don't feel like taking a tour," his wife said. "I want to know when we're going to *leave*."

The old man gripped her arm. "The tour'll be good for you, Emma," he said.

Aaron excused himself. He said he was tired and needed to lie down.

"Is it your stomach?" Sophie said. "Do you want a pill? I'll stay here with you."

Sophie fussing over him wasn't what he wanted now. He had to be alone, with nobody asking him things, expecting things from him. "Go ahead, go ahead. There's nothing wrong with me."

"Don't worry about him," old Schwarzkopf said. "We all know about Aaron's stomach by this time, don't we?"

And finally they left, and Aaron stretched out on the bed and shut his eyes. He kept thinking about what old Schwarzkopf had said. "We all know about Aaron's stomach by this time—" In one form or another, the old man was always making this joke at his expense.

It *was* absurd, this "delicate health" which had plagued him all his life. Never anything seriously wrong with him, but always *something* wrong with him. As a child, he remembered, he was constantly having colds, coming down with unexplained fevers. He spent a great deal of time in bed, reading one book after another, sipping the weak tea that his mother brought him at all hours of the day, gazing out the window at the quiet treelined street and the children playing in the little park. And every winter, because of his health, his mother used to take him to the mountains, and his father joined them on weekends. Until his father's business failed, and they couldn't afford to leave Berlin any more. . . .

This delicate health of his, this difficult stomach that never revealed its difficulties in an X-ray—it was all tied up with the timidity, the cautiousness for which old Schwarzkopf felt such contempt. Yes, he *was* cautious. He knew he had none of the daring and imagination that had made the old man so successful in business. If you grow up in a family that's always short of money while all its friends and connections are rich—if you go to a school full of boys who are better dressed than you, with whom you can't go out on weekends because you don't have enough pocket money to join in their amusements—if you can never invite friends to your home because they'll see how sparse and shabby the furniture is—well, what else can you be but cautious? Cautiousness is a lesson you *have* to learn when the slightest recklessness might lead to disaster.

But he had always told himself that cautiousness had its value, too. At least he wasn't like so many other men in the business world, a predatory beast whose headstrong ambition led him to devour everyone around him. He was kind, he was generous, he treated other people decently. He loved his family and took care of them conscientiously. Furthermore, his cautiousness wasn't entirely a liability in business, either —once or twice it had helped to keep the store out of serious trouble.

And if he had been listened to a few years ago— But of course his father-in-law had dismissed all his warnings. "Believe me, this won't go on much longer," he had said. "I have it on the highest authority, Hitler will modify his racial policies in a month or two. The pressure is on from the big industrialists, they've come to realize how much they need us—"

And Aaron had given in. Against his judgment he had given in. What else could he have done? It was part of the unspoken bargain he had made twenty years ago when he married into the Schwarzkopf family. The old man had done him a great favor—giving his only child to the son of a bankrupt, to a nearsighted twenty-two-year-old nobody with no money and no prospects, nothing but vague ambitions about medical school; giving him an executive position in the store at a time when so many men were out of work. Aaron had known from the start what his part of the bargain must be. Work hard and make good, of course—but also keep his mouth shut, let the old man have his way.

All right, what was so wrong about that? He wasn't the violent type. He had a weak stomach. He couldn't be effective by shouting and brandishing his fists. Giving in to the old man on certain things had enabled him—in his quiet way, working behind the scenes—to do a great deal of good. He had slowly but surely improved the wages and working conditions of the store's employees; he had corrected many individual injustices; he had increased the store's involvement in charitable activities and projects for the benefit of the community. A more aggressive person could never have accomplished these things—he would have quarreled with the old man from the start and lost his place.

There was a soft knock on the cabin door. Aaron got up from the bed and opened the door to David.

"I wanted to talk to you, Papa. I know you're tired, and I don't want to disturb—"

"It's all right, I'm not that tired." Aaron stepped aside, then sat on the edge of the bed.

David went on standing. When he spoke he was careful to keep his eyes turned away. "There's something you ought to

21

know about, Papa. On the dock this morning—you remember, when Grandpa's hat got knocked off, just before the customs men got to us?"

"I remember. What about it?"

"Well, I picked it up for Grandpa, and while I was handing it back to him—I saw something inside it. Pinned to the lining. It looked like a hundred-mark note."

Aaron sighed. It didn't really surprise him that the old man should have tried to take money out of the country illegally, or even that he should have had money to take, money which he had never told his family about. But to be so reckless about it, so foolhardy— If the customs men had found that note, the whole family could have been detained, sent back to Berlin. The old man really ought to be told . . .

"Did you mention this to your grandfather?"

"No. I thought I'd better tell you—"

"You did the right thing. It was very responsible of you. Don't mention it to him, David. Don't mention this to anybody. It's over now and no harm done, so we'll just keep it to ourselves."

"You can count on me, Papa." David's expression was solemn. He looked much younger than nineteen.

Aaron's heart went out to him. These last years had been terrible for the boy—looking forward so eagerly to the university, to medical school, then finding out there would be nothing. But when did he ever complain? When was he ever anything but quiet and well-behaved?

There was a shrill whistling sound from the passageway. Then a voice came barking through the loudspeaker. David opened the cabin door so they could hear the voice more clearly. "The gangway goes up in five minutes. All passengers are requested to come aboard."

The ship was really leaving? The dream was going on?

Aaron took David by the arm. "Let's go up on deck. It's always interesting to watch a ship pull away from the dock."

As they climbed the two flights of stairs, he thought again about that unspoken bargain he had made with old Schwarzkopf. After all, it had been justified by the results, hadn't it? Without the bargain there would have been no job, no security all through the inflation years. Sophie would have married him anyway, of course, but how well would she have adjusted to living a life of genteel poverty? And how would it have been for David and Joshua, growing up poor instead of well-to-do?

He knew the answer to that. He had grown up that way from the age of seven. He remembered, for instance, what it was like at Dr. Waldheim's Academy—he remembered those days more vividly than many things which had happened much more recently. How miserable he had been at that school! How often he had made up his mind to go to his father and beg to be taken out of that school! But he never could bring himself to do it. He knew how much it meant to his father that he had won that scholarship. Once he had overheard his father saying to his mother, "At least he's got the school. That's one thing I didn't steal from him." His parents had wanted him to have the best possible education—that was how Aaron used to explain their enthusiasm for Dr. Waldheim's Academy. Underneath, though, he had always understood the truth. It wasn't the education they were so desperate for him to have but the social prestige, the toehold on respectable society. For this they were more than willing to sacrifice his happiness, his boyhood.

And the same thing would have happened to *his* sons if he hadn't made certain decisions, recognized certain hard facts, at the age of twenty-two. He couldn't blame himself today for doing what he had thought was right, what he *still* thought was right.

David and he stepped out to the main deck. It was already swarming with people. They found a place at the railing, squeezed in between a middle-aged couple with a cluster of children and a tall man who had only one arm, whose left sleeve was pinned to his coat.

The noise was terrific. With much creaking and groaning the gangway was being hauled in. Ropes were being pulled away from the pier, and stevedores on shore were shouting at sailors on the ship. Every few minutes hoarse blasts and hoots came from the smokestacks. Above it all the band could be heard, blowing and banging away as if their lives depended on it. "O Fatherland, dear Fatherland."

Only the crowd at the railing was quiet. As if it were frozen there, Aaron thought. Ice people, staring ahead and waiting.

The minutes stretched out, the silence hung in the air. And then Aaron felt a small shudder under his feet. The ship's engines were beginning to pump. A cry, almost a gasp, broke out of the crowd. "We're moving," somebody said. Like an echo the words were taken up all along the railing. "We're moving! We're moving away from the dock!"

The ship moved slowly at first. Inch by inch, painful and slow. Then it began to move faster; the shuddering grew more pronounced. Now the dock was feet away, yards away, and you could see the water churning against the side of the ship. The smokestacks gave a few more blasts.

Aaron looked around him. He saw that the crowd had snapped out of its trance. It was alive now, bursting, overflowing with its emotions. The tall one-armed man had tears in his eyes—you couldn't tell if they were tears of joy or sorrow. The little married couple, surrounded by their children, were clasping hands tightly. Everybody seemed to be laughing wildly or sobbing even more wildly or throwing his arms around somebody.

David, at his side, was shaking his head and laughing and saying, "Papa, look—we're moving—"

Aaron wanted to join in. It wasn't a dream after all. The nightmare was finally over. He had come out of the darkness into the light. At this glorious moment he wanted to be happy, to laugh and cry like everyone else.

He stood at the railing a while longer. He saw the dock grow smaller and smaller, until it was nothing but a gray speck swallowed up by the late afternoon light. He just couldn't feel what everyone else was feeling. That sensation of unreality was stronger in him than ever. It seemed as if he were being sucked into a whirlpool, he was spinning round and round, soon he would be flung into space—and where would he land? The unknown lay before him, frightening, making his stomach throb—but maybe a little bit tantalizing, too.

"Shouldn't we get back to the cabin?" David said. "Mama will be worried about us."

"Yes, of course. We mustn't worry your mother."

As Aaron turned away from the railing, he heard the band come out with one last oom-pah-pah, and then it was still.

*   *   *

Rabbi Max Einhorn stood at the railing with his son and his daughter until there was nothing to see on the horizon except the long blue line where the sea was joined to the sky. As he finally turned away, he noticed that Naomi's eyes were full of tears. He didn't ask her about this, of course—she would have been too embarrassed. He put his hand gently on Peter's arm and held him back a little on the pretext of asking him the number of their cabin. Naomi was able to walk ahead of them, safe from their prying eyes.

It took such tact, the rabbi thought, such superhuman tact to bring up two children all by oneself. And especially in these last six years. What a terrible conjunction of tragedies had fallen on his poor boy and girl—Hitler and adolescence, both at the same time! Things had been so much easier for *him* when he was growing up. Loving parents, a gracious, cultivated household where books and music were valued—and where there was always enough money to obtain them. A household devoted to Judaism, to Sabbath dinners and blessings and even to kosher food—though the rabbi had stopped feeling the need of this particular custom many years ago. A genuinely pious atmosphere—but what was even rarer, there was *joy* in his parents' piety. His desire to become a rabbi had received nothing but encouragement from them. His way had been smoothed from the start. This hardly made him the most appropriate person to bring up children in this age of continual disaster.

He wondered what sort of job he had done with them. They seemed to be good young people, polite, intelligent, responsible. There *was* Naomi's daydreaming and Peter's provoking ideas—but there was no meanness in either of them, and surely that was what really mattered. And yet, how can one ever be *sure* about one's children? If only Miriam were alive. Even now, after ten years, there were moments when he longed to turn to her, to explain his problems to her and ask for her advice.

Perhaps he should have remarried, as so many people had urged him to do. After all, he was only forty-five when Miriam died. But in those first few years he simply couldn't bring himself to think about it, and then came Hitler and the Nazis. There was so much to do then, so much to worry about, so many people to talk to. People had always found him easy to talk to, but in these last six years more of them had come to him than in all his previous years as a rabbi. Businessmen, professional men, ladies of social position—people who, though they may have belonged to his congregation, would never have considered taking their problems to a rabbi. But now they came—to ask him questions about the

Torah, to hear him say that there really *was* a God, to pour out their troubles without even caring for his answers.

And of course, during these six years there was the constant fear. Night and day it hung over the synagogue. Fear of the thugs in the street who at any moment might start smashing windows, smearing obscenities on the doors. Fear of the official thugs in uniform who might descend without warning like the plague. And one day they *did* descend, and the synagogue was locked and bolted for good. . . . The rabbi had known people who somehow, in spite of the fear, managed to get married during these years—and even to bring children into the world. There had been such people in his own congregation. He had performed the wedding service a dozen times, said the familiar blessings as if no change had taken place in the world since they were first written. But for himself personally, marriage under such circumstances had never been conceivable.

Did that show a weakness in his faith, a rejection of life just when life needed to be affirmed most vigorously? He hoped this wasn't so. He sincerely believed it wasn't so. What would Miriam have said? She would have reminded him, he suspected, of the advice that old Rabbi Hirsch, his philosophy professor at the seminary, was fond of giving. About not splitting hairs with oneself over the strength or weakness of one's faith. "Have faith that you have faith," old Hirsch used to say, "and go on about your business."

But *had* he gone on about his business in these last six years? No business could be closer to him than his own son and daughter, and there was a real question in his mind as to whether he hadn't neglected them for the sake of strangers. Already, at the age of nineteen, Peter was one step from being an atheist. On the train just a few hours ago he had made one of his upsetting remarks. And as for Naomi—she lived in romantic fantasies. Normal enough, perhaps, for a girl of seventeen, but how much place was there in her heart and her imagination for the God of Abraham, Isaac, and Jacob?

And in the United States of America their rejection of the faith of their fathers would proceed even more rapidly and efficiently, there could hardly be any doubt about that. The rabbi had heard stories about what happened to even the most religious young people in America. Was he fated to be one of those rabbis whose own children have turned away from Judaism? He had known several such rabbis, and it had been clear that they were deeply unhappy men.

If he was in danger of joining their ranks, the fault couldn't be his son's and his daughter's. If Judaism meant nothing to them, this must be because he had failed to *make* it mean something to them. His doubts must be greater than he had suspected; his faith must be weaker than he had feared. And he *had* feared for his faith—many times in these last six years. Many times he had looked at the world around him, at his beloved Germany, and he had asked himself what kind of a God could have created *this*. Many times, as he watched the sufferings of his fellow Jews—and saw, as the years passed, that those sufferings increased, that there seemed to be no end to them—

These thoughts came to him only fleetingly, of course. They crept up on him when he was tired or discouraged. Always, sooner or later, he was able to drive them away. The Lord is good, he was able to tell himself. Good will come out of this somehow. But lately—especially in the last few months, since the synagogue had been barred to him—these fleeting moods had been staying with him longer and longer, and it took a harder and harder effort to rid himself of them.

Was this the reason why, when Peter had made that remark to him on the train, he had been unable to answer it with nearly enough force and conviction? The answer sprang to his lips right now, the answer he should have given hours ago—and the force and conviction were in him, too. "If being a Jew is no more than a political phenomenon—if it has no spiritual significance—".

He was on the verge of bringing it out in his most pompous oratorical manner—the manner Peter hated so, the manner which made his sermons (as he knew too well) so boring to his congregation. But God came to his rescue and restored his sense of humor.

Instead of haranguing Peter, he smiled at him and patted his arm and made some remark about how beautifully the ship was decorated. And the boy looked surprised, blushed a little, grinned—as if the innocuous remark had been an expression of endearment, a fatherly kiss. Which it had been, of course, in a way. . . .

Naomi Einhorn left her father and Peter at the door of their cabin and started down the passageway to her own.

27

She wondered if they had seen her crying up on deck. If they had, she hoped they had thought she was crying for the same reasons that everyone else was.

But the truth was she had been crying because of Wolfgang. Poor little Wolfgang Amadeus Mozart with his muddy gray fur and one eye larger than the other, so that his face always seemed to have a shifty look on it, like a criminal's. Peter was always saying to her, "That's undoubtedly the *least* charming animal I've ever run across. I can't understand what you see in him." What she saw in him, she supposed, was just exactly that he *was* so uncharming. She always *did* have a weakness for underdogs. Undercats?

And now she missed poor Wolfgang terribly. She knew Mrs. Bloch would be kind to him. Mrs. Bloch was the half-deaf, half-blind old lady who lived in the apartment above theirs, who could have left Germany with her son three years ago but said she was just too old to change her ways. Mrs. Bloch loved cats—she already had three females, and Wolfgang was on *very* good terms with all of them. Obviously he wasn't going to miss Naomi one bit.

And yet all she had to do was think of him now, and tears came to her eyes. It was so silly really. She was as upset about Wolfgang as she was about her friends who had stayed behind—Nikki and Hans and Tony Schick and the Horstmann girls and so many others—and nobody knew what would happen to *any* of them.

She got to her cabin and went inside. The lady who shared it with her was lying on the bottom berth. Her eyes were shut, and she had a damp washcloth on her forehead.

"Don't make any noise, dear," she said the moment Naomi stepped in. "I've got a dreadful headache."

Her name was Mrs. Fischel, and she was fifty or so, as old as Naomi's father. She had been very rich once—as she had let Naomi know two minutes after they met—and she had a way of ordering people around as if they were all her servants. Naomi had no intention of being ordered around like a servant—still, Mrs. Fischel *did* have a headache, so Naomi unpacked her suitcase and put her things away with as little noise as possible, practically walking on tiptoe.

Meanwhile, she kept thinking about the silly tears she had shed up on deck. Crying over a disagreeable cat when the whole world was turning upside down. What was wrong with her, anyway, that she just couldn't seem to concentrate on

28

serious things? Her father was dedicated to Judaism and to being a rabbi—if he couldn't find a synagogue in America, he'd be miserable. And Peter was dedicated to his "cause," to the homeland and Zionism and all. But what was *she* dedicated to? Nothing. There was no steady goal or purpose or anything in her life. She just drifted along from day to day, listening to music and humming it to herself, stroking a cat, gorging herself on candy and then starving herself for a week, combing her hair, reading poetry. Mostly Heine and Goethe, but not even their really profound and *important* things. It was their love lyrics that she knew by heart and recited over and over to herself—silently when she was in a room full of people, or out loud when she was alone.

> *"When two part from each other,*
> *Hand reaches out to hand,*
> *And then begins the weeping,*
> *The sighing without end—"*

"Please! My head!" Mrs. Fischel called out from the bed.

Naomi blushed and apologized. Yes, there *was* something wrong with her. What kind of person recites poetry out loud when there's nobody around who wants to listen and floats off into foolish daydreams at the drop of a hat? Daydreams about handsome men who sweep her off her feet. Silly *un-original* daydreams.

There was a knock on the door, a timid little knock, and then a small, elderly lady came into the cabin. She looked like a bird who had fallen out of her nest. This was Mrs. Moritz, a friend of Mrs. Fischel—they had met on the train a few hours ago. Mrs. Moritz was also a widow.

"Were you able to arrange it, Gertrude?" Mrs. Moritz said.

"Of course I arranged it." Mrs. Fischel sat up, pulling the washcloth from her forehead. "That steward tried to tell me the table was all filled up and there was no room for you. I told him to switch somebody to another table, and I wouldn't budge until he did it."

Mrs. Moritz thanked her, and looked at her like the Dog of Flanders looking up at his young master in that book Naomi used to love as a child.

"God knows how you'll get along in America, Rosa, if you don't learn to assert yourself," Mrs. Fischel went on. "What are you going to do there? How are you going to earn a living?"

"My sister's been there for three years, she's got a little dressmaking business. I'm sure I can learn to sew. I used to do a lot of sewing before my marriage."

"It'll be a struggle," Mrs. Fischel said. "I tell you what— I've got some good friends in America, wealthy and important ladies whose husbands are in the shoe business, like my late husband was. We were very nice to them in the old days, whenever they came to Germany, and they'll be returning the kindness as soon as I get to New York. I'll talk them into giving a little of their dressmaking to you and your sister."

"Would you do that, Gertrude? That would be wonderful of you!"

"Think nothing of it, no trouble at all." Mrs. Fischel went on talking about her late husband's good friends in America. She explained how she used to help him in the designing end of his business when he was alive, and how one of those American friends had practically promised her a position in his store—

Naomi had heard this story before. Mrs. Fischel had told it to her earlier this afternoon. So she excused herself and went out to the passageway. Once again she could feel the tears coming to her eyes. Those poor old ladies, full of hopes about the future, trying to believe that things would turn out fine! How awful it must be to lose everything and start all over again when you're old! How lucky she was to be seventeen!

And suddenly, in the middle of feeling sad, her heart gave a jump, and she was feeling happy. I'm going to America, she thought. All the bad times are over now. I'm starting a new life. I'm free—

She sighed. She was at it again. *Where* had she got this frivolous mind of hers? Certainly not from Father. She must have got it from her mother, then. She had been six years old when her mother died, and the memories were all mixed up in her head—but she did remember Father shaking his head once and saying, "Miriam, my dear, can't you *ever* understand that certain things are no laughing matter?" This memory always made Naomi feel very close to her mother. It usually sent her off on one of her favorite daydreams, the one where she imagined what her life might be like if her mother were still alive—

And again her eyes were full of tears.

Oh, this is ridiculous, she told herself. Can't you think of anything else to do with your freedom except cry your eyes out?

She started down the passageway toward Father's cabin. What she had to do was stop *thinking* for a while. Maybe Peter would join her in exploring the ship. . . .

Peter Einhorn followed his sister around the ship. He listened to her chatter, and he even answered her from time to time, but his mind was on other things. In his pocket he had the name and address that Wilhelm had given him a year ago. That was just a few weeks before Wilhelm—

It was a New York address. He would write to this man as soon as he was off the ship. In America the government doesn't open your letters. This man in New York would be able to tell him what to do next, how to get to the homeland. There were ways, he knew. Dangerous and illegal, but it *could* be done. Wilhelm had known many people who did it. Some of them were even *younger* than nineteen.

He hoped it wouldn't take too long. He could hardly wait for the time to come. It seemed to him that this was what he had been waiting for all his life—it wasn't possible that only three years had passed since he had met Wilhelm and had started thinking about these ideas. "Patience, patience," Wilhelm had often said to him—and he *had* been patient. But now the time was so close. It was just over the horizon—the homeland was waiting for him there. And the crawling, the whispering, the trembling with fear would finally come to an end. He could have his pride then. For the first time in his life he could start being a Jew.

Then he thought of his father. Poor Father who believed that being a Jew meant going into a synagogue and reading some Hebrew from the Torah and making a speech full of respectable sentiments about charity and faith. Being a Jew was something you had to *fight* for. But Father would never be able to understand that.

When he finally went to the homeland, would he be able to persuade Father and Naomi to come with him? She was just a child—who knows what she might think in a year or so, or even in a month or so? But Father— No, he didn't

31

think Father would do it in the end. He was too old, too set in his ways, too bogged down with prejudice and fear.

And then Peter wondered why it should matter to him if Father went with him or not. When you're building a new world, you must be able to stand on your own feet. You don't need old men to lean on. Why then should he feel this sudden pain at his heart when he thought of the new world without Father?

Impatiently he pushed the pain aside and followed Naomi out to the deck. I'm free, he told himself. This is freedom, this is what it's like. But I mustn't waste it on childish emotions. I must use it for the good of the cause.

*   *   *

A sudden roll of the ship jarred Dr. Carl Bender's hand as he was tying his necktie. So he carefully started over again.

How very methodical of me, he thought. How very German. And he smiled the soft, rather wry smile which, he knew, was his most characteristic trait. It used to make Hannah, his first wife, so furious. "Stop laughing at me! I'm not that funny!" Poor Hannah—always so intense, taking everything so seriously. Born to be a victim.

His second wife, Julia, didn't mind the smile. There weren't many things that Julia minded.

Suddenly he was thinking about old Berkholz. Why? Oh yes—Berkholz used to say to him, "When you smile at me like that, Carl, I feel that you have no respect for me at all."

This from one of the leading Freudian psychiatrists in Europe, a senior lecturer on the medical faculty, a distinguished man, and also Bender's own teacher, who had been responsible twenty years ago for leading him into psychiatric practice. Yet it *was* a fact that he had always thought Berkholz slightly ridiculous, brilliant in his field but something of a dunderhead in every other department of life.

And how sadly this judgment had been confirmed. When the authorities quietly arranged for Berkholz' dismissal from the medical faculty, where on earth did he get the supreme muddleheaded vanity to take the stand he took? Writing to the newspapers, instituting a civil suit, circulating a petition! "I will call this to the attention of the public!" he kept saying. "I am not exactly an undistinguished person! Once the facts are known, the responsible scientific community will put a stop to this outrage!"

Poor Berkholz. To court martyrdom at his age—a potbellied, Jewish Don Quixote. He was actually surprised when the newspapers refused to print his letters, when the court dismissed his suit, when nobody signed his petition. And finally, when he made his grand gesture—arriving at his lecture room at the scheduled hour and refusing to move from the platform after his replacement appeared—the police were called, the distinguished professor was dragged away shouting and struggling. Nobody ever found out what became of him —even his wife could get no information from the authorities.

And not a word of protest was heard from "the responsible scientific community."

Bender's own approach to life was rather different. He believed in being reasonable, using his good sense, calculating the consequences of his actions. He had always admired that French bishop who was asked, "What did *you* do during the siege of Paris?"—and replied, "I survived."

In my own case, however, Bender told himself as he turned away from the mirror, it's been somewhat too close for comfort. If it weren't for the completely unexpected gift of this ship . . . Why *had* he waited so long? Why had he postponed his decision, given himself excuses, listened to the optimistic rumors that were circulating long after sensible people had seen the writing on the wall? Perhaps it was because of Julia. Subconsciously he may have hoped that being married to a Christian woman would exempt him from the fate of others. If so, he must have some hidden weakness which had allowed him to entertain such a fatuous hope. He would have to consider this very carefully. He couldn't make such a crucial error a second time.

The door opened and his cabin mate came in. Bender would much rather have shared a cabin with Julia, of course, but Eva was ten years old—too young, Julia felt, to be separated from her mother and quartered with a stranger, too old to sleep in the same cabin with her stepfather. He had to admit that Julia was right. When it came to her daughter's welfare, Julia could be a remarkably clear thinker.

His cabin mate was a young man named Liebling, an accountant who was joining his fiancée in America. He was afflicted by a compulsive urge to tell his life story; three times already Bender had heard about his future father-in-law who had left Germany several years ago, become a successful manufacturer of costume jewelry in Chicago, made the arrangements and advanced the money for Liebling to travel on this ship. "All my life I'll be grateful for his generosity," Liebling had said three times. "To embrace my beautiful Lottie—my fiancée's name is Lottie—for more than two years I've lived for nothing else."

Such romantic ardor coming from such a stiff, correct young man was rather touching. But then he had started talking about the job he would have in America. "At first I must work for my father-in-law as a salesman. This will stop, of course, as soon as I pass the American accountancy examinations."

"Why of course? A salesman can make a good living in America."

Liebling smiled gently, and his tone couldn't have been easier and more amiable. "I'm an accountant, doctor. Accountancy is a respected profession, just like medicine. Accountants aren't salesmen of costume jewelry."

Romanticism and snobbery in equal parts, Bender thought. A typically German mixture. What a dreadful people we are, after all! And the Jews among us are as bad as the pure-blooded Aryans—there's the huge, grotesque irony of this whole Hitler madness.

And what of himself? No, he had very little right to look down his nose at this pompous young man. If he hadn't been lucky enough to get the offer from the medical school in Boston—if he were faced in America with the prospect of becoming a costume jewelry salesman—howls of injured dignity would unquestionably be heard from him.

The dinner gong sounded, so he didn't have to listen to young Liebling's tale all over again. He left the cabin and went down to the foyer outside the dining room. He was meeting Julia and the girl here, but of course they hadn't arrived yet. In the eight years of their married life Julia had seldom been on time for anything.

He settled into an armchair, lit a cigarette, and watched the people moving through the dining room doors. The aging matrons trying to make their dresses look less shabby than they really were; the heads of families with grave faces; the timid little daughters and polite young sons—a perfect cross section of middle-class Germany.

Would people be any different in America? He rather suspected not. Nor in England, France, or anywhere else. The whole world today was rapidly becoming German.

Julia appeared with Eva by her side. The child always seemed a little paler and gawkier than usual, in contrast to Julia's radiance and poise. Like everyone else on this ship, Julia had brought only one small suitcase, had left behind most of her clothes, jewelry, makeup articles. Yet even now she managed to look like a queen at a royal ball.

She kissed him on the cheek. "I'm not late, am I, darling?"

The dining room was nearly full. He could see his fellow passengers gaping at the astonishing sight—walls lined with mirrors, ceiling painted with Rubenesque cherubs and held up by golden columns, clusters of balloons hanging from the chandeliers. On each table was a bowl of red and white roses, setting off the gleaming silverware and sparkling cut glass. And there were bottles of wine, also. Strange, very strange. Behind the arrangements on this ship one got the impression of a mind at work. Whose mind? The captain's? At any rate, a very strange mind indeed.

Julia, Eva, and he were the last to arrive at their table. They exchanged introductions with their fellow diners. The tall, white-haired man with the soft voice and the rather formal manner of speech was a rabbi named Einhorn. He was traveling with his two children, a dark-haired boy of nineteen and a girl a few years younger, sweet-faced, with that air of floating halfway between earth and heaven which is characteristic of adolescent females. There didn't seem to be any Mrs. Einhorn. Bender guessed that she was dead; men like the rabbi don't get divorced.

The other two people at the table were sitting across from Bender. The plump, talkative little blonde—her name was Tannenbaum—was in her late twenties. She was six or seven months pregnant. The little man next to her—fortyish, perhaps fiftyish—was obviously not her husband. Despite his confident smile and his checked sport jacket which proclaimed what a dashing man of the world he was, Bender recognized him as one of the unmarriageables, the perpetual bachelors who skip along on the surface of life.

"Monsky," said the little man. "Leon. So you're a psychoanalyst. Personally, I believe in it, no matter what people say."

"I'm glad to hear it."

"I didn't always feel that way. For a long time I was skepti-

35

cal. But a few years ago I met this Dr. Sigmund Freud—he's a cousin of some friends of mine, he visited them whenever he came to Berlin—and he argued with me till two in the morning, and finally I was convinced. A remarkable man."

"So I've always thought," Bender said, "though I never had the privilege of meeting him."

The waiter came with the first course, smoked salmon with capers and lemon and slices of black bread. Bender could almost hear the gasps of amazement from all over the room. It had been a long time since most of them could afford salmon like this.

"It really looks excellent, doesn't it?" Rabbi Einhorn said, but he lifted his fork to his mouth warily—and so, Bender noticed, did most of the other people around him, as if they expected this salmon to turn to ashes as soon as it touched their lips.

Only Monsky crammed the food into his mouth with any demonstration of pleasure.

Stewards came and poured the wine. "A toast, a toast," Monsky said, raising his glass. "Happiness and success to all our enterprises in America!"

Rabbi Einhorn raised his glass, too. "Perhaps I might add to that—thanks to God for His mercy and lovingkindness in delivering us from evil."

Mrs. Tannenbaum said, "Amen."

The waiter whisked away their plates and reappeared a few minutes later with soup—a thick lentil soup with frankfurter slices in it and a delicious aroma rising from it. There must be people on this ship, Bender thought, who observe the dietary laws. Will they be obliged to starve throughout this voyage—or does Talmudic law give them a special dispensation? The rabbi, he noticed, was eating his soup without hesitation. He was a Reformed rabbi, then, a progressive rabbi—what Bender's father used to refer to as "one of those goyische rabbis." Was he passing his progressive ways down to his children, or would they react against his liberalism as Bender had reacted against his father's Orthodoxy? He had spent his adolescence eating pork sausage in secret, had stopped going to synagogue from the day he left home, had studied psychiatry in the face of his father's belief that this was an "ungodly" subject. And he had ended up—fortunately after both his parents were dead—committing the crime of crimes, marrying a Gentile. A rather sad story, really. All that religious fervor in his home—and what had it come to in the end?

The conversation turned to the subject of America. Bender became the center of attention because he had been there several times—in 1928 he had taught for one semester at Columbia University, and he and Hannah had occupied an apartment in New York. Everyone at the table had questions to ask him about life there, about employment opportunities, the prices of food and clothing, the kinds of places in which people lived.

"Remember, of course, that I was there ten years ago," he said. "New York must have changed since then. America has had her economic troubles, too."

"Compared to us," Monsky said, "the Americans don't know what economic troubles are."

"I wonder, is it expensive to go to concerts and operas in New York?" Rabbi Einhorn said. "Naomi and I would be most unhappy if we couldn't hear a little Mozart or Beethoven on occasion."

He smiled at his daughter, and for a moment she descended from her cloud and smiled back at him. The next moment she floated up again.

"Excuse me, doctor," Mrs. Tannenbaum said. "Is it possible that you're familiar with Camden, New Jersey? Have you ever visited that city?" Her husband, she explained, was living now in Camden. He was a designer of fabrics and had gone to America six months before, when his uncle, who manufactured drapes and slipcovers, arranged for him to have a job. At the last moment, however, she had been forced to stay behind because of her mother's sudden illness. By the time her mother died, though it was only a month later, nobody was allowed to leave the country anymore; only by a miracle had her husband and his uncle been able to arrange this passage for her. "Now he has a house in Camden, New Jersey," she said, "and I've been so worried if this will be a nice place to live. In his letters Martin writes only about work and about money. He never says if the people are friendly, if there are small children nearby."

Bender had to tell her that he had never been to Camden, New Jersey. But it was his impression that life could be very pleasant in many of these small American towns.

"*I've* been to Camden," Monsky said. "A few years ago, when business took me to the USA. Several leading merchants of Camden entertained me in their homes. I assure you, young lady, it's one of the prettiest little towns in the whole country. Cows grazing on the hills, white fences, picturesque old windmills—just like a painting. And the people couldn't be friendlier."

Mrs. Tannenbaum's face creased with smiles. She suddenly looked rather pretty and girlish and eager, with an expression that belongs only to pregnant women. For a moment Bender felt a twinge of regret that Hannah had never been able to have any children. It was years since he had felt such a twinge.

The main course was served—a beautiful Beef Wellington with soufflé potatoes. Monsky rubbed his hands and proceeded to devour it with enthusiasm. And the others raised and lowered their forks with a little less caution than before. How long would it be, Bender wondered, before the good food and wine loosened them up completely and made them all forget that such creatures as Nazis existed? One week? One day? It would be interesting to watch the process taking place.

Rabbi Einhorn asked Mrs. Tannenbaum when the baby was due and whether her husband would come to Havana to be with her. She answered that her husband's uncle planned to give him a whole month's vacation as soon as the baby arrived and to pay his fare to Cuba, too. She started talking about how wonderful it is to have a generous, loving family.

As Mrs. Tannenbaum gently jabbered away, Bender looked at Julia. She was yawning, and there was a sinister glitter in her eye. He recognized that glitter. In a moment she would bring out some quiet, sarcastic remark designed to crush poor little Mrs. Tannenbaum. This was how Julia reacted when people bored her. In the first months of their marriage Bender had often urged her to be more tolerant of people's foibles, but she had merely patted him on the cheek and said, "Now you're just not being reasonable, darling. Are their foibles tolerant of *me*?" After awhile he had stopped trying to reform Julia—in this respect as in all others. She was, in fact, exactly what he wanted in a wife. He had lived for ten years with the other kind of woman, the kind whose heart bleeds for suffering humanity, who throws all her feelings into everything—who forces you to give yourself up to her, to care so much—

In her own best interests, then, he interrupted Mrs. Tannenbaum by addressing himself to the rabbi's daughter. "Since you're interested in music, Miss Einhorn, you must be excited about our famous passenger."

"What passenger?" The words dropped out of her from a great height; obviously she was still up in her cloud.

"I thought everyone knew. Emil Karlweis is on this ship."

"The *conductor?*" With amusement Bender saw Naomi Einhorn come swooping down to earth, her eyes shining. "He's *here?* In this *room?*"

"I shouldn't be surprised." Bender began to look around.

"Karlweis aboard this ship?" Rabbi Einhorn shook his head. "It's amazing! I was sure he had managed to get out a long time ago. After he resigned from the Munich Opera—"

"There he is," Bender said. "The table by the window."

There was no mistaking him, with his long nose and that wild shock of snow-white hair, almost the Karlweis trademark. He must have been in his sixties, but his face looked surprisingly young.

"Yes, it *is!*" The girl was craning her neck. "He's marvelous-looking, isn't he? Like one of the Prophets!"

Her father smiled at her. "With some girls it's film stars. With Naomi it's musicians."

"What *I* can't understand," said his son, "is how anybody can call that conceited old matinee idol a musician."

His sister turned on him. "Nothing means *anything* to you. You have to tear down *everything.*"

The boy gave a grin and a shrug. "I prefer to save my admiration for people who work and fight for something worthwhile. Not overpaid clothing-store dummies who wave a stick and make old ladies swoon."

"*I'm* not an old lady—"

Her eyes were flashing, her cheeks were flushed—and yet as the argument went on, Bender began to realize that her anger didn't really go deep. Teasing and being teased was clearly a favorite ritual between this brother and sister. No doubt it gave them both a lot of pleasure.

Monsky said, "Karlweis is good, but I've always preferred Bruno Walter. Of course, I admit I'm influenced by personal considerations. Walter and I got along very nicely a few years ago when we ran into each other in the course of business."

"What *is* your business exactly, Mr. Monsky?" Julia looked straight at him, and put on her wide-eyed "innocent" expression, an infallible warning that she was about to pounce. This time Bender felt no impulse to interrupt. Monsky, he thought, was strictly fair game.

Monsky answered, "I've had various enterprises, Mrs. Bender. At the time of my meeting with Maestro Walter, I was in music stands. Manufacturing and selling. You look surprised, of course. It never occurs to people that *somebody* has to manufacture music stands."

"But what's your business *today*, Mr. Monsky?"

Monsky laughed and spread his hands. "Today? The same business as everybody else on this ship. Getting away as fast as I can. Hoping for the best."

In a way you had to admire him, Bender thought. When it came to a *hutzpah* contest, not many people were a match for Julia.

The waiter served the salad now, and Bender refilled his wine glass.

"Rabbi *Max* Einhorn?" Monsky said. "You were the Reformed synagogue on Hindenburgstrasse, weren't you?"

"Quite so. You attended services there?"

"Who, me?" Monsky laughed. "Only the cream of society patronized your establishment, Rabbi. I never had any illusions that I could move in such exalted circles."

"I'm sorry you felt that way, Mr. Monsky. The truth is that anybody was welcome to join our congregation, anybody at all. The only requirement was a desire to identify with the Jewish heritage."

"Are you sure everybody in your congregation met that requirement? One of your former members is on this boat with us—Bruno Schwarzkopf, the department store man— you remember him?"

"I know his name, of course. But I don't believe I ever had the pleasure of his acquaintance—"

"We used to do business together a long time ago, Schwarzkopf and me. I'll introduce you to him. Ask him how much desire he ever had to be Jewish. I'd be interested to hear his answer."

The rabbi had turned a little pale. He just looked at Monsky for a moment. When he spoke again, his voice was louder. "Mr. Monsky, let me tell you something you may not know. During the past three years, until we were forced last spring to shut our doors, attendance at our services more than tripled. On the Sabbath it was almost impossible to find a seat—yet people came and stood up. How do you account for this, Mr. Monsky? In this period of time was it easier or harder to be a Jew in Germany?" The rabbi's last words reverberated around the table.

"Rabbi, Rabbi," Monsky said, without a dent in his good-humored smile, "you're not telling me anything I'm surprised to hear. Naturally, when the ax is falling, people panic and revert to their childhood superstitions."

"Mr. Monsky," Mrs. Tannenbaum broke in, "you're not an *atheist?*"

"Why not? Most of the Jews I know are atheists."

"That's absolutely right." Rabbi Einhorn seemed to have regained his composure. He was smiling again. "My apologies for speaking sharply to you, Mr. Monsky. I forgot for a moment that in denouncing your people and denying your religion you're following one of the oldest, most valuable Jewish traditions. We're always drawn strength from our apostates as well as our faithful. That's one reason why we've survived for four thousand years."

"You think we'll go on surviving?" Bender said. "You think we'll make it through the next ten years?"

"I'm sure of it, Doctor.'

"And what's your evidence for that?"

"My evidence?" The rabbi looked very grave. "I'm not a superstitious man, in spite of Mr. Monsky's accusation, but I can't believe that God's ways are *quite* without purpose or reason. If a great people who have contributed for four thousand years to the literature, the art, the ethical and spiritual values of civilization can be wiped out overnight by an ignorant paperhanger—then what kind of world do we live in? It can only be a nightmare—a maniac's nightmare."

The waiter brought dessert, a strawberry tart overflowing with custard. As he started pouring their coffee, they heard shushing noises from across the dining room. Bender looked where everybody was looking, toward a table by the wall at which several men in uniform were sitting—the ship's officers, Bender supposed. One of them, a tall young man with a sallow, scowling face, was clinking his spoon against a glass. When the crowd was finally silent, the young officer stood up and spoke in a sharp clear voice with almost no emotion.

"My name is Muller. I am the first officer aboard this ship.

The captain cannot unfortunately take his meal here tonight, but he has asked me to welcome you to the *Franz Joseph.*"

There was a low buzzing sound from the crowd. Others, Bender realized, were as disappointed as he that they wouldn't be getting a look at the captain of this strange ship.

"The captain feels sure," Muller went on, "that you are wondering about the treatment you will receive during this voyage. You have become accustomed to a certain kind of treatment, according to the laws of the state—" He paused. When he continued, though his voice was as flat as before, Bender distinctly felt a sharpness underneath. "The captain wishes to assure you that *he* is the supreme authority aboard this ship. Here the laws are *his* laws. He has always treated his passengers in a certain way, and you will receive the same treatment, nothing less—that is his responsibility as he sees it. Therefore, he has instructed the stewards, the members of the crew, and the officers—including myself—to make your comfort their first concern. If anyone should fall short of this standard, or convey by word or action the least disrespect to any of you, the captain urges you to report the matter to me as his representative. The offender will be properly disciplined."

Abruptly, with no formal conclusion, not even a "thank you," Muller sat down. There was a moment of silence, then the low buzzing rose again all over the room. Bender could guess what people were thinking. The captain's message was against nature; a thing like this just couldn't happen—therefore nobody was quite willing to believe that it *was* happening. Madness, Bender had noticed before, often has that effect on the inexperienced. It takes a long time to accept the reality of madness.

And the captain must be mad—no other hypothesis, at the moment, would account for all of the facts. It might be instructive, Bender thought, to try to diagnose the specific nature of this madness. A pity that his opportunities to observe the captain would be so severely limited.

The meal was over. All around the dining room people were pulling away from their tables. As Bender escorted Julia and Eva out to the foyer, the loudspeaker announced that there would be a bingo game in the main lounge and dancing in the nightclub.

Bender saw the eager look on Eva's face, though it disappeared a moment later and was replaced by a shadow of

42

uncertainty. He could almost read the words in her mind—"Is it all right to enjoy myself?"

Bender turned to Julia and said, "Would the bingo game amuse you? I have a feeling Eva would like to try it."

"You two go along, then," Julia said. "I've got some underthings to wash out. It's a bore, but it has to be done. And frankly I can't think of anything deadlier than bingo."

"Very well, then. Eva and I will be desperate gamblers together. I'll return her to you when it's her bedtime. And then perhaps you and I can look in on the nightclub."

"Oh, not tonight, darling. I'm really so exhausted. You don't mind too much, do you?"

"Certainly not. It's been a hard day for me, too." He gave Julia a kiss, then took Eva by the arm and turned away.

With complete success he forced down his momentary disappointment. It was strictly a reflex, it had no importance at all. The day he first met Julia—at that luncheon for the Hospital Fund with all those stupid, homely rich ladies, among whom this one clever, beautiful rich lady stood out like a swan among geese—he had had enough of emotional involvement. He had been looking for detachment, and in Julia he had found it. He had absolutely nothing to complain of. . . .

As she walked up the stairs, Julia Bender could still see the look that had flashed over Carl's face when she'd told him how exhausted she was. As if it really mattered to him— But that was impossible, of course. She knew Carl inside out—how kind he was, how intelligent and amusing, how polite and considerate; and how careful always to do precisely what he wished to do and nothing else. He had made it clear from the start how few demands he would make and how few he would expect *her* to make. And she had accepted the terms gladly—with the utmost relief. After her hellish four years of total war with Gunther, she wasn't likely to be in the mood for the same damn thing all over again. Easy, relaxed, friendly, undemanding—nothing could be better for her, for Carl, and for Eva. Above all, for Eva.

Only sometimes, very seldom but sometimes, Julia would feel a vague wish— Utter nonsense! She had nothing to wish for, there was no reason to feel a thing. Exhaustion was confusing her tonight, playing havoc with her imagination. Only natural after the day she had been through. Up at the

43

crack of dawn, that hideous train ride, those policemen on the dock . . .

Yet the cause of her exhaustion went deeper. She knew what was *really* bothering her—though perhaps she hadn't quite admitted it to herself until now. She was frightened. For a long time now, literally for years, it had been building up in her. And today, as she waited for the ship to sail, her fear had reached its climax—it had left her weak, shaking, imagining all sorts of horrors, like a child.

She wondered if Carl had guessed this about her. There was very little he didn't guess about her. Nevertheless, she had been trying hard to conceal this from him. She didn't care to expose herself to his smile, his soft, amused, all-knowing smile.

She gave a sigh, the easiest, most relaxed sound she had been able to manage all day. The ship was at sea, the night-mare was over—her fear wasn't necessary anymore. She ought to be happy—she ought to be ecstatic. Later in the evening, in fact, she might have a few dances with Carl after all.

* * *

"Monsky, you talk too much. Your voice is too loud, you interrupt people in the middle of sentences, and why do you have to disagree with what everybody else says? It doesn't matter what the subject is, you always take the opposite side of it. Believe me, you're not going to make friends *that* way. Furthermore, Monsky, you're a liar. There's no use denying it—you'll tell lies at the drop of a hat. You invent conversations with people you never met. You give detailed descriptions of places you've never been to. And why? To build up your ego, pure and simple. To make yourself look like a big shot in the eyes of people whose opinion you've got no respect for. And the worst of it is the lies you tell aren't even plausible. Selling music stands to Bruno Walter! Arguing about psychoanalysis with Sigmund Freud! Nobody in his right mind could possibly believe such stories. So tell me, Monsky, when are you going to break yourself of these rotten habits? When are you going to start acting like a man?"

Off and on for the last twenty-five years or so Leon Monsky had been giving himself this lecture, more or less in the same words. Sometimes he gave it angrily, disgusted with himself—

44

sometimes on the verge of tears, sorry for himself. But to-night, as he sat in the smoking room off the main lounge and puffed his after-dinner cigar, he couldn't keep from feeling pleased with himself. The harder the insults he heaped on his head, the more pleased he felt. Each piece of evidence in the indictment was accompanied by an unspoken little quali-fication: "All right, Monsky, so you're not perfect. But you're still a pretty fine fellow."

This feeling of well-being had been growing in him all day. He had awakened with it this morning. It had seen him through a big breakfast of eggs and kidneys and one last duel of wits with his landlady, Mrs. Blaumeister, that scrawny, scratchy-voiced female who looked like a malevolent chicken. As usual, she had poured out her vitriol on him. What a pleasure it was to get rid of him at last! Now she could rent the room to some *respectable* gentleman who paid up on time and didn't leave things in such a mess! In times like these, too, when Jews ought to behave *better* than other peo-ple! As her late husband always used to say, "It's a few bad ones who make it hard for the rest of us." In reply to all this Monsky had pretended to believe that she didn't mean a word of it, that her nasty manner concealed a feminine tenderness for him, that she was actually flirting with him in her own peculiar way and was brokenhearted to see him leave.

This strategy drove her wild and sent him off to the rail-way station in a better mood than ever, such a good mood that nothing could spoil it, not even the train ride, not even the customs inspection on the dock. As a matter of fact, that inspection had *raised* his spirits. He had taken two dozen cigars—the best Havanas, a special going-away present to himself; he didn't like to think of the finagling he had done to get them—and distributed them one by one in various parts of his clothing. And those stupid policemen hadn't nosed out a single one.

A good omen, he told himself. A preview of what the future's going to be like. Because he thought he knew why he was feeling so wonderful today, so positively on top of the world. Everybody else on this ship had mixed feelings about leaving Germany. They were thankful to get away with their lives, but also they were frightened about the future, about starting all over again in a strange country where the language was different and they had no money and their

45

prospects looked dim at best. But Monsky wasn't frightened, Monsky wasn't sad. He had *never* had any money. He had *never* had any prospects. Of all the passengers, he and he alone left nothing at all behind, not even happy memories.

The orchestra conductor, Karlweis, appeared in one doorway of the smoking room. A tall old man with crazy white hair and a long nose. As he started across the room, Monsky stood up and held out his hand. "How are you, Maestro? It's a pleasure to see you again."

Karlweis wrinkled up his nose, as if he were smelling something that bothered him. "Excuse me, I don't—"

"Monsky. Leon. We met a few years ago in Vienna, at a dinner for the Bruno Walters. We talked about Beethoven's symphonies. You were kind enough to agree with my opinion of Toscanini."

"Oh yes, I believe I recall—" And there was nothing Karlweis could do but shake Monsky's hand.

"Well, it's nice that you're on this boat. Maybe we'll continue that discussion." Monsky patted him on the arm and returned to his chair and his cigar. Karlweis hurried out the other doorway.

Monsky couldn't stop himself from chuckling a little. Vienna. Now that was a city he'd like to visit someday.

He took a puff from his cigar and let out the smoke slowly, savoring it. The truth was, he had always had expensive tastes. If he could have had the income to go with them, what a happy man he would have been. "Monsky," he often told himself, "you were born into the wrong family."

By nature, intellect, and inclination he belonged in the aristocracy—or at least in the upper bourgeoisie. Instead, his parents had been a couple of Polish immigrants, peasants till the day they died, even though they had spent the last forty years of their lives trying to squeeze a living out of their dingy little tailor shop. With all those nights that he pored over his Hebrew books, Papa was strictly an ignoramus. His head was full of windy Talmudic phrases that he didn't understand, and he never *had* been able to speak German without an accent.

And Mama was even worse. To this day Monsky could make himself wince just by remembering the fancy tricks she had played to keep people from finding out she couldn't read. Pretending she had mislaid her glasses, and so on. So naturally everybody guessed the truth anyway. And then there were his sisters and brothers, seven of them, all older than he was, all carbon copies of Papa and Mama. It was years since he had set eyes on any of them, but he couldn't say this made him feel deprived.

Though he did have to admit, if it wasn't for his sister Sadie in Detroit, Michigan, and her rich American husband, he wouldn't be on this ship now. . . .

Anyway, coming from such a family, no wonder he'd had his troubles. How could he ever go to the university, for instance? He was a lot smarter than the rich dummies who slept through classes for four years and collected degrees at the end of it, but where was he going to find the money?

So for the rest of his life this injustice had followed him, barking at his heels, keeping him from ever getting the kind of job that suited a man of his intellectual capacity. And the kind of woman who suited him, too. All right, along those lines his tastes had always been expensive and discriminating. Why not? He wasn't going to settle down for life with some drudge who was too stupid and middle-class to share the interests of a man like him. The type of woman who *could* appreciate him he could never get to meet, on account of the social barriers—that family of his again. Better to go to prostitutes. Better the most slovenly and disgusting street-walker—and he had known some pretty slovenly and disgusting ones—than being chained forever to a mediocrity. And it was the same with all the other troubles in his life—the money that people claimed he owed them, the landladies who kept throwing him out in the street, the business enterprises that always seemed to collapse as soon as he got involved in them. Was *he* to blame for the bad luck which had dogged him since the day he was born? In all fairness, was *he* to blame?

In all fairness, Monsky told himself—producing another cloud of smoke from his cigar—he was absolutely and completely to blame. He himself. Nobody else had any right to share the credit.

Oh yes, he knew the truth about himself well enough. Immigrants or no immigrants, Mama and Papa had managed to send him through school. He had ended up—let's face the facts—with better opportunities than most boys get. He had thrown away those opportunities. All his life he had made the worst out of every good thing that happened to him. Whenever he got his hands on a little money, he squandered it. Whenever he met a nice girl who seemed to care for him, he found some way of turning her against him. Whenever he made a friend who wanted to help him, he managed somehow to undermine the benefits of that help. Almost as if he did it on purpose. Destroying his own life on purpose. Now what would the great Dr. Sigmund Freud—or the not-so-great Dr. Carl Bender—make of *that*?

And now what happens to me? Monsky wondered. Now that I'm sailing away from all that, putting the Atlantic Ocean between me and myself, making a fresh start in America thanks to my rich brother-in-law, will I become a changed man? Will I turn over a new leaf?

"Mr. Monsky, you're not playing bingo?"

He looked up and saw Mrs. Tannenbaum, the girl from his dining room table. "I'm not the gambling type," he said, getting to his feet. "I prefer to sit here and relax with my cigar and think about life."

"Martin's that way, too," she said. "He has a very philosophical mind. He reads Spinoza. He thinks playing cards and so on is a terrible waste of time."

"A man after my own heart." To himself Monsky added: Playing cards certainly *would* be a waste of time on this ship, since nobody was allowed to take more than five marks out of the country. Another example of his terrible luck. Any other ocean liner would be full of fat, stupid millionaires, perfect targets for certain skills he had picked up in his younger days, when he was still playing cards at the cafés. But *this* ocean liner, the first and only ocean liner he had ever sailed on, was carrying a cargo of paupers.

"I have to confess, though," Mrs. Tannenbaum said, "I *do* enjoy a little game of rummy once in a while. Or making a bet on something or other. It's exciting, for a change, that is—"

She laughed, and Monsky could see she was blushing. A nice girl, he thought. Not so bright or sophisticated or beautiful maybe, but she was in love with her husband—which was a nice change nowadays. And the way she was looking forward to having her baby— How old was she, he wondered. Twenty-seven, twenty-eight maybe? If he had got married around that age, he could have a daughter right now who wasn't much younger than she. Now *there* was a thought to spoil a man's whole day.

"Well, I think I'll look in on the bingo," she said. "I'm

going to do everything there *is* to do on this ship. It's the only way I'll get through the week, till I see Martin."

"Your husband will be meeting you in Havana?"

"Isn't it wonderful? His uncle is letting him out of work for a few days. He'll have to go right back, of course—and my American visa won't be good for eight months—"

Though she was smiling, Monsky could see tears in her eyes. For just a second he felt a sharp pang somewhere inside him. No woman had ever felt like crying such tears over him.

The pang went away. He was annoyed at himself, and annoyed at this silly girl, too. What business did she have barging in on him and spoiling a good cigar?

A few moments later she moved toward the bingo game. Monsky took a puff or two from his cigar and regained his mood of contentment. So where was he? Oh yes, he had been going over the failures in his life. A long, impressive list. It wasn't easy to decide which item was the most inexcusable, which was the most irresponsible act he had ever committed.

Maybe it was that business with Bruno Schwarzkopf a dozen or so years ago. Monsky had just been fired by that company that made buttons, and things had looked pretty black until a pal of his, a floorwalker at Schwarzkopf's Department Store, had got him a job as a clerk in the administrative office. He hated it there. Especially he hated it every afternoon when the great Schwarzkopf himself came in for his daily snooping expedition. Looking over everybody's shoulder, checking up whether they were pounding their adding machines to his satisfaction, and ending up in the doorway, rocking on his heels, looking like he thought his shit was made of diamonds. "Carry on, ladies and gentlemen!" was what he always said. "You're doing a fine job, and Schwarzkopf's appreciates it!"

That fat, smug little tyrant! Day in and day out Monsky felt that breath down his neck and listened to that asinine speech, and the impulse grew in him to answer back. He began to do a lot of thinking about what he should say exactly. He would have only one chance, so he'd better make the best of it. Several devastating rejoinders occurred to him, until he settled on "As far as I'm concerned, Mr. Schwarzkopf, you can take your appreciation and stick it up your *tokas!*" But after five or six months, when he was finally ready to quit, Monsky decided that this remark wasn't good

49

enough. It was crude, overemotional. So he contented himself with simply not showing up for work the next morning.

Naturally, Schwarzkopf wouldn't have any memory of him today. If he went up to Schwarzkopf and said hello, all he'd get for his trouble would be a fishy stare. And later on he could imagine what Schwarzkopf would say about him to his idiot wife and family. "What's that Pole doing on this ship, anyway? It's disgraceful he should take up space that could be occupied by a good German."

My God, how Monsky hated them, these good German Jews! Yes, this was the deepest feeling in him—maybe the *only* deep feeling in him. He hated them more than the Nazis. More than Hitler, even. He was filled with rage and hatred for every one of them—for Schwarzkopf, his fat stupid wife, that pompous rabbi, that Dr. Bender with ice water in his veins.

And now he understood, *really* understood, why he was in such a wonderful mood today. "Monsky, this is the happiest day of your life," he told himself, "because at last, at long last, you're equal to those damn Germans. They've come down to join you at the bottom of the barrel. The pack is being reshuffled, the cards are being dealt all over again— who says *you* shouldn't have the good hands this time around?"

Suddenly he had an idea, a wonderful way to celebrate his great discovery. He could go into the lounge where the bingo game was, where he had seen Schwarzkopf and his whole family going a few minutes before. He could walk right up to the old man and smile at him and say, "Schwarzkopf, I'm glad to see you again. The time has come for me to tell you what I think of you." Two minutes it would take—not even that long—and he could enjoy the memory for the rest of his life. Why not, why not? Absolutely nothing was stopping him.

"Mr. Monsky?"

He looked up. Standing over him was the man he shared his cabin with. Arthur Stieffel—a big man in his fifties, some kind of banker or stockbroker. "Mr. Monsky, a few of us are trying to get a bridge game started, and we were wondering if you'd like to be the fourth."

Another good omen. Only a minute ago hadn't he been thinking about packs of cards? It was as if God were saying to him, "Monsky, I'm listening to you. It's taken a long time, but finally you've got my attention." A man would have to be crazy to ignore an omen like this. His big idea, his big confrontation with Schwarzkopf, would just have to wait till later.

"My pleasure, Mr. Stieffel," he said, stubbing out his cigar and getting to his feet. "A nice game of bridge is exactly what I've been needing."

As he followed Stieffel out of the smoking room, he made up his mind to show these big shots how the game was played. If necessary, he would give lady luck a helping hand— True enough, there wouldn't be any money in it for him. But money isn't everything. Sometimes a man has to do things just for the fun of it.

*   *   *

The chief steward, a fat little man who never stopped grinning, stood on a platform at the end of the lounge and called out numbers. "Twelve-B! Twenty-one-I! Forty-seven-G!"

People sat at tables and sofas all over the large room watching their cards, listening to the numbers. And yet, it didn't seem to David Peyser that most of them were any more interested in the game than he was. Nobody was smiling much, nobody cried out happily when his number was called or groaned when it wasn't, everybody just seemed to be going through the motions. Even Joshua, who usually got so excited over games.

Still, people *were* paying attention while the numbers were called out. And so, bored as he was, David knew enough to keep quiet. You have to have good manners and show consideration for others, Papa always said, otherwise you're no better than the Nazi beasts.

Grandpa—as David had noticed a long time ago—had never learned any manners. While everyone around him was trying to hear the numbers, Grandpa just went on talking. "Take my word for it," he said, "there wouldn't be any problem today if some of us had been allowed to have our way ten years ago. We saw those people pouring into the country by the thousands, we knew what was bound to happen. Ignorant foreigners! They didn't talk the language, they had no respect for our German customs and traditions. They didn't even spend their money within our borders. Seventy-five percent of what they made they sent right out of the country to their relatives in Warsaw or Odessa or God knows where. People resented it, what could be more natural? And of course they blamed the Jews as a whole. The average man doesn't make a distinction between them and us. As far as he's concerned, all Jews are alike."

This was Grandpa's favorite topic of conversation. For years David had been hearing him make speeches about it. Lately the speeches seemed to be getting longer, and he seemed to be making them more often. This morning on the train he went through the whole thing with the old lady who was sitting across from him, though she looked as if she were over eighty, and probably she was deaf. And he did it all over again for the people at their dining room table, Mr. and Mrs. Buberman, when anybody could see they weren't a bit interested—they had just got married, and all they did was look at each other, and they left the dining room together ahead of everyone else. But Grandpa didn't notice, he kept on talking anyway.

"So I ask you, what's the cause of all the trouble?" Grandpa was coming to the part where he always raised his voice. "The German Jewish community! You don't think those immigrants could have lasted a week in our country if our own charitable organizations hadn't fed them and clothed them and given them handouts. *Some* of us saw what was going on, believe me. As far back as nineteen twenty-six I stood up at a meeting of the Berlin Jewish Council and warned them what would happen, begged them to stop cutting their throats before it was too late. Yes, I begged them, I practically got down on my knees."

Grandpa on his knees, Grandpa begging anybody for anything? David couldn't even imagine this.

"But naturally they wouldn't listen to me. Jews, God help them, have no sense in their heads. So now we're paying for our stupidity."

But the worst of it, David thought, wasn't Grandpa's loud talk. It was Papa's silence. David knew what Papa thought of Grandpa's opinions. Papa had told him many times that you have to help those who are less fortunate than you, that this is the most important thing about being a Jew and it has to be remembered even by people like themselves who aren't very religious. But Papa never had the courage to say any of these things to Grandpa.

Somebody ought to put Grandpa in his place. It wasn't right that he should go on bullying and bragging without ever being punished for it. Listening now to that harsh, ugly voice, David could imagine the punishment. He could see the rope around Grandpa's neck, his thick neck with all that flabby flesh. He could see the beads of sweat on Grandpa's face, the terrified look in his eyes. Then the signal was given, the trap was sprung, Grandpa's fat body dropped into empty space. The rope tightened, dug into those folds of flesh, made his eyes bulge and his tongue stick out. That's how people like Grandpa ought to be taken care of. That's what ought to be done with every one of them—

"David, David!" He looked up and saw Mama leaning towards him. "Are you all right, darling? You don't look so well."

"What is it?" Papa said. "You look as if somebody frightened you."

"Bingo!" somebody shouted.

A little later a new game began, the steward called out more numbers. David found himself yearning to see a movie tonight. Would there be movies on this ship? It was important to him—he couldn't tell anybody how important it was.

For the last two years there hadn't been much for him to do all day except go to the movies. Papa had taken him out of school before graduation—things had got so bad that David hadn't been able to hold out anymore. After that he was supposed to read and study on his own, but how much reading and studying can you do all alone in your room when you know it isn't going to lead you anywhere? So four or five times a week, when he told Mama and Papa he was going out for a walk, he ended up at the movies. And it wasn't easy to do, either. He had to pay for it with the pocket money he was supposed to use for lunches when he met his friends—and the risk was terrible, since Jews weren't allowed in places of public entertainment. If he had ever been caught . . .

If they did show movies on this ship, he hoped there would be newsreels along with them, the kind he'd been seeing in theaters in Berlin—the kind the government made, with soldiers marching, airplanes flying in formation, the Führer making speeches while the crowds cheered. When he got to America, it wouldn't be possible to see such newsreels any more. That would be the end of it—out of his life forever.

53

He wondered if he could stand that. For almost two years he had been watching them, sitting without moving a muscle as the marching and the shouting and the loud music blasted out at him. He remembered one newsreel particularly. Every day for a week he went to the same theater just to see it, though the main film wasn't any good. That newsreel showed a youth rally in Munich, where Borman and Göring and finally the Führer himself had spoken. There were many close-ups of the boys in their seats listening so intently, their eyes shining with inspiration. And when the Führer finished speaking, how they all jumped to their feet, raised their arms in the salute, and called out *Sieg Heil! Sieg Heil!* until they were hoarse. One boy kept showing up in the camera, a thin boy with dark hair who still had a few pimples on his face and who was wearing glasses, thick, pale-rimmed glasses, the same kind that David wore. How excited and happy that boy was as he raised his arm and cried out *Sieg Heil!* That boy is me, David used to say to himself. That's me at that rally. The Führer is speaking to me. I am his son, the fatherland's son, and all these boys are my brothers.

He got to his feet. "It's stuffy in here. Please—could I go out on the deck?"

Mama was sure he was sick. She put her hand on his forehead, declared that he had a fever, insisted on taking him back to the cabin. Papa told her to let him alone. "Go on, go out on deck," Papa said. "Don't come to bed too late tonight, though."

David kissed Mama and Grandma and gave his little bow to Grandpa and Papa. And finally he escaped.

On deck he walked quickly to the end of the ship, where there were no other people. He went to the railing and took in big gulps of air, cold and fresh, with the tang of salt in it. Far below he saw the black water, streaked with white foam. Thank God he was alone. The dream was about to start, and it was never right unless he was alone.

It started, as always, with that day in school when Professor Klein told him to sit in the back of the room. "From now on, Peyser, you will be apart from the rest of the class. You will talk to nobody, and nobody will talk to you. We can't make you leave this school, but at least we can make sure that good German youth isn't contaminated by you."

Then the dream moved ahead to the future—not too far in the future—to the time when the truth would finally be revealed. The world would learn then that David Peyser wasn't a Jew at all. His mother and father had been pure Aryans, but in infancy he had been stolen by Jews who pretended to be his parents, and they had brought him up as one of themselves. Suddenly he discovered the terrible thing that had been done to him, and he went to Professor Klein with the evidence. He was congratulated, but also he was told, "You must prove to us that your life among the Jews hasn't contaminated you. You must perform some splendid heroic deed which will show us that you're worthy to sit with the class once more."

There was only one deed, he knew, which could possibly satisfy them. And so in the middle of the night he got up from his bed and silently entered the room where his false mother and father were sleeping. There was a gun in his hand —where it came from wasn't clear—and he stood over their sleeping bodies and squeezed the trigger, and squeezed and squeezed. . . .

He felt drained, exhausted, as he always did when the dream reached its climax. Then, bit by bit, the exhaustion left him, and he was filled with horror and disgust. He was dizzy, nauseated. He had to grip the railing, or he might have stumbled to his knees.

Slowly he became aware of music. It was faint and tinny, it seemed to be coming from the deck above. They must be dancing in the nightclub. He felt a wish to be up there, to watch the dancers and listen to the music. With people around him, the sick feeling might go away.

He climbed the outside stairway to the upper deck and went into the small, dimly lighted bar that led to the nightclub. Through the entranceway he could see the dancers turning slowly to the moaning of saxophones while Chinese lanterns gave out an eerie orange light over their heads. Men and women were pressed together, bodies touching, faces touching. He felt himself trembling a little. If he had a girl to press her body against him, to put her cheek against his . . . In his whole life he had never really *done* anything with a girl, though he had imagined it often enough. In his whole life he had hardly ever been alone with a girl. How could he have been? If she wasn't Jewish, she wouldn't have anything to do with you. If she *was* Jewish, she didn't dare go out with you at night, you had to sit in her parents' living room and listen to her father talk about political conditions until her mother brought out the family photograph album. He wanted to go out with girls in America. He was afraid it might be too late now. After two years of wandering alone, of hiding himself in dark movie theaters, he was afraid he had made himself so clumsy and strange that no girl would be able to stand him.

"I don't blame you for getting out of there."

It was a moment before he realized that these words had been addressed to him. The speaker moved out of the shadows, and he recognized the boy who had stood behind him in the line this afternoon, when Joshua and he were making dining room reservations. A tall boy about his own age, with dark hair that wasn't very neat. They hadn't exchanged two words this afternoon, yet somehow it didn't seem strange for this boy to be speaking to him now.

"Getting out of where?" David said.

"The lounge, the bingo game. We just left ourselves. It *is* discouraging. The people on this ship have been through so much—only a few weeks ago they had no hope at all. So how do they celebrate their miraculous deliverance? They play bingo."

"What else should they do?" From the shadows behind the tall boy another figure appeared, a girl of seventeen or so. Her hair was dark, too, she wore hardly any makeup, her eyes were very large—the first thing David had noticed about her was her eyes. "It's no crime for people to enjoy themselves a little. They've got a right to after what they've been through."

"Don't they have any sense of—of dignity?" the boy said. "I mean, they're *not* just ordinary people. They stand for something. They're—the descendants of the Israelites wandering in the wilderness looking for the Promised Land. They're fulfilling their tragic destiny, and they don't even know it."

"Maybe they don't *want* a tragic destiny," the girl said. "Maybe they just want to lead their lives, like everybody else."

The boy gave a sigh. "You're right, I'm being unreasonable. By this time I ought to know that people are going to go on being people, no matter how much I'd like them to be heroes." He laughed, and the tenseness seemed to have gone out of him. "Well, as long as everybody else is wallowing in triviality tonight—why don't we sit down here and have a drink?"

"I'm afraid I don't have any money," David said.

"Who has money on this ship? Fortunately, beer is included in the price of our ticket."

They sat at a round table in the corner. The waiter hurried over to them and took their orders for three bottles of beer. "This service is heartwarming, isn't it?" said the boy. "Everybody making our comfort their first concern. And I had an idea the Nazis didn't like us."

They all introduced themselves. The boy was Peter Einhorn, and the girl was his sister, Naomi. They were traveling with their father who was a rabbi—his synagogue was the one Grandpa and Grandma used to belong to.

"Naomi and I have just been having an argument," Peter said. "I'd like to get your opinion about this. Our father is in his cabin just now, writing a sermon—"

"Because tomorrow is Friday," Naomi said, "and he's going to hold a Sabbath service. I don't see what's so strange—"

"A Sabbath service!" Peter said. "So we can all thank God for His kindness in giving us Adolf Hitler! No, it isn't strange at all. It's typical. The way Jews can deceive themselves, shut their eyes to reality—"

"A lot of people will come to the service," his sister said. "It'll be a real comfort to them."

"So is cocaine to some people. And incidentally, what were you telling me the other day, about the doubts you've been having?"

She blushed. "You promised you wouldn't repeat that. If Father ever found out—" She glanced quickly in David's direction, as if she were afraid he might be shocked at this revelation about her. She was sort of pretty when she was upset, he thought. "Maybe that *is* how I feel," she said. "With everything that's happening in the world— But that doesn't mean I think *everybody* ought to feel the same way. If people are able to believe in God, if it makes them happy to say the prayers and read from the Torah, why isn't that a good thing? It brings them a little peace of mind, and it certainly doesn't do any harm—"

"Who says so?" Peter broke in. "Isn't it harmful to turn people into sleepwalkers? What Jews need right now isn't praying but action. If we're satisfied with the way things are, we'll never make them any better."

"In other words, we're all supposed to go to Palestine, the

way *you* want to do? Well, that's all right, you're entitled to your opinion, but you have to be tolerant of people who feel differently—"

Peter threw up his hands. "There it is again—the old safe, timid, do-nothing philosophy. Sit around and be tolerant, while the anti-Semites annihilate us. Don't you understand, Jews can't afford that sort of thing any more, not until we've got a country of our own, some kind of freedom and security. Tolerance is a luxury of the strong."

"Now you sound like your friend Wilhelm Keitl," she said. "I'll bet those are exactly his words."

Peter reddened. "All right, suppose they are. Wilhelm made more sense than anybody I ever met. I hope I *can* carry on what he believed." He turned suddenly to David. "What do you think, Peyser? Am I right or wrong?"

"Well, I haven't really thought it out—"

It always made David nervous when people asked him for an opinion. He was glad that Peter Einhorn preferred talking to listening. He didn't wait for anything else from David but pushed right on. "It's the inertia, the apathy, the stubborn attachment to old, outworn beliefs—that's what drives you crazy sometimes. The state *can* be established in Palestine if we all work together. It's just a question of waking people up, making them understand—I mean, every Jew is a Zionist at heart. All right, all right, Wilhelm used to say that, but it happens to be true."

"I don't think you could include my grandfather in that," David said. "You should hear what he says about Zionism."

"Your grandfather is the fat man who was talking so loudly during the bingo game?" Peter grinned. "Well, I admit he sounded like a difficult case. A very common type. My father's congregation was full of them. . . ."

David knew it was wrong of him to listen to this kind of talk. It was disrespectful, disloyal. If you're not loyal to your own family . . . But as the words came out of Peter's mouth, a funny kind of thrill went through him. And he didn't say a thing in Grandpa's defense.

The ship rolled gently. The bottles of beer were emptied and replaced. Accompanied by that tinny music from the next room, Peter went on talking and talking. He talked about politics, about religion, about people he had met on this ship, about America. He talked about the life he had been leading for the last few years. Like David, he had found himself out of school with nothing to do, with no prospects for the future. He had spent the time reading all the books on Zionism and Jewish history he could get hold of. And some of his friends and he used to meet together in one another's homes to talk about what was happening to them and what Jews could do to fight back.

David remembered how *he* had spent these last few years. "I've always wanted to be a doctor," he put in quickly, "so I could spend my life helping people. I've been reading books on medicine since I left school—"

He stopped talking, lowered his eyes. He was aware of the rolling of the ship. He realized that the music had stopped. The nightclub was dark—the Chinese lanterns had been turned off, the dancers had gone away. He took a sip of beer, and it was flat.

"It's midnight," said Peter, looking at his watch. "I've been talking too much, as usual. Why don't we all turn in?"

When he got to his feet, David felt a touch of dizziness. Was he drunk from too much beer? Or from sitting here listening to the wild, dangerous words of this boy his own age? Or from knowing every single moment, even when he wasn't looking at her, that the girl was next to him, that her body was only a few inches away from his?

They left the bar, went down to the main deck, and walked through the lounge. Most of the lights were off, and only a few people could be seen. A man and a woman sat close together on a sofa, talking in low voices. An old man was in a chair near the door, his head hunched down, his hands clasped in his lap. He was shivering, though there wasn't any cold.

They walked down the stairs to A deck, where Peter and Naomi had their cabins. In the foyer David said good night to them, and they all stood and looked at each other, and then Naomi said, "At breakfast we're allowed to sit at any table we like. So if you wanted to meet us in the dining room tomorrow morning—"

David blinked in surprise for a moment, then he nodded. "Yes—I'd like to . . ."

Then Naomi and Peter were gone, and David stood still, feeling dizzy again. A girl like that—intelligent, serious-minded, full of high ideals— If a girl like that could ever care for him—

Or what if a girl like that should reach out to him, stroke his face, kiss him? What if she should open her dress for him and show him her naked body and let him do things to her? He could see her body right now, he could see himself doing those things—

He gave a shake of his head. He was revolting. He was a revolting person. He didn't deserve to be friends with a girl like that.

He hurried down the stairs to B deck. He got to the door of his cabin and opened it slowly. He tiptoed inside so that he wouldn't wake Joshua, and he undressed himself in the darkness. Then he went into the little bathroom. He finished brushing his teeth but stayed at the sink staring at himself in the mirror. He stared and stared, asking himself the question he asked nearly every night: Do I look Jewish? Could anybody tell if they didn't know it already? All right, I've got dark hair. But so does Hitler. And my nose isn't hooked or anything, and my lips aren't thick, in fact they're more on the thin side.

There was one way, though, that everyone could tell he was a Jew. He had often thought about this, staring at himself in the mirror and hating what he saw. If only he had been born a girl! Or if you could take a knife and make it look as if some kind of accident had happened to you—

He pulled away from the mirror. He left the bathroom and tiptoed up to the double-decker bed. But he didn't get in yet. He stood and looked at Joshua sprawled on his back in the upper bunk. His arm was flung over his forehead, his mouth was slightly open. His breathing was so soft you could hardly hear it.

How easy it would be to make him stop breathing, David thought. Just slip the pillow from under his head, then clamp it down over his face. He might thrash around a little, but he was small and skinny, he wouldn't have the strength to last more than a few minutes. And when it was over—*then* they'd have to trust you. They couldn't say you were contaminated *then*. Once you showed them that you didn't think any more about killing one little Jewboy than you did about stepping on an ant—

David looked away from Joshua's face. He got into the lower bunk and pulled the covers up to his chin. He lay on his back for a long time, his teeth chattering. God forgive me, he kept saying to himself. Please, please forgive me. I'm not really like that at all. . . .

*   *   *

A wind came up that night. It troubled the sea. Large rolling waves like hills lifted the *Franz Joseph* up and up, held it trembling for a moment or two, then let it plunge down again.

A thousand people were in their beds now, rising and falling with the motion of the ship. Some slept as soundly as corpses. Some tossed fitfully and gave out low, anguished sighs that they wouldn't remember in the morning.

Suddenly one of the sleepers opened his eyes wide, gave a cry, sat up staring into the darkness. For a few moments his nightmare seemed real to him, then gradually he realized where he was. That pitching motion, that shadowy porthole across the room—yes, he was on the ship after all. This was reality. His nightmare had been—just a nightmare.

With a smile he let his head sink back on the pillow. And yet he wouldn't close his eyes again. For as long as he could, he fought the heaviness that was pressing down on his eyelids. Anything was better than being sucked back into that dream.

THREE

DR. Emmanuel Rabal was the leader of the Jewish community in Havana, Cuba. He held this position for both official and unofficial reasons.

Officially, he had many titles attached to his name. He was president of the largest synagogue in Havana. He was chairman of the board of the Jewish Home for the Aged. He was a permanent arbitrator on the Jewish Court, an informal body which settled private disputes on a voluntary basis. Most important of all, he was chairman of the Hebrew Community Council, which raised money for Cuban Jews in need. His function was to speak at public affairs and have his picture published in the newspapers, thus giving the organization an unimpeachable stamp of dignity and integrity.

Unofficially, Dr. Rabal was leader of the Jewish community by virtue of his unique place in the non-Jewish community. He was far from being the wealthiest Jew in Havana, but he was certainly the best known and the most highly respected. For more than ten years he had been chief of staff in the government hospital—the only representative of his faith ever to hold this post—and for many years before that he had been the president's personal physician. He and his family had *entrée* to the highest social circles. They attended the balls and dinners to which most of Havana's wealthy class, Jew and gentile alike, would have given years of their lives to be invited. Regardless of which political faction was in power, the most influential men dined with Dr. Rabal at his home. When difficulties arose between the Jewish community and the Cuban government, it was seldom that Dr. Rabal, with a quiet little dinner or two, couldn't smooth them over.

It was to Dr. Rabal, then, that Morrie Feldman turned for help with his problem.

The problem didn't come up till his third day in Havana.

62

Everything went perfectly till then. Within twenty-four hours of his arrival he established credit at the largest local bank, so that at short notice he could draw emergency funds for food, clothing, and medical supplies. Then, in a day of dashing around the city in taxicabs and sweating constantly in the unrelenting heat, he found several dozen boarding houses and private homes where guests might be put up for several weeks at minimal rates. Not ideal, but these places would do as a stopgap measure. Then he turned his attention to the delicate question of providing employment for the refugees. Many of them were trained professionals or people with expert business experience; there certainly ought to be work for them, at least on a temporary basis.

So Morrie went to the Ministry of Labor, which issued work permits to visitors and aliens. He talked to an official who explained that a small fee would be required from each applicant, a mere trifle, as well as certain extra charges for clerical work; and of course, there was the usual tax for the old-age pension. No matter that none of these people would be staying in Cuba long enough to collect an old-age pension: it was simply, the official explained, a question of the regulations.

Adding up all these items and multiplying by one thousand, Morrie decided that an immediate cablegram to Al Margolinski was in order. Al cabled back: "TELL MINLABOR OK. AJDA WILL FIND MONEY."

Next Morrie saw Senor Benites, the chief of the Bureau of Immigration. Much smiling, bowing, and handshaking—but the chief became very serious when they got to the subject of the *Franz Joseph*. He spoke at length about "those poor homeless people" and expressed the "deep sympathies of the Cuban government and of the entire population of our island, from the lowliest peasant up to the president himself." He mentioned that his wife had cried for hours when he first told her the story of the *Franz Joseph*. He shook his head grimly as he referred to "the mad dog Adolf Hitler." Then, to Morrie's relief—for this had been the whole point of the visit—he confirmed that all the passengers' visas were in order and had been fully paid for in Germany.

In the taxicab riding back to the hotel Morrie felt rather pleased with himself. Only two days, and most of the technical obstacles had melted away. Who said you couldn't get things done in a Latin country?

He knew, of course, that he couldn't have done it without Esther Berkowitz. She was the "expert" Al had assigned to help him. An American citizen whose husband worked for the Havana branch of a New York bank, she had served for nearly three years as liaison between AJDA and the Hebrew Community Council. She was about Morrie's age and had received the same social work training that he had, but from the start he was impressed by her energy, resourcefulness, and knowledgeability. She seemed to know everybody; all doors were open to her; people relaxed and talked frankly when she was present. She accompanied Morrie on all his interviews, not only translating difficult phrases but frequently suggesting the right questions to ask.

Her most important qualification for this job, however, was that she herself was a German refugee. Her parents had come to America in 1933 among the first Jews to get out of Germany. Morrie would never have guessed this about her. She had gone to college and graduate school in America, and spoke English with no trace of an accent.

She was a quiet girl, tense and unsmiling, a little uncomfortable to be with. Morrie much preferred the warm, *hamische* type, like his wife, Ruth, the type who couldn't keep her mouth shut. To his surprise Esther's husband, Jerry Berkowitz (they all had dinner together on Morrie's second night in Havana), turned out to be hearty, good-natured, and totally nonpolitical—a former All-American halfback from Cornell whose eyes lit up with excitement when he talked about "debentures."

And then, out of nowhere, the big problem came up.

His first day in Havana Morrie had got in touch with the local office of the Hamburg Line. It was run by an elderly little man named Gruber, half German and half Cuban in parentage, but all Cuban in his easygoing, cheerful manner. Senor Gruber had assured Morrie of the line's complete cooperation when the ship was in dock. Senor Feldman and his charming associate would be permitted to go aboard and talk to the passengers; a special section of the pier would be cordoned off for people who were meeting the unfortunate refugees. On his third afternoon in Havana, less than three days before the *Franz Joseph* was due, Morrie called up Gruber again to remind him of his promise of cooperation.

Gruber was very nervous over the phone. He stammered,

coughed, interrupted himself. Finally he blurted out, "Senor Feldman, don't talk to *me* about these matters! I am only a businessman, a most unimportant businessman! Talk to the Bureau of Immigration!" And he hung up.

Morrie called the bureau immediately and asked for Senor Benites. There was a long delay. Once he was disconnected and had to put in the call again. At last a sharp voice came on the line and introduced itself as the assistant chief. Senor Benites was engaged in an important conference, he was unavailable. Would he be available later in the day? Could an appointment be made? Impossible. Senor Benites could see nobody till tomorrow morning at the earliest. Even then he had a heavy schedule. Perhaps with luck he could give the American a few minutes around eleven.

At eleven the next morning Morrie and Esther got to Benites' office. They cooled their heels for an hour. Then a young man appeared, businesslike and cold, and handed Morrie an envelope. "The chief cannot see you today. This communication will explain itself. It will not be necessary for you to call him for additional information."

The note in the envelope stated, in formal, spare language, that the Cuban entrance visas of the passengers arriving Wednesday morning on the German liner *Franz Joseph* were hereby cancelled until further notice. Unofficial information to this effect, the note went on, had been given to the local representative of the Hamburg Line. Official information would soon be given by radio to the captain of the *Franz Joseph*.

For the rest of the day all Morrie's efforts to talk to Benites failed. Finally, late in the afternoon, he called Al in New York. It was a terrible connection. Through the wheezing and crackling he barely heard Al say, "Okay, you'd better call Esther. Tell her to get you an appointment with Emmanuel Rabal."

* * *

After dinner Dr. Rabal's car and chauffeur came for Morrie at the hotel, then picked up Esther at her apartment building. The drive took them out of the city, through softly rolling hills, under canopies of palm trees. All of a sudden the air was cool, and miraculously, Morrie's shirt wasn't sticking to his back. At last the car turned into a crescent-shaped driveway enclosing an expanse of lawn that glowed palely in the moonlight. The house was large and white, with Roman columns in front and flowering shrubs all around. An elderly butler led Morrie and Esther down a long hall into a wood-paneled room full of old overstuffed furniture.

Dr. Rabal rose to greet them from a high-backed armchair near the fireplace. He was a small man with thinning white hair and small, delicate hands. He was wearing evening clothes, and on his head was a black skullcap. This surprised Morrie—in New York you didn't see too many *yarmulkes* any more. Morrie's Brooklyn grandfather still wore one, but *he* didn't even own evening clothes.

Dr. Rabal kissed Esther on the cheek in a benign and fatherly manner and shook Morrie's hand. "You're surprised that I keep my head covered, Mr. Feldman? Purely an atavistic remnant of my childhood. Though I wear the *kepot* here in my own home, in the world outside I remove it. And even here, when the world comes to me. I'm afraid my late father would be horrified at my inconsistency. 'Be a Jew or don't be a Jew,' he'd say to me. 'Stop pussyfooting.'" Dr. Rabal smiled, and his face became very gentle, almost cherubic. "For the two of you, however, I feel sure I can keep my head covered in perfect safety. You'll join me for coffee and brandy, won't you?"

He rang a bell, and the elderly butler entered wheeling a coffee table. "My wife would like to have met you," Dr. Rabal said, as they were served. "She's very interested in your country, and especially in her fellow Jews among you. She has heard that in New York City the synagogues have signs in front of them, right out on the public street, proclaiming what they are to the whole world. She can hardly bring herself to believe this, and would like to see for herself. I, of course, have visited your country many times, and so I know that these marvels really exist. You'll have sugar, Mr. Feldman? It's as well for a newcomer to take a great deal of sugar in our Cuban coffee. Well, as I was saying, my wife unfortunately won't be joining us tonight. We have a limited amount of time—half an hour, to be exact, before my next guest arrives—and we mustn't waste any of it."

He took a sip of coffee and a sip of brandy, shut his eyes for a moment, then went on. "Since I talked to Esther on the phone, I've made a few inquiries among friends of mine in government circles. I had, of course, heard something about the ship which is scheduled to arrive Wednesday, and frankly I'm not surprised to hear that difficulties have arisen. My friends merely confirm my own suspicions."

"Why have the difficulties arisen?" Morrie said.

Dr. Rabal pursed his lips. "I'm going to speak quite candidly, Mr. Feldman. I know and respect your organization, and Esther vouches for your discretion. I assume you'll be careful about repeating my words outside this room. Very well, then—let me give you a brief lecture on the Cuban political situation. As you may know, our country was plagued for many years by revolutions, a polite name for pirates fighting among themselves for the spoils. That period is over now. We have a stable, unified government in which all leading factions are represented, with no serious threat from outside dissidents. In other words, the pirates have learned to live together and divide the spoils.

"You must understand, however, even within this unity and stability there are tensions, conflicts, little disagreements as to the equity of the division. We have a president, Senor Bru, and we have a gray eminence, General Batista. But Senor Bru, though he looks like a figurehead, is not entirely without muscle, and General Batista, though he appears to be all muscle, is not entirely without his vulnerable spots. And between these two are countless lesser fry who constantly shift allegiance, pursue self-contradictory policies, depending on their estimate of the current balance of power. This is the political web, I'm sorry to say, in which the passengers on the *Franz Joseph* have become entangled."

He took another sip of coffee. His expression was sad now, but still gentle. "When the Hamburg Line sent out feelers about obtaining visas for these thousand people, certain Cuban officials—above all Senor Benites in the Bureau of Immigration, a Bru man—saw a chance to realize a nice profit. By issuing those visas, he was guilty of a clear violation of the immigration code, a highly restrictive one which was passed last year with the apparent support of both Bru and Batista forces. Not that an official of our government would precisely be setting a precedent by violating the law—it *has* been known to happen before—but everything depends on how much fuss his enemies are prepared to make over the violation. At the moment there are indications that certain important Batista people are prepared to make quite a considerable fuss over this matter of the visas, with the object of effecting a change of power in the Bureau of Immigration. And so, in an effort to extricate himself from his indiscretion before it's too late, Senor Benites has cancelled those visas."

"What hope is there, then?" Morrie said. "If his enemies are determined to use this to get rid of him——"

"But are they? In Cuban politics nothing is ever quite that obvious. The Batista people *say* they wish to get rid of Benites, but is that their real object? Are they, in fact, Batista people at all, or merely independent agents who are piqued because no share of the profits has been offered to them?"

"You think they might be willing to overlook Benites' racket if he gives them some of the money?"

"Well—not exactly."

"Then I don't understand. If it isn't money they want——"

"Oh yes, it *is* money they want, we may take that as certain. Not Senor Benites' money, however. His profits from the sale of those visas have already been safely stowed away in his bank account—and not, I suspect, a Cuban bank account. It's most unlikely that the opposing parties have hopes of extracting anything from Senor Benites. Their hopes, I would think, are turned in another direction."

Dr. Rabal paused, and in the silence that followed Morrie began to understand what he was being told. "They expect to get money out of the passengers?"

"I can think of no other possibility. I shall learn more about it, of course, when my next guest arrives—another twelve minutes, if he's on time, so we really must move on——"

"Dr. Rabal, those people don't have any more money to give. Most of them used their last savings on earth to get on that ship. They've been squeezed dry."

"I'm aware of it. I imagine that the men we're talking about, the Batista people, are aware of it too. They don't expect to get money from the passengers directly."

"Where *do* they expect to get it from?"

"Well"—Dr. Rabal spread his hands, an expressive little gesture of resignation—"I rather suppose they expect to get it from you. Oh, not from you personally, don't be alarmed, but from the organization you represent."

"They can't assume that the American Jewish Defense Agency is going to——"

"I assure you, Mr. Feldman, they know nothing whatever about the American Jewish Defense Agency. I doubt if any of them ever heard of it until a few days ago. But you see—you arrived in Havana, you opened a bank account, you spoke to various officials, you indicated your willingness to spend money to help those refugees. It's hardly surprising, is it, if the thought should come into some people's heads that you might be willing to spend a good deal more?"

For a while Morrie couldn't say anything. When he finally spoke, it wasn't easy to bring out the words. "Are you saying that if I hadn't come down here and handled things so badly —those people would be able to land without any trouble?"

"It would be most unjust of me to say any such thing. Your activities here have caused the situation to take a certain turn. Had you proceeded in a different manner, or had you not come here at all, who is to say that the situation might not have taken a far more unfortunate turn? Surely the Batista people would still have found out about Benites and his visas—and seeing no way to make money out of this information, they might well have decided to use it as a lever to force Benites out of office. Your fortuitous appearance on the scene has given them an alternative. Instead of being faced with an irreversible cancellation of those visas, we now have room in which to maneuver. Your presence in Havana may well have provided the people on the *Franz Joseph* with their only hope."

"I wish I could be sure—"

"In this world nobody can ever be sure of anything. Except that it's quite useless to condemn oneself for the past. Our task now is to make the best possible arrangements for the future. That's why my next guest is coming here tonight to discuss the whole question with me. A very important personage, a key figure in the Batista camp. Yes, I should certainly call him a key figure." Dr. Rabal smiled to himself for a moment. "I've told him, of course, that I have absolutely no official status. I can't speak for your organization any more than he can speak for his. Our conversation will be nothing but an informal exchange of views between close friends."

"I understand that."

"Good. Well, I'm truly sorry about this, but I shall have to ask you to leave before he gets here. He'd rather not let it be known that he's taking a personal interest in this matter. He gets these attacks of shyness occasionally. But you haven't finished your brandy—I'm truly upset! Esther, my dear, won't you assure Mr. Feldman that my hospitality isn't usually so atrocious?"

He got to his feet, so Morrie and Esther did, too. "I'll see you to the door, no need to disturb my servant." He took each of them by the arm and led them out of the living room. "You'll be at your hotel all night? I'll call you as soon as I have anything to tell you."

They were at the front door now, but Dr. Rabal still held on to their arms. "You find this all quite strange, don't you, Mr. Feldman? Mysterious visitors, conversations that aren't really conversations, secrets behind closed doors—what a distasteful and slightly farcical way to deal with a problem that involves the lives of human beings! And possibly my part in all this seems more distasteful to you than anything else."

"No, of course not—"

Dr. Rabal lifted his hand. "Of course it does. Don't you know what I am? A figure totally unknown to you in the United States—a legendary figure common once in most countries of the civilized world but generally believed to have disappeared with the Middle Ages. I am the State Jew. Yes, there's really no other name to describe me. It's not a very enviable role—especially when I'm among my own people. Everybody treats me with respect, but nobody respects me except a few despicable toadies whose respect I could gladly do without. At times, to be frank with you, I even feel a certain contempt for myself."

He paused, then went on in a lower voice, "Why do I do it, then? That's the question in your mind, of course, the question you're too polite to ask. My dear sir, the sad truth is that it must be done by somebody. There are forty thousand Jews in Cuba, an infinitesimal percentage of the population. Most of us are middle-class people, as we are everywhere else—small shopkeepers, business people, a few doctors and lawyers. We own no land, we hold no official titles, we live from day to day by the intelligence God gave us. Where do we belong? The upper classes snub us. The peasants never come in contact with us and no doubt think of a Jew as a devil with horns. The middle classes, among whom we find ourselves, are jealous of our industry and success, as they have been through the ages. Our position here is precarious. We hold onto it in the only ways we can."

He lifted his head again. "Yes, yes, I know what you wish

to say. Why don't we band together and fight for our rights, as you do in the United States? Why are we content to beg crumbs from the Christian's table? Well, this is not the United States, I regret to say. In a country like this—an easygoing, corrupt, incompetent dictatorship—anti-Semitism takes a special form. There is, of course, a great deal of it, in this respect we're no different from the rest of the world, but our people are lazy about it, as they are about most things. Nobody goes out of his way to persecute Jews. There are no pogroms, no concentration camps. The existence of the Jew is a matter of indifference to everyone. If those in power felt that it was convenient to sacrifice Cuba's Jews tomorrow, we would be sacrificed tomorrow. This would be done, you understand, not as an act of sadism or moral righteousness or religious fanaticism, but simply because it would be easier to do than not to do.

"How can we protect ourselves in such circumstances? Unified action, publicity, vigorous support of pro-Jewish candidates in elections? Reasonable tactics in your country, perhaps, but not here. Among many other reasons, Cuba *has* no elections. We must fall back on that contemptible old scoundrel, the State Jew. We need him to slink in his abject way behind the scenes making himself indispensable to those in power, reminding them that we do exist, tipping the balance in moments of danger so that it becomes more inconvenient to sacrifice the Jews than to leave them alone."

He broke off as the sound of a motor was heard from outside. "I've talked too long, he's here now! You *must* be going—" He opened the door for them. His car pulled up, and they got inside. "Don't be too hard on me, Mr. Feldman," Dr. Rabal said, lingering at the car window for another moment. "Don't condemn me utterly, as Esther does. Oh yes, my dear—you never say anything, but I know how you feel. Remember, Mr. Feldman—if I lived in your country, I should undoubtedly be one of the most active supporters of your admirable organization."

Their car pulled away just as another car was turning into the driveway behind them. Morrie saw Dr. Rabal quickly pull the *yamalke* from his head and stuff it into his pocket. . . .

Two hours later Dr. Rabal called Morrie at the hotel. He said that his guest and he had had a most productive talk. Certain suggestions were made as to how the passengers on the *Franz Joseph* might get their visas reactivated. A certain sum of money was mentioned, as well as a time limit for producing it. The time limit was ten days, and the sum of money was half a million dollars.

"My reaction was the same as yours, Mr. Feldman," Dr. Rabal said. "I told my guest that this seemed like a rather high price to pay. He couldn't be persuaded to lower it, however. He seems to be under the impression that all Jews in the United States are millionaires with philanthropic inclinations. It's really rather a flattering notion, isn't it? Well, I told him it isn't true, of course, but—how do you convince a Christian to give up any of his preconceived ideas about Jews?" And Morrie could imagine the doctor gently spreading his hands.

"One thing I can reassure you about, however," Dr. Rabal went on. "If my guest says that half a million dollars will do the trick, then for half a million dollars the trick *will* be done. You can trust him completely. He's an honest man."

*   *   *

Shortly after midnight Morrie called Al in New York. He knew Al wouldn't mind being awakened on a matter of importance. Al never minded waking other people on matters of importance.

Morrie explained the situation in detail, and Al told him to wait for instructions. At three o'clock in the morning Al called back; he had located Dan Wechsler and several other important members of AJDA, and it had been decided that Morrie should fly back to New York as soon as possible and make his report in person.

"I've already told you the whole story," Morrie said.

"You'll tell it again. You'll be sick of telling it before you're through. We're going to take you around to a lot of different places just so you can tell your story."

"What's the idea?"

"The idea is we've got ten days to raise half a million dollars."

For a second or two Morrie couldn't say anything. He felt a wave of relief pass over him. It's going to be all right, he told himself. AJDA is going to take care of everything.

"You still there?" Al's voice was barking into his ear.

"Yes—of course. One more thing I was wondering about,

Al. When the people on that ship get the news about their visas, the shock is going to be— Well, what I mean is don't you think we ought to let them know as soon as possible that their situation isn't hopeless, that AJDA is doing what it can for them? Maybe we could send them a radiogram— and talk to one of them as soon as the ship is in wireless range—"

"Not a bad idea," Al said. "What we need is a contact on that ship, somebody to act as liaison between us and the rest of the passengers. I wonder if any of those people has a friend or relation who belongs to AJDA— Let me take a look at Bernie's list of sponsors, and we'll talk about this again in New York."

So Al hung up, and as Morrie lowered the receiver he realized for the first time how terribly worried he'd been during these last twenty-four hours, how far he'd let himself drift toward expecting the worst—maybe even toward expecting AJDA itself to abandon those passengers. Crazy, absolutely crazy. All because he had run across a few greedy bastards who were willing to make a profit off somebody else's misery. Was he still a naïve kid who didn't know what the hell went on in the world? After all, life in Brooklyn hadn't been *that* sheltered.

In the morning, as soon as he knew what plane he would be on, he sent a wire to Ruth. At eleven he took a cab out to the airport, and Esther Berkowitz went with him. It was another scorcher of a day. Before he even got out of the cab he felt like changing his shirt. In the airport he sat next to Esther on a hard bench, waited for his flight to be called, and went over some of the things she would have to take care of in his absence.

Then he yawned and said, "I'm dead tired. But it doesn't matter, I still can't fall asleep on planes."

"I can fall asleep anywhere," she said. "It's the first thing you learn when you're leaving a country quickly and don't know whether or not they've given orders to get you back again."

"That's what happened to you when you left Germany?"

"My father was more than a Jew, you understand. He was also 'political.' He taught at the University of Leipzig— anthropology was his subject. He said things about the origins of the races which contradicted the official theories. A friend of ours—a former student of my father's who worked in the mayor's office—saw the papers ordering my father's arrest. He warned us, and we escaped that night."

"Where does your father teach now?" Morrie asked.

"He gives private lessons, German language lessons. In New York City. He couldn't get a post at an American college."

"I'm sorry—"

She gave a shrug. "It was his fault, you know. In some unconscious way he didn't *want* any school to hire him. The truth is he stopped believing in himself as a teacher."

"He thought he'd lost his ability to teach?"

"No, no, not his ability. What he had lost was—his belief in the value of truth. All his life he had struggled to understand what the truth is and to present it as honestly as he could to his students. As a result his world collapsed, his career was ruined. Something happened inside of him—something was damaged that couldn't be seen from the outside. He felt himself growing cautious, pulling back from his ideas—as a child pulls back from the hot stove which has burned his hand. He found himself, almost instinctively, modifying not only his opinions but even his knowledge of the facts. He was frightened of becoming the thing he had always despised the most, a dishonest teacher. Before this could happen to him, he stopped teaching."

It was the longest speech Morrie had ever heard her make. Yet her voice remained matter-of-fact, uninflected, as if she were describing a situation with which she had no involvement whatever.

"And there's something else," she went on. "He never admitted this to me, because he doesn't exactly know it himself. He was also frightened of being a Jew. Before Hitler he hardly ever gave a thought to it, in our house there was no religious observance at all—but after his troubles at the university, especially when so many of his colleagues and old friends turned their eyes away from him, he began to believe that being a Jew made him unfit. He believed that he couldn't teach young people any more because all of them would be jeering at him behind his back and calling him 'dirty Jew.' "

"But in America—"

"He didn't believe that America would be different." She paused, then went on in the same matter-of-fact voice. "He isn't wrong."

"You don't really mean that, do you? You don't see any

difference between anti-Semitism in America and what you were up against in Germany?"

"The differences are superficial. Yes, I know what you're thinking—on those superficial differences people can live or die. But I mean the—the internal differences, the differences in our minds. To suspect that even one person is calling you 'dirty Jew,' that's enough to poison everything. For a Jew the existence of that one anti-Semite—no, even the *possibility* of his existence—is morally and psychologically the same as if he lived in a crowd of anti-Semites, in a nation of anti-Semites. No Jew will ever be at peace with himself until he lives and works where he can positively *know* that there are no anti-Semites."

"There *is* no such place."

"Not now. Someday, however, there will be. When we finally have a state of our own."

"Oh, I see—you're a Zionist!"

"How smugly you say that word. You've got me in my pigeonhole, you don't have to think about me any longer. Yes, I *am* a Zionist. For no mystical reasons, you understand. For hard, practical reasons—for reasons of my health."

"Your health—?"

"You heard Dr. Rabal last night, didn't you? A fine man— in many ways a superior man. But when you listened to him talk, didn't it fill you with shame? To hear what a Jew must go through, what indignities he must commit on himself, in order to survive in a Christian country! No, it isn't good for us to have such feelings. It isn't good for our minds. Some-day, when there's a state, I'll go there to regain my health."

"You *could* go to Palestine right now. Plenty of Jews are doing it."

"If my father and mother weren't alive—if my husband shared my convictions— But as it is, I do what I can right here. And next year, when Jerry is transferred back to New York, I'll do even more."

"But aren't you working for the wrong organization? AJDA's been accused of a lot of things, but nobody ever accused it of being Zionist."

"Nobody ever accused it of being without influence, either. A few discreet doses of Zionism injected into its bloodstream might have a beneficial effect."

"So that's it—you're a spy in enemy headquarters!" He smiled, but he was feeling a little uneasy. "Well, I won't give

75

you away—as long as your work on this project isn't affected."

"Why should my work be affected?"

"Well, if we do get those people off the ship—I don't think AJDA's Board of Trustees would appreciate your proselytizing—"

"Believe me, I have no intention of proselytizing. To tell you frankly, I doubt if the *Franz Joseph* has too many passengers who would suit our purposes."

"I don't follow that. If Palestine is to be a homeland for the Jewish people—"

"Most of these German Jews are lost to the Jewish people already. The ones over the age of twenty-five to thirty certainly. They're too assimilated, too uncomfortable about their Jewishness. Most of all, they're too incurably middle-class. That's why they've chosen to come to America rather than to Palestine. What they want from their new homeland is precisely what they had in their old one—a nice, safe, conventional, bourgeois existence with no cause to fight for except the cause of their own bankbooks. If they escape from Germany, or if they stay and get butchered—what difference does it really make?"

He stared at her. "What *difference* does it make?"

"Oh, a great deal, of course, from the humanitarian point of view. Each human life has its unique importance. I certainly believe that. But from the point of view of the Jewish people and its ultimate survival—well, what's the good of telling lies to oneself? If I had to choose between saving a thousand of the old ones who want to go to America or a hundred of the young ones who want to go to Palestine, I know which I'd have to choose."

"And you could make that choice without any hesitation?"

"Without *any* hesitation? No, I suppose I would hesitate. But this would simply be my own sentimental weakness. I would try hard to overcome it, and I'm confident that I would succeed."

He shook his head. "It's a damn cold-blooded attitude—"

"Not at all. It's *your* atttitude that's cold-blooded. I don't like to think how much innocent blood will be shed if your kind of well-meaning, unrealistic benevolence prevails. It's a simple matter of self-defense—this is what so many American Jews can't see. Sooner or later the holocaust which goes on today in Germany and Austria will spread to the whole world.

Even if war comes this year or next, even if Hitler is eventually destroyed, what he has set loose, his anti-Semitic virus, will go on spreading. Yes, even to the United States. And when that day comes, there had better be a Jewish state in Palestine, or Jews will have nowhere to go—and soon there won't be any more Jews."

She turned her eyes away, as if she were embarrassed at having shown so much feeling.

A few minutes later it was announced that Morrie's flight was ready.

As the plane took off her words kept going through his head. Did he believe what she had said? It was such an easy thing to believe. The fear of such a thing hovered in the back of every Jew's mind. Even one like himself, who had never experienced much anti-Semitism, was always more or less expecting the pogroms to begin.

As he had predicted, he got no sleep at all during the flight.

But his spirits lifted when he got to New York. Al was waiting for him at the airport, and the first words Al said were, "We've found an AJDA man who knows one of the people on that ship. Now it's up to you to write that radio-gram. Do it while we're driving into the city so you won't waste any time."

FOUR

FRITZ Hochschwender, the chief steward on the *Franz Joseph*, had been devoting himself for years to the task— sometimes he thought of it as the art—of keeping passengers happy. His secret, which he never hesitated to reveal, was to occupy them with such a steady supply of games and sports and diversions, both physical and cultural, that they had no chance to notice if they were bored or not. He knew and loved his job, and he welcomed difficult challenges.

From the very beginning of this particular sailing, it was clear to Hochschwender that the challenge would be a difficult one indeed. He couldn't remember when the first day aboard had gone so slowly, so discouragingly. As an example, nobody at all had signed up for the tournaments—not for deck tennis, shuffleboard, chess, or bridge. But Hochschwender was not one to lose heart. He persisted in offering the passengers the very best that his experience and natural good humor could provide.

Fortunately, the weather cooperated with his efforts. It held perfectly for the full six days at sea. There were sunny mornings and afternoons, cool, mild nights, and only enough rolling and pitching to serve as a pleasant reminder that this was a ship and not a luxury hotel. Seasickness, Hochschwender had often observed, tends to dampen the gaiety of passengers; but on this voyage there was very little reason for anybody to be seasick.

And so day by day, and indeed hour by hour, the passengers thawed. Hochschwender could see smiles on more and more faces. He noted, in the daily commissary reports, that more and more food and beer were being consumed. His tournaments began to do well—they ran somewhat below their normal popularity, but not enough to cause him deep concern. Walkers could be seen in the early hours pumping through their laps around the deck, and the outdoor swimming pool grew popular from morning till sunset, especially among the younger people. The card rooms and writing rooms were occupied constantly. Best of all was the response to the special entertainment events which Hochschwender had arranged. Every afternoon in the main lounge the band gave a concert of operetta music while coffee and cakes were served. After dinner every night there was bingo, dancing, and a showing of one of the latest films. On two evenings a string quartet (four members of the band, with the lady harpist playing viola) presented an all-Beethoven and an all-Brahms program. All these events, Hochschwender noted, were very well attended.

Anxiety and restraint among the passengers didn't melt away completely. From time to time—perhaps in the middle of a bridge hand or during the slow movement of a Beethoven quartet—Hochschwender was distressed to see a grimace of pain on somebody's face. This made him genuinely unhappy, for it suggested that he wasn't doing his job as successfully as he ought. No passenger must be permitted to feel pain during an ocean voyage—whatever he might feel before or afterward. And it *was* consoling to Hochschwender that these grimaces seemed to grow fewer as the end of the voyage approached.

And so this afternoon, the last afternoon before the arrival in Havana, Hochschwender strolled around the ship gazing with satisfaction at the happy, relaxed faces around him. Soon the final rounds of the tournaments would be played, and tonight at the gala after-dinner celebration prizes would be awarded—bottles of champagne for the winners, of course, and amusing little novelties for the runners-up. What a merry occasion this gala would be! Full of jokes and tricks! Hochschwender was proud of his ingenuity in thinking up jokes and tricks.

He had another thing to be proud of. He had thrown himself as diligently into serving this group of passengers as he had ever done for any group in the past. That they were Jews, he flattered himself, had made no difference in his behavior. The captain had given his orders, and it was Hochschwender's duty to obey. A man must do his duty. Hochschwender had learned this from his father and had taught it to his own son, who had just recently been given an excellent position on the security staff of a concentration camp. . . .

* * *

Among those who had signed up for the bridge tournament was Bruno Schwarzkopf. Ordinarily bridge wasn't for him. He preferred games where he didn't have to be saddled with a partner, some bumbler to drag him down and keep him from showing the best he could do. His favorite game was poker. Himself against the whole table, figuring odds, bluffing, driving the weak sisters to the wall, staking large sums on the draw of a card.

For twenty years he had been part of a regular Thursday night poker game with Schroeder, Eisenstadt, Walter Reining, and some of the other big men in the department store world —gentiles, every one of them. Right up to the end of '38 that game had gone on, Hitler or no Hitler—with Schwarzkopf's winnings running well ahead of his losses—till that night a week after Krystallnacht when he got to Reining's house and the butler told him nobody was home. Though he could see for himself that Schroeder's car, and Eisenstadt's too, were parked along the street. . . .

He had learned bridge after the war, when it began to be important socially. He could never take it seriously, though —that he left to Emma. It was the perfect game for her, a game for women who wanted to do more gossiping than playing. There was a time in her life when she played bridge four or five days a week. If she wasn't shopping, she was playing bridge. Not lately, though. These last few years, with no more giggling females to play bridge with, no more charge accounts at the shops, what did she do with herself all day? God forbid she should be forced to read a newspaper or think a thought for once in her life!

But he hadn't been able to let himself worry about that. Whatever Emma had been going through these last few years, he had had his own worries, and they were a lot more serious. They closed in on him, weighed him down with aggravation every time he went to the office. Yes, to the end the Nazis never took his office away from him—thanks to certain connections of his—though for all practical purposes the store had stopped belonging to him a long time ago. Even before its name was changed . . .

He drew himself up, made himself stop thinking about the past. A practical man doesn't moon over the past. Leave that to the "poetic" types, the dreamers, like his son-in-law Aaron. A practical man makes plans for the future. That's why Schwarzkopf was sitting now in the card room off the main lounge. Five days of careful planning had brought him to this place at this time. In a few minutes Stieffel would arrive.

The moment he'd seen Stieffel's name on the passenger list—that first night aboard ship—he had made up his mind what to do. Let's be realistic, he had told himself. All his life he had been realistic. That's how he had been able to take over his father's dry goods store—a good enough business, maybe, but strictly second class—and build it into one of the biggest retail operations in Germany. All right, then, realistically it was necessary to admit that he had made a mistake. He hadn't got out of Germany fast enough. His son-in-law, Aaron, had been right for once. No credit to him for *that*. If you predict an earthquake around every corner, sooner or later you'll come to a corner where there *is* an earthquake.

So the fact was, as a result of waiting too long they had no resources now, no funds to draw on, nothing but a few thousand dollars deposited in American banks in the name of the store. And the two large bills—carefully saved in case of emergency—which he had smuggled through customs. If Bruno Schwarzkopf wasn't a match for some stupid policeman— But to pull himself up again, to be on top again, he would need backing.

Then he saw Stieffel's name on the passenger list. He had heard a rumor weeks before that Stieffel was in trouble, that the government was cracking down on him, making no more distinctions. He couldn't bring himself to believe such a rumor. Stieffel and Bauer was the most important brokerage firm in the country—with connections in the government (according to the joke people told) that were better than Hitler's own connections. It wasn't possible that anything could happen to Stieffel. He was not only Bauer's partner, he was married to his sister—and Bauer was a cousin of Julius Streicher himself.

But here he was on this ship, the great Arthur Stieffel. And alone, no Mrs. Stieffel listed with him. The first night in the dining room Schwarzkopf got a glimpse of him—tall, gray hair, gray clipped mustache, distinguished-looking—no different from the way he had looked the other times Schwarzkopf had seen him through the years, in the lobby at the opera or strolling down the Unter den Linden on a Sunday morning swinging his cane.

The Jews of Germany must be even worse off than anybody had thought if that madman Hitler could take an Arthur Stieffel and put him here on this ship, make him just like all the rest of them.

Not quite like all the rest of them, though. This was the important point, the point that Schwarzkopf had grasped right away. For everyone else on this ship nothing, or almost nothing, was waiting for him in America. No money to speak of. No backing. Everything he had done in his life till now, every success and every struggle—it all had to be done over again. But for Stieffel, for him alone, no such problem existed. Stieffel had a brother—everybody knew about him. After the war he had gone to America, because he had married an American woman, according to the story, and Berlin society wouldn't accept her. Stieffel's brother had set up his own brokerage house in America, and the money behind it had come from Stieffel himself. Today that American firm was no less than Stieffel, Weissberger, and Harris of New York. And Arthur Stieffel was on his way right now to take over his share of the business he had started.

Backing—this was what Stieffel could give. This was what he and nobody else on this ship was in a position to give. So suppose he met somebody with ability and experience who was escaping from the Nazis the same as *he* was. Suppose he trusted this somebody from the business point of view and felt at the same time a certain friendly sympathy for him because they were going through the same trouble together. After that, all kinds of things could happen. No limit to what a man like Stieffel might do if he got it into his head to give somebody a helping hand.

Funny that Schwarzkopf had never been introduced to Stieffel in Berlin. All those years, with plenty of mutual acquaintances, you'd think they might have run into each other once or twice. Frankly, it was bad luck that they hadn't. But there's no law that bad luck can't be converted into good luck. Schwarzkopf didn't believe in luck, anyway. A man makes his own luck. A thousand times he had pointed that out to his employees, his family, his friends—to his son-in-law Aaron, especially. So there was no good reason why by the end of this voyage Schwarzkopf shouldn't be as close to Stieffel as if they'd been friends all their lives. It was only a question of handling him right. Not too obvious. Don't be eager, don't let him think you need him. If people think you need them, they kick you in the ass.

But Schwarzkopf had no doubts about his ability to handle Stieffel. He had cracked tougher nuts in the past, hardheaded wholesalers and manufacturers who wouldn't give him the price he wanted. Butter them up a little, play on their weaknesses—in the end he always had such people eating out of his hand.

The first contact was important. The best way to meet people aboard ship is to sit at their table in the dining room. If the ocean isn't too rough, they'll be in a good mood whenever you see them. Too bad he hadn't known, before Sophie's boys made the dining room reservation, that Stieffel was aboard. He could have fixed it up with the steward to put Stieffel at their table—instead of that stupid honeymoon couple who couldn't keep their hands off each other and never listened to what anybody else was saying. All right, no use crying over spilled milk.

So his first day on the ship he went to every event—the bingo game, the band concert, the film—hoping to run into Stieffel. He even went to Rabbi Einhorn's Sabbath service, though it was years since he'd sat through a service that wasn't on the High Holidays. But Stieffel didn't show up for any of these events.

He found out the number of Stieffel's cabin. No reason why he couldn't just go there and introduce himself, mentioning the name of a mutual friend. So he did it that night before dinner.

It didn't work out right. Stieffel was polite enough, but he wouldn't open his mouth, a regular iceberg. And his cabin mate was there all the time, a fellow named Monsky—what kind of a German name is that?—one look, you could tell he was a bum. Schwarzkopf said he had an urgent appointment and got out of there.

So he did some more poking around, and he found out that Stieffel was a bridge player. After every meal, while other people were swimming or seeing movies, Stieffel was playing bridge. So I'll join that bridge game, Schwarzkopf decided. He went to the card room after lunch.

Stieffel had three players with him already—one of them was that Monsky fellow, another was the fellow with one arm, the fellow that used to be a soldier. Schwarzkopf sat behind Stieffel's chair, watched the game, made a remark from time to time. Nobody answered his remarks, and Stieffel never even looked at him. After a while he stood up and said he had an urgent appointment.

"Another one?" Monsky said. "Are you running a branch store on this ship, Schwarzkopf?"

Schwarzkopf walked out without a word. Bums like that aren't worth answering.

Later that day he saw the list of people signed up for the individual bridge tournament. Stieffel's name was on the list. Right away Schwarzkopf knew that this was his chance. It always comes along if you keep your eyes open and if you have the brains to recognize it when you see it. A man makes his own luck.

So he signed up for the bridge tournament, and he pushed his way through match after match—six, seven hours a day of that stupid game—but he was getting what he wanted out of it. He was seeing Stieffel every day, sometimes as an opponent, sometimes as a partner, and they were on friendly terms now—as friendly as you could get with such a cold fish.

The only trouble was, they never seemed to have any time alone with each other, any time for a nice confidential talk. "Let's have a beer," Schwarzkopf would say after every game—but either Stieffel had to run off somewhere, or one of the other players insisted on joining them. A couple of times Stieffel invited him down to his cabin—and Monsky was there sprawled in a chair, making sarcastic remarks. Once Schwarzkopf invited Stieffel down to *his* cabin—and Emma had to pick that afternoon to have a sick headache. And the trip was nearly over, tomorrow they'd be getting off the ship.

This afternoon was his last chance to tell Stieffel what was on his mind. In a few minutes they'd be partners for the last time during the tournament.

For Stieffel it had to be an enjoyable game. He had to get up from the table in a good frame of mind. This meant strategy, Schwarzkopf knew, and he had his strategy all planned. Not a word against Stieffel's bidding, no matter how rotten it was. No complaints when Stieffel made a bad play. And after the game nothing could be more natural than the two partners going off to the bar together, having a beer together, and in this friendly atmosphere talking a little business together.

He looked at his watch. Ten minutes to three. It bothered him that he had come so early. He certainly wasn't in the habit of getting to appointments early. That's what people do when they need something from you, when they don't have the self-control to hide how hungry they are.

The opponents arrived. Two ladies, Mrs. Moritz and Mrs. Fischel. Moritz was a nobody. Fischel talked too much, let you know every time she opened her mouth how many servants she used to have. Funny about women like her, women who were brought up all their lives with money. She was ugly as sin, she had positively no personality—but she acted as if she expected you to kiss her ass, and the chances were that plenty of people *did*. Emma had the same habit, and Sophie, too, with all her mousiness. Money made them take it for granted that they were special.

What happens to such people if they lose their money? How long before they lose that special feeling, too?

He looked at his watch again. Five after three.

"If your partner doesn't show up pretty soon," the Fischel woman said in a sweet voice, sweet like poison, "I'm terribly afraid you'll have to forfeit the match."

The door opened, and Monsky came in. He was wearing that loud, checked sport jacket, smirking like he owned the world—when that bum probably didn't even own the shirt on his back.

"Ladies and gentlemen," Monsky said, "I've got bad news and good news. My roommate, Arthur Stieffel, is suffering from a slight indisposition—too many sausages at lunch, if you ask me—so he won't be able to play bridge this afternoon. That's the bad news. The good news is he asked me to take his place, and I agreed with pleasure." He sat down at the table and turned his smirk directly on Schwarzkopf. "So who deals, partner?"

For a moment Schwarzkopf couldn't say anything. Then he kept his voice low, because he couldn't trust himself not to explode. "Let the ladies deal. Let's be gentlemen for once."

He got through the match somehow. The ladies slaughtered

him, of course, but he didn't care. As soon as it was over, he walked out of the room. He didn't answer Monsky's suggestion that they have a beer together.

He went back to his cabin. Emma wasn't there, thank God. He sat down, but he couldn't stay seated. He started pacing. So it's all over now, he told himself. Never again would he have a chance at Stieffel. After all these years his luck was finally running out—

He shook his head hard. Damn fool—blaming luck for his own stupidity. Why the hell had he wasted the whole afternoon on a bridge game? Knowing that Stieffel was alone in his cabin, he should have walked right out on Monsky and those two women, gone straight down to Stieffel and told him what he wanted from him in the way of backing, made a definite proposition to him. A man like Stieffel appreciates determination and self-confidence.

He couldn't understand why he hadn't done this. Only in his sixties, was he suddenly getting timid, losing his nerve?

He sank into a chair. I'm turning into a weak sister, he told himself. I'm as bad as my impractical son-in-law. All the jokes I've made at him, and now I'm the biggest joke of all.

Emma returned. "Do you like my hair, Bruno? I just washed it and set it, because we're getting to Havana tomorrow."

"Frankly, it doesn't look any better," he said. "With some things there's no room for improvement."

As soon as these words were out of his mouth, he was annoyed at himself. Sarcasm for Emma—it was too easy. A practical man doesn't solve his problems by shooting at sitting ducks. That's how people act when they're desperate, when they're ready to give up.

Bruno Schwarzkopf doesn't give up, he told himself, as Emma disappeared into the bathroom. That's why he had stayed in Germany longer than he should have—that's why he hadn't listened to Aaron's advice two years ago. Because he wouldn't give up, because he had his pride. Yes, pride—that and nothing else had kept him from scuttling off the sinking ship like so many rats of his acquaintance. Germany was his home, his country—*his* country just as much as any other German's. A pack of hoodlums tell him he's not a real German, and for this reason he's supposed to throw away everything, the business he sweated all his life to build

86

up? If he *had* run away when the rats did, when his son-in-law told him to, he would've been proving that the hoodlums were right about him, that the things he owned didn't belong to him, that his whole life hadn't amounted to a damn thing. Pride! What's a man got if he loses his pride? But people like the hoodlums had taken everything away from him by force. Better to stay and stay and refuse to budge an inch until his spineless son-in-law could never understand such a thing in a million years. . . .

So if he hadn't been a quitter two years ago, when the pressure was really on, he sure as hell wasn't going to be one now. All right, so what if he *had* missed his chance with Stieffel this afternoon? They were all going to be sitting in Havana together for a long time, for six months, maybe a year. And Stieffel would feel like playing a lot of bridge.

He isn't God Almighty, Schwarzkopf thought. He can be handled. All it takes is a little shrewdness, some careful planning—and most of all, guts.

Nobody could say that Bruno Schwarzkopf didn't have guts. How else did he get where he was today?

* * *

Aaron Peyser sat in a deck chair by the outdoor swimming pool. It was almost four o'clock; the sun was still hot, but a light breeze made it bearable. Aaron's shirt was open at the neck, and he wore sunglasses, a cheap pair clipped to his regular glasses. Sophie had packed them in his suitcase despite his protests that this wouldn't be "some kind of cruise on a millionaire's yacht."

Sitting here now, he almost felt like a millionaire on his yacht—or as he imagined that millionaire might feel. Above the world, floating on his own private cloud. The strange unreal feeling was still with him—it was even stronger than it had been five days ago. He felt as if the world were magically turning into a different place from what he had always known it to be. In such a place things could happen to him that never could have happened before.

Right now, for instance, he was discussing politics with Carl Bender, who sat in the deck chair next to his.

Under ordinary conditions he had never been good at making friends. He had had a few close ones in his school days, but they had all dropped out of his life years ago. In Berlin, since his marriage, the people he saw most often were Sophie's friends, married couples with whom she exchanged regular dinner invitations. They were all well-to-do, respectable people—businessmen, a doctor and a lawyer or two; nice people, certainly, but conventional, a little dull. Aaron had always got along with them, of course, because he was conventional and dull himself. As for taking the initiative, finding friends of his own who were stimulating and unusual—he knew perfectly well he could never do it.

Yet he wasn't on this ship forty-eight hours before he was on good terms with Carl Bender. The second night out they sat next to each other at the film, something about American gangsters. Afterward they exchanged a few words, and because both their wives were busy doing other things, they had a beer together in the bar. They had been conversing at great length ever since.

It was quite impossible, Aaron told himself. The two of them could hardly have been more different from each other. Carl was a scientist, a man of culture and education, a man of the world. His views of life were totally unconventional, even rather shocking by the standards Aaron had always accepted. Carl had turned his back on religion years ago, while Aaron, though he didn't consider himself a religious man, could hardly imagine life without the synagogue, *some* synagogue, hovering in the background. Carl moved, or had until recent years, in a world of scientists, artists, intellectuals where the distinctions between Jew and gentile were largely ignored—and though he sometimes made wry allusions to this world, to the swiftness with which his "old friends" had capitulated to the general anti-Semitism, Aaron knew in his heart that *he* would never have ventured into such a world in the first place.

Most of all, a year after his first wife's death Carl had married a gentile woman. Her manner toward Aaron during this voyage was pleasant enough, yet he always felt uncomfortable in her presence. Since his boyhood gentile women had frightened him. They were touched with mystery, with horror, even—like statues of the Crucifixion or the Virgin Mary.

And so there was no logical reason why Carl Bender should take the slightest interest in the conversation of a narrow, uncultured, untraveled department store executive.

Nevertheless, here they were on this warm afternoon sitting next to each other in deck chairs and discussing politics.

"You must understand about Fascism," Carl was saying. "Primarily it's a psychological phenomenon, not a political one. It represents the innate urge in all human beings to give up their freedom, to relieve themselves of the terrible burden of individual responsibility, to merge the self which they despise in the larger entity of the State, the Leader. Each of us has a cringing little slave inside him somewhere, desperately digging away, trying to undermine the superstructure of his individuality. Today we call this Fascism, Nazism, Bolshevism. Five hundred years ago we called it the Church. A hundred years from now we'll call it—what? The Community of the Mentally Healthy and Emotionally Stable, perhaps, with a committee of leading psychiatrists making the rules. Under one name or another it's always existed and always will exist, because it's a basic fact of human nature."

"But why should it be so strong today?" Aaron said. "Why should it threaten to overwhelm the whole world just at a time when democracy is spreading to every civilized nation, when the common man is finally coming into his own?"

"You've answered your own question," Carl said. "Democracy is a dangerous blessing. To your common man it sometimes seems more like a curse. After all, if he's 'free,' if he 'comes into his own,' he can no longer blame anyone but himself for his inadequacies. It's the very growth of democracy, you see, that makes him embrace Fascism. And it's his frustration and desperation that cause this embrace to take such violent, barbaric forms."

"If you're right," Aaron said, "there's no way out for us. The better the world becomes for people, the more they'll feel compelled to destroy it. I don't see how I could go on living if I believed that."

"It's not a bit difficult, really." Carl smiled, that soft, ironic smile which had disconcerted Aaron at first but which he had lately become rather fond of. "Once your eyes have been opened to reality, once you've accepted the very worst, you can relax. You've freed yourself from suspense and anxiety. You can sit back and enjoy the show."

Then Carl gave a small sigh. "But I mustn't claim too much for my pessimism. In the long run reason tells me there isn't any hope—but in the short run I snatch at fleeting consolations just like everyone else. Even in hopelessness there are degrees. What lies ahead for most of us on this ship? Nothing very good, I'm afraid. But when we compare it with what's behind us . . . A perfect illustration is provided by our two young animals there." He pointed at the swimming pool, where his stepdaughter, Eva, and Aaron's son Joshua were romping. "Those two were scarcely out of diapers when the Nazis came to power. By all normal standards their childhood has been a nightmare. Yet look what a few days in the sun with no Storm Troopers lurking around the corner have done for them. And we're all like that, more or less. The human mind contains a mechanism which anesthetizes it against reality. Too much raw reality would destroy us."

Aaron watched the children. No doubt of it, Joshua was livelier these last few days than Aaron had ever seen him. Much more like a twelve-year-old boy.

Then Aaron saw David running across the deck toward them.

"Papa, a steward was in the cabin looking for you. He says it's very important, the captain wants to see you right away. The steward is waiting for you in the lounge."

"The captain? But I've never talked to him, I've never even set eyes on him!"

"Who has?" Carl said. "You're being given a unique opportunity, my friend—a private interview with the Supreme Mystery. You can tell us whether or not this ship really *has* a captain. Some of us are beginning to wonder. My own view is that if the captain didn't exist, it would be necessary for us to invent him."

Aaron smiled, but he wasn't really in the mood to find this funny. Common sense told him he didn't have to be anxious about this interview. By this time the captain had surely demonstrated his benevolence towards his passengers. But the idea of being called in to see an official, *any* official, was enough in itself to make Aaron uneasy. This was one of the things that the last six years had done to him.

"Should I tell Mama where you've gone?" David asked, as they headed for the lounge. "Or maybe it would worry her."

"Yes, you'd better not mention it to her just yet."

What a paragon the boy was, Aaron thought. Always helpful and considerate. And then a peculiar thought came into his head. Did the boy ever get tired of being a paragon? Did he ever feel like pushing through those layers of good manners and letting something else out? Every human being has to have something else, doesn't he? Deep at the center of him, there has to be that little kernel—of desire, ambition, dissatisfaction—which belongs to him alone, which sets him apart from everybody else on earth, which *is* him. From the day you're born the world starts clawing at you, trying to tear that kernel out of you—and mostly, before you're through, you let the world take it. But not when you're just a boy, not when you're as young as David. At nineteen you should still be fighting back.

"David," Aaron said, "we haven't had much chance to talk on this trip."

"No, we haven't, Papa."

"Now that it's almost over, how do you feel about things?"

"What things?"

"About what's going to happen to you—America—the kind of life you're going to have? You think about that, don't you?"

"Yes, of course."

"Does it trouble you very much? Are you afraid?"

"Papa, have I given that impression? Have I done anything—"

"No, no, not a thing."

"I don't want you to worry about me. You have so many worries already. I know how much you're doing for us."

"You're all right then, are you?"

"Yes, Papa. Of course I am."

They arrived at the lounge, and David squeezed his arm and left him. And Aaron felt a little ashamed of himself. Obviously there was no need to be concerned about the boy. Just because he was quiet and unassuming didn't mean he had no spirit, no—no little kernel. Once they were safe in America, who could doubt that David would show his spirit? He would go to college and to medical school—Aaron would find the money somehow—and he would become a doctor, as he had always wanted to do.

One of the assistant stewards—a boy not much older than David—led Aaron up several stairways, higher than any of the passengers were permitted to go. They went through a door marked "Keep Out" and along a corridor to an office. The young steward knocked, and as soon as a voice said "Come in," Aaron went through the door alone. He found himself in a plain, undecorated room, nothing in it but a desk, a filing cabinet, several hard-backed chairs, and some charts on the walls. Sitting behind the desk was First Officer Muller, the young man with the yellowish complexion and the perpetual scowl.

"Aaron Peyser?"

"Yes, that's me."

"The captain finds that he is unable to see you personally, as he originally intended. He has an important request to make of you, and he has asked me to explain it to you. First, however, are you able to read English?"

"Yes—if it isn't too difficult—"

"Then you'd better read this radiogram which arrived for you an hour ago." From the desk in front of him Muller picked up a square of yellow paper. "You must understand, Mr. Peyser, that this radiogram has already been examined by the captain. As a matter of course our wireless operator shows him all messages of any importance."

"Yes, I understand. But—isn't there some mistake? I'm not expecting to hear from anybody."

"You're the only Aaron Peyser on the passenger list."

"Yes, that's true—"

"Then there's no mistake. Read it, please."

Muller held out the piece of paper. He neglected, Aaron noticed, to ask him to sit down.

Aaron took the paper. He began to read slowly:

"AARON PEYSER—

WE ARE CONTACTING YOU BECAUSE YOUR AMERICAN SPONSOR, GUSTAV SELIG, SELIG AND KEPLER SPORTING GOODS, BELONGS TO OUR ORGANIZATION, AMERICAN JEWISH DEFENSE AGENCY. WE HOPE THIS REACHES YOU BEFORE YOU RECEIVE THE NEWS THAT CUBAN ENTRANCE VISAS FOR ONE THOUSAND AND FOUR PASSENGERS ON YOUR SHIP HAVE BEEN CANCELLED. YOU WILL NOT BE PERMITTED TO LAND IN HAVANA UPON ARRIVAL WEDNESDAY MORNING. . . ."

Aaron stopped reading. A wave of dizziness came over him. He stood very still, waiting for it to pass. Then he made himself start reading again.

". . . THIS SETBACK IS TEMPORARY. REPEAT, TEMPORARY. AJDA IS NOW WORKING TO REMOVE DIFFICULTIES AND

GET VISAS REACTIVATED. CHANCES ARE EXCELLENT. DELAY IS UNLIKELY TO CONTINUE LONGER THAN TEN DAYS, TWO WEEKS AT MOST. URGE YOU TO INFORM YOUR FELLOW PASSENGERS OF THE SITUATION, REASSURE THEM ABOUT HOPEFUL FUTURE PROSPECTS.

WILL ATTEMPT TO MAKE RADIO CONTACT WITH YOU IN HAVANA HARBOR WITHIN SEVERAL DAYS, REPORT ON PROGRESS AT THAT TIME.

OUR HOPES ARE HIGH.

MORRIS FELDMAN."

Aaron read this radiogram a second time, even more slowly. He read it a third time. The words began to blur before his eyes. So this, he kept thinking, was what that feeling of unreality had meant all along. This ship was a dream, and now he was about to wake up.

He realized that Muller was talking to him. "You'll be interested to know, Mr. Peyser, that shortly after the arrival of that radiogram the information contained in it was confirmed—the captain received a message directly from the immigration authorities in Havana. It is his wish, therefore, that this news be given to the passengers as soon as possible. An announcement must be made at dinner tonight. The captain would do this himself, but he feels that it will come better from one of your own number. In his view this would be more diplomatic, less harsh." The way Muller pronounced this last word made it clear how he felt about the captain's scruples. "He suggests that since you are already in possession of this information, you are the one to make the announcement."

Aaron could feel his stomach tightening. "No—I don't think I could do that. I have no authority with the passengers —hardly anybody knows me."

"Are *any* of you particularly well known to the others?"

"Well, probably not. But even so—I have no special position—it's only an accident that these people got in touch with me."

Muller shrugged. "It's up to you. I'm simply repeating the captain's request. I suppose you may entrust the job to someone else, if you wish. Personally, I think the captain's going about this in an unnecessarily complicated way. *My* suggestion was that we announce the news over the loudspeaker every hour between now and midnight. He saw fit to

93

reject this suggestion—but if none of you people are willing to accept the responsibility, I'm sure I could persuade him to reconsider my suggestion—"

"No, don't do that!" And then Aaron heard himself saying yes—yes, of course, he would make the announcement at dinner tonight, he would take care of everything.

And then he was leaving Muller's office. How steadily he walked. How carefully he shut the door behind him. But after a step or two he came to a stop with a sharp burning pain in his stomach, and he cursed himself for his stupidity.

How could he have let himself in for this? Why hadn't he stuck to his first reaction, kept insisting that somebody else was needed, somebody with a cool head, a reassuring manner, with the courage and self-discipline to keep his own panic from showing, from spreading to the others? The perfect choice would have been Carl Bender. . . .

He went down the stairs, through the door marked "Keep Out," and back to the sun deck lounge, back to home territory. He blinked around at the wicker chairs, the blue drapes, the cheerful murals with their tigers and monkeys. This *was* home, in a way. If home means a place where you're safe among your own kind, shut off from the hostile world. Yes, this could be the last home that he or any of them would ever know.

He sat down in the nearest chair. The lounge was almost empty. People must be in their cabins dressing up for tonight's gala, making themselves elegant despite the lack of materials. Making bricks out of straw—an ancient accomplishment of the Jews. That was how they had occupied themselves before that other exodus, the first exodus four thousand years ago. But the Red Sea had opened then, the children of Israel didn't have to go back to the land of bondage. . . .

Dear God, I don't like this game, Aaron thought. My stomach hurts, I need my pills. Please, let somebody else be the diplomat.

Across the lounge he saw two figures facing each other over a small table. One was Emil Karlweis, the great conductor. The other was Rabbi Einhorn. They were playing chess, as they had done every afternoon since the first day at sea. Nobody could figure out exactly how they had started, for they hadn't known each other before the voyage, and Karlweis had kept aloof from all the other passengers. The rabbi is the man to break the bad news, Aaron thought. That's the perfect job for a rabbi. I'll take him aside and unload this thing on his shoulders. A man gets tired, a man has to stop fighting someday. . . .

Where had he heard those words before? Somebody had said them to him a long time ago.

He remembered now. He was twenty-two years old, his last month at the university. He was sitting in the executive office at Schwarzkopf's Department Store, and Sophie's father was peering at him from across the desk. That was his first time inside that office—he had come to know it well in the years that followed. "Medical school?" Sophie's father had said to him. "Well, that's out of the question now, of course. How are you going to support a wife if you're in medical school? In times like these a young fellow has to be independently wealthy to afford that sort of career. You come into the store with me—you'll start at the bottom, don't make any mistake about *that*—but I'll be keeping my eye on you, and if you show any ability, there's a big future for you here. Believe me, you'll end up with a hell of a lot more money than if you became a doctor." And Aaron had gone home that night to think it over—to remember all the years since his boyhood when he had yearned to be a doctor, all the jobs he had held after school hours, the work he had put in for his scholarships, the dreams that had kept him going—and then Sophie, her little-girl smile, what he had felt if she touched his cheek— And underneath, something had stirred in him so faintly—uncertainty, fear, most of all fatigue. A man can't go on forever driving himself, giving up everything pleasant in life. A man gets tired, he has to stop fighting someday.

Yes, he remembered now. It was he who had said those words—said them to himself over and over through that long sleepless night more than twenty years ago. He had made his decision, and he had never regretted it. His life with Sophie had been a good one—and a useful one, too. If a man does the best he can for the people he loves, if he behaves decently to others, if he isn't cruel or greedy, what more can you ask of him?

"I've been looking for you everywhere."

Sophie was standing over him. She was out of breath, and her eyes were shining. "We have to hurry—they're serving coffee in the main lounge, and the band is giving its final concert! Franz Lehar—*The Land of Smiles.*"

What would she do if he told her the news, if he broke it to her right now—we're turning around and going back to Germany, there won't be any Land of Smiles. He could imagine the hysterics, the sobbing and wailing. He *couldn't* be the one to bring that on, to deliver that death blow to Sophie, to his children, to all these people. It wasn't fair that he should carry such a burden. It was hard enough to carry his own fear, his own despair—

And then a feeling of revulsion gripped him. It made him wince. His *own* fear, his *own* despair? Was that all he could think about, what *he* was going through? There were a thousand people on this ship, and for every one of them this news was going to be as terrible as it was for him. For Carl Bender, for Rabbi Einhorn, for anybody else who might have to do his job for him. If one of *them* could carry the burden, *he* could carry it, too. What was he, after all—a grown man with a wife and a family, or that sickly little boy who sipped tea in his bed while his mother told him how delicate he was? There *had* been a time in his life when he was able to fight against that contemptible "delicacy," a few years when he had overcome his squeamishness, worked at jobs he hated, hoped against hope, because he had wanted to be a doctor so badly. Eventually he had given up that dream—all right, for sensible, honorable reasons—but surely he was still capable of fighting if he had to. He could still do a job he hated—especially if he didn't have to go on with it for too long. . . .

With amazement he realized that he had made a decision. He had no idea what his reasons were, but he *would* make that announcement at dinner tonight. He would stand up in front of a thousand people and tell them the truth, and do it calmly and steadily. He would put hope and strength into his voice—regardless of his own feelings—so that the others could feel hopeful and strong. And if his stomach was killing him, he would simply ignore the pain.

And afterward, after that announcement was off his chest, he would sit down and retire without a single regret into private life. Gratefully he would give himself up again to worrying and taking pills and minding his own business, as he had been born to do.

He stood up and took Sophie by the arm. "Let's go listen to the music," he said. And he even managed to put a smile on his face.

*   *   *

It was Carl Bender's custom to take a stroll on deck every night after dinner. The fresh air and the exercise aided his digestion and soothed his nerves. And sometimes, if his step-daughter Eva decided to go off to the film or to play with Joshua Peyser, Julia would accompany him on his stroll.

He looked forward to these occasions. It was always pleasant to be with her. Her conversation was always charming, and her silences, too. Unfortunately, there hadn't been too many opportunities, in the course of this voyage, to see her and talk to her in privacy. Somehow she was always rushing off somewhere—to play deck tennis or watch a film or do something to her hair.

Tonight, however—what was supposed to have been their last night aboard—she walked with him when dinner was over, and so did Eva. On a night like this, he knew, families cling together, close in on themselves, shut out the rest of the world. It was a basic instinct; one could see it with small animals, too, burrowing into their mother's fur when they smelled danger. Bender felt nothing but pity for anyone on this ship who had no family.

And so the three of them moved slowly along the deck together. He held Julia by the arm, and she kept her other arm around Eva's shoulder. They pressed close to one another as if for protection from the cold. But there was no cold. The night was as mild and pleasant as all the other nights had been. The moon shone down as softly. What right did this night have to be so beautiful? Laughing in their faces, turning the knife in the wound.

"If we don't go to Havana, Mother," Eva said, "will we go back home instead?"

Julia said nothing. Bender could feel her fingers tighten on his arm.

"I'm sure Mr. Peyser was telling the truth," he said. "When we get to port tomorrow, there's a very good chance something will be worked out. It's quite likely they'll let us stay."

"Even if we don't go to Havana, Eva darling," Julia said, "that simply means we'll be going straight to the United States. We'll get to Boston a few months earlier than we expected to, that's all."

They went on walking. Occasionally they passed a small group of figures huddled in deck chairs or leaning together by the railing. They turned a corner and found themselves face to face with Mrs. Tannenbaum. The young woman

97

seemed to be out of breath, and her voice was high and agitated.

"Oh doctor—Mrs. Bender! I'm looking for Mr. Monsky—have you seen him anywhere?"

They told her that they hadn't seen him.

She shook her head and said, "I've been wanting to ask him something. Maybe you can tell me, doctor—you've done a lot of traveling. I know we won't be allowed off the boat tomorrow, but what about people who have come to meet us? People on the dock—will they be allowed to come *on* the boat? What do you think, doctor, will we be allowed to talk to them?"

He told her he couldn't answer her question. He had never found himself in a situation like this, he had no idea what the usual procedure might be.

"I'll ask Mr. Monsky," she said. "Mr. Monsky's been all over the world, he's been on a dozen different ships. He'll be able to tell me. I'll look for him in the card room—"

She moved past them shaking her head.

They went on walking. They came to the stern of the ship. To cross it they had to pick their way through the rows of deck chairs. In the center was the outdoor swimming pool, sealed up now with its large metal cover.

A small group of people could be seen standing on this metal cover, silhouetted against the moon-drenched sky.

At first the faces were blurs; there was only a discord of angry voices. Coming closer, Bender could see six people in the group, all boys in their late teens, all talking at once. Some of these boys he knew by name, some he had seen only at a distance. In the center of the group was Rabbi Einhorn's son, Peter, and next to him was that thin red-headed boy, the one traveling with his mother. His voice was loud and sharp. "I don't know about anybody else! *I'm* not going back! They can't make *me* go back!"

From some of the others gathered around him came a low muttering, urgent and confused, like a chorus of conspirators in a melodramatic opera. "How?" "What can you do?" "There's no way!" "How?"

Then came Peter Einhorn's voice, firmer, more controlled than the others. "If we stick together—if we all make up our minds to fight—"

As Bender drew level with the group, Peter's voice stopped abruptly. Six pairs of eyes shifted away. But one of these pairs caught Bender's for just a moment, flickered in recognition before shifting away, too. Aaron Peyser's boy—David, his oldest.

They went on walking—past the swimming pool, across the stern, leaving the group of boys behind them.

They turned another corner and started down the other side of the ship. They came to the wide glass doors that led into the main lounge. From inside came a ring of light, a buzz of voices. They paused, hesitated. Did they want to follow the light inside? Were they ready to be with people again?

Not a word was spoken between them, but a moment later they started walking again. The night had turned cooler. Julia reached down to button the collar of Eva's coat. A brisk, efficient gesture—the hands of a *couturière*, not a mother, you might have thought. But Bender was never fooled; he could always sense the tenderness under the briskness when Julia reached out to her little girl.

If she hadn't been left with this little girl when her husband walked out on her, would she ever have cared to get married again? He often asked himself this question. Pointlessly, for of course he knew the answer.

From behind them they heard a voice. "Dr. Bender! Mrs. Bender! Excuse me—"

They stopped and let Rabbi Einhorn catch up with them. His eyes were red. He looked as if he hadn't slept for a week. Yet at dinner tonight, hardly an hour ago, he had been vigorous and smiling.

"Please excuse me, doctor," he said. "I don't wish to intrude on your family and yourself. But I've been talking to as many people as I possibly could, and since I happened to see you through the window . . . Well, tomorrow morning—quite early, before we reach port—we're planning to hold a religious service. It won't be long, it will be quite brief, but it seemed to be the right thing to do—"

"You'll have a *minyan* without my help, won't you, Rabbi?"

"Yes, of course. I expect a great many people to attend."

"Please excuse me, then. We've discussed my feelings on these questions, you know."

"We have—certainly—but I assumed under the circumstances you'd probably—"

"I'm sorry, Rabbi—the circumstances haven't turned up any evidence that would lead me to change my views. I'll be

99

happy to pass the word about your service. But I'm afraid I won't be there."

"Yes—I see—you mustn't do anything that seems wrong to you. I can't help feeling it might give you—but these are matters for the individual conscience." The rabbi shook his head and said, "If you'll excuse me, I'd better be looking for—"

He hurried away from them, and Bender gave a sigh. Poor Max Einhorn—it didn't really seem possible to him that somebody could take a logical position and stick to it. Like most people, he didn't believe in logic at all. He believed in emotions, in magic, in the power of hope to conquer unpleasant facts.

They went on walking. They came to the point, near the front of the ship, beyond which no passengers were allowed. Here they had to turn and walk single file along a narrow passageway while holding on to a railing. Below this railing, stretching forward to the bow, was the foresection of the main deck. Oil drums, coils of rope, large crates squatted there, assuming strange animal shapes in the darkness. Beyond was the water, sliced in half by the oncoming bow, flecked with foam and moonbeams. A lovely sight. They stopped halfway along the passageway to look out at it.

Julia's hand was on the railing, only an inch from Bender's. Her fingers, long and graceful, had seemed beautiful to him from the first moment he met her. He could remember her sitting next to him at that tedious luncheon where a number of distinguished medical men made speeches. Those speeches had slipped out of his memory long ago, but what he could still call up before his mind's eye was the image of Julia eating an artichoke, delicately but firmly plucking up each leaf and turning it in her beautiful fingers. Even at the time he had realized that she was perfectly aware of what she was doing. She had deliberately transformed her artichoke-eating into an elaborate finger-ballet just to arouse his interest.

If Julia had only known where her casual flirtation would eventually lead her, how promptly she would have put down that artichoke, with what businesslike speed she would have diverted her attentions to the dinner partner on her other side. Or would she? For there was something in her, Bender knew, which made it necessary for her to live dangerously. There was a part of her nature, and no small part, either, which enjoyed playing with fire. Wasn't it inevitable, then, that some day she should be burned? Wasn't her present fate closely bound up with her character—as one's fate always is?

And yet—it did seem hard that she should have to pay such a high price for such a small fault. For Julia and Eva to be caught in this whirlpool and sucked down with all the others—this was gratuitous cruelty, injustice beyond the limits of a good joke. It may be an old truth of human existence that the innocent must suffer with the guilty, but nothing will ever make this easy to bear.

He had to smile at himself. Who were "the guilty"? All these people on this ship, himself included—what were they guilty of, except being Jewish? Observe how easily, how naturally he was already falling into the habit of thinking of this as a crime. He was familiar, of course, with the theories of Freud and Lewin and others, to the effect that the victims of persecution tend to accept their persecutors' evaluation of them. But only now, only in this last year or two, had he begun to feel and taste this bitter truth by watching its operation within himself.

But Julia and her daughter shared none of this "guilt"— there was no reason for *them* to be punished. Reason? Surely this word had no conceivable application to a world in which an accident of birth automatically makes one guilty of a non-existent crime. . . .

Eva shivered.

"We'd better walk again," Julia said.

They continued along the narrow passageway until they reached the other side of the ship. The deck was dark and empty—no, empty only if you didn't look hard enough, peer into the shadows until you could make out the figures hidden there. The normal reflex of the cornered beast, Bender thought, is to find a dark hole and crawl into it and hope that nobody will see him there. Human beings are different from other beasts only in being more ingenious—they're able to find a great many more dark holes, some of them inside their own heads.

"Good evening, doctor. Good evening, Mrs. Bender."

This precise, earnest voice could only belong to his cabin mate, young Liebling. The tall, stiff figure loomed up in the darkness and shook their hands politely. A well-mannered son of the fatherland to the very end. A credit to the brotherhood of accountancy.

"I've just come from the cabin to get a breath of air," Liebling said. "I'm happy to say that my suitcase is now packed."

Bender looked at him curiously. "You expect to be leaving the ship tomorrow?"

"We paid money for our passage, didn't we? Our contract stipulates that we are to disembark in the port of Havana, and visas were provided for that purpose, at considerable additional cost. The Hamburg Line is an old and reputable firm—I have every confidence, therefore, that they'll straighten out this misunderstanding."

"You have an optimistic view of life, Mr. Liebling."

"Yes, I *am* optimistic. I went to great trouble to get on this ship. Others went to great trouble on my behalf. Lottie—my fiancée—will be waiting for me on the dock. Her father, too. They've made the long journey especially to meet me. It's unthinkable that I should disappoint them."

"Circumstances sometimes oblige us to disappoint people."

The young man shook his head. "It's unthinkable. Quite unthinkable." He wished them good evening and strode off into the darkness.

They went on walking in silence. Madness, Bender thought. All around him was madness. And who could tell, perhaps the greatest madmen of all were those who tried to hold on to their sanity.

Nevertheless, he intended to try. Somehow he would snatch a few scraps of reason out of the tidal wave of unreason that was about to inundate the world. And he saw, dimly, how it might be done.

He believed in survival. It made sense, it was logical. His own survival first, of course—but once it became impossible for him to survive, the next logical step was surely to make the effort for someone else. This wouldn't be an act of altruism—altruism *never* made sense, as the case of Hannah, his first wife, had clearly shown—but rather an act of self-defense, a willful assertion of his individual identity. To save one beautiful, vain woman and one commonplace little girl out of all the thousands upon thousands—obviously no gesture could be more futile. And yet he had no other means of proving that he wasn't entirely at the mercy of an irrational universe.

And so, frowning, Bender began to formulate a certain idea. . . .

"We're back where we started from," Julia said. "And Eva's cold. I think we'd better go in now. You don't have to come with us, of course. If you'd rather stay out here."

"Would you prefer me to stay out here?"

She gave a little yawn. "Really, it doesn't matter to me either way. Whatever you wish."

He smiled—even more wryly than usual, no doubt. The irrational universe, he noted, was kindly making things easier for him. "In that case," he said, "I'll take another turn around the deck."

He kissed Julia on the cheek and Eva on the forehead, and then he went on walking. . . .

And Julia, watching him until he disappeared in the darkness, gave a little sigh. She shouldn't have forced herself on him after dinner tonight. No matter how sharp it was, this ache of terror inside her, she should have remembered that he preferred to be alone.

*　　*　　*

At seven o'clock in the morning the *Franz Joseph* sailed into Havana Harbor.

Naomi Einhorn stood at the railing on the main deck. She saw the ancient fortress of Morro Castle glowering down from its clifftop perch. She watched the ragged landscape slipping by muffled in mist. She couldn't see any definite objects; trees and bushes and telephone poles, all looked as if they were covered by thick layers of gauze. And then, far ahead, a tiny shape could be seen, and another, and then another. Soon the shapes began to spread and turn into rooftops, smokestacks, lampposts, the rigging and masts of ships. The shrieking of seagulls could be heard and a flapping of wings in the air. And suddenly it all fanned out before Naomi's eyes, an immense sweep of bay and ships and hills dotted with little houses. And in the center of this picture she saw the port itself, rows and stacks of tiny buildings, like the doll village she used to play with when she was a girl.

It was so beautiful, sparkling through its shroud of mist. She felt tears coming to her eyes. She glanced around guiltily, but she was all alone on the deck. She wasn't the only passenger awake at this hour—not many people had felt like sleeping late today—but not many people had felt like looking at scenery, either. Most were still at their breakfasts, or they were in the lounge while Father conducted his service.

She knew she ought to be at the service, too. The news that had come last night—she shouldn't have been able to think of anything else. But this morning they were sailing into Havana, into a whole new country. She had to see that, didn't she? And so when Father and Peter had started for the main lounge to set up the altar, she had excused herself for a breath of fresh air—hoping they wouldn't notice if she didn't come back.

"It isn't as big as I thought it would be."

She gave a start. David Peyser was standing next to her. She hadn't heard him coming.

"I'm sorry, I didn't mean to frighten you. I was at the service, but it got so warm in there. I'm really sorry—"

He could never just apologize for anything. He always had to fall all over himself. Did he really think so little of himself, or did he just want people to feel sorry for him? "What's not as big as you thought it would be?"

"This harbor. Havana. Everything in America is supposed to be so tremendous, but this isn't even as big as Hamburg."

"I was thinking it's just the right size. Pretty houses, and lots of room for trees. Have you ever seen palm trees before?"

"Only in the movies."

"I haven't, either. They're supposed to have coconuts on them. People split open the coconuts and drink the milk right out of them—" She knew she was running on and on, saying any silly thing that came into her head. She always had trouble carrying on a conversation with somebody who made her uncomfortable.

"It sounds sort of unsanitary," David said.

"I'd like to try it though, wouldn't you? When we go ashore—"

She stopped talking. She could see from his face that he was thinking what she was thinking. *Would* they ever taste coconut milk?

A shudder went through her. She didn't want to go back. These last two years had been so awful. Though she had tried not to complain—not even when she had to leave school and so many of her friends had stopped seeing her. Father gave her lessons at home—she had told herself that she learned a lot more that way than when she was in school. And

Peter had spent a lot of time with her. He talked to her about the books he was reading—sometimes she read them, too, and they argued about Zionism and religion. She used to get so angry and upset at the things Peter said, she used to burst into tears nearly every week. But she didn't know how she could have got through the last two years without those arguments. . . .

Remembering all this, she felt badly about David Peyser. If *she* was feeling awful about going back, *he* couldn't be feeling any better. He was facing the same things she was facing. Like her he was frightened and lonely, and needed all the friends he could get.

Why couldn't she be kind and understanding, as Peter was? The other day he had spoken sharply to her about her "rudeness"—because David had asked her a question, and she had pretended she didn't hear him. "It's your crazy romanticism," Peter had said to her. "He likes you a lot—don't pretend you haven't noticed—but you're offended because he doesn't fit your image of the great hero you deserve. You expect life to be like a movie. Every time you're with a boy there have to be violins throbbing in the background."

The mist was lifting now. The rays of the sun were beginning to pierce that gauze curtain, to strike sparks from the water. The port still looked tiny, because it was far away, but some details stood out clearly—a glint of silver on a metal rooftop, a splash of red from a flowering tree. And more people were coming out on deck now. They were leaning against the railing, pointing out at the harbor.

The services must be over, she thought. In a moment Father and Peter wouuld appear, and she wouldn't be able to talk to David any more. Suddenly it was important to tell him something. To tell him she would try to do better—

She put her hand on his arm. "I don't know what's going to happen, David. But we'll go on being friends—even if we have to go back—"

She couldn't say any more. There was a look of surprise, almost of panic, on David's face. She was glad, a moment later, when Peter came out of the lounge. Though he was frowning and hardly seemed to know she was there. . . .

I shouldn't have said it, Peter thought. It was a cruel thing to say—even if it was true. And it hurt Father—you could see the pain on his face. All right, Father *could* make such infuriating remarks sometimes, but that was no reason to—

Peter stopped himself with a stab of anger and shame. He remembered something that Wilhelm used to say. "Sometimes you have to hurt people. It isn't nice, but you have to do it. So do it, and don't waste your time feeling sorry for yourself or for them. Otherwise nothing will be accomplished." Wilhelm had never let personal feelings stand in the way of what he knew was right. He had cut himself off from his family, his friends, the girl he was once engaged to. He had risked his life every day for the cause—and other people's lives, too. It wasn't that he hadn't cared about people but that he *had* cared and he had known he was helping them in the long run.

And right up to the very end, Peter thought, Wilhelm tried to make *me* be like that. He tried to make me purge myself of confusion and weakness and shortsightedness. And look how I'm justifying his faith in me!

He was so disgusted with himself that he could hardly say a word to Naomi and David when he saw them on deck. He nodded at them, then went to the railing and looked out at the misty harbor that was coming closer and closer. He saw rooftops, palm trees, splotches of color.

I was right to lose my patience with Father, he told himself, I've got no reason to apologize for it. The Hebrew was what did it, of course. Father's voice rising and falling in the old familiar prayers. The voices of the other passengers chanting and mumbling along with Father's. Older people mostly, hardly a young face in the crowd—just as it had been at home when Father had his own synagogue. Tired old people halfway to the grave.

Yet Peter loved those Hebrew prayers. He had known them from childhood. His happiest memories—Sabbath dinners, mother lighting the candles, all of them saying the blessings together—sitting in the front row of the synagogue on the High Holidays, looking up at Father while he intoned the adoration in his rich, beautiful voice, looking up at him with such love and admiration. They were beautiful prayers, and it was a beautiful language. It was *the* language—the language of the homeland—someday all Jews would speak it.

Yes, but that was all the more reason why it shouldn't be corrupted, subverted, forced to serve the old dead ways, to reinforce the old hopeless apathy. That was why he had spoken cruelly to Father this morning. How could he help himself, with the tension that had been building up in him ever since Mr. Peyser's announcement last night?

He remembered talking with the other boys last night on deck by the deserted swimming pool. They were all feeling the tension, showing it in different ways. Kurt Halevy exploding with anger—"*I'm* not going back! They can't make *me* go back!" And David silent, always silent, with his eyes on Peter every moment—as if he couldn't decide what to feel or think till Peter told him.

But for Peter himself, his feeling had been a kind of excitement, impatience, a burning desire to *do* something. He had snapped back at Halevy, "How can you *stop* them from taking you back? Talking is no good, don't you see?" And Halevy had said, "You're so much better, Einhorn? Have *you* got any brilliant ideas?" And Peter had said, "Yes, I do——" These words had come bursting out of him, and only then did he realize that they were true. His mind was working faster than it had ever worked before—ideas were swarming in on him. For the first time in months, in years, he wasn't thinking about the homeland. Not because he had stopped caring about the homeland, but because the moment he'd been looking forward to for such a long time—the moment of freedom, the moment when he took his life into his own hands—seemed to be on him *now*.

The others sensed that there was something special, unusual in him. They lowered their voices instantly. They all started looking at him a little bit the way David had been looking at him. It came over him with a shiver that this was war, they were going to fight now, and he was their leader.

On deck they were too much out in the open—they moved into the music room, where people could listen to phonograph records. It had comfortable chairs, and when the door was shut you couldn't be heard outside. Peter started telling them some of his plans. . . .

Today they would meet again. They would settle on a plan. They would work out the details. They were *doing* something—while Father was chanting Hebrew, praying, abasing himself to God.

After the service Father had come up to him and said, "It went well, I think. It did some good, don't you agree?"

And that was when Peter had said the cruel thing. "We're about to be thrown to the wolves, and all you can do is read Hebrew. We're not going to *pray* the Nazis out of existence. Sometimes I think Hitler is right about us. If we don't have the guts to defend ourselves, we *deserve* to be destroyed!"

He hadn't meant it—not the way it sounded—but Father had turned white. He couldn't have looked more wounded if he had been struck in the face. But I won't waste time feeling sorry, Peter thought. Sometimes you have to hurt people. What really matters is the cause. . . .

David's family came out on deck—they had all been at the service. Peter roused himself to say good morning to David's parents, his grandparents, his little brother. "Your father gives a nice service," said David's grandfather, Mr. Schwarzkopf. "Lots of dignity. Not like these newfangled rabbis nowadays. When your father talks it doesn't sound like ordinary conversation. It sounds *religious.*"

Peter didn't like Mr. Schwarzkopf. He was always laying down the law, acting as if his approval were needed before anybody had a right to an opinion. But in a way Peter found him sad, too. Because nobody really listened to him when he talked.

David's little brother was pointing at something out on the water. "I think they're coming *here!*"

Other people were pointing, too, all along the deck. Peter looked, and way off he saw a small boat skimming through the water, heading toward them. A flag was flying from the front of it, and a man in uniform was standing on the deck.

Then Peter noticed that the ship had stopped moving.

Mr. Schwarzkopf rubbed his hands together. "Well, it's about time. They finally sent someone out to do business with us." He chuckled. "It's what I've been saying all along—this is a bluff by the Cuban government. What they want is a small financial transaction under the table—"

Peter could hardly bear to listen to this. Buy your way out or pray your way out—that's what everyone on this ship seemed to believe. Why couldn't they realize that the only chance they had now was to *fight* their way out?

Those talks he'd been having with Father for the last year or two—they all came back to him. "Jews are a peace-loving people—we don't believe in settling our problems with our fists. Our strength lies in our horror of violence. This is why we've survived so long." But Father was wrong, it wasn't true about Jews at all. You just had to read the Torah—Samson slaying the Philistines with the jawbone of an ass, David bashing in Goliath's head, Joshua razing the walls of Jericho and slaughtering all its inhabitants. Those men in the Torah were Jews—their faith was Judaism as much as the soft, timid "peace" that Father believed in. A lazy religion for rich people whose lives have been too easy, who have too much to lose. "The man who won't fight for his rights," Wilhelm used to say, "doesn't have any."

Wilhelm had been willing to fight for his rights. Wilhelm had—

"The boat's tying up," said Mr. Peyser, David's father, "they're coming aboard."

Peter saw the small boat bobbing in the water far below. Then a long metal ladder was dropped from the deck, and two men started to climb up it. They climbed slowly, hand over hand. They wore white suits and straw hats. These two foolish-looking men would decide if a thousand people went back to Germany? Peter could feel the anger stirring in him.

Farther down the deck the crowd began to heave and sway, and then it seemed to break in two. Peter saw that a passage was being cleared for the two men who had just come aboard. With a couple of ship's officers in front of them—the yellow-faced one named Muller and the boyish-looking one named Dietrich—they walked briskly along the deck. They were both short men, one fat and one thin, and they both had black hair and sideburns and little black mustaches, and they both carried briefcases. They kept their eyes straight ahead—no sign at all that they knew anybody else was on the deck with them.

Peter felt like shouting out at them: Look at us, you bastards! We're not invisible! We're here! We're human beings, just like you!

"Out of the way, out of the way," Muller said, looking as if he hoped somebody would disobey him, while Dietrich fidgeted and didn't seem to know where to look.

The two men in white suits disappeared through the glass doors. Then there was a buzz of talk from the crowd on the deck.

"Somebody ought to go in there," Mr. Schwarzkopf said. "Talk to them before it's too late—look out for our interests!"

"How about you, Schwarzkopf?" It was Mr. Monsky, pushing out from the crowd. He stepped right up to Mr. Schwarzkopf, grinning, looking as pleased with himself as always, wearing that funny loud sports jacket. "You should be the perfect man for the job, with all your experience back home dealing with people in high places."

Mr. Schwarzkopf had turned his head away. He was pretending he hadn't heard what Mr. Monsky said.

The lounge doors opened, and Peter saw Father come out. He went straight up to David's father. "I'm sorry to trouble you, Mr. Peyser. The first officer, Mr. Muller, just asked me to find you. The immigration officials are with the captain now, and the captain thinks you should talk to them after they leave him. As our representative, to report back to the rest of us—"

"I'm not anybody's representative, Rabbi," said David's father. "You're a much more appropriate person—"

Mr. Peyser was pleading with Father, Peter could hear it in his voice. He saw Father lower his eyes apologetically.

"No, I really don't think— The fact is that you already have the passengers' confidence, Mr. Peyser. You showed last night that you can communicate with people. That's always been my problem with my congregations. They believe in my sincerity, but I have difficulty communicating . . ."

Father's voice trailed off, and he still wouldn't look Mr. Peyser in the face. Peter ached with pity for him. He had known for a long time how distrustful Father was of himself. This was something that had been growing worse in him during the last few years. And how, Peter asked himself, have I been helping him? Sneering at everything he holds dear, haranguing him with ideas that he can't understand.

Then he asked himself what he *should* have done. Changed his ideas? Kept them hidden, pretended to believe what he didn't believe? No, that would have been inexcusable. The old sloppy myth that a man who cares about humanity has to be weak—Wilhelm had taught him a long time ago how wrong that was. "The more you care," Wilhelm used to say, "the colder you must be."

He had to be cold about Father. If he couldn't harden himself up right now, how would he behave when the moment for action arrived? He had to be one of the *old* Jews, the strong Jews—purge himself once and for all of the guilts and confusions that centuries of weeping and wailing in exile had instilled in his people.

Mrs. Peyser had her hand on Mr. Peyser's arm now. "You

don't have to do this, Aaron. You were awake all last night, your stomach's never been so bad." She turned to Mr. Schwarzkopf. "Papa, since it's a question of talking to officials, why can't *you*—"

Mr. Schwarzkopf drew himself up and started to say something, but Mr. Peyser spoke first. "All right, Rabbi, I might as well get it over with." He squeezed his wife's arm, then hurried into the lounge.

There was a long silence. Mrs. Peyser shook her head. "I'm tired—I'll wait in the cabin. David, when your father comes out again, tell him where I am."

"Do you need me, Mama?" David said.

"No. Stay here, keep your eye on Joshua—"

"Mrs. Peyser—" Father stepped up to her. "Let me see you to your cabin."

She looked at him a moment, and it seemed to Peter that there was a kind of weary anger in her eyes. But then she nodded and let Father take her by the arm and escort her off the deck. That's what he's good at, Peter thought. Not congregations, but individual people—they feel his kindness, they're comforted by him.

Mrs. Tannenbaum came pushing out of the crowd. She pulled at Mr. Monsky's sleeve. "What's happening? Will they let us off the ship?"

"The big powers are negotiating behind the scenes," Mr. Monsky said. "Our own League of Nations."

It always puzzled Peter, the way Mrs. Tannenbaum hung on Mr. Monsky's words, actually took him seriously. And she had been spending so much time with him, too, since this trip began—going to concerts and movies with him, having coffee with him while the band played.

"So how about it, Schwarzkopf?" Mr. Monsky was saying. "If the negotiations break down, are you going to get us out of this mess? Why don't you make some urgent appointments with influential Cubans?"

Mr. Schwarzkopf took Mrs. Schwarzkopf by the arm, and they walked off the deck together.

Mr. Monsky laughed.

A cry rose up from the crowd The ship had started moving again. Faster than before, Peter thought. The houses in the distance were getting larger and more distinct.

"Do you suppose they're letting us in after all?" Naomi said.

111

The faces of the other people on deck were tense, turned toward the port. Everyone was asking Naomi's question, Peter knew. He was asking it, too, saying it to himself silently over and over again. If the ship docked in Havana, he wouldn't have to meet with the boys again, they wouldn't have to make their plan, the moment of action—of violence, maybe—wouldn't come. Was he scared of that moment, scared of how he would behave? Wilhelm used to talk a lot about violence, and Peter had listened enthusiastically. But Wilhelm had *known* violence—he had been to the homeland twice, had thrown a hand grenade from ambush, though he was only three years older than Peter. Wilhelm had slipped in and out of Germany several times to do his job, to recruit young Jews for the cause. Every time he appeared on the street or sat at a café or went to Peter's apartment to talk to his friends, he had known that he was risking his life. When they finally picked him up at the entrance to the park and dragged him into their car beating him with their clubs, it couldn't have come as a surprise to him. But Peter—he had never so much as struck another person and drawn blood. He had never even held a weapon in his hand and pointed it at somebody. How could he be sure, when the moment came, that he wouldn't be his father's son?

The mist had lifted completely. In the bright morning sun it was possible to make out more and more details of the port. The dock was jutting out into the water, and there was a crowd of people on it. You couldn't see any individual features, but you could tell that those were faces, rows and rows of faces.

"Mr. Monsky," said Mrs. Tannenbaum, "do you think Martin could be there?"

"It's too far away," Mr. Monsky said. "Even if he were there, you couldn't see him."

"Please—could we go closer to the railing?"

With a shrug Mr. Monsky followed her. He was by her side as she pushed against the railing, thrust her head forward, shaded her eyes with her hand.

Suddenly there was a deep rumbling noise. It set the deck shaking, seemed to be coming from all around them. Peter recognized that noise, though he had heard it seldom. It was the ship's anchor being unwound. Then he saw that the dock in the distance and the crowd of people on it weren't growing any larger. The ship had stopped moving.

He saw David's hand tighten on Naomi's arm. He saw Naomi's face turn pale.

The lounge doors opened, and the two ship's officers, Muller and Dietrich, stepped through with those Cuban officials behind them. Their white suits looked a little rumpled, and there was perspiration on their faces. But as they moved through the crowd, which again divided in two for them, their eyes still didn't flicker to the left or right.

"I'd like an explanation, if you please!"

Somebody had stepped out from the crowd and stood right in the path of the men in white suits. Peter saw that it was Mrs. Fischel, the lady who shared Naomi's cabin with her. Naomi was always saying what a terrible old nuisance Mrs. Fischel was—hanging her wet stockings all over the bathroom, taking up most of the medicine cabinet with her pills and her creams, but quick to complain if she found so much as a hairpin of Naomi's on her side of the dressing table.

An angry gleam was in Mrs. Fischel's eye as she faced the Cubans. Her chin was up in the air, and her voice was as shrill as the voices of the seagulls wheeling above the ship. "If I'm not mistaken, every person aboard this ship paid money for certain visas. Certain promises were made. We were led to expect that those visas would permit us to land in Havana and remain there for at least one year—"

"Please move aside, madam," Muller said. "These gentlemen wish to leave the ship."

She didn't even look at Muller. She kept her sharp little chin pointed at the Cubans.

"Certain rumors came to our ears last night. We were told we wouldn't be allowed to land as agreed upon. If those rumors are true, you will please explain how you can justify such highhanded, illegal behavior. If they aren't true, kindly give orders for this ship to put into dock at once—"

"Madam, please," Muller said.

"Don't madam me, young man! I won't submit to this outrage—"

It wasn't clear what happened next. Did Mrs. Fischel push past Muller, or did he try to push her out of the way? Did she lose her balance accidentally, or did he grab hold of her with too much violence? It all happened so quickly, a flurry of arms and legs, a lot of shouting, and then Mrs. Fischel was lying on her back on the deck. A black smear was on her cheek, and heavy gasping sounds were coming out of her. Her friend Mrs. Moritz, who was also in the crowd, began to cry, "Gertrude! Gertrude!"

Muller looked down at Mrs. Fischel, breathing hard, as if he couldn't decide if he should help her to her feet or give her a kick. Finally, with a shake of his head, he muttered, "She's all right—somebody pick her up—gentlemen, if you'll follow me, please—"

Dietrich seemed about to reach down to her, but Muller stopped him with a look. They led the Cubans past Mrs. Fischel. The fat one, Peter saw, couldn't keep himself from glancing down quickly. Just as quickly he raised his eyes again and hurried after his partner.

And for a moment, his cheeks stinging, Peter was on the verge of crying out—telling those Nazi animals what he thought of them, rushing at them, smashing his fists into their faces. That selfish, egotistical, absurd old woman had shamed them all. She hadn't been afraid to step forward, to speak her mind, while the rest of them stood around and gaped and fidgeted and congratulated themselves on how "peace-loving" they were.

He held himself in. He didn't do anything foolish. What good would it do to get himself in trouble now, when everything might depend on him and his plan? But he was glad this incident had occurred. He had learned something from it. You had to fight, no matter *how* you felt about it. You might doubt yourself, you might be full of fears, but you had to fight just the same. In ethical terms, in human terms, Father was worth a thousand Mrs. Fischels. But right now, today, on this ship, Peter hoped against hope that he would turn out to be like her, not like him. . . .

Slowly Naomi let out her breath. For a few moments she had been really afraid. She had seen Peter's face tightening, his lips trembling—she had realized he was about to do something crazy. She could understand how he felt—sometimes it seemed to her as if *nothing* would help except to scream and scream—but thank God Peter had got hold of himself at last. He had kept his mouth shut, and the two men in white suits disappeared now through the crowd.

As soon as they were gone, people rushed up to Mrs. Fischel. She was lifted to her feet. Several hands supported her under her arms, while sympathetic ladies clucked at her. After a few minutes, though, she gave a snort, shook off the hands, and snapped out, "I'm quite all right, *thank* you!"

114

Then she turned to Mrs. Moritz, who was sobbing fitfully. "Rosa, you're making a damned fool of yourself!" And then she went stamping off the deck.

Now everyone was talking, gesturing, shaking heads angrily or gloomily. Mrs. Tannenbaum had turned away from the railing; she was leaning on Mr. Monsky's arm. The sympathetic ladies, frustrated in their efforts to comfort Mrs. Fischel, were comforting Mrs. Moritz. Several of them led her away to the lounge. Three or four children were clutching at their parents, asking questions in frightened voices.

Naomi turned to look at David, standing by her side. He was staring straight ahead, and his face was very still, almost rigid. As if no thoughts were going on inside his head.

What *was* going on inside him when he got that look on his face? All her doubts about him rushed over her again.

But she couldn't think about this any longer—a voice came booming out through the loudspeaker. They all knew this voice very well—for six days it had been telling them what tonight's film would be and when the bingo game was scheduled. Now the voice said, "Passengers will not be permitted to leave the ship until further notice. This is by order of the harbor police. Please do not attempt to disobey this order. There will be no exceptions."

And as if this announcement had been a signal, a loud buzzing, sputtering noise was heard now beyond the railing. Everyone looked and saw a heavy boat chopping through the clear blue water about a hundred yards away. It seemed to be approaching the ship, then it veered off to the side, then it turned away from the ship, then it veered to the side again. It was going in circles, around and around. "Look—the guns!" somebody called out. And Naomi saw them, two large black objects with long, cylindrical snouts. They seemed to be fastened to the deck of the circling boat, one in front and one in the stern. They were pointed out over the water.

The crowd was suddenly silent. The only sound was the buzzing and sputtering of that engine.

And then at Naomi's side Peter began to speak in a very low voice. *"And the Lord said unto Moses, This is the land which I sware unto Abraham, unto Isaac, and unto Jacob, saying, I have caused thee to see it with thine eyes, but thou shalt not go over thither."*

She felt Peter's hand reaching for her own, pressing it

tightly. A moment later he laughed and said, "You see, I'm not a rabbi's son for nothing."

The boat with the guns on it kept going around and around.

But the harbor is beautiful, Naomi told herself. Yes, it *is* beautiful. That's not my imagination. That's real, just as real as anything else. Nothing can take that away.

*   *   *

At noon the luncheon gong sounded. The deck was cleared quickly. Word had spread that an announcement would be made, that answers would be given to everybody's questions.

The sun, high in the sky now, beat down on the boards of the deck and on the empty chairs. It beat down on Albert Liebling, the only passenger who still stood at the railing. He wore his best suit, his only suit—dark gray, double-breasted, with vest to match. Conservative, respectable, looking as if it had cost much more than it really had. He flattered himself that he knew the correct way to dress, that his clothes might not be expensive but would always be appropriate to the occasion. His mother had trained him in this from earliest childhood—his poor mother, widow of a civil servant, struggling on her small pension to provide an education, a decent start in life, for her only son. She had made him understand the importance of maintaining one's dignity, keeping up appearances.

His suitcase was on the deck at his feet. It was neatly packed—Lottie always said that she had never met a man who packed a suitcase as neatly as he. A pair of leather straps were tied around it, just to be on the safe side. It appeared, however, that he wouldn't be able to bring it ashore with him. A pity to leave it behind on the ship. Heaven knows there was nothing of any great value in it—the small leatherbound Bible which his mother had given him did have sentimental value, but he had transferred it to his trousers pocket this morning. Yet there would be a certain inconvenience in arriving at the dock with no possessions, not even a toothbrush or a razor. He would have to draw even further on the generosity of Lottie's father, and though the amounts would be negligible, the necessity was distasteful to him.

Shading his eyes from the sun, he stared out across the

water, as he had been doing since early morning. He stared at the crowd of people gathered on the dock, far off in the distance. How great a distance? At most it could hardly be more than a quarter of a mile. For a young man in reasonably good physical condition a quarter of a mile wouldn't present insuperable difficulties. He was grateful now for those summers at the seashore, those happy boyhood summers for which his mother had somehow managed to scrape together the money.

He stared at the mass of people on the dock. If he stared hard enough, he might be able to distinguish one face from another. He might be able to pick out Lottie from the rest.

He strained his eyes till the beams of light seemed to dance before them. *That* was Lottie—over there near the front of the crowd, the dark hair, the oval face! No, he couldn't really be sure. He couldn't tell one face from another. Perhaps he wouldn't recognize her face even if he *could* tell. He had seen it in his dreams for the last two years. And he carried her snapshot in his wallet, that fuzzy snapshot that was taken by a photographer on the street. Yet the terrible suspicion came to him sometimes that he had forgotten what Lottie looked like.

If *he* could forget, so could *she*. Perhaps she wasn't on the dock at all, then. Perhaps she and her father hadn't bothered to come to Havana. In providing the money for his passage they had fulfilled their obligation, and nobody could blame them for washing their hands of him now. Who wants to be burdened with a penniless refugee, an unemployed accountant who has no license to practice his profession, who can hardly even talk English, much less pass the examinations?

But these thoughts were foolish. These moods of discouragement had troubled him before, and he had always managed to overcome them. One must use willpower, one must assert one's common sense. Lottie's father was an honorable man, a conscientious man, like Liebling himself, despite the slight inferiority of his social position. And for Lottie herself—she loved him. He was sure she loved him. She *was* there on that dock.

She was there, and she was reaching out to him, beckoning to him. Albert, I'm here, I'm waiting for you, why don't you come to me? Yes, he could almost see her, even from this distance. Why did he hesitate? In his whole life he had

117

never been one to shirk his responsibility. Did he want his faithful Lottie to think that his love for her wasn't strong enough?

He took off his jacket and his vest and folded them carefully before unstrapping the suitcase and placing them inside. He took off his shoes and set them down next to the suitcase. He could have squeezed them in, but in doing so he might crush his jacket. There was still a great deal of wear in that jacket, and the Hamburg Line would surely return his property to him someday.

Should he not remove his shirt and trousers, too? He would find it much easier to swim without them. But no—Lottie would be waiting for him on the dock. Out of the question to appear before her in his underclothes.

He threw one leg over the railing, then the other leg. Holding on with his hands, his back against the railing, he looked down at the water. It suddenly seemed much farther away than it had a few minutes ago. He felt a lump in his throat.

He swallowed quickly, shut his eyes, and let go of the railing.

First came the pounding of air against his ears, the sensation that his stomach was rising into his chest. Then came the shock, like a block of stone slamming into his face. The cold gripped him, the water closed over his head, a terrible choking grew in him—all this he had expected, had allowed for. Yet it was worse than he had expected, and it seemed to last forever, until he went shooting up to the surface. He gasped for air, and water filled his mouth, ran out of his nose, started him coughing violently.

He got the coughing under control. He began to swim. Arms over his head, legs kicking, a steady, even stroke. The important thing is not to think about what you're doing, turn yourself into a machine, keep moving until you reach your destination.

There was a noise in his ears. Shouting—people shouting. They must be shouting at him from the dock. Urging him on. He focused as best he could, though his eyes were streaming with water. The dock was closer, Lottie was shouting at him. Hurry, Albert, I'm waiting! But why then did the shouts seem to come from behind him, from both sides of him, from everywhere except in front of him?

He kept on swimming. His arms were beginning to ache.

No, he must not let them ache. Fatigue was not permissible. It wasn't part of his plan.

A new noise came to his ears. It was all mixed up with the shouts. A loud buzzing noise—and then someone was setting off fireworks. Bang-bang-bang, a whole string of them, and it kept on going, it didn't come to an end. They hurt his ears—he had never heard such loud firecrackers. Something struck the water in front of him. It splashed into his face, stinging his eyes.

Suddenly he understood. But they're shooting at me. Those are bullets hitting the water. That patrol boat, with its big black guns—how could it be shooting at *me?* It was impossible—such things don't happen to people, not to respectable people who have been careful and law-abiding all their lives. He had to swim faster, he had to keep on swimming until he got to Lottie. He must discuss this matter with her, explain to her that he wasn't in the habit of being shot at and pursued by police officers—that this wasn't his manner of life at all but some terrible, incomprehensible, embarrassing accident. He must make it clear to her, and also to her father, that their confidence in him hadn't been misplaced—

Pain shot through his right leg. It made him kick, made him retch—in his whole life he had never felt such pain. Then his leg was hanging from him, a dead weight, pulling him down, pulling him under the water. He kicked with his other leg, he flailed his arms, anything to keep his head above the water.

More pain—his shoulder. He was flung around in the water; he couldn't seem to move his arm anymore. There was a taste in his mouth—strange, metallic—the taste of blood? He tried to spit it out while he flapped his good arm. Then something exploded in his chest, and a hot flame went through his whole body, rushed up through the top of his head—the faces on the dock were spinning before his eyes, a giant wheel against the sky. He knew that a scream was coming out of him. Don't leave me, Lottie! Everything will be fine for us, you'll see! I'll carry out my responsibility—

*   *   *

The noise of the guns was heard in the dining room below. Some of the passengers ran out to see what was happening. By the time they climbed the stairs and reached the deck, the patrol boat had cut its engine, and the surface of the water was smooth again and lightly flecked with blood.

Among these passengers was Aaron Peyser. Instinctively—he couldn't have explained why—he raised his eyes and squinted through his glasses at the window of the captain's office way up on the bridge. Behind that window did he see a motionless figure standing? Had the captain seen everything, the whole terrible thing that had happened? What were his thoughts and his feelings as he listened to the guns and the screams mingling with the shrieking of the sea gulls? Was he filled with pity, with anger? Was he calm? Was he indifferent?

The sunlight, striking fire off the glass, made it impossible for Aaron to be sure that the captain was standing there at all.

FIVE

M ORRIE'S conviction that disaster lay ahead began to ease as soon as he saw Al at La Guardia Airport. The radiogram he wrote to Aaron Peyser on the *Franz Joseph* was a tonic for his spirits. A few hours in the city completed his cure. He looked around at the tall buildings, the yellow cabs, the subway ads in English; he listened to his friends and his family talking about the same things they had been talking about before he left—and he just couldn't go on thinking of the world as a nightmare place in which everything or everybody was suddenly liable to turn horrible.

And the next day he had no more time to be gloomy. With Al by his side he was plunged into a nonstop round of briefings, conferences, visits. For the first time since he had come to work for AJDA he was able to observe at close quarters how the really big givers were approached when money was needed quickly.

To begin with, the prospects—six or seven of AJDA's wealthiest supporters, male and female—were called on individually by Al or Dan Wechsler. Each prospect was told that a grave emergency had arisen, that a committee was being formed to advise the AJDA staff on how to deal with it, and that everybody hoped he would be interested in joining. Nobody turned down the request. Then Morrie was made to tell his story in detail. "Sure, I could tell it to them myself," Al said, "but the effect wouldn't be as good. These are important people—you can't let them think they're getting their facts secondhand."

The day after these opening talks Al or Dan phoned up each prospect and told him that a committee meeting was set for the following morning. The situation in Havana, it was explained, had grown more urgent, and quick action was needed. The prospect *had* to show up for tomorrow's meeting, because there was reason to believe that certain congenitally

121

cautious members of the committee might be planning to drag their feet. Each prospect was given exactly this same speech—so who, Morrie wondered, were those "congenitally cautious" members supposed to be?

Another thing puzzled him. Finally he asked Al about it. "So far nobody's mentioned where the money's coming from. You haven't told these people you're expecting to get it from *them.*"

"My God, this is a sensitive group. We can't insult them by telling them we're only interested in their bank accounts."

"But they *are* generous people. Are you sure they have to be hoodwinked?"

"Who's being hoodwinked? After all these years don't you get the point yet about Jewish fund-raising? They *know* we're out to get money from them. They knew *that* the moment we started talking to them—after all, they're not exactly damned fools. And they intend to give the money, too, that goes without saying. But they expect us to work hard for it, just the same. Otherwise, how can they be sure we really think this is such an important matter? It's by watching *us* that they decide how much *they* ought to give."

Morrie was up early the next morning. He had to be at the office at nine for Dan's last briefing to the staff before the ten o'clock meeting. At breakfast he couldn't eat a thing. When his kids—Joanie, who was five, and Billy, who was three—started quarreling over a piece of raisin-bread toast, he bawled them out in the voice he usually reserved for major misdemeanors. "Darling, there's no reason to be nervous," Ruth said. "You know nothing can go wrong."

"Sure I know it," he said. "So why don't I believe it?"

And he realized that all his irrational fears had returned to him. He was filled again with the conviction that disaster lay ahead.

An hour later in Dan's office he was amazed at how calm everybody seemed to be. Nobody acted as if there were any reason in the world to be tense. Somebody made a comment about the weather—summer was definitely around the corner, any day now the first heat wave would strike and the city would become unbearable. Somebody mentioned the double-header which the Yankees had dropped to Cleveland yesterday. Somebody said that he didn't much like the reports that Ribbentrop was planning to go on a diplomatic mission to Moscow; if Hitler could neutralize Russia, there wouldn't be anything to stop him from invading Poland and the Balkans. Professor Seymour Schwartz, the public-opinion expert, who was the closest thing AJDA had to a genuine Marxist, declared that the Soviet Union would never under any circumstances make a pact with Germany. "In Russia today there are no crypto-Fascists waiting for their chance to take over, as there are in the so-called democracies. What do you think Stalin's purge trials were all about?"

"They were all about one set of gangsters grabbing power from another set of gangsters," said Bernie Kramer, who was supposed to have been a Trotskyite when he was a lot younger.

Professor Schwartz sighed. "Political naïveté—the curse of our benighted country."

Dan didn't join in this conversation. He never talked about trivial things, though he kindly tolerated this weakness in others. With his gray hair, his conservative suits, his slow manner of speech—weighing every word as if the fate of nations depended on it—he always reminded Morrie of the wise old father in those Andy Hardy movies. ("Come along, son, I think it's time we had a man-to-man talk.") Only after he had been working at AJDA a long time did Morrie come to realize how carefully Dan himself cultivated his paternal image.

Al got to the office fifteen minutes late, which was about par for him. As soon as he was seated, Dan settled down to giving them detailed instructions on the procedures for the ten-thirty meeting. Then they all went down the corridor together to the executive boardroom, which was full of leather upholstery and oak paneling and dominated by a long mahogany table that wouldn't have disgraced the boardroom of U.S. Steel.

Some of the prospective donors were already sitting at this table, and within ten minutes all the rest had arrived.

* * *

Senator Friedkin opened the meeting with a few remarks on the seriousness of the problem they were about to consider. His voice trembled, his face showed pain and compassion. Yet it seemed to Morrie that the horrors, as they came out of the senator's mouth, didn't sound very horrifying but rather bland and remote. This had been the secret of his

123

success (until the last disastrous Democratic landslide) among Jewish voters and many non-Jewish ones, too: He was everybody's warm, friendly uncle; he never flinched from dealing with deeply serious subjects, but he always made them come out soothing.

At the end of his speech he turned the meeting over to "our good friend and executive director—the man, let's face it, who *is* the American Jewish Defense Agency—Dan Wechsler."

In his quiet, unhurried way Dan was a highly effective speaker. By the time he got through laying out the facts of the *Franz Joseph*'s voyage and of her present predicament, the horror that had eluded the senator was clearly before their eyes. "Now there's no point beating around the bush," Dan ended up. "We don't have time for elaborate plans, public functions, protracted debates. If we're going to help those people, we have to do it now. Before you leave this room today, ladies and gentlemen, you have to raise half a million dollars among you. Furthermore, what you give now has to be over and above your regular yearly contributions to AJDA. Your pledge this afternoon can't be considered, even partially, as a substitute for what you intended to give later on anyway. Our regular budget is just as urgently needed as ever to finance our regular programs. More urgently, in fact, because of the extra strain of providing for the needs of these thousand people once we *do* get them off that ship."

"Just a moment, please." This interruption came from Ben Zuckerman, speaking quietly with all the authority he must have used in presiding over the board of the Continental Radio Network. His dry, metallic voice, his rimless glasses, his skin as gray as steel plate made him seem to Morrie more like a machine than a human being. "Don't we provide an annual budget for our Department of Refugee Affairs? That budget, as I recall, is a lot higher than some of us think it should be. Now you seem to be implying that it isn't adequate to take care of these people in Cuba. What else is that budget for, I'd like to know, if not for emergencies like this?"

"Ben is right," said Sigmund Wolff, the fur man, trying to sound hard and machinelike, too, but badly handicapped by his high-pitched voice and his slight lisp. "That budget was approved on the express understanding—" Why did Sigmund Wolff agree with everything Ben Zuckerman ever said? He had absolutely nothing to gain from being Zuckerman's number one slave. His fur business, inherited from his father, was highly successful, and as far as anyone knew he had no dealings with the Continental Radio Network and no social connections with Ben Zuckerman; they never even saw each other except at AJDA board meetings. "Siggie," Al used to say, "seems to be one of the rare cases of completely unselfish, altruistic ass-licking."

"You're quite correct, gentlemen," Dan said, unruffled as always. "The Department of Refugee Affairs *does* have an adequate budget, under ordinary circumstances. It was never contemplated, however, that we would have to maintain a thousand people in a foreign country all at the same time. This unforeseen emergency comes to us courtesy of the Nazi government. It's a headache, no doubt, but I'm sure nobody in this room would prefer that those people *hadn't* been let out of Germany."

His eyes rested gently on each of them in turn. He gave no more time to Ben Zuckerman and Sigmund Wolff than to anybody else.

Judge Goodfreund cleared his throat. He had two public manners, Morrie had noticed, his easygoing, anecdotal one and his solemn, oratorical one. Clearing his throat was a sure sign that he was about to be solemn and oratorical. "You've put the matter as clearly and succinctly as possible, Dan. None of us could possibly add to or improve on your words." Then for another ten minutes the judge proceeded to add to and improve on them, with frequent references to "the traditional spirit of Jewish giving" and several Biblical quotations, a habit he indulged in only when there was no rabbi present. "It's obvious to me, therefore, as it must be to all of you, that we cannot fail to underwrite this sum of money, large as it is, and with the utmost speed. If I were in the position to do so, I'd gladly guarantee the entire sum myself. Unfortunately, as you know, I happen to be the 'poor man' among you—"

The judge gave a discreet little laugh. In a way, Morrie thought, his statement was true. His great grandfather, the German peddler who had founded the Goodfreund fortune, had handed down a considerable amount of money to his heirs, but it wasn't quite so considerable by the time it reached the judge, and the chances were that he hadn't added anything to it himself.

"But you may count on me to pledge as much as I can afford, and possibly a bit more."

"I'm with you, Judge, I'm with you a hundred percent!"

It was Reuben Levinson who spoke up now. He was in the leather goods business, a little bald-headed man in his fifties, never to be seen without a half-chewed cigar in his mouth. Ordinarily, because he was a comparatively new member of AJDA, he wouldn't have been summoned to such an urgent meeting. But Dan and Al had thought they ought to have as many completely loyal allies as possible.

"What are we going to do," Mr. Levinson went on, "let those people go back to Hitler, to that mad dog? We're going to let them rot away in concentration camps—women and children, too? My God, on that ship are babies, little babies, the same age as my grandkids! If a man is too stingy to use his money to save the lives of little children, what's he got money for, that's what *I'd* like to know?"

"Excuse me," said Ben Zuckerman, "but it isn't a question of stinginess. Everybody here has demonstrated his generosity many times over in the past. If some of us feel doubts about this project, those doubts are based on sound businesslike considerations."

"What considerations, what? Tell me please just one consideration that's more important than a little child's life!"

"The lives of a great many children," said Zuckerman, looking him straight in the eye. "We have, after all, something to consider besides the fate of those thousand people. We have to consider the fate of the Jewish community in the United States—which happens to be closer to five million people. Thank God we Jews in this country aren't in danger of the same persecution which is going on in Germany— and I assume we'd all like to keep it that way."

"Is that relevant, Ben?" said the judge. "If we help the passengers on the *Franz Joseph,* how could that possibly jeopardize our own—"

"You haven't thought this through carefully enough, Judge. What is it that protects the Jews in this country? It's the government—law and order—the democratic system. That's the only thing stands between us and another Hitler. And what is AJDA planning to do with this half-million? Let's not mince words about it—we're planning to bribe an official of the Cuban government for the purpose of influencing Cuban policy. What the hell do you think *that* would look

126

like if it ever came out? It would look as if the Jews of America—and this organization *does* represent the Jews of America, even though a lot of them aren't too crazy about us—were interfering in Latin-American affairs, maybe even undermining this country's relations with a friendly power. All for the sake of a bunch of foreign nationals."

"Persecuted people," Mr. Levinson put in, "with nobody else to help them."

"We see them as persecuted people, but everyone else will see them as Germans, foreigners. Haven't the Jews of America fought hard enough—with AJDA being a leader in the fight—to get people to recognize that we're Americans first and Jews after that? We'll be giving the anti-Semites a perfect chance to say that a Jew isn't capable of loyalty to his country if we turn over this half-million to Cuba."

There were a few seconds of silence after that. Then Sigmund Wolff began nodding. "Yes, that's absolutely true, Ben. We'll be playing into the hands of the anti-Semites."

"I don't agree with that for a minute," Judge Goodfreund said. "I think you're building something up way out of proportion, Ben. But in fairness, there *is* somebody here who knows about the workings of the government and diplomatic relations and so forth. Senator, you had twenty years in Washington—and you'll be starting on your next twenty right after the forty-two election, I'm confident of that—so is there anything to what Ben's worried about? Is the State Department liable to think we're interfering in foreign policy?"

"Well, now—that's not an easy question to answer." The senator frowned, his thick black eyebrows almost meeting above his nose. "On the one hand, plenty of organizations and private individuals are constantly engaging in various financial transactions, not all of them of a public nature, with representatives of foreign powers. To be honest about it, how do you think some of our biggest corporations managed to obtain their franchises abroad? So it might be said that there's nothing irregular about engaging, for humanitarian purposes, in the same kind of activity that others engage in for profit-making purposes. On the other hand, it might also be said that an organization like ours—which, as Ben Zuckerman quite justly reminded us, does have a certain quasi-representational character—is obligated to maintain a higher standard of behavior than if it operated on a strictly private level."

127

"In other words, Jews have to be better than other people or what will the *goyim* say?"

These words came from a corner of the room, where Willie Levy was sprawled in a leather chair. Willie Levy was William K. Levy the criminal lawyer, a man in his sixties, tall and burly and vaguely disreputable-looking even when he was washed and shaved and wearing his best business suit. Next to Ben Zuckerman, he was probably the richest man in the room. According to rumors, his money came not from his courtroom activities but from half a dozen enterprises that his clients, some of whom belonged to the highest branches of underworld society, had allowed him to invest in. He was also one of the few AJDA big shots who had grown up on the Lower East Side; his parents had brought him over from Lithuania when he was a young boy.

"You'd like to comment on the discussion, Willie?" the judge said. They were old friends and had tangled in court many times. "You don't agree with Ben Zuckerman's analysis of the problem?"

Morrie could understand the note of hope in the judge's voice. If he could get Willie Levy on his side, there was a chance that the half-million could be raised without the help of Ben Zuckerman or Sigmund Wolff or any of the other dissidents.

"Now I didn't say that, your Honor." Willie Levy gave one of his broad grins. "For all I know, there's a lot of merit to Ben's analysis. Or maybe there isn't. I'd like to do a little more listening." And he settled back contentedly in his chair.

"I'd like to explain how *I* feel about all this," said Mrs. Sylvia Fingerhood, the widow of the department store owner, who was one of the two ladies in the room. "I'd be more sympathetic to those refugees if they weren't all so arrogant. They think they're too good for us vulgar Americans. They absolutely refuse to recognize that they're not in their own country any more, on top of the heap. They think they can still walk all over people the way they used to do."

"But it must be so terrible for them here," said Mrs. Selma Slotnick, the widow of the kosher frankfurter king, and before him of Arnstein the toy manufacturer. "People who were brought up with money and servants and never had to work for a living—and all of a sudden they don't have anything or anybody. Being poor is much harder for

128

people who *had* money once than for people who were *born* poor and never knew anything else." Mrs. Slotnick, before her marriages, had worked behind the lingerie counter at Macy's.

"That's ridiculous," said Mrs. Fingerhood, whose personal acquaintance with poor people, Morrie suspected, was limited to her own servants. "It's obvious to me that it's *much* worse to be born poor and *never* have any of the advantages. I've got no patience with these spoiled women who used to be rich and are constantly whining that they can't adjust to poverty. If your refugees can't adjust, let them go back to Germany."

Mrs. Slotnick gave a gasp. "You don't mean that, Sylvia! You *can't* mean such a thing!"

"You heard me, Selma." But Mrs. Fingerhood's voice was wobbling, and it was easy to see that she had frightened herself a little.

For another hour the discussion went on. Ben Zuckerman moved rapidly from point to point, slapping each one down on the table hard but scarcely even bothering to defend it against attack. He was using a form of boardroom infighting that Al had explained to Morrie many times. "Toss out as many different arguments as you can, even if some of them contradict each other. That way you've got a chance of convincing a lot of different people. After all, we hear the arguments we want to hear, and the contradictory ones we ignore."

Most of Ben Zuckerman's arguments were variations on old familiar prejudices against refugees. But one of his arguments made Morrie squirm. "With all this fine-sounding idealism and sentimental rhetoric," Ben Zuckerman said, "we're losing all sense of business. How was the figure of half a million dollars arrived at? What sort of negotiations went on? As far as I can tell, the very first figure named was immediately agreed to—and that doesn't strike me as very smart tactics. Furthermore, after we turn over our money to this nameless Cuban politician, what guarantees do we have that we'll get value received? Maybe this is all a racket—some Cuban swindler will pocket our half-million, and the people on that ship will be sent back to Germany anyway. In short, I'm not impressed by the way this affair has been handled up to now, and I think we should postpone our final decision until somebody with proven business ability can go down to Havana and look into the situation."

Al's answer was that his assistant, Mr. Morris Feldman, had gone to Havana and personally conducted all the negotiations. And Al had complete faith in Mr. Feldman's judgment and experience. ("What judgment, what experience?" Morrie asked himself with a sinking heart.)

Then Reuben Levinson broke in angrily. "What is this, some kind of business deal where you calculate the ins and outs ahead of time? You want to save those people, you have to run some risks. In a mess like this there are no insurance policies."

"Excuse me, Mr. Levinson," said Ben Zuckerman, "but a certain amount of prudence—"

"Prudence!" Mr. Levinson threw his arms up. "*I'm* talking about people's lives, *you're* talking about prudence! I don't understand it! The mentality of some of you! Are you Jews, or are you traveling under false pretenses?"

His anger seemed to spread around the room like a flash fire, and suddenly everybody was talking at once. Mr. Levinson shouted at Ben Zuckerman, who growled back at him. Mrs. Fingerhood and Mrs. Slotnick resumed their disagreement over the arrogance of German refugees. Sigmund Wolff squeaked and lisped at anyone who would listen to him. Professor Schwartz and Bernie Kramer for some reason started up their earlier argument about Stalin's purge trials. And Senator Friedkin kept calling out, "Ladies, gentlemen, please come to order!" But he didn't seem to be addressing those words to anybody in particular. Meanwhile, Morrie noticed, Willie Levy was sitting back and watching the fracas with a grin on his face.

At last, as usually happens, everybody's energy burned itself out, and one by one people fell silent.

Then Dan spoke. His voice was as even and controlled as ever. Morrie wondered how many in the room noticed the veins standing out on his forehead, the tightness at the corners of his eyes. Only recently had Morrie himself begun to suspect that Dan's perpetually soft, judicious manner was maintained at the cost of tremendous inner strain. "Ladies and gentlemen," Dan said, "we've covered most of the pros and cons, I think. It's getting late. The time has come to take some positive action. We've got half a million dollars to raise. I'm going to ask each of you, one by one, if you're willing to take on the responsibility for any of this money."

"I pledge fifty thousand," said Mr. Levinson before the last word was out of Dan's mouth. "And believe me, if I could give more, I'd give it. I'm not acting coy, and I'm not playing games." He nodded, and his mouth snapped shut.

Dan turned to Mrs. Slotnick, who was sitting on Mr. Levinson's right. She blushed and fidgeted and then, almost apologetically, she pledged thirty-five thousand dollars.

Judge Goodfreund, on her right, pledged ten thousand in a deep, portentous voice which somehow raised his pledge to at least ten times its face value.

Senator Friedkin pledged five thousand dollars, though Dan and the judge immediately told him he didn't have to. It was no secret that the senator had used up most of his savings on his last campaign. "No, no, I really want to do this," he said, "I wouldn't feel right if I didn't. Don't worry, I'll make good political capital out of it in 1942."

A hundred thousand already. Not a bad start, Morrie thought. Except that all of Dan's big allies had been heard from. It was Willie Levy's turn now, and after him only the open opposition remained.

A long sigh came out of Willie Levy, and he hitched himself forward in his chair. "Seems to be up to me now, doesn't it?"

He grinned around at them all. "I've been listening with interest to all the arguments. Brilliant! Ingenious! But most of them don't mean a thing to me. Take *your* various points of view, Ben. They sound fine—only thing wrong with them is they don't happen to make sense. First of all, why shouldn't a Jew have as much right as anybody else to do a little finagling behind the government's back? Second of all, I'm not a bit worried about those crooks in Cuba taking our money and not delivering the goods. That's their business down there, bribery. If they get the reputation for double-crossing their customers, they'll go out of business. So I'm sorry to say, Ben, none of your arguments got much consideration from me while I was making up my mind what to do.

"On the other hand, Senator, that humanitarian line doesn't cut much ice with me, either. There's all kinds of humanity, you know. You're asking me to pay out my good money so a thousand Germans can come into this country,

131

when in my opinion we've already got all the Germans we need. I was ten years old, an immigrant kid with six younger brothers and sisters, when I met my first *allrightnik*—that's what we used to call those uptown Germans, you remember? Individually, of course, I've run into *some* nice ones. Including everybody in this room, that goes without saying. In fact, I'd go so far as to say that some of my best friends are Germans. Still, in the aggregate, I don't like them. Well, the reason I'm telling you all this is I want to be sure you understand and appreciate what I'm about to do."

He gave them all another grin, and then he said, "I'm pledging a hundred and fifty thousand dollars." And while people were still gaping at him, he turned directly to Ben Zuckerman, who was on his right. "So how about it, Ben? Is that rhetoric sentimental enough for you?"

Zuckerman's face didn't show a thing. It wasn't even any paler than usual. From looking at him and listening to his steady voice, no outsider would ever have guessed what everybody in the room must have known, that he was furious, that his insides were churning.

"That seems to be that, doesn't it?" he said. "You've heard my views, and apparently you've decided to reject them. All right. This is a democracy. If we start going against the will of the majority, no matter how ill-advised it may be, what we'll get is anarchy. And anarchy has never been any good for the Jews. All right—I'll pledge as much as I feel I can, in all conscience. Two hundred thousand dollars."

The look he flashed at Willie Levy was a mixture of anger and triumph.

It was Mrs. Fingerhood's turn next. She shook her head, muttered something about "arrogance," and said, "How much have we got already? Four hundred and fifty thousand? Well, it's absurd to leave it hanging. I'll pledge the last fifty thousand."

There was a long, low sigh all around the table.

"Thank you, ladies and gentlemen," Dan said. "I hope, due to the urgency of this matter, that all of you can give me your checks before noon tomorrow morning. We'd like to send Mr. Feldman back to Havana tomorrow afternoon prepared to deposit the money in our account down there—"

"Stop! Wait a minute!" Sigmund Wolff's voice rose up, high and shrill, and his lisp was more pronounced than usual. "What about *me*? You didn't ask for *my* pledge."

132

"It won't be necessary, Mr. Wolff," Dan said. "We've raised enough money already. And since you did express your opposition—"

"Never mind my opposition. What's my opposition got to do with it? I've got a right to make a pledge, too."

"But we don't need any more money. If you'd like to increase your *regular* contribution to AJDA—"

"I'm not talking about my regular contribution. I don't mind saying I think it's disgraceful when somebody who's been a member in good standing for fifteen years, and who's always been more than generous in his support, and who's served on the board and donated his time and effort without a cent of pay—"

"I tell you what, Siggie," said Willie Levy, "I'll do you a favor. I'll let you take over fifty thousand dollars of my pledge. That is, if it's okay with Dan."

"*We* certainly have no objection," Dan said.

"Well, there it is, Siggie. Fifty thousand, take it or leave it. Going, going—"

"All right, I accept your offer. But I must repeat, this misunderstanding should never have occurred—"

While Sigmund Wolff went on grumbling, Willie Levy settled back in his chair and folded his hands over his stomach. His grin was bigger than ever.

The meeting ended a few minutes later. Morrie and Al were the last people out of the room.

"So how did you enjoy the show?" Al said, as they walked down the corridor together.

"Kind of nerve-wracking," Morrie said. "It was touch and go for awhile."

"Touch and go!" Al laughed. "My God, the thing was a shoo-in from the beginning. Not even any opposition, to speak of. Easiest, most routine fund-raising session I've ever been to."

* * *

As soon as Morrie got to Havana, he notified Dr. Rabal that the money was in the bank. Dr. Rabal sent back a message that he had informed his "friend," the machinery was in motion, and all they could do now was wait. And suddenly, after the rush and fever of those four days in New York, life seemed to come to a standstill.

It wasn't easy for Morrie to get through the time. He was too jumpy to read anything except American newspapers, always three days old. He soon got tired of walking around the city. He wouldn't go out to nightclubs or theaters because while he was gone Dr. Rabal might try to get in touch with him. Twice Esther and Jerry Berkowitz had him for dinner in their little flat in one of the new housing developments. The food was good and the company was pleasant, but each time he did very little talking and left early.

Two or three times a day Al rang him up long distance to ask what was happening and to give advice. Once Dan himself got on the line—clear evidence of how much pressure the AJDA big shots, led by Ben Zuckerman, must be putting on him. Well, Morrie couldn't blame them. They had a sizable investment in all this. They couldn't have been any more worried about their money than he was.

Often he felt an overwhelming need to talk to Ruth. On two occasions, very late at night, he gave in to this need and called her up in New York. He wasn't able to discuss his business with her over the phone, but just the sound of her voice kept the spark of hope alive in him.

He spent most of his waking hours at the harbor. He stood by the railing of the dock and watched that long, sleek, white form floating motionless off in the distance. From noon till late afternoon, when the air was clear and the sun was brightest, he could see the ship so distinctly that he could almost count the portholes. At such times the black and red flag flying from its topmast was unmistakably a swastika and sent a chill through Morrie every time he saw it. Sometimes he could make out small figures on the deck. He wondered if they were watching him as intently as he was watching them.

There was always a crowd on the dock with him, standing by the railing and watching the ship just as he was doing. It was easy to tell, from the clothes and the faces, that most of this crowd wasn't Cuban. These were friends and relations of the refugees, he supposed. Many of them looked as if it wasn't long since they had been refugees themselves. In the middle of the afternoon, when the crowd was thick, Morrie would give his place at the railing to one of them. They needed to be there much more than he did.

His first day at the dock he had been puzzled by the large number of small boats, rowboats mostly, that kept moving from the landings, heading out towards the *Franz Joseph*, then bobbing up and down by its side. But soon Morrie realized what was happening. People were hiring these small boats to take them close to the ship so that they could make contact with their loved ones on board. What kind of contact could it be? No real conversation was possible; they could hope only to shout or wave, to see and be seen.

During his second afternoon at the dock—toward five, when most of the crowd had drifted away—Morrie was approached by a young man in his twenties. He wore a gray suit, old and cheap and too heavy for the heat. His face was beaded with sweat. He spoke in a thick German accent, often hesitating because he wasn't sure of the right word.

"Excuse me, I don't wish to disturb. On the ship out there is someone you meet?"

"Well, in a way."

"Ah, good!" The young man smiled. "There is someone that I also meet. My wife, she comes from Germany in this ship. And I have been hoping—I have talked to many who come here, but nobody can help—"

"If you'd tell me what the problem is—"

The young man took a deep breath. "You see the little boats, the people who go to the ship in these little boats? I wish to rent one so that I may see my wife. But you see, there are not many, and they are wanted by many people, and so it is very expensive. Twenty American dollars for one hour only. I have come here with not much money—I hope for someone who also wishes a boat and will share with me the cost. I have talked to many people—some share already, and some have not the money to pay even half—and one was so rich that he had no need to share. But it is most important that I see my wife. She is—she is—how do you say, when a baby is to come?"

"Your wife is pregnant?"

"Yes—for seven months. Since before I leave Germany. And so, you see, if I can know that she is well—"

"But if you get a boat," Morrie said, "how can you be sure your wife will be on deck when you go out there looking for her?"

"Messages can be sent. There is a radio operator here on the dock, he speaks every day to the ship. This is how everyone does it. It's necessary, of course, to give him money."

"It turns out to be quite expensive, doesn't it?"

The young man's lips trembled slightly. "This is too expensive for you? Yes, I understand. Money is difficult for all of us. It is perhaps foolish of me—childish—to spend it in this way."

"I don't think it's childish. Look, let me arrange for a boat. How about tomorrow morning at ten o'clock? And I'll get the message to your wife, too."

"Thank you. You are most— Thank you so much. My name is Martin Tannenbaum. My wife is Betsy—Elizabeth Tannenbaum. We will be always grateful." He reached into his pocket. "I will give you now my share of the money."

"Never mind that. I think I can handle this so it won't cost you anything."

"I am able to pay my share. I do not require charity—"

"Believe me, whatever it costs, you'll pay half. But I know some people, I may be able to work something out."

Because Martin Tannenbaum still looked dubious, it was on the tip of Morrie's tongue to explain who he was and what he was doing in Havana. But some instinct kept him from speaking. If he let one person know who he was, pretty soon everyone would know, and friends and relations of the passengers would never stop besieging him for favors, information, reassurances. His caution made him feel a little guilty—he was here to help these people, and already he was deceiving them, treating them like enemies. But he didn't see what else he could do.

So all he said was, "Trust me, will you?" and then he invited Martin Tannenbaum to have a beer with him at the café across from the dock.

This café turned out to be full of people Martin Tannenbaum knew, people like himself who had come to meet the *Franz Joseph*. Soon there were half a dozen men at the table with Morrie; they ranged in age from a sixteen-year-old boy to an old man who might have been in his eighties. They all talked with great animation, mostly in German, sometimes slipping into English in deference to Morrie. As far as he could tell, they had only one subject—the passengers on the *Franz Joseph*: who they were, how they had managed to get out of Germany, what prospects they had in America. In all their talk, Morrie noticed, nobody expressed the smallest doubt that the passengers would eventually be allowed to land; they all seemed to take it for granted that everything would turn out all right. Why was it then that a feeling of pessimism, of resigned hopelessness, hung so heavily over this group? Soon it was more than Morrie could bear. He excused himself and left the café.

Back in his hotel he called Senor Gruber, the little old man who represented the Hamburg Line in Havana. First he arranged to have a dinghy at his disposal; it would meet him at the pier at ten o'clock in the morning. Then he asked for a permit which would allow him to use the ship-to-shore radio in the harbor master's shack whenever he needed to. Though he had no definite news to give, he felt that the time had come to talk to Aaron Peyser, AJDA's contact aboard the ship. The passengers, he thought, would appreciate hearing a friendly voice from the outside world, even if that voice had nothing particular to say.

Gruber said he could fix this up easily, and so at eight o'clock that night Morrie and Esther were in the harbor master's shack talking to the radio operator on the *Franz Joseph.* The conversation was painfully slow because Esther had to translate everything from English to German and back again. Then they were put through to an officer named Muller—a cold voice, even through this dehumanizing machine that made *every* voice sound cold. Then Muller left to take up the matter with the captain and there was a long wait, and at last the radio operator's voice was heard again. The captain, he said, had given orders that Mr. Feldman was to be allowed to call the ship whenever he pleased—and Mr. Aaron Peyser was standing by to speak to him right now.

Another voice was heard. Morrie knew, from the information given to AJDA by old Gustav Selig in New York, that Aaron Peyser was in his forties; but through the crackling of the radio his voice sounded neither young nor old. It spoke English carefully and hesitatingly. "This is Aaron Peyser here."

"This is Morris Feldman, Mr. Peyser. I sent you a radiogram—about our organization, the American Jewish Defense Agency. Your sponsor, Mr. Selig, is a member."

"Yes, I received your radiogram."

"Do you know anything about our organization, Mr. Peyser?"

"I know you wish to help us."

"Arrangements *are* being made. I can't give you the details, but as I said in my radiogram, there's a chance you'll be allowed to land in Havana after all."

"Excuse me, Mr. Feldman—do you mean a *real* chance? Or are you saying this only that we should not feel badly?"

"It's a real chance. We're all very optimistic about it."

"Thank you. I must be sure of this because here on this ship there is much—much—" He hesitated, then he said a German word.

"Anxiety," said Esther. "Fearful anxiety would be even more accurate."

Aaron Peyser's voice came again. "If this continues much longer, you understand, I cannot say what will happen. What people will do. You heard of the young man, Albert Liebling?"

"The chances *are* good," Morrie said. "Tell people that. Tell them to be patient—we'll know for sure any day now."

There was a long silence. Morrie wondered if they had been cut off. Then the voice came, hollow, disembodied. "I will tell them. I will believe you."

The conversation went on a while longer, and then Morrie said, "We'll speak again tomorrow—and in a day or two we'll be meeting face to face."

And we will, I'm sure we will, Morrie kept telling himself all the way back to his hotel.

* * *

Three days later a call came from Dr. Rabal's house. A servant's voice informed Morrie that Dr. Rabal would like to see him at his hotel in one hour and that he hoped Esther Berkowitz would be present at the meeting.

The news was bad: Morrie knew it right away. If it had been good, Dr. Rabal would have talked to him himself, would have invited Esther and him out to his house to celebrate.

An hour later Dr. Rabal was sitting in an armchair in Morrie's hotel room. He was quietly but elegantly dressed, perfectly at ease, suggesting somehow that he was the host and they were his guests. But his face was grayer than before, and for the first time he looked to Morrie like a very old man. The words that came out of him were no surprise at all.

"The very worst has happened," he said. "The newspapers learned several days ago that efforts were being made to let these people into Cuba. Was this information intentionally leaked to them? We shall never know. It hardly matters. The harm has been done. The effect has been disastrous."

He shut his eyes for a moment, then went on quietly. "The editorials. The speeches on the radio. The comments everywhere. Letters and phone calls have been pouring in to officials of the government. Many of these men are friends of mine, and so of course they have told me about the letters and the phone calls. Everyone says the same thing—the Jews must not be permitted to enter, to take the food from the mouths of Cuban babies, to make trouble here as they have made trouble in Germany. That these are only a thousand people, that they will stay here no more than a year, that their own organizations will feed them and shelter them— none of this, it seems, makes any difference. That terrible persecution awaits them if they return to their homeland— this makes no difference, either."

"But the man you talked to last week—you said he was a key figure, you said his promise could be depended on."

"Yes, I said that. I believed it. But it appears that he is like all the others. Nobody dares to help those people. Even those who would take the money you have raised. Their desire for money is strong, but their fear is stronger." Dr. Rabal broke off, and a shudder went through him. "It isn't the anti-Semitism that surprises me. A certain amount of anti-Semitism—one soon learns to live with that. But the intensity of it, the—the malignancy. A few days ago, Mr. Feldman, I would have sworn to you that such malignancy was not possible here. That I, in my small way, had helped to create a certain atmosphere—"

He shuddered again. He rose slowly to his feet. Polite and formal as ever, he shook their hands and left the room.

"What else did he expect?" Esther said in a low voice. "Has he grown so spoiled that he's forgotten what it means to be a Jew?"

An hour later Morrie was in the harbor master's shack. He had to break the news to Aaron Peyser—he couldn't let it come from any other source. In his whole life he had never had to do anything more painful. Somehow he cared very deeply about the feelings, the good opinion of this man whose face he had never seen, whose life and character were completely unknown to him.

He came out with it as quickly as he could, and then he made his voice cheerful. "I've talked to my office in New

York," he said. "AJDA is in touch with Washington already, we're requesting the Bureau of Immigration to accept your American entry permits a few months ahead of schedule. My boss is confident of an affirmative response, he thinks it's merely a formality. So you see, this may turn out to be a blessing in disguise. You'll get into the United States that much sooner—" Even as he said these words, Morrie felt ashamed of himself for sounding so stupid, so shallow.

"I will explain this to the others," Aaron Peyser said.

Morrie pushed on. "The only problem is it'll take a few days to make these arrangements, and what we're a little worried about is— Well, your ship hasn't been ordered straight back to Germany, has it?"

There was a long pause, then Aaron Peyser's voice came. "I don't know. This is possible. I will try to find out."

"If you can possibly persuade the captain to hold off awhile, to sail up the east coast and put into New York Harbor until we get the final word from Washington. If you're right there on the spot, I can keep in touch with you by radio, and as soon as I know anything—"

"I will submit this request to the captain," Aaron Peyser said. "When are we to leave Havana?"

"The harbor master just got his orders; he hasn't even relayed them to your captain yet. Your deadline is tomorrow morning at eight."

"Tomorrow morning? Yes—I must speak to the captain tonight. Perhaps we should say good-bye, Mr. Feldman."

"We'll talk again, Mr. Peyser. I'll be flying back to New York tomorrow. We'll talk to each other there."

"Yes, no doubt we will."

Morrie left the harbor master's shack and started across the deck. The sun was still bright but lower in the sky. Lengthening shadows from the palm trees cut across the path like sentries barring his way.

He saw Martin Tannenbaum leaning against the railing, looking out at the water.

Morrie hesitated, then went up to him. "You saw your wife again this morning?"

"Yes, the boat was there, as usual. But it troubles me that you never come with me. Is there nobody that you—"

"Don't let it trouble you," Morrie said. "What I wanted to tell you—your boat will be coming for you much earlier tomorrow. At seven in the morning."

"So early? Will Betsy be up?"

"She'll be up. I'm sorry about this, but it's the only possible time."

He didn't see why he should tell Martin Tannenbaum anything more. The bad news would be all over the place soon enough.

The next morning Morrie didn't leave his hotel. He didn't go down to the dock to watch the ship disappearing over the horizon. He didn't want to see the faces of all those people. Instead he lay in his bed wide awake, staring up at the ceiling.

What he saw in his mind's eye was Martin Tannenbaum standing in his little boat, shouting up at the girl on the deck, smiling at her, clasping his hands together in a gesture of hope and encouragement, mouthing the same words over and over. "We'll meet again—we'll meet again—we'll meet again—"

SIX

AS the *Franz Joseph* steamed out of Havana Harbor, the band sat on the quarterdeck and played a medley of Latin-American tunes. This was its regular routine on a cruise; for each arrival and departure native music was supposed to put the passengers in a properly adventurous mood. And so this morning Edelmann automatically assembled his men (and his one woman) for this purpose.

For half an hour the cheerful, syncopated strains rose through the silvery morning mist. Then Dietrich, the second officer, came running out on deck, waving his arms and shouting something. A moment later Edelmann gave a signal, and the music stopped suddenly—and Dietrich's voice could be heard, loud and pleading: "—bad taste and gratuitous cruelty! He says you ought to have better judgment!"

Most of the passengers didn't notice the blunder. Many didn't even come on deck when the ship left the harbor. They stayed in their cabins or in the public rooms; they talked in low voices, turned the pages of books, and carefully kept their eyes away from portholes and windows. Those who did gather on the deck crowded at the railing, peering out at the dock in the distance, trying to make out faces. Or else they engaged in frantic pantomimes at the little boats in the water far below. They waved, nodded, cupped their hands around their mouths to give out cries that were lost in the roaring of the ship's engines.

Like some wild game of charades at a drunken party, thought Emil Karlweis.

Nevertheless, he remained on deck until the bitter end. The last faint outline of the harbor was snuffed out by the mist, and most of the crowd had melted away, but Karlweis still stood at the railing—slightly apart from everyone else, as he had been since the beginning of the voyage. Even in the middle of a crowd, with people jostling him from all sides, he somehow managed to hold himself aloof. Yes, he felt a certain distaste for these people, but that wasn't the main thing. Mostly he felt what he had felt all his life—indifference. He had his own world, his own concerns. The impingements of this outside world were irrelevant.

Yet he did stand here and watch, and he couldn't quite understand why. During his first days aboard he had spent much more time alone in his cabin. Or when he was driven out by the rather irritating presence of his cabin mate, a strange man with one arm missing, he had made a point of stationing himself, on deck or in the lounge, in a chair as far as possible from other people. From time to time, of course, attentions were forced on him. Somebody gushed at him over "that beautiful concert" he had given somewhere or other. Several times he was asked for his autograph. (Such was the power of human inanity to assert itself even on the brink of disaster.) This was only to be expected. He dealt with these nuisances as politely and icily as was his custom, and in the last week or so they had pretty much ceased. His fellow passengers, it seemed, had grown accustomed to having him among them—just as people who live within sight of some spectacular natural phenomenon, such as a mountain or a waterfall, will eventually stop gaping at it and go about their business as if it didn't exist.

And yet instead of welcoming this respite from their unwelcome attentions, Karlweis had to admit that he was being somewhat less distant with the people around him. He was moving among them more frequently, observing their activities, listening to—though not, of course, joining—their conversations. His motives presented a perplexing problem to him. For the next few days, as the ship sailed north to New York, he found himself considering that problem. For some reason it seemed important to him that he should unravel the secret of his own behavior before the ship dropped anchor again.

On the last night he slept very little, and he got out of bed at six o'clock—his one-armed cabin mate still breathing heavily in the lower bunk—to go up on deck. It was a foggy morning, no buildings or stretches of shoreline were yet in sight. He began to take his daily constitutional, five times around the deck at a steady but not unduly hurried pace. In his work it was essential to keep oneself in good physical condition—especially now during this period of enforced idleness.

While he walked, he summed up in his mind the conclusions he had come to about himself. He understood now why he had recently grown less indifferent to his fellow passengers. It was, of course, his famous vanity again. While the crowd was pressing him with its vulgar curiosity, he had snubbed it; now that it was leaving him alone, he felt neglected. The truth seemed to be that he craved the admiration he professed to scorn.

"Part magnificent artist, part circus horse"—that was what Lichtheim, the critic for the Berlin *Zeitung,* had written about him once. How furious this description had made him! He had cut Lichtheim dead at the party after the War Veterans Concert in 1930, and even two years later he had referred to Lichtheim in a magazine interview as "one of those parasites of the arts who attempts to compensate, with sarcasm and personal abuse, for what he lacks in taste and knowledge." No, he had never been the type of man who can easily forgive a slur.

Yet all the time he had known in his heart that Lichtheim wasn't far off the mark. His "personal abuse" was no worse than what Bella had said many times, in her gentle, amused, slightly mischievous way. "Emil, darling, the Bruckner sounded beautiful tonight, but why did you have to do that Russian dance all through the finale?" "I was worried about you during the slow movement, dear, you seemed to be in such terrible pain." From Bella, of course, he had always been able to take things that he would have tolerated from no other human being.

With a frown he broke his stride around the deck. He wondered if his attacks could have been responsible for Lichtheim's sudden disappearance from the music page of the *Zeitung.* This was most unlikely, he decided. There were so many other, more common reasons for the disappearance of public figures nowadays. Actors, writers, artists, people whose names were household words would suddenly drop out of the world; overnight it would be as if nobody had ever heard of them. Surely it wasn't possible that they were *all* Jews or that they all had some Jewish grandmother tucked away somewhere in their past. He remembered how his mother used to point to the most unlikely names in the newspapers—statesmen, generals, members of the nobility, even an archbishop once—and announce, "He's a Jew, you know!" And Karlweis, amused but always on the edge of exasperation—his normal state in the family circle, as a young man—used to accuse her of believing that everybody in the whole world was Jewish. But now, with this mysterious oblivion blotting out so many well-known people, it began to look as if his mother had been right all along.

He wondered if such a fate—official, government-sponsored nonexistence—was in store for himself. In a few months or weeks people might well be saying to one another, "Karlweis, Karlweis? Sorry, I don't remember anybody of that name. He used to conduct an orchestra, you say? You're sure you didn't imagine him?"

Perhaps this fate had overtaken him already. Perhaps it had happened a year ago, when he was finally forced to give up his post at the Munich opera (though it had been a year before that since he had been allowed to conduct a performance). Perhaps he was blotted out already and his vanity prevented him from realizing it.

His thoughts were interrupted by a dreadful sight. Edelmann, the pompous ramrod who conducted—or, to be accurate, drilled—the ship's orchestra, was bearing down on him, and there was a familiar gleam in his eye. Since the first day aboard, Edelmann had been buttonholing him, trying to inveigle him into musical discussions.

"Maestro, did you hear our arrangement of the *Meistersinger* overture yesterday afternoon? It's a great presumption, of course, for our humble group to tackle such noble music. I wonder if you'd tell me, honestly and frankly—"

"I didn't hear the concert yesterday, Mr. Edelmann."

"Then let me explain what I was trying to do—"

"I haven't had my breakfast yet. I never think about music until I've had my morning coffee."

"But how can that be? I should have thought that music was in your head at all times of the day or night. Constantly with you, like the air you breathe."

"You should have been wrong. The truth is, I think of music as infrequently as possible, and only when I am obliged to by the necessities of earning my living. My dislike of music is equalled only by my dislike of musicians. If you'll excuse me, sir."

He moved past Edelmann and continued down the deck until he reached the first door into the lounge. His constitutional wasn't over yet, but it seemed essential to remove himself from the sight of that poisonous bore.

The lounge was still empty. It had the desolate air of a concert hall before the musicians or the audience have arrived. Karlweis sat down and tried to calm himself. He was still annoyed at the unspeakable Edelmann, and this led him to think about persecution. All his life he had been dogged by persecution of one sort or another; Hitler was only the most dramatic example. There were always small-minded, empty-headed, mean-spirited people who delighted in making life miserable for the artist, for any man who stood above the faceless mob. Sometimes they snapped at you and spat on you, eaten up with envy, furious because your very existence was a galling reminder to them of their own mediocrity. Sometimes they tried to suck your blood and pick your brains in the name of admiration, appreciation, even worship. It was hard to say which persecutor was more tormenting, the spitter or the worshiper. Extraordinary, in fact, how quickly one could often be transformed into the other.

Yes, Edelmann was merely the latest in a long line of persecutors dedicated to the task of distracting Karlweis, destroying his peace of mind, pulling him away from his music. Before Edelmann there had been a whole parade of critics, managers, talentless orchestra players, stupid rich ladies on boards and committees. Earlier still there had been his teachers at the academy and his fellow students, not to mention landladies nagging him for their rent and tradesmen making threats. And before all of this—right from the very beginning—there had been Mama and Papa and their whole gang of accomplices, of aunts and uncles, brothers and sisters, rabbis—

But he was letting himself slip too far into the past. Fits of memory—you could hardly call it nostalgia—had a way of coming over him when he allowed his mind to drift. He had to guard himself against this habit, because the past—that earliest part of it, anyway—was distasteful to him at best. And at worst— The point was that his life had been lived by two people, two separate and distinct individuals, and the dividing line between them was sharp and clear. It had come somewhere in his sixteenth year. Suddenly, with all the force and finality of a descending ax, the truth had struck him. You are a man now, it announced to him, and the time has come to put away childish nonsense and take your life

146

seriously. Music is your life. Nothing means more to you than your career in music. You must fight for this career, and you must fight to win, regardless of the consequences. Nobody must be allowed to stand in your way.

And so the ax fell, the existence of the old Emil Karlweis was terminated, and the new Emil Karlweis, the present Emil Karlweis, took his place.

A gong sounded and gave him the excuse he needed to leave the lounge. Breakfast was being served. The only tolerable meal of the day—largely because he didn't have to sit at his assigned table, badgered by that dreadful Fischel woman whose screech of a voice reminded him of the flutes and piccolos in some atonal "masterpiece." And almost as distressing, at his assigned table was the empty seat which had been occupied by that sad young idiot who had tried to escape from the ship in Havana. For the first week of the voyage he had bored them all with endless tales of his fiancée in America. How heartily they had all wished that he would shut up! But now his silence—like the silences in certain symphonies of Beethoven or operas of Verdi—was louder and more compelling than his noise had ever been.

The dining room, as he entered it now, was much less crowded than usual. A general loss of appetite had afflicted his fellow passengers since the departure from Havana. During their stay in Havana Harbor it had been clear that the departure must inevitably take place—but few had been able to accept this fact, to rid themselves of impossible hopes. To most of these people the truth could be brought home only by some concrete physical event, something they could actually see—in this case, the disappearance of the harbor over the horizon. Today the ship would get to New York and sit there for several days more—and Karlweis felt sure that all the impossible hopes would be revived. Eagerly people would grasp at the words which Aaron Peyser had spoken in the dining room the other night—"a blessing in disguise," "the United States Immigration Bureau may very well permit us—" Wishful thinking, nothing more. But Karlweis had found out long ago that facing facts was beyond the capacity of most of his fellow men.

And what of me? he asked himself, as he slipped into a seat at an empty table near the door. Am *I* so free of self-deception? Have *I* got no delusions which I cling to with contemptible blindness?

The shoe fit quite snugly indeed. He knew what his delusion was. He recognized the insane chimera to which he had dedicated his life, for which he had stayed in Germany years after the truth was obvious, years longer than any of his colleagues and friends who were equally threatened. So long, in fact, that he had come perilously close to letting even this ship, this final lifeline, slip out of his grasp. If his old friend Kristella the opera composer, the most talented of all his protégés, hadn't insisted that he go down to the Hamburg Line office, hadn't practically dragged him there and done all the talking himself—

Oh, yes, he had no trouble identifying his grotesque and ridiculous delusion. Its name was Culture—sacred, hallowed, eternal German Culture. The name itself called up a roll of august figures from the past—Bach and Handel, Beethoven, Brahms and Wagner, Goethe and Schiller and Lessing—*his* Germany, the most civilized nation in Western history. Yes, German Culture had always been the air he breathed—to use that moron Edelmann's phrase—and a man could hardly lose faith in the very air. In this pure clean air, above politics, factionalism, prejudice, violence, it was impossible to believe that anything terrible could *really* happen. For instance, in the whole course of his life—once his talent was recognized, once his mastery of the baton had imposed itself—he had never been held back because he was born a Jew. In *his* world there were no Jews and Christians, only good artists and bad ones.

And this world was the *real* Germany, he had always felt sure of that. There might be upheavals, aberrations, outbursts of madness, but surely all of these could only be temporary; in the final analysis Germany was her culture, her artists and musicians, her thinkers and her great humanists. The spirit of Germany was expressed by the people who came to his concerts, wept at the tragic lament of Beethoven's Ninth, stood and cheered as the last chord crashed out. The pure, spontaneous joy which brought these people to their feet was *bound* to sweep away the Hitlers and their like.

"Now there," Karlweis told himself, as he took a sip of coffee, "you have a delusion that *is* a delusion! There you have a fantasy that makes the ones around you look like sober collections of statistics!"

He was finishing his breakfast when Max Einhorn entered the dining room with his son and daughter. Max saw him, smiled, and came up to him, but the young people didn't come, too. They didn't approve of him, Karlweis knew. Justifiably, perhaps. Max's little girl was one of the people he had firmly snubbed on the first day of the voyage when she tried to tell him how much she admired him. He wouldn't have done it, he supposed, if he had been friendly with her father then.

"A game of chess later this morning?" Max said.

"Why not?"

"Will ten o'clock be too late? I'm holding a service this morning."

"I'll be waiting for you after your service."

"You might even *come* to the service, Emil. It wouldn't hurt you a bit."

"I'll sacrifice myself and stay away."

There must have been some sharpness in his voice, because Max looked concerned. "I was only teasing you. I certainly wouldn't try to—"

"Excuse me, Max," Karlweis said, with a smile. "I didn't realize you were making a joke. Not being a rabbi, I don't consider Judaism a laughing matter."

As he left the dining room a few minutes later, he marveled at the whimsical fate which had brought him and Max Einhorn together. Their first encounter had been an accident. On the second morning out Karlweis had taken a seat in the lounge and had found a chess set on the table next to him. Idly he had started playing with the pieces, reconstructing the trap he had fallen into a year ago, the last time he played chess with Gerhardi the cellist—safe in London now, thank God. For a year he hadn't given a thought to that chess game, and suddenly here it was again, the position of every piece indelibly marked in his memory, just as the score of a symphony he hadn't conducted in years would spring full-blown into his mind the moment he looked at the title page— or sometimes even when he heard somebody whistling one of the melodies on the street.

And then Max Einhorn had suddenly appeared at the other side of the table, saying, "I wonder if the king's knight shouldn't beat a retreat before it's too late." After that it was only natural that Max should suggest they have a game. True enough, Karlweis had determined to avoid any relationships with his fellow passengers—but after all, playing chess with a man could hardly be construed as a "relationship."

He had played with Max every day since then. Tough, enjoyable games that went on for hours because they were so evenly matched. And something like a relationship *had* been established. It was amazing, in fact, how well you could come to know a man merely by playing chess with him for a week or two. Karlweis was able to infer all of Max's virtues and faults from his resigned sigh when he was in trouble and his apologetic smile when he was giving trouble.

Was Max, he wondered, finding out as much about *him?*

There were times when Karlweis told himself that he ought to resent these chess games. Quite early it became clear that Max's interest was professional—could that be the right word? —as well as sporting. From time to time, between moves, Max would slip in bits of propaganda for his organization. He really seemed to think he could make a dent in Karlweis' infinite indifference to the whole question of religion. Furthermore, Karlweis wouldn't have been surprised to learn that Max's concern for his soul wasn't entirely altruistic. Perhaps Max was calculating what a feather in his cap it would be, what a splendid and useful introduction to the American rabbinical jungle, if he could claim the credit for leading the world-famous maestro back into the fold.

Well, so what? Even if Max's motives *were* impure, Karlweis felt no resentment. How could he condemn a man for attempting to advance his own interests? He could remember very well those days when he was out to get his appointment to the opera. He could remember the intriguing he had done, the stupid people he had flattered, the dull parties he had pretended to enjoy, the absurd opinions he had pretended to espouse. Looking back on all this, he felt not the slightest twinge of shame. No man should be ashamed of the things he does deliberately, with his eyes open, in order to achieve his authentic goals. It was necessary for Karlweis to conduct at the opera. It was necessary for himself, and it was necessary for the opera. He had taken the appropriate steps to get the appointment, and everybody involved had benefited.

Men should feel shame, he believed, only for confusion, vacillation, cross-purposes. Selfishness is a fault only when it is pursued so sloppily and halfheartedly that it might as well be self-sacrifice. This, of course, was precisely poor Max's trouble. His efforts at snaring Karlweis' soul were tentative, fumbling—and rather funny, if the truth were known. No sooner did he throw out a hint than he withdrew it, tumbling all over himself with blushes and apologies, as full of guilt as a respectable young man who makes improper advances to a young lady.

Nevertheless, Karlweis had come to look forward to their chess games together. Despite his incompetence as an intriguer, Max was a pleasant fellow. He was a gentleman, that rare phenomenon in this world of boors and clods. Rarer still, he was a genuine lover of music. His mother, it seemed, had played the piano for him when he was a boy, and she had passed on her fondness for Mozart and Schubert to him. He hummed his favorite melodies often—slightly off key, but joyously. And he never mouthed pretentious ignorant gobble-dygook about "diminished sevenths" and "daring modulations."

"Oh Maestro, Maestro!" Karlweis had turned a corner, and there was the horrid Fischel woman. "What do *you* think? Is there anything to this rumor that's going around?"

"I haven't heard any rumor—"

"That the United States has already decided not to take us in. That they've sent a mesage to the captain ordering us to turn around or they'll send out a Navy boat to escort us."

"Where do you find your rumors, Mrs. Fischel, in bad American films?"

"You're an optimist, Maestro. Well, you can afford to be, I guess. They can't turn *you* away, whatever happens to the rest of us. One of the most distinguished Jews alive today!"

What he felt like answering was, "Musician, madam. Distinguished musician. Jew is not a description. It tells nothing about what a man is. It's merely a label, and a rather inaccurate one." But he held his tongue, nodded coldly, and moved past her. Just as well he had kept silent. She wouldn't have understood. She would gleefully have spread the word that Karlweis was "ashamed of being Jewish." He could never have explained himself to her or any of the people on this ship—possibly not even to Max Einhorn.

He had married a Jew—even a comparatively devout one —and had lived with her happily for twenty-eight years. He had permitted his daughters to make their own choices in the matter—nor was it his fault that both of them had married gentiles, one in the United States and one in Brazil. His chief attitude toward the fact of being a Jew wasn't shame but supreme indifference. What troubled him about losing his post at the opera, leaving Germany, facing an uncertain future was not the hardship of it—for he had endured hardships before —but the fact that once again he was being labeled, pigeonholed. Once again his persecutors were trying to squeeze the individuality out of him.

A sudden yearning came over him. There was a music room on this ship, and in it was a phonograph and a collection of records. He yearned to hear some music, to go there now and shut the door and lean back in a comfortable chair. . . . He had kept away from music during this voyage. He had attended none of the concerts. He had tried to banish, though without much success, the scraps of melody which were always turning and twisting in his head. Music couldn't be listened to in a vacuum, cut off from what one was thinking, feeling, enduring. Every note that he heard on this ship would call up memories—faces, voices, people he had known and loved, who had loved him too, or he thought they had. Even worse, it would call up concerts he had conducted—and his fingers would start trembling and closing around an invisible baton. This mustn't be allowed to happen. It would be too painful. He wasn't afraid of pain, but useless pain ought to be avoided. It was better to listen to no music at all.

But now, this morning, the yearning was suddenly too much for him. He felt that he had to take the risk.

He went to the music room, which was blessedly empty. On the shelf he found Mozart's Jupiter Symphony—his own recording, the one he had made with the Berlin Philharmonic! Though nearly ten years old, it was still the best version that had ever been recorded.

As he took the first record out of the album, he noticed something. He had seen this once before, many months ago, in a large music store in Munich. Wherever his name appeared—on the album cover, on the label of each record —it had been carefully inked out or gummed over. Some zealous hand had expunged all evidence of his pernicious non-Aryan contribution to this performance.

He pushed the album away. He went out on deck for some fresh air. He wasn't alone anymore. A lot of people were at the railing, pointing at the wide expanse of white-hot sea and sky which was spread out endlessly in all directions. "When are we going to see the Statue of Liberty?" said a little girl, and her mother hushed her quickly.

What's wrong with me, Karlweis thought, why am I trembling? Something strange was happening to him today, he could no longer hide it from himself. He was losing that perfect calm, that steady control over his emotions which he had been able to maintain throughout this voyage, throughout these last years of madness, for that matter. He wondered if he was beginning to be afraid.

But that, of course, was impossible. It had never occurred to him for a moment that he wouldn't come out of all this safe and sound. "They can't turn *you* away," the Fischel woman had said, and he quite agreed with her. He was one of the three or four greatest conductors in the world today. This wasn't modesty, perhaps, but it was the truth. A man like him simply doesn't get turned away.

*   *   *

"When are we going to see the Statue of Liberty?"

The little girl, Carl Bender's stepdaughter, asked this question in a high, piping voice that carried all around the deck. Out of the mouths of babes, thought Monsky, come the questions that everybody else is scared to ask.

The Statue of Liberty should have been in sight a couple of hours ago. It was ten o'clock already, and the ship should have pulled into New York Harbor at eight. That's what Aaron Peyser had announced at dinner last night, and Aaron Peyser had the inside track to the captain. But instead, the ship had suddenly come to a stop here in the middle of nowhere, with nothing to look at except some shapes way off on the horizon—so far off that you couldn't tell if they were real islands or shadows on the water. The deck was full of people, some of them milling around and talking in voices that were either too loud or too soft, some of them fastened to the railing, staring out at the horizon as if they thought they could make skyscrapers appear there through sheer willpower. When that little girl's question came ringing out, Monsky could imagine the sick thud in the pit of everybody's stomach. Imagine it? He was feeling it himself.

Or maybe it was just fatigue that was upsetting his stomach. The last week or so Monsky had been having his troubles getting to sleep—which he blamed on Stieffel's snoring from the upper bunk. (Monsky had made a point of boarding the ship early so he could commandeer the bottom bunk.) When he finally *did* get to sleep, he had been having a lot of crazy dreams, mostly about Betsy Tannenbaum. No, not about Betsy actually, but about her baby, the one that wasn't even born yet. Sometimes, in these dreams, it was a girl and sometimes it was a boy, but always it was kicking its little feet and screaming its lungs out until Monsky took it up in his arms, and then right away it was gooing and gurgling with contentment.

Betsy came up to him through the crowd. She had gone down to her cabin after breakfast to fetch her knitting, and she was carrying it now in that little red knitting bag which he had become so familiar with during this trip.

"I thought I might as well make some progress," she said as she came up to him now. "Since we can't do anything but wait."

"Maybe you'd be more comfortable sitting down," Monsky said. He took her by the arm, and they started towards the lounge.

"Did we move at all?" she said. "While I was down in my cabin?"

"Not an inch. But it's nothing to worry about, believe me. These transportation monopolies always rush you and rush you so they can stop and make you twiddle your thumbs. The idea is to reduce the customers to nervous wrecks so nobody will have the strength to complain about the high fares."

"It's a shame you have to be so cynical, Mr. Monsky. Martin always says that it's unhappiness which makes people lose their faith in people."

He felt her hand on his arm. He heard the gentleness in her voice and saw it in the half-timid smile she was turning on him. He could feel himself blushing a little. He, Leon Monsky, who hadn't given a real blush since he was seven years old. At his age, with his experience of life, this little girl was making him feel like a—he didn't know what. He knew only that none of it made any sense. A girl who was young enough to be his daughter.

As they got to the door of the lounge, Stieffel was coming through, and with him, holding onto his arm like his oldest pal in the world, was Bruno Schwarzkopf. Naturally Schwarzkopf was doing the talking. He was telling some kind of funny story, judging from the chuckles coming out of him. A story about how he once made a financial killing or put some inferior in his place; what other kind of story did Schwarzkopf tell? And Stieffel was listening very politely, looking interested but not putting in many words. After all this time, sharing the same cabin with him, Monsky still couldn't figure Stieffel out. Why was it that he practically never opened his mouth, a man in his position who must have been used to talking and being listened to? And no matter how nice and polite he was, he always seemed to have something on his mind that was taking away half his attention.

"Good morning, Schwarzkopf," Monsky said. "Are you looking forward to getting to New York today? Is it true that a delegation of leading businessmen will be meeting you on the dock?"

Schwarzkopf laughed jovially, as if he had never heard a more hilarious remark in his life. When Stieffel was around, butter wouldn't melt in Schwarzkopf's mouth—you could get away with saying practically anything to him. Monsky had a pretty good idea what Schwarzkopf was up to. He was sucking around Stieffel because he figured that Stieffel was still an important big shot and could give him some kind of help in America.

Monsky gave Schwarzkopf a friendly nod and escorted Betsy into the lounge. It was crowded, as if every passenger on the ship who wasn't out on deck were in here. On a morning like this it would take a pretty cold-blooded character to sleep late. The only chairs Betsy and he could find were in the middle of a group of women including the gorgon Fischel, who definitely wasn't one of Monsky's favorites.

"There's no question about it," Fischel was saying as they sat down. "I'm on good terms with one of the stewardesses—she used to work for me as a chambermaid some years ago—and she tells me that the word came through early this morning. The reason why this ship has stopped moving is the New York authorities aren't going to let us into the harbor. Until the government decides if we can enter the country or not, we have to stay right here beyond the ten-mile limit."

"That sounds pretty farfetched to me," Monsky said. "Why *shouldn't* the authorities let us into the harbor?"

"I assure you, my information comes to me from a completely reliable source."

Monsky spread his hands. "If I had a hundred marks for every lie that was ever told by a completely reliable source, I'd be a richer man than Rothschild." He kept a big grin on his face, and all the time he was wishing that Fischel would shut her mouth. Her rumor was prabably true, but what was the point in sounding off about it at the top of her voice? All she could do was scare people. Already he could see that she was scaring Betsy—and a woman in such a delicate condition, you have to handle her with kid gloves.

Was that *his* job, to handle her with kid gloves? This question came into his mind occasionally and confused him a little, but always he pushed it out again. If not his job, then who else's? *Somebody* had to watch out for her while her husband wasn't around. Like a father or mother would do, for instance, if a girl was having a baby and her man went off to war.

For a moment there flashed into Monsky's mind the face of Betsy's husband. Back in Havana Harbor Monsky had caught a glimpse of that face two or three times. Each time Martin Tannenbaum was in his little rowboat way down by the side of the ship, and it was quite a distance; you couldn't actually see anybody's features too clearly. Besides which, Monsky had looked at that face only until he was sure Betsy saw it too, and then he had turned away and taken a stroll around the deck, figuring she was entitled to privacy when she talked to her husband. Some privacy, since she was out on deck with a hundred people all around! The two or three glimpses Monsky got of Martin Tannenbaum he hadn't been particularly impressed. A very ordinary-looking fellow. Average. Probably pretty dull. Why not? After all, was Betsy so out of the ordinary herself?

"But they'll let us into the harbor eventually, won't they?" Betsy was saying. "Even if we can't get off the ship—it'll be like Havana, won't it? People will be able to hire little boats—"

"Don't count on it," Fischel said. "New York is a modern, up-to-date city, they don't do things sloppily and inefficiently there, like those Latin countries. They won't allow a lot of dirty rowboats to clutter up the harbor, endangering lives."

Fischel still hadn't got over those rowboats. Nothing that had happened to her so far, not even the treachery of the Cuban government, seemed to have infuriated her as much as those rowboats. Disorder of any kind offended her, Monsky had noticed. She went into a rage if everything around her wasn't done strictly according to the rules.

"Sloppiness and inefficiency are international commodities,"

Monsky said. "New York has its share of it, too, I'll bet on that. An hour from now the rowboats will show up—and think how foolish you'll look."

Fischel produced a small smile. "I don't imagine *that's* very likely," she said.

"Why don't we ask Mr. Peyser why we've stopped here? Mr. Peyser always knows what's happening." This suggestion was made in a shaky voice by little Mrs. Moritz, Fischel's shadow.

"There's too much talk around here about Aaron Peyser," Fischel said. "Who is he, anyway? Why should we take *his* word for anything? Just because he's Bruno Schwarzkopf's son-in-law? I don't consider *that* much of a recommendation. My late husband used to tell me plenty about Bruno Schwarzkopf. 'On the day Schwarzkopf stops lying,' he used to say, 'the Messiah will come!'"

"I'm sure Mr. Peyser wouldn't lie to us," said Mrs. Moritz.

"And you're an expert on human nature, aren't you, Rosa dear? You've had such a wide experience of life."

Moritz was no match for Fischel's sarcasm. She turned pale, bit her lip, and retreated from the field.

Suddenly Fischel pointed across the room, wagging her finger. "I don't imagine *she's* losing much sleep over our problems!"

She was pointing at Carl Bender's wife, who was just passing through the lounge with her little girl. To Monsky Julia Bender looked as if she'd been losing a *lot* of sleep lately. There were dark circles under her eyes, and her cheeks were drawn.

When he remarked on this, Fischel gave one of her snorts. "Don't worry about *that* one, Mr. Monsky. You can always count on *her* to look after herself. They say you can't have your cake and eat it too, but *she'll* manage it, all right."

"I'm not sure I follow you, Mrs. Fischel." These words came from a lady who hadn't spoken till now, Mrs. Halevy. She was in her forties, traveling with her eighteen-year-old son, and of course she was a widow. This ship, Monsky had noticed, was positively loaded with widows.

"It's very simple," Fischel said. "Not all of us are lucky enough to be covered *both* ways, like the Bender woman is. If she gets to America, she'll have a very nice position as the wife of a successful psychiatrist. If she *doesn't* get to America —well, Hitler doesn't have anything against people of *her* persuasion, does he? Providing she sheds such inconvenient baggage as Jewish husbands and so forth. Which I can't see *that* one hesitating to do."

"You have no right to say that," said Mrs. Halevy. "You don't know anything about her.'"

Fischel drew herself up and glared, but Halevy was no pushover like Mrs. Moritz. Underneath her quiet manner, she gave the definite impression of having reserves of strength. She never played cards or joined in on the gossip; she spent much of her time reading books. She always wore a plain black dress, very little makeup, and no jewelry except a wedding band, though it was obvious to an experienced eye—and what other kind of eye did Monsky have?—that she could have been a highly attractive woman if only she had taken a little trouble with herself.

"And *you* know something about her, I suppose?" Fischel said. "You're old childhood friends, I suppose?"

"We met for the first time on this ship. Her cabin is across the corridor from mine."

"And that's it, that's the whole relationship? That's the basis of your profound understanding of her character?"

"You don't always have to know people for a long time in order to understand their character. Some people give themselves away the minute they open their mouth." Halevy's lips quivered in a tiny smile.

Fischel reddened and gulped. Her vexation did Monsky's heart good, but it didn't take her long to recover herself. "Nobody could accuse *you* of giving yourself away, could they, Mrs. Halevy? You're quite an enigma to most of us on this ship."

For a while Halevy just looked at Fischel. Then, as steadily as ever, she said, "The enigma isn't worth solving, I'm afraid. My life has been very uneventful."

"You're from Dresden, aren't you? It seems to me I saw that on the passenger list." Fischel's eyes glittered. "You didn't happen to know the Steuers in Dresden, did you? Ludwig Steuer—the elastic business—my late husband, who made ladies' shoes, had dealings with him. They went to America a few years ago, but they used to be acquainted with *all* the finest Jewish families in Dresden."

"I imagine we moved in different circles, my husband was an artist, a painter."

"Was he? I don't believe I ever heard of him. I used to

158

visit the Berlin galleries regularly, a few years ago. What school did he belong to?"

"A school that had greater appeal to his fellow artists than to buyers with money. Rich collectors, you know, are generally less interested in art than in showing off to their friends."

Fischel gave no sign that she had heard this remark. "How sad for you, dear. A husband who couldn't make a living from his work—how on earth did you get along?"

"I contributed to the family income," Halevy said quietly. "For a great many years I worked as a social secretary."

"A social secretary! That's very interesting. I never had one myself, but some of my friends did. Whose social secretary were you?"

"I had several different employers. Wealthy, ill-bred women who enjoyed the feeling of power. You don't have to sympathize with me, however. I've always known how to handle that type." Then Halevy rose to her feet, easy and unhurried. "I find it chilly in here. I think I'll go down to my cabin and get my sweater. You'll all excuse me, won't you?" And she began to walk across the lounge.

Monsky felt like applauding. And Fischel's face was a study. But pretty soon, when Halevy was out of sight, Fischel managed to give her loudest snort yet. "There's something *about* that woman. She's got something to hide, believe me. Don't worry, though—I'll find out what it is before we leave this ship."

"In my opinion," Monsky said, and he was all set to make a remark about people who don't have any respect for other people's privacy—but before he could get it out, Betsy stood up, clutching her bag of knitting. "It's so stuffy—I have to get some air——" And she turned without a look at any of them and started out of the room.

"Ladies, excuse me," Monsky said, standing up. "Do me a favor, Mrs. Fischel. Don't tell any interesting stories about me until I'm around to hear them."

Before she could answer him, he turned his back on her and was hurrying to catch up with Betsy.

"Are you sick? Can I get anything for you?"

She waited until they were out on deck again, then she took a tight hold on his arm. "She isn't right, is she, Mr. Monsky? We'll never get any closer to New York? There won't be any rowboats this time?"

In his whole life this was the first woman who had ever turned such a look on him. Women had looked at him with anger, with amusement, with exasperation—plenty of *that*— and even occasionally with desire (though the world was full of people who would never believe it). But until this moment no woman had ever looked at him as if she was absolutely, without question, *depending* on him. On *him*. On Monsky the deadbeat, the no-good, the bum.

This look gave him a glow, no getting around that. He wanted to get hold of various members of the Down With Leon Monsky Club (starting with certain uncles and aunts and brothers and moving on through the years to people like Bruno Schwarzkopf) and shout at them, "So you're wrong about me, the whole bunch of you! There *are* impartial observers who appreciate my value!"

"She's just a windbag, that Fischel," he said. "But to ease your mind—I've got a contact on this ship, somebody who's very close to the captain and knows exactly what's going on. I'll find my contact and ask him what he's heard."

"Would you, Mr. Monsky? Right away?"

"Absolutely. It's my pleasure."

He found himself patting her hand. A silly gesture—like the Understanding Father in some rotten sentimental play. Yet he kept on doing it, he actually *enjoyed* doing it.

He stopped doing it fast, gave her a smile, and left her.

His "contact" worked in the radio room. He was the assistant to the radio operator, and he was an eighteen-year-old kid. A Nazi, of course, but also a simpleton who believed whatever you told him. He believed, for instance, that Monsky had been an important film producer back in Germany, and he listened goggle-eyed to Monsky's intimate behind-the-scenes revelations about great stars. That was one advantage of being a passenger on this particular ship—you could tell people anything about yourself, and no matter how down-at-the-heels you looked, there was no reason why you couldn't be telling the truth.

So Monsky got to the upper deck, walked through a door marked "Keep Out," and started down the corridor to the radio room. He walked nonchalantly, with his chin up; it was his experience that you can go almost anywhere if you look as if you belong there. With this method he had crashed some tremendous parties in his younger days.

Luckily, his "contact" was alone in the radio room when

Monsky stepped in. Ten minutes' casual conversation confirmed, beyond a doubt, the accuracy of Fischel's information. The *Franz Joseph* would stay at anchor right here, surrounded by nothing but empty ocean, until further instructions came from New York. The authorities knew about that crazy Liebling who had tried to swim ashore in Havana, and they didn't intend to let anybody repeat Liebling's gesture in American waters.

Walking down the stairs again, Monsky was a little puzzled at his feelings. This news should have depressed him; his heart should be pounding with fear. It *was* pounding, he *was* depressed—but at the same time, though this didn't seem possible, he was positively cheerful. All the way up to the radio room he had been remembering how it had been in Havana, how Betsy had scanned the water for that little boat with her husband in it, how her face had lighted up as soon as she saw it. And he had remembered the heaviness in his heart. . . . But now, with this news from his "contact," he knew he wouldn't be feeling that heaviness today. Betsy's face wouldn't be lighting up. Not, at least, for anyone but him.

He saw her at a distance, waiting in the same place on deck where he had left her. She was staring out at the ocean, and the breeze was gently ruffling her hair. Somehow she looked terribly young—somehow this made him feel terribly old.

He composed his face before he went marching up to her. He kept any trace of a smile from showing on it, any hint of satisfaction from creeping into his voice as he told her the bad news. When she began to sob—quite softly, like a little girl—he took her hand and comforted her and made himself sound as if he couldn't feel any worse about this news than she did.

It was a peculiar sensation, drowning his feelings to make things easier for someone else. He wondered if this was the sort of thing fathers and mothers were always doing for their children. If so, no wonder they sometimes went berserk and murdered the little monsters.

As soon as he could get away from Betsy he found a secluded corner and lit up a cigar. He didn't have too many of them left and was rationing himself to one a day—after dinner, when his urge was usually strongest. But he was up against an emergency situation this morning. His nerves needed soothing right now.

"Monsky, what's come over you?" he asked himself, puffing away. "Stop acting like a schlemiel. Remember who you are."

* * *

On the sofa outside the dining room Rabbi Einhorn waited for his children. Though he was many minutes early and the dining room doors hadn't even been opened yet, he kept looking at his watch. He knew perfectly well why he was so nervous. Last night, for the second time, Peter had slipped out of the cabin in the middle of the night. The rabbi had awakened to find him gone and hadn't heard him come back until two o'clock in the morning.

The first time this happened, three or four nights ago, he had asked Peter about it. Peter had answered him with some story about the heat, the motion of the ship, insomnia—well, it was possible, of course, though the boy had always been an unusually sound sleeper. Under the strain of the present situation, one's sleeping habits *could* change. And so when Peter slipped back into the cabin this morning, the rabbi had pretended to be asleep. Why question the boy, since there was nothing whatever to worry about? He had even mentioned the matter to Naomi after breakfast, and she too was sure that there was nothing to worry about.

Still, he didn't stop worrying. Keeping it to himself, hiding his uneasiness from the boy—this just made it a great deal worse. He had always been open and honest with his children. All his life he had hated deception, equivocation. He must face up to this anxiety, then. He must have this out with Peter in a forthright manner—that's what Miriam would have advised. She had always known how easy it was for him to shut his eyes to unpleasant facts. Since his days at the seminary he had been aware of this temptation to wrap himself up in a warm, cozy blanket and pretend there was no world outside. Was this the price one had to pay for a happy childhood? Did everything afterward suffer by comparison?

"Father—"

He looked up and saw Peter standing over him. He hadn't seen the boy come into the room.

"Where were you a moment ago?" Peter said, sitting down next to him. "You certainly weren't here in this room."

The boy was smiling in that slightly mocking way he had —not unkindly, though, not without fondness. It was very odd, the rabbi thought, that the moments when he felt surest of Peter's affection were the moments when Peter was making fun of him.

"I was thinking about your mother," he said.

A troubled frown passed quickly over Peter's face. The rabbi had noticed this reaction in him before when Miriam was mentioned. At the time of her death Peter had been nearly nine years old. He had missed her terribly for a while—once, hardly three months afterwards, he had burst into a terrible tantrum, screaming out that his mother was "a bad person" because she had left him.

"Did you and Mother ever go on a cruise together?" Peter said.

"We talked about it once or twice. We thought of sailing through the Mediterranean to the holy land. But somehow there were always too many other things to do."

"It's too bad," Peter said. "I was thinking last night, looking at that full moon—Mother would have loved traveling on a ship like this. Well, not like *this*—but you know what I mean."

"What makes you think she would've loved it?"

"She was sort of romantic, wasn't she? Always up in the clouds. That's where Naomi and I get it from, I guess."

In contrast, the rabbi thought, to your plodding, unimaginative, earthbound old father, whose life revolves around synagogue budgets, *bar mitzvah* classes, and other such trivialities. Yes, he was most familiar with this attitude. Miriam had been so emotional, she had loved music and recited poetry out loud and cried so easily at plays and concerts, even in the middle of the services, or when somebody told her a sad story. Everyone had assumed that she was the flighty one, the giddy child who depended on his solid, reliable, dull approach to life. Nobody ever guessed how completely he had depended on *her*, how he used to talk over all his plans and problems with her, how he had counted on her to keep him from making a fool of himself. He remembered that terrible Saturday, his second year on the pulpit, when he gave the same sermon word for word that he had given the week before. After that he always showed his sermons to Miriam the day before.

He could almost hear her now, whispering into his ear, You've got something to ask the boy, Max. Ask it. Get it off your chest. Don't you see how pointless it is to go on dodging the issue?

"Peter," he said.

"What is it, Father?"

He looked into the boy's face. Those clear, earnest eyes— blue, like Miriam's eyes. Naomi's eyes were brown, like his own—it was Peter who in so many ways was the image of his mother. The way his mouth quivered at the corners before he smiled— But other things could come into his eyes, the rabbi knew, things that were never seen in Miriam's. Flashes of anger, a glitter of scorn.

"They're opening the doors of the dining room," said the rabbi. "I'm very hungry. I hope your sister won't be too late—"

He was talking to the air so that he wouldn't have to talk to the boy. Why couldn't he tell his own son what was on his mind? He *used* to be able to talk to his children—nothing easier. When they were very small, they would come to him in his study. "Papa, can I ask you something? Can I sit on your lap and ask you—" And then a small, soft bundle of child would be curled up in his arms, sobbing into his chest. Deep, racking sobs at first, but always growing gentler, more comfortable before too much time had passed. Because the sound of his voice had soothed them then. . . .

He knew why he couldn't talk to Peter now, couldn't ask him where he had been at two o'clock in the morning. He was afraid of being rebuffed. He was afraid that Peter would sneer at him, or snap at him angrily, or worst of all press his lips together and coldly turn away. That couldn't be allowed to hapepn now. He couldn't run the risk of losing his children's love.

Was it because he had lost everything else? Was he finally admitting the truth about himself, that his faith was dead, that he didn't believe anymore?

But it wasn't true. His faith was as strong as ever, he was as good a Jew as ever. How furious Miriam would be at him for this surrender to imaginary fears. . . .

Naomi arrived, and the three of them went into the dining room. Toward the end of the meal Aaron Peyser rose to his feet and announced that the ship wouldn't be entering New York Harbor until further notice. Once again He's abandoned us? the rabbi thought, and everything grew confused in his mind. What was he feeling, what did he believe? Could a man devote his whole life to an ideal and then discover, in his middle fifties, that the ideal may have been an illusion all along?

I have to be sure, he thought. I can't go on like this, not knowing what's happening inside me. There must be some way of testing myself. . . .

Lunch was over. With the rest of the crowd he started out of the dining room. Peter seemed restless—he muttered that he had someone to see and hurried ahead and out the door. The rabbi made no effort to detain him. Until he knew where he stood with himself, what could he say to his son?

* * *

David was worried. Papa's announcement at lunch had driven everything out of his mind except one question— would he and the other boys have to give up their plan? He had to talk to Peter.

After lunch Peter came up to him in the foyer. "The meeting place, in half an hour," Peter said quickly. "I'll tell the others." Then he slipped away through the crowd.

The meeting place was still the music room. Nearly every day, since the ship had got to Havana, the six of them had gathered there. They had done a lot of arguing—though David never argued, he was willing to do whatever Peter said—and finally they had managed to hammer out a plan they could all agree on.

It was a very simple plan. The first night in New York Harbor they would wait till everyone was asleep and the public rooms were dark and deserted, then they would sneak out on deck, lower one of the lifeboats, and row as fast as they could to the shore. Once on American soil they would submit to arrest and claim political asylum, not only for themselves but for all the other passengers. They knew that the American authorities would reject their claim at first, but the newspapers would write about them, and their pictures would be published—"Six helpless children," Peter said, "fighting against the Nazi machine to save their lives and the lives of their families!" Sympathy would be aroused for them; public opinion would force the authorities to let them stay, and everyone else from the ship, too. America was a democratic country; the voice of the people wasn't stifled there.

As this plan developed, David had grown more and more excited. In his whole life nothing had ever filled him with so much excitement. It was a great temptation to tell everybody around him—his parents, his brother, above all Peter's sister, Naomi. But Peter had made them all swear to keep their mouths shut and had given David a special warning against saying anything to Naomi—"You just can't tell how she might react to things." And so David had fought against the temptation and had overcome it. A man can't be any use to the cause unless he has willpower and can train himself to subdue his personal desires. This was what the Führer always said.

David didn't think about the Führer very much these days, though. That terrible dream—going into Mama's and Papa's bedroom with a gun in his hand—hadn't come to him for almost two weeks. The plan had pushed everything else out of his head.

And they hadn't just been *talking* about the plan, either, they had been *doing* things about it, too. In preparation for the big night each of them had had a special job. Schlossberg and Altdorf, because they were the strongest and heaviest, had spent the last few days striking up an acquaintance with one of the sailors who looked after the lifeboats. From him they had learned how to operate a boat, how to lower it smoothly and quickly into the water. Halevy and the small, pale boy called Paul, whose last name David hadn't caught, had been assigned to find out as much as possible about New York Harbor. By carefully pumping various members of the crew and a few passengers, too, they had learned how large the harbor was, how it was laid out, which piers were nearest, whether the tide was likely to be heavy.

The trickiest job had been left to David and Peter. The success of the plan required perfect timing; the lifeboat had to be lowered while the sailor on guard duty was patrolling the opposite side of the ship. So it was important to find out who *would* be on guard duty that night and to observe his habits—how long it took him to make a circuit of the deck, where and when he stopped to rest on the way. To gather this information Peter had penetrated the heart of enemy territory; three nights ago he had made his way, without being seen, to the bulletin board outside First Officer Muller's office and had discovered from the duty roster that a certain Strassvogel would be on guard from midnight to four A.M. on their first night in New York. This Strassvogel had been on guard last night, too, so very late Peter and David had slipped out of their cabins, gone up on deck, and delberately shown themselves to Strassvogel. They had told him they were suffering from insomnia and had accompanied him on his rounds for the next hour, timing him while they engaged him in friendly conversation. He was fat and gray-haired, older than most of the crew, and he wasn't a bit suspicious of them. In fact, he was glad to have the company and more than willing to talk about himself, his wife and children back in Hamburg, and the girl he always visited in the German section of New York.

It had really seemed as if their plan was going to work—until suddenly the ship stopped moving, and Papa made his announcement. . . .

Half an hour after lunch the six of them were in the music room. Everyone was weighed down with gloom. Halevy was pacing. Altdorf was slumped in a chair, frowning. Schlossberg just kept shaking his head. Finally Paul, the pale boy, said, "Well, that's the end of it. Ten miles in a lifeboat—in the middle of the night—"

"I'm pretty good at rowing," Schlossberg said. That was Schlossberg—willing, good-natured, and a little bit thick.

"We appreciate that, Ernst," Peter said. "Your rowing may come in handy when we've got our alternative plan."

David could see them all looking up at this, reacting to the confidence in Peter's voice. When *he* was confident, so was everybody else.

"There's no alternative," Paul said. "We tried, and we failed—that's all there is to it."

"Thanks a lot," Halevy said. "So now we can march into the concentration camp with the satisfaction of knowing we did our best." Halevy frightened David a little with his constant sarcasm, his anger. He was an artist, and a few years ago he had been all set to get a scholarship to the Academy of Design, but then it had been taken away from him. He made up for his disappointment by lashing out at the people around him.

"We don't have to march into any concentration camp," Paul said. "The time has come to do what we should've done from the start."

His face was pale, and his eyes were glowing. David had never seen him so excited about anything.

"What should we have done from the start?" Peter said.

"The Jews of Germany have to face the truth, don't you see? We can't fight the Nazi by ourselves—nobody else is going to help us—so we have to make a gesture, a great meaningful gesture to arouse the guilt feelings of the world. If the Jews of Germany had any real courage and weren't as—as decadent and corrupt as all other Germans, don't you see that we'd band together and commit mass suicide? Yes, I mean it. All together, the same day, the same minute—announcing ahead of time what we're going to do. The message would be clear, the whole world would understand it—'*We've* lost! *Our* lives are doomed! But at least our deaths can have meaning, as a warning and an accusation to humanity!'"

For a long time everybody stared at Paul.

Halevy broke the silence with one of his sharp laughs. "That's a beautiful operatic finale. The only trouble is, how are you going to get a couple of million people to agree about this *Götterdämmerung?*"

"We'll do this ourselves, just the six of us. It would be a beginning, don't you see? We're symbols—being on this ship and being so young. The symbolic suicide of six promising young men, with their lives before them—it could have a tremendous effect. Providing, of course, we leave behind a really effective Statement of Principles. Our deaths would touch off a wave of suicides all over Germany—I'm positive of that."

"Excuse me," Halevy said, "but I don't think I'll join you in this project. You don't really need me. Five suicides will be just as symbolic as six. I'll be happy to help you draw up the Statement of Principles, of course—"

"Your idea wouldn't work, Paul," Peter said without a trace of sarcasm, as if he were really giving it serious consideration. "There *have* been plenty of suicides in Germany since Hitler. Two or three thousand a year, my father has seen the figures—but somehow humanity doesn't seem to be going through any pangs of guilt."

"Suicide is a terrible thing," said Altdorf, who was the only Orthodox Jew among them, the only one who really believed in all the laws and the rituals. "It's a sin, no matter how desperate you are. The Torah tells us to choose life."

"A man is allowed to kill himself in order to save the lives of others," Paul said. "That's in the Torah, too."

"But if *all* the Jews in Germany killed themselves," Altdorf said, "whose lives would they be saving?"

"I don't want to do it," Schlossberg said. "I *like* being alive."

"I don't want to do it, either," David said. He could imagine what it would be like, the first flash of unbearable pain, and after that never knowing anything again— He was terribly frightened of dying. He couldn't think of anything more frightening.

"Since most of us don't much feel like killing ourselves," said Halevy, "suppose we get back to discussing how we're going to save ourselves."

"What do you think, Peter?" Altdorf said.

Peter didn't answer for a moment, and David could feel the anxiety in the air.

"What we have to do," he finally said, "is take as much as we can from the old plan and adapt it to the new conditions. The basic principle, after all, is still valid. If we can once row ashore and get ourselves arrested—"

"That's just what we *can't* do anymore," Paul said.

"Why not? Let's examine the problem analytically. What *are* the new conditions? First, we'll have to row ten miles rather than half a mile. Well, who says we can't do it? We're all young, and our health is good. Second, it'll be dark, and there's a risk of losing our way. All right, we wouldn't be the first seafarers in history who had to navigate in the dark. It's just a question of getting hold of a compass."

Altdorf broke in, already sounding much less gloomy than he had a few minutes ago. "The busboy at my dining-room table has a pocket compass, a present from his brother in the Navy. It's quite good, I think, much more than a toy."

"And how are you going to get it away from him?" Paul said. "Hit him on the head and steal it?"

"I think I could make a trade with him," Altdorf said. "I have a knife he admires, a pocketknife with three blades and a corkscrew."

Halevy gave his laugh. "You're still carrying things like that? Like a fifteen-year-old kid?"

Altdorf blushed a little. "We gave them to each of the boys in the League—this one was left over."

For a moment nobody said anything. The League—its full name was the League for the Cultural and Spiritual Renewal of German Jewish Youth—had been founded a few years ago by a group of rabbis. Its purpose was to train teen-age boys in skills that would be useful to them under the Nazi regime. Since they could no longer enter the business world, the professions, or the government service, they must learn to live much more simply, to support themselves through agriculture or manual trades like carpentry, to renew their roots in God's earth. In this manner they would retain that pride in themselves as Jews which persecution and deprivation could so easily destroy in them. To prepare for this future the boys took trips into the country, hikes through the woods, visits to farms, under the leadership of boys not much older than themselves, with not much more experience of "nature." But the League had never really caught on, and after struggling along for a year or two it had finally died out.

Last week Altdorf had mentioned that he was once a leader in the League, and Halevy had made a remark about "the Jewish Boy Scouts—those glorious crusaders who thought they could stop Hitler by planting tomatoes!" And Altdorf had replied, "No, it wasn't like that. We were trying to hold on to something. We couldn't think of any other way—yes, we were very foolish." He had lowered his head, and since then it had seemed safer to steer clear of the subject of the League.

Peter, as usual, smoothed over the moment of awkwardness. "It's a good thing Franz still *has* that pocketknife. Can you talk to your busboy at dinner tonight and make the trade with him?"

"I m sure he'll be agreeable. My knife is worth a lot more than his compass, and he strikes me as a very practical boy."

"Even if that compass works, by some miracle," Paul said, "it won't help us any. What good is it for us to simply get off the ship? We have to reach shore before anybody can catch up to us and bring us back. As soon as they know we're gone, they'll send a fast boat after us."

"Then the trick," Peter said, "is to keep them from knowing we're gone—at least until we've got a few hours' start on them."

"There's one thing you ought to understand, Peter," Altdorf said. "It's quite noisy lowering those lifeboats. Ernst and I watched them doing it during one of the drills."

"It's noisy if you lower the boat quickly—as we would have done for our original plan. But what if you lower it slowly and carefully and ease it into the water instead of letting it drop with a splash?"

"That would cut down *some* of the noise, I suppose. But it couldn't be done in absolute silence."

"As long as the noise doesn't carry more than a few yards along the deck—"

Paul broke in again. "Have you any idea how *long* it would take to lower one of those boats 'slowly and carefully'? Fifteen minutes? Half an hour? It doesn't matter, because the sailor who's on duty tonight—Strassvogel, isn't it?—is *bound* to come along while we're still at it. He'll raise the alarm—and there goes our plan."

Everybody looked at Peter, not very hopefully. Even David wasn't so sure.

Peter gave a sigh. "I guess we had to get to this eventually," he said. "What we're trying to do is important, isn't it? Well, I hope we're all old enough and tough enough to realize that important results sometimes require drastic methods. We don't *want* to use them—and with our original plan they wouldn't have been necessary—"

Halevy spoke up, his eyes shining. "But that plan won't work any more. So we can't afford to be squeamish, right? We'll wait in the shadows of the lifeboat until Strassvogel comes along on his patrol—"

Paul's face had gone white. "You aren't saying we have to *kill* him, are you?"

Halevy turned to him sharply. "If that's the only way—"

"If that were the only way," Peter put in quietly, "then God knows we'd have to do it. But the fact is, we have to make damned sure we *don't* kill him. We're trying to arouse the sympathy of the American public. We'll defeat our whole purpose if we appear before them as common murderers instead of helpless victims. So we'll knock this fellow out and take him in the lifeboat with us, give him a free ride to New York. He'll probably be grateful to us—he'll get to see his girlfriend that much sooner."

David could see the relief on all their faces. Yes, even on Halevy's. He was relieved himself—it would have been terrible if they had had to kill somebody. He wondered if Peter would have done it himself. Or if the six of them would have drawn lots. He wondered how he would have felt if *he* had been the one . . .

"We can't keep talking about this forever," Peter said. "It's time to make a decision, yes or no."

He turned to each of them in turn. Everybody said yes—Paul, too, though the word came out of him in a whisper. As the last "yes" was spoken, there welled up in David a feeling of warmth, of love, even, for these five friends of his. In his whole life he had never had such close friends, and he knew he never would again. They were joined together by the strongest of all bonds. Together they would risk their lives for a cause, for something that was more important than any of them.

Peter nodded and said, "Good." Then he arranged to meet them all on deck at two o'clock in the morning, and then he unlocked the door, and they all filed out of the room, nobody saying another word.

Later that afternoon David was reading in the lounge when Naomi sat down next to him.

"Am I bothering you?" she said. "I wanted to talk to you about something."

How could she bother him? He was always hoping she would want to talk to him, instead of the other way around, as it usually was—him wanting to talk to her and half the time feeling that she was being polite but wasn't really much interested.

"It's about Peter," she said. "Is everything all right with him?"

David wondered if he would *ever* get over his habit of blushing and fidgeting when he had a bad conscience. "He's all right, I guess."

"He doesn't talk to me anymore. He used to talk to me *all* the time—he used to tell me how he felt about things and get into arguments with me and tell me what childish ideas I have. Now he always seems to be going somewhere else—"

"I don't think it's anything special," David said. "He's worried about what's going to happen. The way everybody is."

"He gets up in the middle of the night. He walks around the ship."

"How do you know that?" David could feel himself trembling.

172

"My father told me. A few nights ago he woke up when Peter was coming back to the cabin. He asked him where he'd been."

"What did he say?"

"That he had insomnia. But Peter *never* gets insomnia—he can fall asleep anywhere, any time, if he's tired enough. I've seen him fall asleep in the middle of a family party, with everybody shouting at everybody else."

"Well, there you are." David felt more relaxed. "That proves he's worried about what's happening to us. Insomnia is a symptom of worry."

She looked into his face a moment, and he managed to meet her gaze. "If there *were* anything else, I know he'd tell you about it," she said. "And I know you'd tell *me*."

She smiled, and he could see that he had made her feel better. That should mean *something,* he told himself. She wouldn't have faith in him if she didn't care about him at *all.*

"Peter can say such crazy things sometimes," she said. "He's so romantic. I guess that sounds funny coming from *me*—but I *know* when I'm up in the clouds, and sometimes I think Peter doesn't. I'm afraid he'll stop talking someday and actually do something—"

"I don't think you have to worry. Peter's awfully smart. He wouldn't do anything foolish."

"Well, anyway, you wouldn't let him. You don't get carried away, David. I know I can always depend on you."

She leaned forward suddenly and kissed him on the cheek. Then she laughed, not at all embarrassed, and hurried out of the lounge.

For a long time afterward he felt that kiss on his cheek. The place seemed to sting a little, almost as if she had slapped him.

Slowly it came to him that she *had* slapped him, in a way. For underneath the pleasure and excitement that was making his heart beat so fast, he began to feel a kind of ache. How could she care about him, *really* care, as long as she thought he was some kind of dull nobody who never got carried away?

And it wasn't true, either; he *did* get carried away! He was just as romantic as she was, as Peter was. Hadn't he been taking part in the secret meetings all week? Wouldn't he be in that lifeboat, too? He almost felt like blurting out the

173

whole plan to her, just so she would know what kind of a person he really was.

He couldn't read his book anymore. He went out on deck and walked, but it didn't help to calm him down. I'll show her, I'll show her, he kept telling himself. She was weak— women are weak. He could *make* her stop looking down on him. He could *force* her to respect him, if he wanted to. He could do anything with her, anything *to* her, if he wanted to.

Before dinner he went down to the cabin to wash up. Joshua was there tying his necktie in front of the mirror, smirking at himself. David had never known anybody who spent so much time *looking* at himself, admiring himself.

"I went swimming today," Joshua said. "It was great. I don't see how you can spend all your time cooped up with your nose in a book."

That was Mama talking, Joshua was a great one for repeating what grown-ups said.

"Why don't you shut your mouth?" David said.

"Suppose I don't want to. Are you going to shut it for me?"

"You think I couldn't?"

David reached out. Joshua flinched and dodged back, but it wasn't necessary; David had already lowered his hand. If he once started hitting the kid— He had let himself go only once, a few years ago, and he still remembered the scare it had given him.

"Why should I waste my strength on you?" David said. "I'll be needing it for tonight."

"What's happening tonight?"

"Never mind what's happening. I just won't have *you* around my neck anymore—"

He broke off as he saw the look of curiosity growing on Joshua's face. What had he said, what had he done?

Quickly he went into the bathroom. He turned on the water in the sink and let it run over his hands. Weakling, weakling, he told himself. Tainted blood was in him. He ought to be punished as a traitor. He had heard stories about some of the things that were done to traitors in the SS. . . .

He wondered how much Joshua had guessed. He wondered what Joshua would do about it. He began to think of different ways he could shut his brother's mouth.

The water from the faucet kept running over his hands.

* * *

To the great distress of Chief Steward Fritz Hochschwender, the *Franz Joseph* had run out of films. Hochschwender always paid special attention to the quality of his films, for he believed that they were unequalled as builders of passenger morale during a cruise. He had often speculated on the reasons for this—his job requiring him to be something of a student of human nature—but he could never really understand the hypnotic effect they had. Personally he found them a waste of time. To sit for hours in a dark room watching the frivolous antics of trivial people—this was no occupation for a serious person. In his opinion even a man's amusements should provide him with food for thought and help him improve his mind. Hochschwender was an avid reader of magazine articles on political, economic, and medical subjects.

Nevertheless, his passengers wanted films, and so he had always made it a point to give them the newest and the best. He had been particularly insistent before *this* cruise, so that nobody should be able to accuse him of any discrimination whatever. Furthermore, he had ordered ten different films, instead of the usual seven, recognizing the remote possibility that technical delays in the port of Havana might extend this voyage a day or two.

But never for a moment had he foreseen the turn of events that actually took place. Already this cruise had lasted a week longer than scheduled. And the end of it was not yet in sight.

Even so, he had done what he could, within the capacity of a human being, to rectify the situation. As soon as he learned of the difficulties which had arisen in Havana, he had made it his business to obtain the name of a Cuban distributor of films, had put himself in communication with this firm, and had arranged for the rental of another ten titles—not precisely the newest or the best, but certainly better than nothing. And then at the last moment the Cuban auhorities had refused permission to bring those films aboard. The unfortunate escape attempt of the gentleman from Cabin A-26—so poorly planned and ill-timed, besides being a most clear-cut violation of the law—had caused the authorities to allow no deliveries of any kind to the ship except for food, water, fuel, and other essentials.

And so with the greatest reluctance Hochschwender was obliged on the twelfth night aboard to do what he had never yet done during his whole tenure as chief steward—he was obliged to repeat a film. This shook him badly, no doubt about it. He knew that no fair-minded person could possibly blame him, yet such was his conscientious nature that he persisted in blaming himself.

And now, this evening, a rumor was spreading that the passengers wouldn't be allowed to enter the United States at all, that the ship would proceed back to Hamburg in a day or two. Nobody aboard could have been more profoundly shocked than Hochschwender. Before this hellish voyage was over, he might have to repeat *all* of his films. Almighty God, he might end up repeating some of them *twice*.

*   *   *

Tonight Carl Bender departed from his usual custom and went to the film with his family.

It was an operetta of the schmaltzy, overdressed type that was particularly obnoxious to him. Its hero, the son of a wealthy industrialist, disguised himself as an impecunious piano student in order to woo a poor but proud young soprano who despised all men with money. At the end of the film the hero proved, by writing a love song which became an overnight success, that he could earn a living without help from his father, and so the girl, though she now knew the truth about him, agreed to marry him anyway.

For Bender the chief interest of this film lay in the comments about it which were made at the end of it by his step-daughter, Eva, and Aaron Peyser's boy Joshua, who had been sitting next to her.

"It wasn't true to life," Joshua Peyser said. "I don't think you *could* make a fortune overnight from just one silly song."

"Who *cares* if it's true to life?" Eva said. "It was a beautiful song, and I cried when she came to his room in the hospital at the end and sang it to him!"

"Oh, women will cry at *anything*," Joshua said.

"Well, what's *wrong* with that?" Eva said.

Julia took Eva down to the cabin now for the complicated ritual of bedtime, and Bender made his way up to the bar to wait for her. He reflected, as he climbed the stairs, that Joshua and Eva had been expressing, in their reactions to this film, several basic human conflicts. The male view of life versus the female view of life. Realism versus romanticism.

The pragmatic versus the ideal. Above all, their disagreement illustrated a certain psychological phenomenon with which Bender had become more and more preoccupied in the last few days. In times of danger the world turns out to be divided into two kinds of people—those who fight and those who hide. Bender had often observed this in his patients, but till now he had never had the opportunity to test the generalization under, so to speak, laboratory conditions.

For the last three days, since it became known that the *Franz Joseph* had to leave Havana, he had carefully watched and listened to his fellow passengers, trying to decide which category each individual belonged to. Sometimes it was difficult to be sure. Obvious fighters, who made loud, aggressive noises at the slightest provocation, turned out on close inspection to be hiders. Timid souls, apparently cowering inside their shells, suddenly revealed the toughest fighting instincts.

And what of himself? His urge to make these speculations, was it a form of fighting or a form of hiding? He might be standing up to the butchers in the only way he could, by asserting his intellectual superiority even as they prodded him into the slaughterhouse—or else he might be seeking to escape from reality by pretending that he was engaged in a "scientific experiment," that he was merely a "researcher" observing the guinea pigs from outside the cage.

He reached the bar. From the adjoining nightclub came the sound of the band prancing its way through an insipid ballad. He sat down at a table with three men whom he knew. They were all nursing glasses of beer; he ordered one, too. They began discussing their future in the United States. A strange discussion, he thought, for none of them, himself included, was asking the only question that was on all their minds—*did* they have a future in the United States?

"You're the lucky one, Doctor," said Gottlieb, the fat little lawyer from Munich. "There's a great demand for psychiatrists in America. I understand that neurosis is a way of life there. You can't hold up your head in good society unless you've had at least one nervous breakdown."

"I should think that mental illness must be increasing everywhere," said Rabbi Einhorn. "How could it be otherwise, considering the world we live in? Is there anybody who doesn't have moments when he wonders about his own sanity?"

The rabbi smiled as he said this, but it seemed to Bender

that only his mouth was smiling. In his eyes was nothing but fatigue.

"You're right about mental illness increasing," Bender said. "Before Hitler it was rising in Germany at a rate of nearly eight percent every year. I'm talking about *certifiable* mental illness, of course."

"And after Hitler it all went away?" This question was asked in a sharp voice by Ehrlich, the man with one arm. He used to own a furniture store in one of the small cities in the north, but he looked very little like a small-town merchant. With his large head, his heavy features, his shaggy mane of gray hair, he reminded Bender of an old lion. Contained rage seemed to flow from him, as it did from the lions who paced back and forth in their cages in the zoo.

"After Hitler," said Gottlieb, "they stopped certifying the lunatics and put them in the government instead."

Rabbi Einhorn laughed—a bit more eagerly, Bender thought, than Gottlieb's mild joke deserved.

"However, I withdraw my remark about the United States," Gottlieb went on. "I admit that people there are no crazier than anywhere else in the world. The fact remains, a psychiatrist fills a need nowadays. He can cross international boundaries, he's welcome wherever he goes—like a traveling priest in the Middle Ages. You can't say that about a lawyer."

"Lawyers run the world, don't they?" Bender said. "Most of my lawyer friends have told me so."

"I thought so once myself." Gottlieb's amiable smile was quite unruffled. "That's why I went into the profession. How wrong I turned out to be! Lawyers do quite nicely in their native soil, but they don't transplant very well. One country's law is another country's disorder. A misdemeanor in German is a hanging matter in English or French. This puts a man like me in a difficult position. What could be more superfluous in the United States today than an expert on the civil code of the Weimar Republic?"

He told his tale of woe in the most cheerful manner. Rabbi Einhorn looked far more concerned than Gottlieb himself did. "Couldn't you take some courses of study, Mr. Gottlieb? Fill in the gaps so you could qualify for the American bar?"

Gottlieb laughed. "I'm afraid it's *all* gaps, Rabbi. I'd have to do more than take some courses. I'd have to start all over again in law school—and in a foreign language that I'm not too secure about at best. No, no, at my age, with a wife to take care of, I can't afford to tilt at windmills. The law and I will part company from now on. I'll go to work for my wife's brother in the hardware business."

"If you need an assistant," Rabbi Einhorn said, "perhaps you'll consider my application."

"You, Rabbi? Nonsense! *You* won't have any trouble in America. From what my brother-in-law writes in his letters, there's a serious rabbi shortage. Synagogues are springing up all over the country. With German refugees alone you could start your own congregation."

"Yes, I imagine there *will* be opportunities," Rabbi Einhorn said. "I've met some distinguished American rabbis at various conferences throughout the years, and I've been in correspondence with several of them. But lately it's been difficult not to feel— So many things are happening in the world, upheavals, changes. Perhaps it isn't possible for a man my age to be an effective spiritual leader. It may take a younger man—"

"There are too many younger men!" said Ehrlich. "Hitler is younger than any of us. So is Göring, Himmler, Hess—all the top Nazis. And the Youth Corps, the SS, the mobs that smash windows— They marched down the street in my own town last year, breaking into every Jewish shop, destroying the merchandise. And when I saw them coming down the street, I said to myself, 'It must be a circus parade—they're all schoolboys.' So don't talk to me about younger men, please. They'll rip the world to pieces like they did my merchandise—that's your younger men!"

For a moment they were all disconcerted by Ehrlich's intensity. Bender felt that he had to speak up; the silence was growing too oppressive. "Mr. Ehrlich, have you decided yet what kind of work you'll do in America?" Among the passengers this had become the standard way of phrasing this particular question. It wasn't considered polite to ask a man pointblank if he had a job lined up.

"Work?" Ehrlich gave a grunt. "I'll dig wells. I'll repair watches. I'll do tricks from the flying trapeze. Don't you think that's the kind of work I'm fit for?" He pointed at his empty left sleeve, which was pinned to the front of his jacket. "The fatherland—if you'll excuse that expression—arranged it nicely so I could do such work. At the front in 1917 I gave them my arm—twenty-two years later they're giving me the

179

toe of their boot." He laughed harshly, but then a look came over his face, a confused, uncertain look, and for a moment he didn't seem to be talking to the rest of them any more. "They let me keep my store to the end. I could go to the shops at any hour of the day—I had a permit. I even kept on getting my disability pension. Because I was a war hero, a special category—" He broke off, then he looked up at them. "You asked me about my work, doctor? My son, who lives in Brooklyn, New York, has a good job with an architect, making blueprints. With the money he's saved he'll help me open a little store."

"Furniture again?"

"What else do I know but furniture? But I really *know* it, you understand. Not just from behind the counter. Before the war I used to go into the shop with a saw and hammer—I won't do too badly. My wife died a few years ago; I've got nobody but myself to keep. The boy will get his money back with interest." Ehrlich gave a sudden shake of his head—the impatient gesture of the lion when he reaches the limits of his cage and has to go back in the other direction. "It's no pleasure to me at my age. Fifty-three years of age, and I never asked help from anybody, I built up my own business from nothing. I served in the Kaiser's army and was decorated for bravery—and now I'm taking money from my children."

"It's nothing to be ashamed of, Mr. Ehrlich," said the rabbi. "In times like these everything is upside down. Fathers and children— Your son will respect you as much as ever, I'm sure."

"Respect me!" Ehrlich flashed a look at the rabbi that was full of rage. "Oh yes, I'm a very respectable type. Disabled soldier of the Reich—a highly special category. You know what I used to tell myself? 'They can't touch *me*—I'm not like the others!' And they *didn't* touch me for a long time— long after everybody else—" The fierceness faded from his face like a quenched fire. "But that's over now. No more special categories when we go back—"

His toneless voice made them all lower their eyes and become occupied with their beers.

Julia suddenly appeared. The men scrambled to their feet and greeted her with pleased, awkward smiles. She always had this effect on a group of normal males. Bender couldn't deny that it gave his ego a boost.

She told them all to sit down. Her manner was tempered, as usual, by a touch of amusement, of mischief, yet somehow it managed to be gracious, too.

"There's a lovely moon tonight, Carl," she said. "Would you care to come out on deck and give it the benefit of your clinical examination?"

After nodding at the others, he went off with Julia. Out on the deck her chatter came to a stop. Silently they stood together at the railing. The moon—almost a full one—lived up to her praise of it. And yet it made him uneasy. From high in the sky it gazed down at its twin, quivering in the yellow-black water way below. There was something sinister about this confrontation. Two mortal enemies seemed to be watching each other silently, warily, before flinging themselves into some titanic struggle.

After a long time Julia broke the silence. "Everybody is an expert on what's going to happen to us. Haven't *you* got a theory, darling?"

She said this in her lightest voice. She might have been asking a casual question about the weather. Yet something made him turn and look at her. Only her profile could be seen. The moon cast a pale glow over her features, drained them of all expression.

"My only theory," he said carefully, "is that all theories are meaningless. We haven't got enough facts in our possession."

"Did your friend Aaron Peyser talk to his American today?"

"Not by dinnertime, which was when I saw him last."

"Does that mean anything, do you think?" She had turned to face him now. "The man promised to get in touch as soon as we reached New York. Isn't that what Aaron told you?"

"Perhaps there was nothing to say. Perhaps nothing has happened yet."

"Perhaps the American and his organization have decided they can't help us."

She was still keeping her voice light and casual, and so he replied to her in the same tone. "That isn't likely. If they were going to abandon us, they would surely tell us first. No, this really seems to be a case of no news is good news."

She turned her head again and stared out at the ocean and the moon. Bender couldn't take his eyes from her face. The words that came out of him now were completely unplanned. The moment he had spoken them, he would have given a great deal if he could have retracted them. "Tell me something, Julia—are you sorry you married me?"

She looked at him again. He could see her eyebrows going up with amusement. "What a question! Must I take an oath on the Bible?"

He had gone this far—he had to push on to the end. "Yes, it *is* an unforgivable lapse of taste. Still, you'll humor me, won't you? Considering the present circumstances, nobody could blame you for feeling certain regrets."

"Well, since you mention it, Carl—I *do* feel certain regrets."

Her voice had become almost solemn—if such a word could be applied to anything connected with Julia. He was aware of a sick feeling inside him, but he wouldn't let anything show on his face.

"I regret—in fact, I *deeply* regret—that a brilliant man like my husband, with his expensive education, should sometimes talk like an absolute idiot." Then she leaned forward, took his face in her hands, and kissed him on the mouth.

He found himself holding her tightly, pressing his mouth against hers. It was more than sexual desire that made him reluctant to let her go. It was as if he were afraid that she might vanish in a puff of smoke once he broke contact with her.

But he soon regained his sense of proportion, and he separated from her gently. "How did you ever come to exist, darling?" he said, putting on his ironic smile—more ironic than usual, perhaps, to make up for his momentary lapse. "An upper-middle-class German lady of conventional education and respectable background—don't you honestly have an ounce of anti-Semitism in you?"

"The truth is"—she was using her light casual voice again —"I rather *like* Jews. They're so much less dull than other people. So much more complicated and neurotic and utterly impossible." She patted him on the cheek.

Then they noticed the sound. It was coming from somewhere nearby, off to their right. A low gulping sound, like somebody struggling for breath. He saw a figure in the shadows ten or twelve feet away—the figure of a woman leaning against the lifeboat.

He took a step toward her but was stopped by Julia's hand

on his arm. "Leave her alone," Julia said, her voice very low.

"I think she's ill—"

"Darling Carl, how many years have you been an analyst? And you still can't tell when a woman is crying?"

She drew him gently along the railing, away from the lifeboat.

"You know her, then?" he said.

"It's Claire Halevy—the cabin across from us. I've seen her like this before. Always at night in the darkness, when she thinks nobody's looking."

"Have you any idea what's troubling her?"

Julia gave the smallest of shrugs. "She's a woman. She has a nineteen-year-old son. She's on this ship. The year is 1939. Any one of those reasons would do nicely, don't you think?"

Even at this distance the soft gulping sounds carried to them through the clear air. So they left the deck and went back inside.

"Just one dance," Julia said, "and then if I don't go to bed, I'll drop with exhaustion."

They went to the nightclub and danced together through a slow, sentimental number. Julia was an excellent dancer, and Bender had been told that he wasn't bad, either. A fact which surprised and disturbed many people; psychiatrists were supposed to be deadly serious types who never indulged in frivolous amusements. Hannah, he remembered, had always believed that. He couldn't recall that she had ever danced with him. Except at their wedding reception . . .

Julia's cheek was cool and soft against his. Her perfume caressed him. She was an extraordinary woman, he thought. Perhaps he was just beginning to realize this. She was full of contradictions, of emotions that couldn't possibly exist within the same person—compassion and selfishness, understanding and indifference, malice and—and love? Was she capable of love? She loved her daughter, there could be no doubt about that. She had probably loved her first husband until he systematically stamped out all traces of it in her. And her present husband? The question was infantile, of course. Nor did she ask it with any seriousness. What she had shown him tonight wasn't love, as he knew perfectly well. It was friendly affection, at most—one might almost say sisterly affection—and in a way it was more precious than love. The sweet delight it had given him was with him still, mingling with the music from the band, making him think again of his "idea," of the plan he was forming for Julia's future and her daughter's. In the last week hardly an hour had gone by without his giving some thought to the "idea." . . .

I married an angel, said the music. Some angel, Julia was thinking, as her cheek rested against Carl's. Oh yes, *I* must certainly be making the heavens sing. Noble, fairminded, blessedly free of vulgar fears and prejudices.

She remembered what the last few years in Berlin had been like, as one by one the doors closed to Carl, the patients disappeared, their old friends dropped away, and eventually they even had to move out of the old neighborhood. She remembered how, though money was growing so much scarcer, she had insisted on paying her weekly visit to Santini's, her hairdresser on the Boulevard. That incredible place with its ersatz gold decorations, its atmosphere of synthetic Hapsburg opulence, its pseudo-French homosexuals pawing and patting at your hair. And Madame Santini herself, moving from dryer to dryer, smiling her sweet smile that didn't for a moment conceal her utter contempt for all her customers. And yet long after she had given up certain necessities, Julia had clung to Santini's.

Was it the very dreadfulness of the place that had made her hold on to it so tenaciously? Its raw ostentatious display of luxury—its air of wallowing in sybaritic waste—the outrageous flattery that was smeared over you, like gobs of honey on a piece of toast, for no other reason than your willingness to pay the price—the stupid, malicious, extravagantly improbable slanders that the high-pitched voices screeched back and forth—the nasty remarks about Jews that dropped from the mouths of customers and employees alike? Toward the end this poison had flowed so easily and naturally that nobody even hesitated; nobody paused to suppress a pang of conscience, because there *were* no more pangs of conscience. And of course no voice was lowered tactfully any more, for Jewish ladies had long since stopped coming to Santini's. Julia could imagine what the "regulars" would have said if they had known about her marriage to Carl. But in fact they didn't know, because she had never told them. She had started going to Santini's in the days when she was Mrs. Gunther von Helmuth, and somehow she had never bothered to mention her second marriage to Madame Santini or Monsieur Antoine or any of the others.

Somehow? She knew well enough how. There at Santini's, for a few hours a week, she could lean back and relax and be a good little Aryan girl again. . . .

The music ended, as this band's arrangements always did, with a dying squeal and a few random beeps. Julia yawned and said that she really must get to bed. She did look exhausted, Bender thought. At the end of her strength.

He took her down to her cabin. Outside the door he kissed her gravely, a bit paternally, then he went out on deck again for a last cigarette. He returned to the place by the railing where Julia and he had been standing earlier. He noticed that her friend Mrs. Halevy was gone.

The moon was veiled now, behind a cloud. It looked a little kinder, a little more human and pliable than before. Perhaps the implacable universe could be reached and softened after all. He intended to do his damnedest, God knows. His "idea" was fully formed now, and all that remained was to put it into effect. Just as soon as the news came definitely from New York—as soon as it was clear that the United States wouldn't take them in—he would make the opening move. If the worst *didn't* happen, of course, and the United States *did* decide to take them in . . .

But he wasn't going to let his mind dwell on that unlikely development. He was determined, above all, not to be a hider.

* * *

Two o'clock in the morning—for Aaron the end of a bad day. Disturbing news from New York. No word from Morris Feldman. Everybody's nerves on edge. Now he was in the small foyer outside the passageway to his cabin. He was sitting in the one chair yawning, struggling to keep his eyes open. And wondering all the time if he wasn't about to make the biggest mistake of his life. . . .

All through dinner that night Aaron knew that something was troubling Joshua. The boy was too silent. Usually he chattered away so steadily that he had to be told to let somebody else talk. And he hardly ate a thing tonight, though the main course was chicken paprika; Aaron had often seen him polish off three large portions of chicken paprika and still have room for two desserts. A normal, healthy twelve-

185

year-old-boy—something of a miracle, all things considered. Aaron had often asked himself how anything normal and healthy could have survived in the Germany of these last few years.

Dinner ended and they all started out of the dining room.

"Papa, can I speak to you alone somewhere?"

Joshua had come up next to Aaron. He talked in a low voice and glanced over his shoulder, as if he were afraid of being overheard. But there was nobody to overhear him. Only David and Sophie, a few feet behind them.

"We'll take a stroll on the deck," Aaron said. He turned around to Sophie and David. "We're getting a little air; this boy looks pale to me. Are you going to the movie tonight, Sophie? Then save a seat for Joshua and me. David, you keep your mother company."

"I wasn't planning to see this picture, Papa."

"You can leave the theater when I get there."

He started up the stairs with Joshua, knowing that Sophie wouldn't follow them. She would wait for the elevator—she never climbed stairs unless she absolutely had to. Through the years she had fallen into bad habits. She had always worked hard on her committees, her boards, her charitable activities, but at the same time she had grown accustomed to thinking of herself as something special and fragile, a valuable object that had to be handled with care. Like so many other people, men *and* women, that Aaron saw on this ship. Whatever happened to them next, it was certain that they would all have to lose that feeling of fragility.

He wondered how many such habits he had fallen into himself without even knowing about them. In the old days he used to get to his office before nine every morning and often stay till seven at night. He had considered it necessary to keep even longer hours, to be even more conscientious, than Schwarzkopf himself—this was the least he could do to justify the old man's faith in him. It had never occurred to him during those years at the store that he was pampering himself, indulging himself; that the hard work a man puts in for most of his life could simply be his way of avoiding the *really* hard work.

Joshua and he were on deck now. They went to the stern, by the swimming pool. People stood at the railing or walked among the empty deck chairs. "Why don't we sit down?" Aaron said. "No reason to be uncomfortable."

186

He stretched out on a deck chair. Joshua perched on the edge of another one, squeezing his hands together in his lap.

"Look at that moon," Aaron said. "When I was your age I used to stare at it as hard as I could, trying to see the man's face in it. It's different with boys today, I suppose. You know all about science. For you the man in the moon is just a lot of craters."

He was running on because he didn't want to get started with this talk. He was afraid that Joshua wanted the same thing from him as everyone else—reassurances, promises that everything was going to be all right. A dozen people had come up to him today, people he didn't even know, and begged him to reassure them. Why him? What made them think he had a crystal ball in his pocket? It was only an accident, a quirk of fate, that they knew his name at all, that he was any less obscure than they were. He wanted to be obscure again. Why wouldn't people let him?

The captain was the worst of all. The captain, the captain —"our mad commander," as Carl Bender called him—my God, how he wished that man would let him alone! Every day since the arrival in Havana Muller had called him to his office and given him some message from the captain. Would Mr. Peyser express to the other passengers the captain's deepest regrets for the tragic death of the young man Albert Liebling? Would Mr. Peyser comment on the morale of the passengers and particularly on how the crew was treating them? Did Mr. Peyser feel that the kind of entertainment being provided for the passengers was appropriate now that certain doubts had arisen as to their ultimate destination?

Aaron had answered this last question in a letter. He had agreed that people weren't much in the mood for diversion these days—but on the other hand, if the diversions were suddenly cut off, alarm and panic might set in. Then Aaron had put a postscript on this letter: "I would like to thank you in person for everything you've done for us. Could I make an appointment with you?" There were so many things he wanted to ask the captain. Why had he treated them with such kindness? What plans did he have for them in the future? In the event that the United States wouldn't take them in . . .

No answer was ever given to his letter. The films and games and concerts hadn't stopped—which proved, Aaron supposed, that the captain had read what he had written,

even valued his opinion. But the request for an appointment—
not a word of acknowledgment, not a hint, nothing. And he
still hadn't set eyes on the captain—nobody had. How could
he resign his office when the authority who kept him in it
was nothing but a blur in the distance, an indistinct shape
behind a pane of glass?

But Joshua was telling his story now—what David had
said to him before dinner tonight, how David had sneaked
out of the cabin after midnight last night, how David and
Peter Einhorn and some other boys kept meeting in the
music room and locking the door. Aaron heard it all the
way through, and somehow it gave him no concern at all.
He told Joshua that there was nothing to worry about, that
there were many possible explanations for David's behavior.
It wasn't in David's character to become involved in some
wild escape plan.

"I guess you're right, Papa," Joshua said. "I shouldn't have
spoken to you. Telling on him behind his back—I *never* do
things like that. Not since I was a little kid."

Joshua looked so unhappy that Aaron put a hand on his
shoulder and assured him that he had done the right thing.

They made their way down to the movie theater. The film
hadn't begun yet. Joshua asked if he could sit with Carl
Bender's little girl, and Aaron went to Sophie.

David stood up immediately. "I'll see you later, Papa."

"You've got plans tonight?"

"Nothing in particular. Naomi and I might listen to some
music. Or I might just read a book and go to bed early."

He *was* a little more nervous than usual, Aaron thought.
First he wouldn't meet Aaron's eye, and then he did meet
it, almost too squarely, as if he were afraid of looking
evasive. Anxiety began to stir in Aaron— But the lights went
out; the film was about to begin.

Two hours later, after the film, Aaron accompanied Sophie
down to the cabin. She said she was tired and wanted to go
right to bed. He noticed that she wasn't humming any of the
tunes from the film she had just seen. Poor sentimental
Sophie—only a very heavy heart could keep her from being
carried away by a pretty tune and a story of young love.

"I'll stay till you're in bed," he said. "Then I'm going up
to the lounge to read."

He watched her undress. Of course she had put on weight
through the years, but to his eyes she wasn't all that different

from the sweet, pretty little girl he had married. He could understand very well why he had fallen in love with her. She had been so full of high spirits, she had brought color into his life at a time when the dreary seriousness of everything was crushing the joy out of him. And of course he had never denied to himself that she had saved him from anxiety as well. Her father's money, the job in her father's store, had meant the end of his haunting fears about the future, about becoming what *his* father had become. All right, but that didn't mean he had married Sophie for her money. He would have loved her even if she hadn't been rich. He was sure of that. By marrying her hadn't he given up as much as he had gained? Hadn't he given up the dream of his life?

She slipped into her nightgown, pink and frilly, the kind of nightgown she had been wearing as long as they had been married. Maybe she was getting a bit too old for it now. A baby—that's what she still was in many ways. So was her mother. Strange how old Schwarzkopf managed to keep his women frozen in infancy. And possibly his men, too.

Aaron reached out and took her hand. "Sophie—why did you ever marry me?"

She looked startled. "But I *always* wanted to marry you. The first time I met you—at that lecture at the university—"

"I couldn't have seemed like much of a catch. No money, no prospects, not exactly the life of the party. And God knows I never fooled myself that I was good-looking."

"You're *very* good-looking. You were always the most *interesting* looking man I knew. Sensitive and sweet—"

"A jellyfish. Your father called me that to my face, if you remember. The day after I proposed to you."

"He changed his mind about you years ago. You know how much he likes you and respects you. Besides"—her voice lowered; her smile was like a shy shadow of the smiles he had loved when he first knew her—"what's wrong with being a jellyfish? All the men that Mama and Papa wanted me to marry were so loud and sure of themselves and—and domineering. Like Papa. I was *sick* of men like that."

She wasn't telling him anything he didn't know. A long time ago he had realized that his gentleness, his unaggressiveness had been part of what made him attractive to her. Not because she was looking for a man she could bully, but because she didn't want to be bullied any more. When this

189

realization first came to him—he was still in his twenties at the time—it had rather pleased him than otherwise. Why feel ashamed of being a kindhearted, gentle sort of person, a *nice* person? The world was too full of strong men already; they were the ones who caused all the trouble. So he used to tell himself.

"You never wished I were a different kind of person?" he said. "You never wanted *me* to be more domineering?"

"Of course I didn't. I like you the way you are." She hesitated, then went on quickly, "I don't want you to change—ever—" He was struck by the peculiar note in her voice. Almost as if she were begging him—had she noticed changes in him lately, changes that worried her? Sometimes he thought he could notice them in himself. Gentleness and kindness didn't seem like such unalloyed virtues to him any more. "He that is slow to anger is better than the mighty. . . ." These words were in the Torah. But what use was it likely to be to anyone, his slowness to anger? All over Germany the synagogues had been broken into, angry men had burned the Torahs—and slow men had just stood by and watched. . . .

A knock on the door, then David looked into the room. "I'm going to bed now. I just wanted you to know I was back." And he pulled his head out before they could ask him any questions.

"He was with that little girl, of course," Sophie said. "She's a sweet girl, but I really wonder, to get serious at his age—"

"What makes you think there's anything serious?"

"He *is* seeing a lot of her. They're together all the time."

"On this ship we're all together all the time."

"But what do we really *know* about her? What's her background, what kind of family?"

"Sophie, Sophie—" Aaron had to give a sigh. "If we had nothing to worry about except David's love life—"

She blinked at him, and then her face seemed to crumple a little, and he could see her eyes growing wet. "I'm sorry—it's all so trivial, I know it is—"

He got to his feet and put his arms around her. He kissed her, held her close. He felt the impulse to go further. It passed almost immediately. It was a long time, many months, since they had been able to enjoy anything like that together. Old age couldn't be the reason. It must be Adolf Hitler.

At last he left the cabin, and in the passageway he glanced at his watch. Eleven fifteen. It was odd that David had made such a point of telling them he was going to bed. He had never done that before.

Aaron felt his anxiety growing. In the foyer at the end of the passageway he saw a chair against the wall. It occurred to him that he might sit here, and if David appeared sometime later . . .

His first instinct told him not to do this. He may not have been the ideal father, but at least he had never spied on his son. Besides, if David *was* involved in some plan to get off the ship, would it be right to stop him? Suppose he could actually carry it out—

Then Aaron remembered what had happened in the harbor at Havana. He had seen the blood on the water, and all through the funeral service conducted by Rabbi Einhorn in the lounge he had imagined what it must have been like for that poor Liebling. Alone in this foyer now, late at night, it was easy to put David's face on that broken, water-soaked body. . . .

He took his place in the chair. Here he would wait until David came. . . .

At two o'clock in the morning Aaron saw David emerge from the dim light of the passageway into the brighter light of the foyer. His suit was rumpled, his shirttail was sticking out, his hair was tumbled over his forehead—it was obvious how hastily he had dressed himself. For a moment he looked to Aaron as he had looked so many times when he was a little boy, shuffling into the house after an afternoon at the playground.

David was halfway to the stairs before he saw Aaron. He stopped short, his eyes wide with surprise, with panic. Then his face grew red, and he looked as if he were going to cry. I just can't do this to him, Aaron thought. I'll believe whatever story he tells me, and I'll go to bed.

But he got hold of himself quickly. He had made his decision. The man who can't stick to a decision isn't really a man at all. Better to do the wrong thing than to be incapable of doing anything.

David put on a strained smile, trying to bluff it out, to pretend that nothing had gone wrong. "I couldn't sleep, Papa. I thought I'd go up on deck and get some air."

"I couldn't sleep, either. Let's get the air together."

David's alarm at this suggestion was evident, but he couldn't seem to think of any way out. So Aaron took the boy's arm, and they started up the stairs. When they reached the main deck, David said, "Wouldn't it be better if we went up a little higher?"

No missing the anxiety in his voice. Whatever he was supposed to be doing, this deck was where he had been intending to do it. "I'm not as young as you are, believe it or not," Aaron said. "All this climbing makes my legs sore. If it's all right with you, let's stay where we are."

Aaron led the boy out to the deck. They walked in silence. The moon was hardly visible now, lost in a blanket of clouds, and the darkness was thick around them. There were no human figures in sight; there was no sound except the soft sound of their feet against the wooden deck. A ship in the middle of the night, when everybody has gone to sleep, is like a piece of the world that's been left behind and forgotten.

They stopped at the railing. Leaning against it, staring out at the black ocean, they could hear the lapping of the water far below. "All right," Aaron said, "tell me what it's all about."

"I don't know what you mean, Papa."

"You know what I mean. What are you doing, what are you planning? You and Peter Einhorn."

The look on David's face told him he had guessed right. "There's nothing; I couldn't sleep—"

"If you don't tell me what this is all about," Aaron said, "we're going inside right now, and I'm calling the officer on watch—"

"Papa, you can't do that!"

"Can't I?" He held his gaze as steady as possible and kept his expression cold and unmoving. David mustn't believe for one moment that his sternness could be thawed. Too often in the years past he had told his sons that they must *positively* do this or that, and then a look of misery or anger in their eyes had made him retreat from his position.

A look of misery was certainly in David's eyes right now. And Aaron was surprised at himself—he felt absolutely no desire to retreat; the cold expression on his face wasn't at all difficult to maintain. There was even a kind of gratification in maintaining it, the gratification of a man who's playing a game and winning. It occurred to Aaron how few games he had played in his life, and how seldom he had won.

After a moment or two he could see David's defenses

crumbling. Unsteadily, repeating himself and interrupting himself, David came out with the whole story.

When he was finished, he looked ashamed, disgusted at himself. No father should ever made his son feel like that, Aaron thought. He chose his next words carefully, hoping to ease the pain he had caused. "It's not such a bad plan at all. It's good, as far as it goes. But you must see that it wouldn't work."

David began to stammer out answers—they had a compass, they would take the deck guard with them, they were young and strong—

"Even if you made it to shore," Aaron said, "what good would it do? You seem to visualize a welcoming committee, newsreel cameras, crowds of well-wishers clamoring to bring your case before the public. It wouldn't be like that at all. The moment your boat touched shore, the police would bundle you off to jail, lock you in a cell until the immigration officers could dispose of your case and send you back to this ship. No pictures, no newspapermen, no crowd—the American people would never cry out at your unjust treatment, because they'd never even learn of your existence."

"But things aren't done that way in America. People aren't hidden away, condemned without a trial—"

"American citizens aren't. But we're not American citizens, any of us. We're refugees—you must understand what that means. Our own country has rejected us, and no other country has taken us in. We belong to nobody, we're protected by nobody. In America, and everywhere else, we have no rights, no privileges, no existence in the eyes of the law. Anything at all can be done with us."

He paused and could see his words sinking in. David was shaking his head, bewildered.

Aaron pushed on ruthlessly, knowing how ruthless he was being. "Your gesture would be useless, don't you see? Worse than useless—harmful! Fatal! Not only to yourselves, but to everyone else on this ship!"

"How could we harm anybody? We want to *help*—"

"We're trying to persuade the Americans to take us into their country. Negotiations are going on right now—difficult, delicate negotiations, based on our assurance that the people on this ship will become useful, law-abiding members of the American community. And in one stroke, by your crazy act of bravado, you'll prove that we're all criminals and adventurers with no sense of responsibility, no respect for the law."

"But Peter says—"

"Peter is an irresponsible dreamer. Don't you understand the risk you're taking? You're trading off some vague future hope, some daydream about 'arousing public sympathy,' against a real substantial *present* chance. For the sake of a romantic gesture, you're ready to throw away the strong possibility—probability, in fact—that we can enter the country in a quiet, orderly manner."

David was shaking his head harder. In another moment, Aaron could see, he would be nodding in agreement.

Then a voice came from behind David. "And what if your 'real substantial probability' is the biggest dream of all?"

From the shadows of a lifeboat several feet away Peter Einhorn appeared. His face looked gray and almost ghostly in the half-darkness. "What you want us to do," he said, "is sit and do nothing, while that 'useful law-abiding community' discusses our fate. And when they finally decide against us, it'll be too late for us to help ourselves."

Aaron faced him squarely. "You're making an insane assumption—yes, I mean insane. You're assuming that the American authorities are indistinguishable from the Nazis, that they have no decent rational feelings, that reason and humanity have no influence on the people who make decisions in this world."

"Can you prove that my assumption is wrong?"

"If what you believe were true, proof would be irrelevant. Civilization would be at an end, reason would be dead—the only sane response would be suicide."

"You're a bigger pessimist than I am, Mr. Peyser. You can't see yourself living in an unreasonable world. Well, *I* can see myself living in *any* kind of world. Fighting to stay alive no matter what, that's *my* idea of sanity. And that's what we intend to do—my friends and I!"

He gave a sweep of his arm, and figures appeared from the shadows behind him. Four young men lined up at his back, motionless, staring at Aaron gravely.

"I'm not against fighting," Aaron said, forcing his voice to remain steady. "I'm glad you want to fight, it would be wrong if you didn't. But *pointless* fighting—reckless actions that can do no good and might destroy the one chance we've got—"

Peter shook his head, sharp and impatient. "The deck

194

guard will be coming around that corner in less than fifteen minutes, Mr. Peyser. What are you going to do? Will you return to your cabin and forget you ever saw us?"

Aaron knew that he couldn't afford to hesitate. "No. What you want to do is wrong. You'll cut your own throats, and what's worse, you'll cut everyone else's, too. I'm not going to let you do it."

"How do you plan to stop us?"

"I can't stop you from getting into that boat. But as soon as you're off the ship, I'll raise the alarm. You won't get very far."

"We might defend ourselves, somebody might get hurt. The captain might punish us, lock us up. You won't let that happen to David."

Aaron gave a quick glance at David. He saw that the boy, his face very white, had taken a few steps away from him, had moved closer to Peter.

"If David won't listen to reason," Aaron said, "he'll have to take his chances."

There was a long silence. The lapping of the water at his back, the low humming of the ship's generator—a sound he had stopped noticing long ago—were suddenly loud in Aaron's ears. The line of boys, half-obscured in the shadows —standing so silently, so devoid of expression—might have been spirits from another world. The thought crossed his mind that he was in danger. Suddenly these weren't five romantic, overgrown schoolboys who stood before him but five strong young monsters whose desires were being thwarted. Five of them? How sure could he be that it wouldn't turn into six?

He waited another moment, then turned to David. "You'll come down to the cabin with me now."

David just stared at him, and his lips were trembling.

Aaron held out his hand. "Come on. It's very late. Nothing's going to happen out here."

David cast an anguished look at Peter. This was the crucial moment, Aaron thought. His stomach began to burn. With great difficulty he kept the pain from showing on his face.

Then the silence was broken. A small, almost inaudible sigh came from one of the boys—the thin one who was smaller than the rest. "Peter—I wonder—"

There was another sigh. A couple of heads started shaking. The line became less solid, more ragged.

And then Peter made a mistake. He turned to them angrily. "He's all wrong! We can't let him weaken us!" The idea that they *were* being weakened should never have been put into words. Till then it was only a threat, something shapeless hanging over them which might have gone away. Now Peter had turned it into a solid, inescapable fact. There was more sighing and fidgeting from the boys, and then a mutter broke out of the redheaded boy, the widow's son. "It's no good even starting! If he reports us as soon as we're off the ship—"

This mutter was taken up by all the others.

Aaron felt like letting out a sigh of relief, giving a smile of triumph. He resisted the impulse. The pride of a teen-age boy is the most tender plant on earth. Just one hint of gloating might harden them all against him again.

He spoke instead with as much sympathy, as much seriousness as he could manage. "We'll get out of this. We'll be all right. That's a promise. My solemn promise." Then he put his hand on David's arm and led him across the deck and through the door.

Behind him he could hear Peter Einhorn breathing softly. To humiliate a boy in front of his friends—this wasn't a nice thing to do. It wasn't what Aaron would ever choose to do of his own free will. His own boyhood had been too full of humiliation. He'll get over it, Aaron thought. He has spirit and pride, but he also has a kind of—of largeness. There isn't anything mean in him, any petty revengeful instincts. Suddenly Aaron was filled with admiration for Peter Einhorn. I'll tell him how sorry I am, Aaron thought. I'll make it up to him someday. When we're off this ship, when we're all safe again . . .

David and he walked down the stairs and came to the foyer again, that empty room with its gilt hangings and its white linoleum floor. Now Aaron had to find the right words, he had to relieve the boy's shame. "I'm proud of you," he said. "It took a great deal of courage—"

What he saw in David's eyes made it impossible for him to go on talking. The boy was looking at him with hatred. It was raw and unconcealed. Nobody had ever hated Aaron before.

The next moment it went away—as if a light had clicked out behind David's eyes. Aaron said, "Well, we're both tired. We'll talk again in the morning." And he wondered, as he walked David to the door of his cabin, how long it would be before they could ever talk again.

A little later Aaron climbed into his bed. Sophie didn't even stir in the berth below. He stared up at the dark ceiling and told himself that he could now afford to lower his defenses; he could let the host of doubts which he had been holding at arm's length all night come rushing in on him. He could let his stomach ache again. Here in the darkness he could be himself again.

He waited for the flood. He told himself what a reckless fool he had been; he asked himself how he could ever face those boys again if his "solemn promise" turned sour. What right did he have to make such a promise, when he was as uncertain about the future as anybody else on this ship? Maybe he had just robbed them of their one chance to be free.

He asked himself all this, but the reaction didn't sweep over him. Instead, way down underneath, he could feel that gratification again, that peculiar excitement which came from knowing he had pulled off an impossible feat. Tonight he had shown that he could master people, that he could control a dangerous situation. He had survived, triumphed, by discovering a core of coldness in himself whose existence he had never even suspected before. After tonight he wasn't doomed to be poor, weak, softhearted Aaron Peyser any more.

So he drifted off to sleep—but when he woke up in the morning and looked out the porthole, he saw the sea and the sky stretching away blankly to the horizon. The ship was no closer to New York than it had been the day before. Things were as bad as ever.

He began to feel a dull throbbing in his stomach. He clenched his fists. He forced himself to remember the words that had been in his mind the night before. I'll be strong, I'll be strong, I'll be . . .

SEVEN

WHEN he got back from Cuba, Morrie was sure that AJDA would never send him to Washington. Nothing could be done now except through very high levels of government, and obviously no young, inexperienced assistant was going to be involved in such important negotiations. Especially after the mess he had made already.

And so on his first morning back at the office he headed straight for Al, intending to ask a favor. Though he could no longer be in on AJDA's efforts to save the passengers, he wanted to go on acting as liaison man with their spokesman, Aaron Peyser. It was important for Peyser to feel that AJDA's representative, the only contact between the passengers and the world of freedom outside, genuinely cared about them—and for Peyser to convey this feeling to the others. Nobody could say what might happen aboard that ship if the idea got around that the outside world no longer gave a damn.

As Morrie stepped into Al's office, he was greeted by a shout from across the desk. "Where the hell have you been? I just called your apartment. We're flying to Washington at noon, meeting Dan at the airport in an hour and a half. We've got a two o'clock appointment with Congressman Lascoff."

"I'm going along?"

"Of course you're going along. The people on that ship trust you. Whatever happens in the next few days, you'll have to break the news to them. So you better be around while the decisions are being made."

Every once in a while Morrie had to admit that AJDA wasn't all Ben Zuckerman's hard head and Sigmund Wolff's childish ego.

"Besides," Al said, "the experience'll be good for you. You'll never be any use to this organization until you find out what the big bad world is like. Until you see some of the powers-that-be up close."

"Are they much different from ordinary human beings?"

"Exactly the same. But their camouflage is better. That's the big lesson you have to learn, not to be fooled by the camouflage. Okay, go home, pick up your suitcase, and get back here in half an hour."

"It might take me a few minutes to pack."

"I told Ruth to have everything ready for you." Al gave one of his sour grins. "I warned her there was no time for tender farewells."

And so at two thirty that afternoon Morrie was in Washington, D.C., sitting in the private office of Representative Saul Lascoff of New York. Al and Dan were there, too, and so was a tall, blond fellow in his thirties named Richard Glenn; nobody had bothered to explain to Morrie just what his position was. He looked like the hero of one of those college football movies. It seemed funny for a *goy* to be present at a behind-the-scenes strategy meeting like this.

Congressman Lascoff, who had served seven terms running from his district in the Bronx, was somebody Morrie had been hearing about ever since he was a kid. "What a fine upstanding fellow," he could remember his father saying. "The son of a Russian peddler, did you know that? Four years old when his parents brought him over on the boat. He worked his way through Columbia Law School, selling encyclopedias, and still he graduated number one in his class."

"Whenever he's in New York," Mama put in, "he goes to visit his mother on the Grand Concourse, and if it's Friday night he takes her to the *schul.*"

"Does he go to *schul* in Washington too?" Morrie had asked.

"Washington," Papa had answered with a sigh, as if to suggest that God Himself couldn't be too particular what His children did in *that* impious place. "The best thing about Saul Lascoff is he never let his success go to his head, he never forgot where he came from. People in his neighborhood, he still calls them by their first names, and if they come to Washington he welcomes them in his office and chats with them about the old days."

"Sounds like a great politician," Morrie had said—a confirmed cynic at the age of sixteen.

But irony—to his constant exasperation throughout his adolescence—always went over his parents' head. Mama just nodded enthusiastically and said, "That's right, a *wonderful* politician, God bless him!"

And here now, sitting across the desk from Morrie, was Saul Lascoff himself—a man in his fifties, short, bald, with a small potbelly, but as full of energy as somebody half his age. "Let's face facts," he was saying, rubbing his hands together briskly. "We don't have time to waste kidding ourselves, making ourselves feel good. We got a real problem. How long can that ship sit in New York Harbor, waiting for the government to make a decision? Three days, four days maybe—then Hitler gets fed up and orders it back to Germany, am I right? And the problem is, you can nudge the United States government into taking action, you can even from time to time inveigle it into changing a policy, but to get it moving in three or four days—to get it off its fat ass in anything less than three or four months—this needs a miracle. Still"—he gave a wide shrug of his shoulders—"the Jews have had miracles before. Who could've predicted that the Red Sea was going to open up? That too must've looked like a bureaucratic impossibility. But Moses pulled a few strings—"

"It seems to me, Saul," said Dan, "that the difficulties may not be quite as formidable as you make out."

"Optimism, optimism!" Lascoff wagged his finger. "Didn't I always warn you about that, Dan? You hang around too long with those allrightniks that pay your salary in AJDA, after a while you pick up their bad habits. They were born with more money than anybody knows what to do with, and all their lives they've had servants, lawyers, trust funds, God knows what else to protect them from the realities of this world, so naturally they're optimists, what else could they be? But let's face facts, here in Washington they don't carry so much weight. This is the bigtime jungle."

"Even so," Dan said, "why must we assume that our problem is with such a grandiose entity as 'the United States government'? Those people *have* been accepted for immigration, their visas *are* in order. It's simply a question of timing. Will they be permitted to enter right now instead of waiting six to twelve months? And this, it seems to me, could be looked at as a matter of mechanical routine. Somewhere in the Bureau of Immigration is an official with enough responsibility to change the dates on those visas. We have to move *him*, not 'the government.' "

"You make it sound like child's play," Lascoff said. "Why

are we even discussing it, since it's as good as done already? The only thing I'd like to say is you don't know the way things work in this town. Sometimes the simplest matters involve the biggest complications. Sometimes it's easier to get a million dollars out of the government for a new bridge than it is to get a hundred dollars for stamps. But okay, your point of view is worth considering. I *have* been considering it. Richard and I spent the whole morning considering it. Go on, Richard, tell them what you've done."

Richard Glenn cleared his throat and spoke in a soft voice with the faintest whiff of a Southern accent.

"There's really only one man with the authority to predate those visas on his own responsibility. If he cares to exercise that authority in favor of the passengers on the *Franz Joseph,* they could be disembarking at Ellis Island within a few hours. But we must face the possibility that he *won't* care to exercise his authority in their favor. He might take the view that it isn't within his province to make such a decision, thus throwing the whole problem back into the realm of official policy—where, as Congressman Lascoff suggested, it could remain in limbo for a long time. In Washington people take a great many actions by simply refusing to take *any* action."

"So if this one man drags his feet," Al said, "we won't be able to do a damn thing for those people?"

"Well, there *is* something else we could try," Glenn said. "Congressmen are permitted to present special bills—that is, bills which aren't intended to add to the body of law but simply to confer some momentary favor or privilege on an individual or a group. One senator I'm thinking of, for instance, presents a special bill every year so that his father-in-law can hunt deer in a national park. Such bills are usually rushed through ahead of weightier business on the agenda— and out of Congressional courtesy they seldom meet with any opposition. Of course, they must first be approved by the chairman of the appropriate committees in the House and the Senate."

"The House won't be any problem," Lascoff said. "The chairman of the Immigration Committee is Charlie McCabe from Massachusetts. A nice fellow, a Harvard graduate and very liberal, even though he *is* stinking rich. We play a little poker sometimes. But the chairman of the Senate Immigration Committee—" Lascoff shook his head.

After a moment Glenn said, "A special bill is a nuisance

201

at best. And we certainly don't have to assume it will be necessary in this case. Our best chance is still Harrison Bliss."

The name meant nothing to Morrie. But he could see from the thoughtful looks on their faces that it wasn't unknown to Al and Dan.

"I thought Bliss had been transferred to the Asiatic desk," Dan said.

"Just a rumor," Glenn said. "He's still in charge of immigration from Western Europe. That's where he's likely to stay, too. He's in his fifties now, and he's been in government service since the Harding administration."

Dan looked vaguely troubled. "We've never actually had any dealings with him. We've just heard a few stories—"

"In Washington you always hear stories," Glenn said. "The wisest policy is to believe absolutely nothing. I've known Harrison Bliss for seven or eight years. He's quiet, respectable, a family man, doesn't get caught up in the party whirl—no gossip, no scandal, no debts, not even any known eccentricities. His father was a small-town doctor in the Midwest somewhere. Bliss came to Washington after he got out of the state university, and he's been here ever since. The government is full of pople like him—honorable, useful, unspectacular ciphers."

"How does he feel about Jews?" Al asked.

"I can't remember ever discussing the matter with him," Glenn said. "I certainly never heard him make an anti-Semitic remark."

"How soon can we see him?" Dan asked.

"Tomorrow morning, ten o'clock," Lascoff said. "Richard already made the appointment."

They congratulated Glenn on his fast work, and the discussion went off into tactical details. It ended an hour later, and there was a general sighing, stretching, and mopping of brows. For the first time Morrie noticed what a hot day it was; everybody was covered with sweat.

"One more question," Al said. "If we can't get what we want from Harrison Bliss, can we go over his head? Does he have a superior who could overrule his decision?"

"Several superiors," Glenn said. "Right up to the Chief of the Bureau, or even the Attorney General himself. But you must understand something—people like Bliss are seldom overruled by their superiors. He has one great advantage going for him."

"Which is?"

"He does the work. He gets things done. He answers the mail, reads the directives, keeps the press of business from becoming unmanageable. If it wasn't for Bliss, his superiors would *never* get out on the golf course. No Cabinet member in the history of the United States could afford to antagonize such a useful subordinate."

The deepening silence was broken by Glenn's clearing his throat and lifting his watch. "Nearly four thirty, Congressman. You've got an appointment with those men from the Longshoremen's Union."

"Oh, yes, thanks for reminding me, Richard. Gentlemen, excuse me for kicking you out, but you don't keep the president of a union waiting nowadays—even if he *is* a no-good racketeer."

Before they knew it, they were out of Lascoff's office. On the way down in the elevator Morrie couldn't hold in his curiosity any more. "Who's Richard Glenn?" he asked.

"Technically he's a lawyer," Al said. "Washington has more lawyers per square foot than any city in the world. Actually, he's a professional lobbyist. Licensed, registered, perfectly legal. He handles half a dozen accounts besides AJDA."

"Is it part of our strategy to use a lobbyist who isn't Jewish?"

"Dick Glenn isn't Jewish?" Al and Dan exchanged amused glances, then Al said, "Don't tell his mother that. She's a pillar of the Reform temple in Savannah, Georgia. There have been Jewish Glenns down there since before the Revolution." He grinned a little. "We don't see too many like them in New York, of course. In their opinion the men who founded AJDA were a bunch of immigrants."

* * *

The appointment with Harrison Bliss was for ten o'clock in the morning. At ten sharp the receptionist told them to step inside.

It was a small office—tiny, it seemed, once the four of them had squeezed into it—and it was located in a back corridor of the Justice Department building. Through the window behind the desk you could see neither the Capitol dome nor the Washington Monument nor a spacious avenue of cherry trees; what you saw was the brick wall of the building next door. Morrie wondered if some terrible mistake hadn't been made. Surely the man who had been shunted away to this obscure little hole couldn't have the power of life and death over a thousand people.

Bliss' appearance did nothing to contradict this impression. He was a neat, graying little man with small features. His mouth, when he pursed his lips, seemed to dwindle to the size of a button. His little eyes, behind rimless glasses, hardly did any blinking at all. Under other circumstances—sitting across from him in a bus, for instance, or next to him in a theater—Morrie would have had no trouble overlooking him completely.

As Congressman Lascoff explained why they had come, Bliss listened with his lips pursed and his hands folded together on the desk in front of him. His desk was as neat as himself. The only superfluous item on it was a gold-framed photograph of a middle-aged lady and two young girls. While the Congressman talked Morrie gazed at this photograph, and after awhile the middle-aged lady and the two girls began to look very much like the man behind the desk. All four faces were touched by the same pale, unblinking dullness.

The Congressman came to the end of his speech. For another second or two Harrison Bliss remained in the same position. Then his hands separated.

"Thank you, Congressman. I *am* familiar with the situation of which you speak. The sailing of the German liner *Franz Joseph* was noted in this department, and we've kept our eye —a semiofficial eye—on the developments in Cuba, though strictly speaking, of course, none of the passengers fall under our jurisdiction until their quota numbers become activated. Furthermore," his hands lifted and his fingers touched together lightly, "when you made this appointment with me yesterday, Congressman, and alluded in a general way to its purpose, I felt that I owed it to you to be as well informed as possible about the matter. And so I spent the evening doing some research into the whole *Franz Joseph* situation and into the status, from the Bureau of Immigration's point of view, of its passengers. I think I can safely say that I now have all the facts at my fingertips." He looked down at his fingertips, which were white and rather pudgy.

Then his hands clasped together again, his head poked forward slightly, and a more businesslike note came into his voice. "The *Franz Joseph* sailed from Hamburg at four twenty-six on the afternoon of June twenty-seventh. It arrived at Havana at five fifty-two on the morning of July fourth. The Cuban authorities refused permission to dock and temporarily revoked the entry visas of all the passengers. After a delay lasting five days the revocation was made permanent, and the *Franz Joseph* was obliged to leave Cuban waters. Its departure occurred two days ago, July tenth, at nine o'clock in the morning. It was due to arrive in New York Harbor this morning at approximately seven thirty. Aboard the ship, when it left Germany, in addition to a crew of one hundred and twenty, were one thousand and four passengers, all German nationals, of whom somewhere between two hundred and ninety and three hundred were minor children. As of today, with its arrival in American waters, the *Franz Joseph* has exactly one thousand and three passengers, one of the original group having perished in Havana Harbor under circumstances with which you gentlemen are no doubt familiar. Now then," he leaned back, smiling softly, "if my information is incomplete or inaccurate in any respect, I do hope you'll correct me."

The spectacular thing about this performance was that Bliss had managed it without stumbling, correcting himself, or consulting notes. He had taken their breath away, and Morrie had the impression that this was just what he had intended to do. Suddenly Morrie wondered if there wasn't something more than a juiceless nonentity behind those unblinking eyes; maybe an ego was hidden down there somewhere.

"Well, you certainly *do* know the situation," Lascoff broke the silence. "Damned if I can think of a single thing to add. Under the circumstances then, you can hardly help but sympathize with—"

"As you say, Congressman." Bliss gave a little nod. "My sympathies are very much engaged. It is, after all, in the tradition of our American ideals to sympathize with the victims of political persecution. Frankly, that's why I've spent so much time on this matter—when my schedule is crowded with other matters that might, from an objective standard, be considered even more important. And that's why"—the hands unclasped and spread open—"I feel so deeply sorry that there isn't anything I can do."

Morrie had been expecting this. Somehow, from the

moment Bliss started reeling off those facts and figures, Morrie had known what the end must be.

"Surely there must be *some* way," Dan said. "After all, those people do have quota numbers. Sooner or later the United States intends to take them in."

"Quite so, Mr.—Wechsler, isn't it? But you must realize that 'sooner or later,' in matters of this sort, isn't merely a form of words. The quota system was designed by Congress for a purpose. Our legally elected representatives felt not only that the total amount of immigration over a long period should be controlled, but that the *flow* of immigration *within* that period should also be controlled. It was important to them that those who were entitled to enter the country 'later' should not, willy-nilly, enter the country 'sooner.' This is the law, and clearly it is the duty of this department to carry it out. As one of those legally elected representatives, Congressman, I'm sure you wouldn't be happy if government agencies arbitrarily flouted your decisions."

...."*I* didn't have much to do with that decision. The law you're talking about was passed back in 1920. It's a disgrace that we haven't brought it up to date—"

"No doubt. That's a matter of opinion. We're all entitled to our opinions in a democracy, but that doesn't absolve us from obeying the law, does it?"

"Excuse me, Mr. Bliss." Al spoke up for the first time, and Bliss cocked his head toward him politely. "As I understand it, even within the provisions of the law, you—your department—is allowed, where you feel that special circumstances warrant it, to supersede some of the rules and regulations."

"That's true, Mr.—excuse me, Margolinski? Am I pronouncing it correctly? It's a rather difficult name, isn't it? Mr. Margolinski, what you say is true. I'm *not* simply a rubber stamp, I *am* entitled to use my discretion."

"Well, I've been doing a little research on this myself, Mr. Bliss. I've looked through the immigration code, and I asked the opinion of a couple of our organization's lawyers, and as far as I can see, if an individual's application for immigration has been approved and he's received a quota number—and those conditions, I'd like to point out, have been met by all the passengers on the *Franz Joseph*—then the actual date of his entry into the country *could* be moved forward by your department."

Bliss gave his thoughtful frown. "I *could* sign a paper and let those people into the country, and no doubt, from your point of view, that's what I ought to do. But these things, as I'm sure you realize, are always simpler to those who don't actually carry the burden of responsibility. *Your* interest in this matter is singleminded and uncomplicated, but *I* have to balance a great many interests one against another. For example, in order to move a thousand people forward on the quota list, I should be obliged to delay the entry of another thousand people—people from England, France, the Scandinavian countries. Does that seem fair to you?"

"Surely it depends on the circumstances," Dan said, and Morrie could feel his effort to keep his voice calm. "It *is* too bad that those people you mention should have to delay their immigration. But since there must be a choice, doesn't it make sense to weigh the comparative urgency of the various cases? Are those people from England or France or the Scandinavian countries in a desperate position? If they don't get to America right now, will they be thrown into concentration camps, possibly killed?"

"Perhaps they will, Mr. Wechsler. I haven't discussed it with them. And perhaps your people won't actually suffer such a terrible fate. Forgive me, but there *is* a tendency, out of your understandable partiality in this matter, to exaggerate certain aspects of it."

Al began to shake his head. "Exaggerate—"

"Please, please." Bliss raised his hand. "We mustn't be distracted by side issues. My point is that I don't *know* what the consequences might be if their immigration were delayed."

"But you *do* know—"

"Excuse me, but I don't. No question as to such consequences appears on any of our immigration forms. As a private person I may *speculate*, but in my official capacity I can have no *knowledge* of what might happen to anybody in the event of his inability to enter this country. Gentlemen, be reasonable. The United States government can't be held responsible for the actions of other governments. This department is competent to evaluate the consequences of letting people *into* the country, not of keeping them *out*. Above all, I must give scrupulous attention to the consequences in connection with our national security."

"National security!" Lascoff broke in loudly, then immediately lowered his voice. "How could those people jeopardize the national security? They've all been vouched for by responsible American citizens. None of them is going to be a public charge."

"I'm sure of that, Congressman. It's well known that you people look after your own, and I for one admire you for it. But I wasn't referring to our economic security. There's another question here, an ominous question to which none of you gentlemen, I suspect, has given any real thought. For well over six months Hitler has allowed no political refugees to leave Germany; suddenly he contravenes his own policy and authorizes the departure of a thousand people. Why? One answer immediately comes to mind. War looms on the horizon. Hitler would unquestionably like to know what our government intends to do in the event of a European conflict. Will we intervene, remain neutral, give aid to Germany's enemies—and if so, how much aid, what form will it take? Is it beyond the realm of possibility, then, that Hitler might be using this ship, the *Franz Joseph*, as a means of introducing espionage agents into the United States?"

"Mr. Bliss," Al said after a moment, "first of all, every one of those passengers was thoroughly investigated by the FBI and your bureau before they got their quota numbers. Second, none of them applied for immigration less than a year ago—which suggests some pretty long-range planning on Hitler's part. Third, they weren't even supposed to get into this country for six months to a year. If things had gone as planned, they'd all be in Cuba now. Fourth, what chance will they get to steal state secrets from our government? Who do you think these people are, high-level diplomats, generals' mistresses? They're going to be running little candy stores, or working for their relatives in the clothing business, or studying for years to qualify as doctors or dentists. If that's the best Hitler can do in the way of espionage, the world might as well stop worrying about him!"

Bliss didn't answer for a moment. He pressed the tips of his fingers lightly together. Finally he said, "The danger I spoke of may be remote, Mr. Margolinski, but as long as it exists at all, my duty requires me to take it into consideration."

Al's voice was getting louder. "There's *always* danger, for God's sake! *Anybody* could be a Nazi agent. What about one of those Scandinavians you're so fond of? At least there are some Aryans among *them*. You could cut off immigration completely, and the Nazis could still find plenty of agents—among a hundred percent native Americans. That whole argument is a blind, and you know it yourself!"

"Mr. Margolinski"—Bliss' tone seemed somehow both softer and sharper than before—"I can't continue this discussion if you're going to raise your voice. I simply won't carry on the affairs of this office in an atmosphere of hysteria, emotionalism, and rudeness." He got to his feet, revealing for the first time what a very short man he was. "It's getting late, and I have other appointments. I see no point in pursuing this matter any further. I've heard your arguments, and I've given them due consideration, and I'm afraid I shall have to act as my best judgment dictates."

"Mr. Bliss." Dan was on his feet, too. "I'm sorry if Mr. Margolinski offended you—he's sorry, too, he had no intention of being rude—but you have to see, this isn't an abstract question to us. People's *lives* are at stake."

"I've told you already how deeply I sympathize. But this, don't you see, is precisely the point I've been trying to make. You gentlemen have an emotional stake in this matter. It's no abstraction to you, therefore you're not capable of judging it impartially. My job, however, is to be objective. I must act not out of loyalty to one particular ethnic or religious group, but for the best interests of the country as a whole."

"There are three hundred children on that ship, Mr. Bliss. Couldn't you make an exception for them?"

Bliss gave a little sigh. "I wish I could. But if this department's position is correct—and needless to say, I'm convinced that it is—then it must be applied equally to everybody. It wouldn't be fair to make exceptions, would it?"

Another sigh from Bliss, and suddenly Morrie heard himself speaking up, his voice sounding high and unnatural in his ears. "If the President knew about your attitude—if he knew what was happening—"

"My dear sir." The look Bliss turned on him was gentle and kindly. "The President is a very busy man. I don't flatter myself that he even knows of my existence. Or cares."

*   *   *

Back at the hotel they found a message from Bernie Kramer in New York. The *Franz Joseph* had arrived, but on

209

orders from the immigration authorities it wasn't being allowed within the ten-mile limit.

"What could be more logical?" Al said. "We can't have those Nazi spies fishing up state secrets out of American waters!"

After lunch Congressman Lascoff called. He had arranged for them to meet late that night with Senator Elmer Landers of Idaho, the chairman of the Senate Immigration Committee, and Representative Charles McCabe of Massachusetts, the chairman of the House Immigration Committee. They would all have a drink together at the D.C. Athletic Club, a kind of no-man's-land in which Washington figures of all parties and persuasions could talk, horse-trade, and take one another's measure without compromising or committing themselves. Morrie told himself that this was good news. Men like Landers and McCabe weren't easy to pin down. That Lascoff had been able to do it on such short notice showed how much personal prestige he had. Surely there was a fighting chance that they would support his special bill.

So they all went with Lascoff to the D.C. Athletic Club that night and found the senator and the congressman in a booth in the dimly lit, oak-paneled Men's Bar. They weren't exactly what Morrie had expected. In his newspaper pictures Senator Landers was a lot fatter, burlier, more sloppily dressed, a caricature of the old-fashioned hinterlands demagogue—he was a Democrat, but more isolationist and bitterly opposed to the New Deal than most Republicans. Here in the Men's Bar he seemed plump and friendly. And Congressman McCabe, nicknamed "the Professor" by Washington columnists, was famous for his high-powered intellect and his collection of modern art. But what Morrie saw was a thin, elegantly dressed man in his forties with a cheery, outgoing manner, who seemed much more likely to spend an evening telling off-color stories than discussing Picasso.

Drinks were ordered, and then the meeting got down to business.

"Real interesting," said Senator Landers, after Lascoff had finished explaining the *Franz Joseph* situation. "A real interesting problem, ain't it? Now I want to be frank with you fellows. That's the only way to get things done—put your cards on the table and play out your hand."

"An excellent method in principle," said Congressman

210

McCabe. "It pays, though, to keep your eye on the player with an ace up his sleeve."

He laughed, and Landers joined in, gruffly but heartily. "Well now, I wouldn't deny it. Some of the poker games I've been in, a little bit of cheating was just a normal act of self-defense. But I don't suspect you fellows of ringing in a cold deck on me, so you can count on me to give you a square deal. Notice I said a *square* deal, not a *new* deal."

More laughter, then Landers grunted a few times and pushed his chin forward, and on his face was that bulldog look Morrie had seen in the newsreels. "Ordinarily, y'unner-stand, I ain't happy with all this immigration. In small doses it's fine enough, but these here liberals and radicals nowadays are going overboard—and I never made any secret that I was agin it."

"You never made any secret," McCabe put in, "that you're 'agin' every progressive idea that's come into the world since 1900."

"Damn right I am. And if it wasn't for me and a few others like me holding the line against your so-called progressive ideas—which is just a fancy name for schemes to pick the American public's pocket—this country would've gone to hell and bankruptcy a long time ago. Not that it ain't heading that way right now, with that lunatic in the White House pretending he's a Democrat, God help us all!"

The senator cleared his throat, then went on. "Anyway, my notions on immigration are pretty well known. The fact of the matter is, I could've had my pick of half a dozen commit-tees, but I decided on immigration becasue I think this just might be the most important and vital question that our nation's had to face since the War between the States. What I mean to say is, it's no more or less than the question of the purity of the American way of life."

"Watch yourself, Elmer," said McCabe. "You go on with that racial purity line, and you'll start sounding like Adolf Hitler."

"I ain't talking about *racial* purity, Charlie, and you know it, because you've heard me sound off on this subject plenty of times before. There ain't no such animal as a pure-blooded human being; we're all mongrels if you go back far enough. But *cultural* purity, *national* purity, that's what keeps civilization going, that's what preserves human progress and holds back the barbarian hordes. You take a hundred different kinds of people with a hundred different histories and backgrounds, customs, ideals, in-com-pat-i-ble ways of looking at life—and you shove them all together in one geographical locality and let them loose on one another, and what the hell *can* you get except everybody stealing from everybody else, hating everybody else, and sooner or later shooting at everybody else? If you want people to live together in peace and harmony, they'll have to start off with certain basic things in common, a language they all talk and goals and ambitions they all take for granted. That's what they never had over there in Europe, and that's why their history is one long orgy of rape and murder. That's what we've got in this country, and I ain't going to see it undermined by letting a lot of immigrants come swarming in."

"Aren't you making a pretty shaky assumption, Elmer?" Lascoff said. "You're assuming that most of those European immigrants are inferior to Americans, culturally and intellectually."

"I ain't assuming anything like that. I didn't say the European was *inferior* to the American, I said he was *different*. I didn't say his ideals and his traditions were worse than ours. Maybe they're better, for all I know. But one thing I can tell you for sure, they don't *mix* with ours. You put together too many elements that don't mix, and before you know it you're going to blow the whole damn laboratory sky high. Hell, any kid that's studying chemistry in high school can tell you that."

"Your case would be more persuasive," McCabe said, "if you weren't ignoring American history. Our founding fathers didn't all come from the same background and tradition. Mixed in with the Anglo-Saxon was plenty of German, French, Scandinavian, Spanish. Alexander Hamilton was the illegitimate son of a West Indian native woman—"

"Listen, Charlie, don't talk to *me* about the founding fathers. I studied a lot of history when I was a young fellow—in fact, I went to college and learned my Latin and collected my sheepskin just like my intellectual colleagues, though it ain't easy to get some of them to believe it. Now the thing about the founding fathers was, wherever they came from they all had the same kind of bringing-up, education, religious training. They read the same books and believed in the same ideas. They operated out of the Anglo-Saxon democratic tradition even when they didn't happen to be Anglo-Saxons."

"That was a hundred and sixty-five years ago," McCabe said. "A lot of other cultural traditions have poured into the mainstream of American life since then. Poles, Italians, Irish, Jews, Orientals—Negroes, since the slaves were set free— and they've all made their own contribution. Didn't anyone ever tell you that America is a melting pot? And every indication is that we're stronger for it."

"Or maybe in *spite* of it. Depends on what indications you're looking at, don't it? From where I sit the evidence shows that all those immigrations have been a threat to us, that they've come pretty close to swamping us more than once, that the only reason we ever survived them was that our original foundation was so strong.'"

"Even if you look at it that way," Lascoff said, "you've just given a pretty good reason for not being afraid to let in more immigrants. Since experience shows we can absorb them without damage—"

"We *have* absorbed them without damage. That don't mean, by God, that we can go on doing it forever. A strong man can take more poison than a weak man—but eventually, even for him, it'll turn out to be unhealthy to take poison. Now the poison this country's been taking into its system is beginning to reach the danger level. You can see the signs all around you. For instance, these radical agitators nowadays— in the unions, in the colleges, right smack in the government itself. Coming out and saying they want to destroy our democratic system—"

"There have always been radicals on the American scene," McCabe said. "As a matter of fact, that was the subject of my undergraduate thesis at Harvard. Thomas Paine himself—"

"It ain't the same nowadays," Landers said. "In the old days they wouldn't admit out and out that they hated America. A hundred years ago a radical had to claim he was a patriot, because he knew he couldn't get a following otherwise. But today your radicals and your intellectuals laugh at patriotism, it's a big joke to them—and there's no shortage of barbarians to enjoy the joke along with them. I ain't saying it's a majority yet—far from it, thank God—but the foreign elements, the in-com-pat-i-bles, are getting more numerous all the time because they breed faster than the rest of us, not believing in small families like Americans do. So what I say is, we better cut them off before they *are* a majority, because then it'll be too late."

He took a big gulp out of his glass and settled back in his chair, like some shaggy old circus animal who's done his tricks and feels he's entitled to rest for a while.

"There may be something in what you say, Elmer," Lascoff said, "but it just doesn't apply to those people on the *Franz Joseph*. They're highly educated, cultivated people—businessmen, professionals, not bums and loafers and agitators. They come from a society that's just as advanced technologically as ours. Incidentally, their families are just as small as ours. Before Hitler, you know, most experts used to say there were a lot of similarities between Germany and America."

"And a lot of differences, too," Landers said.

"Sure there are. But because Germans are so much like Americans, there's a good chance those refugees will be able to learn our ways and fit in with our traditions pretty quickly."

"The whole problem won't even come up, will it, if we don't let them into the country in the first place?" Landers gave his low rumbling laugh. "But don't get me wrong, Saul. I'm not saying I'm absolutely opposed to what you're asking."

"You're giving a pretty good imitation of it," Lascoff said, but Morrie could see an alert little gleam in his eyes.

"Fact is, though, I'm a lot more agreeable than I've been sounding, maybe. We've been talking up to now about principles—and I don't back down from principles. But now we're talking about a thousand people. A mere handful. I don't reckon my principles are so wishy-washy that any mere handful is going to make them crumble away. You want to present a special bill to let those people in, and you can't do it if I'm agin it. Well, I'm tempted to give you my support. Yes, sir, it's a real temptation. You want to know why? Because that thin-lipped, bloodless bastard in the Immigration Bureau told you to go to hell. Now, I never set eyes on the bastard in my life, y'unnerstand, but I know he's got thin lips and no blood, because that's what they're all like, those Gawdamn bureaucrats. Your maniac friend in the White House likes them that way, he feels safer if he's surrounded by adding machines instead of grown men with brains. Just to give one in the eye to him and his whole Gawdamn bureaucracy, it'd be a pleasure to support your bill."

"Well, Elmer, I appreciate—"

"Only I ain't going to do it." The famous Landers smirk was on his face as he shook his head back and forth. "Much as I'd enjoy myself, sometimes a man has to put his country above his personal feelings. If I came out in favor of your bill, that'd put me in a hell of a position the next time I had to stand up and be counted on some *important* immigration issue. I'd look like I was contradicting myself—which I've been doing all my life, but the trick is not to *look* it. So here's as far as I'll go for you—I won't support your bill, but I won't squash it, either. I'll keep my mouth shut about it, and when the vote comes up, I'll be absent on urgent business. With Charlie here pushing for you, you ought to be able to get it through. Now I couldn't be fairer than that, could I?"

A big grin was on Lascoff's face. He said thanks a few times, and Dan and Al and Morrie joined in.

Then Landers put down his drink and lumbered to his feet. "Have to be turning in now. Never *have* got used to these Washington hours—and I've been in this town over thirty years. Camping out in the wide open spaces—up at sunrise, snoring at sunset—that's more *my* kind of life. Should've been a rancher, a cowboy, like I started out to be. Never should've been a U.S. Senator at all. I'd quit the job tomorrow, if it wasn't for one thing."

"Please, Elmer," McCabe said, "spare us your campaign speech about sacrificing yourself to the service of your fellow citizens."

"I was about to say, Charlie"—Landers fixed his heavy-lidded eyes on McCabe and scowled—"I'd quit the job tomorrow, only I just love to hear myself talk."

He brought out a big booming laugh, shook hands all around, then crossed the room with a ponderous rolling motion and disappeared through the door.

McCabe looked at his watch. "Good Heavens, it's past *my* bedtime, too. Committee meeting at eight in the morning."

"Shouldn't we work out a few details, Charlie?" Lascoff said. "If I could show you a draft sometime tomorrow and get your okay, there might be a chance of bringing it to the floor the next day—"

McCabe's forehead creased. "I'm sorry, Saul. I'm really sorry. I don't think I can support your bill. In fact, my position is much more difficult than Elmer's—I'm afraid I'd have to come out against it."

There was a moment of silence.

"But you don't believe in Elmer's crap," Lascoff said. "You've always been in favor of immigration—"

"That's why this is such a painful decision for me to make. Of course we should take those people in. That's what the American idea is all about—a haven for the persecuted peoples of the world."

"So okay, in that case, why don't you—"

"Saul, there's a big difference between what *ought* to be done and what *can* be done. You've been in this game longer than I have, you know better than I do that politics is the art of the possible. If I were a free agent, if it were up to me alone, obviously those people would be in the country tomorrow—and all others who were lucky enough to escape from that madman in Germany. But I'm *not* a free agent, am I, any more than you are? I'm an elected representative, and I have to go back to my district and stand for reelection next year. If I support your bill, have you any idea how quickly and enthusiastically my enemies will bring it up against me?"

"So what? Your constituents have always gone along with your liberal ideas. A lot of union members, minority ethnic groups, college graduates—"

"It's different with this particular issue. The old liberal-conservative distinctions are breaking down on this. The fact is people are scared to death just now of the possibility of war. Hardly anybody thinks that it won't break out in Europe and that we won't be pulled into it eventually—but hardly anybody wants to admit this to himself. So nobody likes refugees—nobody wants to look at refugees, think about refugees, or know that refugees even exist, because this knowledge might destroy their illusion that there isn't going to be a war. You don't see it in *your* district, Saul—frankly, your people have a special ax to grind—but believe me, this is what's going on."

"But you've always been a leader, not a follower, Charlie. Isn't it up to you to prepare your constituents for facing the truth?

"Good Heavens, *I* don't have to do that for them. Circumstances will take care of that soon enough. In a year or two there won't be an adult in the United States who hasn't been obliged, like it or not, to face the fact of World War Two. *My* efforts, in the meantime, must be to protect myself. Right now my constituents are making your German refugees a scapegoat for their own fears. If I support your bill—if I do anything except *oppose* your bill—they're liable to identify *me* with the scapegoat."

"Elmer Landers seems to be willing to take that chance."

"Oh, come now, Saul, don't be disingenuous. You know as well as I do that Elmer's position is quite different from mine—or yours, for that matter. He's a senator. He has to go back to his constituents only every six years, not every other year as we do. In six years you can do a lot of things that the voters will forget about. Whose memory could be shorter than a voter's? Furthermore, Elmer is a tradition in Idaho—he's more than a tradition, he's a natural phenomenon, he's the state's biggest claim to fame next to the potato. No matter *what* he does, the average Idahoan would no more vote against Elmer Landers than he'd vote against God or motherhood or the Grand Canyon. But it's not quite the same in *my* district. The voters are watching me like hawks, *waiting* for me to make a mistake. Do you want to see me lose my seat next year?"

"Of course not. But meanwhile, the passengers on the *Franz Joseph*—"

"There are going to be a lot of refugees after this bunch. If I lose my seat in Congress, it'll probably be taken by some died-in-the-wool reactionary, and what kind of immigration policy do you think *he'll* vote for? It may be necessary to sacrifice those thousand people for the sake of the tens of thousands who come after them."

"This isn't a problem in arithmetic," Lascoff burst out. "Those thousand people are real. You can't be sure about the future, but you *can* be sure what will happen to them if you don't try to help—"

"Saul, Saul, who's ever sure of *anything* in this world? You make your decisions according to your evaluation of the evidence, and you hope for the best." McCabe smiled sadly and spread his hands—the identical gesture, Morrie realized, that Harrison Bliss had used earlier today. "I'm sorry, Saul—sorry, gentlemen—but that's how it is."

McCabe rose to his feet and put a bill on the table. "You must let me pay for the drinks—no, no, I insist." He gave them a friendly smile, and then he walked away.

*   *   *

217

They weren't scheduled to leave Washington until the following afternoon. Lascoff wouldn't give up hope. He and Richard Glenn had some ideas about people to see, strings to pull. Even as they outlined these ideas, Morrie could tell they didn't have much faith in them. But to give themselves the illusion of leaving no stone unturned they were determined to spend another morning of frantic running around.

Morrie asked if he could be excused for the morning. He was grateful to Dan for giving his permission. The truth was that Morrie wanted to be by himself for a few hours—no congressmen, lobbyists, civil servants, or AJDA agents to keep him from sorting out his thoughts.

He decided to see something of Washington. The last time he had been here he had been ten years old, and his father's rich brother, Uncle Hyman, had treated him and his cousin Marvin to a weekend trip. What he mostly remembered about that weekend was Marvin's ingenious efforts to keep from doing the things that Uncle Hyman had wanted them to do. But now, twenty years later, Morrie felt in the mood to be a tourist.

So he got up early and visited all the places that tourists always visit. He craned his neck at the base of the Washington Monument. He peered at the Declaration of Independence under glass. He sat with a group of Kansas matrons and Maryland Boy Scouts in the Senate gallery (no session was on, so they had the handsome, high-ceilinged chamber to themselves) and dutifully gasped when the tour guide told them the height, circumference, and total cost of the rotunda. He trudged along the wide, treelined avenues, staring at vistas which he had seen a hundred times in movies and history books. And all the time his mind was somewhere else.

At first he could do nothing but chew on his anger and his frustration. Anti-Semites, he kept telling himself. That's all they were, the whole crowd of them! Harrison Bliss with his prissy, cold-blooded humility—Senator Landers with his gruffness and bluffness, and those "ain'ts" that came and went at his convenience—Congressman McCabe full of sympathy and liberal platitudes, but without batting an eye he was willing to send a thousand Jews to the concentration camp.

Then Morrie turned his anger inward, turned it on Dan and Lascoff and Al, and on himself, too. What were they *doing* about the anti-Semites, anyway? Trotting from one to the other, begging for crumbs, smiling and saying thank you for every kick in the face! And when the chips were down, when they had a chance to do something more than grovel—

Over and over in his head Morrie carried on the argument he had had in Dan's hotel room last night. He had paced up and down while he talked, he had accompanied his words with lots of wide excited gestures, even though his mother *had* told him all through his boyhood not to talk with his hands. The suggestion he had made was obvious enough— you'd think it *couldn't* be turned down. The people on the *Franz Joseph* weren't going to be helped by AJDA's present strategy. Appeals to the consciences of influential gentiles weren't going to work. Nobody pays attention to the weak and powerless in this world. Victims don't get justice just by being victims. The Bible said it a long time ago—"To him who hath shall be given. From him who hath not shall be taken away." So what AJDA needed, Morrie had said, was some leverage to exert for these refugees, some pressure to use on their behalf. And there was one pressure they hadn't tried yet—the electorate. The voice of the people—ordinary people who hadn't become so callous or cautious with the exercise of power that they had lost all their decent human feelings.

In other words, the time had come for AJDA to release the *Franz Joseph* story to the newspapers. It was pointless to keep it under wraps any longer. If the facts could be splashed over front pages around the country, with plenty of horrendous details about innocent children and helpless old people huddling on deck, the effect might be tremendous. Clergymen would preach sermons about it, newspapers would be swamped with indignant letters, voters would send telegrams to their congressmen, mass meetings would be organized, consciences all over the country would be aroused—and in the end Harrison Bliss' superiors (with an eye on the 1940 national elections) might be forced to take time off from their golf and countermand his directive. Anyway, it was worth a try, wasn't it? What alternative did they have?

When Morrie got to the end of this speech, there had been a long silence, then a few throat-clearings, and then everybody had quietly jumped on him. Dan had explained that any such action as Morrie recommended would have to be approved by the AJDA board and that the board would be reluctant to reverse the organization's traditional policy of working behind the scenes, creating a minimum of fuss. Lascoff had said that in his opinion Morrie's plan would boomerang disastrously; a hue and cry started by a Jewish organization could only stir up latent feelings of anti-Semitism in a lot of people, which God knows wasn't what the Jews needed at a time like this.

Then Morrie had turned hopefully to Al—and Al had given a sigh that was almost a groan. "This is the real world, Morrie. What you're saying might make sense in some ideal world that could come into existence someday—but today, in the middle of July, 1939, in the United States of America, the last thing you'll get any Jew to do is make a nuisance of himself."

And a little later came the worst part of all, the part that Morrie had been wincing at ever since. He had given in. He had shaken his head and said, "I don't know, I wish I could be sure . . ." But in his heart he had known why he was letting himself be convinced. Because he was glad of the excuse to stop fighting, because he was infected by their fears.

So what's the use of cursing the anti-Semites? he asked himself. What's the use of inveighing against the enemy? *Everybody* is the enemy. Everybody in the world is corrupt or weak or callous—there's no hope at all for the whole filthy human race.

But now, late in the morning, he wasn't so sure any more. He was on Pennsylvania Avenue, standing by the high iron gates outside the White House lawn. The line of people to go inside stretched for blocks—he decided to content himself with staring at that graceful, gleaming mansion from a distance. It was nothing like its pictures, he thought. It was smaller, not nearly so imposing—you couldn't really hear the stirring Beethoven-like music that was always played in the background when the newsreels showed it. What it lost in majesty, though, it made up in warmth, in a kind of quiet humanity—and yes, in spite of the guards and the gates and the lines of people, in a curious feeling of accessibility. This was a house for people, not statues, to live in. Inside it, if you could ever get there, were simple, compassionate, decent human beings.

And slowly Morrie realized how unjust he had been to Dan and Al and the congressman, to his fellow Jews, to his fellow Americans. Ordinary people want to live their lives in peace and quiet. It goes against their nature to shout, make de-

220

mands, shake their fists. They assume that other men, even their leaders, are like themselves—and can be trusted to act decently and compassionately, too. And in the long run is this assumption really wrong?

Morrie wondered how he ever could have given in to such shallow cynicism, such hysterical despair. His own father, without the benefit of an education, had been a lot smarter than he. So had those hundreds of thousands of people like his father, Jews from the ghettos of East Europe, who had poured into America, who had fallen in love with it at first sight. Even *before* first sight—as Papa had said to him once, "We were good Americans before we got off the boat." Had America changed since then? It was still the land of the free, the home of the brave, wasn't it? Madness to think that America was nothing but isolationist senators, spineless liberals, coldhearted bureaucrats.

The flag was flying over the White House. Morrie watched it flapping in a sudden gust of wind. He remembered how he had loved that flag when he was a small boy, with what solemn, sacred feelings he had placed his hand on his heart and repeated the pledge of allegiance at morning assembly in P.S. 69. He remembered how when he was eleven years old he had saved money for a whole summer from working at Mr. Rabinowitz' soda fountain so that he could buy his parents a present for their anniversary—and the present he had chosen was a big American flag.

How naïve, how positively corny those feelings had come to seem through the years—especially when he went to college, when he started talking politics with his friends, signing petitions against the lynchings down South, cheering from the balcony at the end of *Waiting for Lefty*. It was easy, as the evidence of injustice and corruption and exploitation piled up, to believe that America was nothing else but these things, easy to sneer at that old, absurd, impossible legend. And yet as he watched the flag now, flying from the roof of that dream of a house . . .

The legend was true. He almost despised himself for believing it, but he *did* believe it. The real America was this flag, this house, and—yes, he was sure of it—the man who lived in this house. He was handsome, kindly, wise, powerful, slightly crippled, rather theatrical—and *he* could save the lives of those thousand people.

Against all logic Morrie felt much better for the rest of the morning. He had a plan now—vague and undeveloped, he certainly wouldn't mention it to his knowledgeable, practical colleagues. His plan was to get to F.D.R. Somehow he would talk to the President, present the case for the passengers—not through intermediaries but directly, face to face. Franklin D. Roosevelt, the President of the United States, the only President Morrie had ever voted for, the man his father used to mention in his prayers every Friday night—*he* wouldn't let those people down.

But when Morrie got back to the hotel at lunchtime, he discovered that his plan would have to wait for a while. Dan and Al were already involved in a new set of arrangements. "How would you like to go to Paris?" Al said to him.

EIGHT

Aaron told himself to be strong, and then he turned away from the porthole.

But what did that mean, being strong? What did it mean right now, at this moment? It meant, he supposed, getting through the day in spite of the fact that the ship was still in limbo, that New York still wasn't in sight. Routine details had to be attended to. Panic had to be kept from showing. And the first step was the most important. If the day could be forced to begin like any other— Clearly what a strong man had to do right now was brush his teeth.

He wondered, as he stood before the mirror in the little washroom, whether people in prisons and concentration camps begin their days by brushing their teeth. How hopeless, how bleak must a man's condition be before he is ready to relinquish this elementary hold on life?

A little later, as he was putting on his pants, there was a knock on the cabin door. One of the ship's messengers, a boy of sixteen, brought a message from the bridge: Mr. Peyser was wanted in the wireless room at once, somebody wished to speak to him over the ship's radio.

Aaron thanked the boy and hurried to finish dressing. He knew who this had to be, of course.

"Do you think it's the American, Aaron?"

Sophie was talking to him from the lower bunk. He had supposed she was still asleep; lately she had been having insomnia, and she usually made up for it by sleeping longer in the mornings.

"It's probably him," Aaron said.

Sophie blinked and rubbed her eyes. "He wouldn't be calling so early, would he, unless the news was good?"

Her eyes were red, her face was white and splotchy. Her hair looked stringy and old, standing up all over her head except for a stray lock that had fallen across an eyebrow.

"Aaron, what *do* you think?"

"I'm sure you're right," he said. "If the news was bad, he'd wait till later. He'd at least let us enjoy our breakfast."

He gave her a kiss and left the cabin quickly so she couldn't get too close a look at his face.

As he passed the cabin next to his, its door opened, and David looked out. Last night came back to Aaron—the shame and anger on the boy's face—and he just stopped himself from blurting out an apology. He mustn't give the boy any reason to believe that he regretted what he did last night. He *didn't* regret it. He was sure he had done the right thing. "Good morning, David. You're up early."

"Good morning, Papa. I didn't sleep very well."

His eyes were lowered. He still feels the humiliation, Aaron thought. He still can't forgive me. All right, he'll just have to live with that. And I'll have to live with it, too.

He left David and made his way up to the wireless room on the bridge. It was a route he knew pretty well by now. The wireless operator greeted him with a noncommittal nod. Usually the man was friendly, but Muller was in the room today, standing stiffly near the door.

"Please make your conversation brief," Muller said. "We're expecting several important communications from Berlin."

What Aaron felt like saying was, "It's lunchtime right now in Berlin. Even the Führer stops occasionally to eat—just like a human being." He restrained himself, though. It would be foolish to make provocative statements, to give Muller ammunition against him. He was sure that Muller never missed a chance to tell the captain how dangerous he was— and who could say how long the captain would resist this pressure? All right, everything so far indicated that he had sympathy for his passengers—but why wouldn't he show himself, explain himself? Inexplicable behavior filled Aaron with distrust. The captain was generous and humane today, but couldn't he easily turn malignant tomorrow?

Muller stalked out of the radio room, and a few minutes later Aaron was listening to Morris Feldman's voice. Metallic, empty of personality, an artificial sound manufactured by a machine. Aaron knew nothing about Morris Feldman—if he was married, if he had children, how old he was. Yet he had never allowed himself to ask any personal questions. He was unfamiliar with American ways; he couldn't be sure that attempts at further intimacy might not be regarded as a breach of manners. For his own sake, for the sake of his fellow passengers, he couldn't take the risk of offending this man. Who else cared if they lived or died?

"How are you, Mr. Peyser? Are you and your family well? The sailing from Cuba wasn't too unpleasant, I hope."

As he listened to these innocuous words and made his innocuous replies, Aaron realized that the news was going to be bad.

There was a pause, and then it came. "I'm sorry about this, Mr. Peyser. I wish I didn't have to tell you—" And he spoke of his trip to Washington, D.C., of his talks with important men, of the different methods of persuasion his organization had attempted.

And Aaron stopped following his words. They became a buzzing in his ears. What would happen to them now? Where on God's earth could they go? And David—Peter Einhorn— those other boys. He shouldn't have interfered with them last night; he shouldn't have robbed them of their chance. He was their murderer now. . . .

"Mr. Peyser, did you hear me?"

"Oh—excuse me, Mr. Feldman. Your voice faded, I missed the last words."

"I said the situation *isn't* hopeless. There's still hope. Do you understand me?"

"Oh yes—still hope. Mr. Feldman, what is this hope?"

"The countries of Europe. France, Belgium, the Netherlands, England—even Russia—the countries that aren't under Fascist domination. There's every reason to hope that some of them will take you in. At least until the United States is ready for you. If each one takes in a few hundred of you— Those countries are much closer to the problem than we are. There's an ignorance, a complacency here—Hitler and the Nazis are so far away. But the European democracies have Hitler on their doorstep, they've seen refugees coming across their borders for years, they're more likely to sympathize with you—"

"Or perhaps," Aaron said, "they are tired and impatient of refugees by now. As their own danger grows closer, they feel less able to care about somebody else's danger."

"No, I'm sure you're wrong about that, Mr. Peyser. God knows you've got every reason to feel pessimistic, but you honestly don't have to."

Even through the inhuman wireless machine it was impossible to miss the concern, the genuine pain in Morris Feld-man's voice. Aaron gave a little sigh. He had no right to inflict his despair on Morris Feldman. This man, after all, had done his best to help them. "I'm sorry. If you say there is hope, I believe you."

"Let me tell you what we're doing, then. We've started working on this already." Then Morris Feldman spoke at length of the influential contacts that his organization had in Europe, of a meeting which these influential people were arranging in Paris with representatives of many European nations, of the important results which were sure to follow.

"One thing we're a bit concerned about, though, Mr. Peyser. Some time this morning our Immigration Bureau will notify your captain officially that you won't be allowed to dock. I don't know what he'll do when he hears this, but we're hoping you can persuade him to take a certain course of action."

"What do you want him to do?"

"He mustn't head straight back to Germany. We have high hopes for this European conference, but it *will* take time. It would be a tragedy if something—irrevocable were done before the various countries announced their decisions."

"How much time will be required?"

"A week—two weeks, maybe. We have to schedule this conference, then the representatives have to report back to their governments—"

"I will present my request to the captain."

"That's not all, though. While the conference is on, it would be a good idea if I could talk to you from time to time—to get information from you about individual passengers, their backgrounds and families, how many might have connections in particular countries. But if you're too far away from where I am, direct radio contact won't be possible. So we're hoping you can persuade your captain to take the ship as close as possible to the French coast—"

"I will do what I can."

"Good—fine. Well, I'll be in touch with you again very soon. From Paris probably—"

The conversation was at an end, yet as usual Morris Feld-man was having trouble cutting himself off—as if he feared in his heart that they would never be able to talk to each other again. That's the fear *I* should be feeling, Aaron thought. *I* should be the one who can't let go of the lifeline.

"Good-bye, Mr. Feldman. Thank you for everything you have done."

"I wish to God I *had*—"

"Good-bye," Aaron said and signalled the wireless operator to break the connection.

He went down to the writing room two decks below. It was deserted at this early hour. He filled a sheet of paper with a summary of Morris Feldman's news and a statement of the two favors he had to ask. Then he sealed the paper in an envelope and climbed two flights again to Muller's office. He knocked without hesitation. A week ago he would have hesitated even if he had been sent for.

The familiar voice, clipped, no emotion in it, told him to come in.

"I hope I'm not intruding," Aaron said, sitting down, as he was now in the habit of doing, because he knew he wouldn't be asked. He held out his sealed envelope. "I have some requests for the captain. I'd appreciate it if you gave him this as soon as possible."

Muller scowled down at the envelope. Aaron knew how little he liked the idea of anything being kept from him. Yet his orders stated that Aaron's requests were to be passed on directly, and he would obey his orders, he wouldn't open the envelope on the way to the captain's office. With all his peculiarities, the captain ran a disciplined ship.

Muller stood up. "Wait here for an answer."

When Muller had gone, the thought of David and those other boys rushed in on Aaron again. But what was the use of feeling guilty for what he *should* have done? His mistake had been an honest one, and now there was only one way to make up for it. Somehow he must get this ship to a safe port; somehow he must save these people in the end. If the outside world couldn't do it, if Morris Feldman's conference in Paris couldn't do it—then *he* must be the one to do it.

He? It was fantastic. What could he do all by himself? Capture the captain and take over the ship? He was being as childish and romantic as Peter Einhorn and his friends.

Muller returned. "The captain showed me your note," he said, not without a trace of satisfaction in his voice. "His answer to both your requests is affirmative. His orders, when he left Germany, were to return to Hamburg after disembarking his passengers. No port of disembarkation was specified, and no time limit was mentioned—therefore, until he receives new orders to the contrary, he sees no reason why the ship can't proceed in a westerly direction and drop anchor in international waters off the northwestern coast of France."

Aaron could feel relief flowing over him, but he was careful not to show it to Muller. "I mentioned in my note that we would need two weeks—"

"The captain feels confident that no new orders will come from Hamburg within the next two weeks. He is willing to put that confidence in the form of a promise."

Muller paused, then his voice took on greater intensity. "Let me add something on my own, however. For your information, Mr. Peyser, the captain isn't the only one aboard this ship who's capable of contacting Hamburg. If his manner of dealing with this situation should appear to conflict with the best interests of the Reich, others can use a radio, too."

"You mean you'd go over his head—"

"He's my captain. I'm obliged to submit to his authority. But there are persons back home to whose authority *he* is obliged to submit, and if those persons felt it necessary to countermand his orders—"

"Mr. Muller, two weeks is a very short time. The interests of the Reich won't be damaged by allowing a few wretched people—"

"What's this, Mr. Peyser? Are you pleading with me?"

Aaron saw the smile on Muller's face, and he felt his cheeks reddening. After a moment he stood up. "Thank you for giving the captain my message. The next time you see him, please tell him that I'm relying on him to keep his promise." Aaron turned and started to the door.

"One moment, Mr. Peyser." Muller's voice brought Aaron to a stop. "This news you just received—the captain wishes to know if you've considered the effect it will have on your fellow passengers."

Aaron frowned. "People will be upset, of course—"

"The captain asks you to face the possibility that your news will move many people to a state of depression, even to despair. And in some cases this may take the form of attempts at self-destruction. The captain is anxious that this should not happen aboard his ship."

"Of course it mustn't happen. But—if a man has made up his mind—"

"The captain suggests that the most obvious form of suicide aboard a ship can be prevented. People can be kept from throwing themselves overboard. Extra patrols can be placed on deck, especially after dark. The captain wishes you to understand, however, that the crew is in no position to undertake this by themselves. They all have essential duties during the day, and they all stand night watch twice a week. They cannot be required to give up any more of their time. It will be necessary, therefore, for the passengers themselves to handle most of the precautions. The captain wants to know if you can find a dozen or so men who would volunteer for this duty."

"Yes, I'm sure I could."

"He wishes to point out that you'll have to choose them very carefully. To minimize the chance that one of *them* might succumb to a suicidal impulse."

"Yes—yes, I see that. I think I know who can help me. All right, I'll make the arrangements."

"Furthermore," Muller said, "the captain realizes that you may need the rest of the day to organize this patrol and that until this is done, your news from New York had better be kept from the other passengers. The captain has instructed the radio operator and myself to say nothing until you have organized your patrol and made your announcement—at dinner tonight. And to further ensure that no premature rumors will spread, he has decided that the ship will not weigh anchor and start out to sea until after dinner. That completes the captain's instructions."

Muller stood up, his usual sign that the interview was over, but Aaron didn't turn away from him. "The captain's been so kind to us. I'd like to thank him personally."

"If the captain wishes to see you, he will so instruct me."

"Why *won't* he see me? Why does he always keep himself hidden from his passengers?"

"He doesn't *always* do anything of the sort. You have no reason to assume that this voyage is typical of any other voyage. So far he has chosen not to mingle among you. This doesn't mean that he couldn't send for you tomorrow, or appear in the dining room at dinner tonight. Nobody on this ship is capable of understanding exactly what goes on in the captain's mind. His moods are unpredictable. Now I'm extremely busy. If you'll shut the door after you—"

By the time Aaron got down to the main lounge, the ship

had come alive. Lots of people were up and about. Many were heading down to the dining room. Aaron followed them and found his whole family at the table waiting to hear about his talk with Morris Feldman. He told them calmly that there was no news; Morris Feldman had simply wanted to reassure him that no adverse decision had yet been made. And then, though he felt like eating nothing at all, Aaron ordered a large breakfast. Nobody could suspect a man with an appetite of having just heard bad news.

After breakfast Aaron found Carl Bender and led him up on deck to a spot as far forward as they could go, where they would be out of earshot of other people. Here they stood at the railing, gazing down at the bright blue water sparkling in the sun—holiday water if Aaron had ever seen any—and he told Carl the news.

As always, he had to admire Carl's extraordinary self-control. A small sigh came out of him, and that was all. No hint that what he had just heard might prove to be his own death sentence. He agreed to give his professional psychiatric advice about choosing the members of the suicide patrol and asked to think the matter over until after lunch. They shook hands, and Carl walked back toward the lounge.

Aaron stayed where he was, looking after him. What wailing and weeping there would have been, he thought, if he had just played this scene with someone in his own family or with any of the friends he had made in the course of his life. Not long ago *he* would have been wailing and weeping, too. But now he was quite steady, quite clear in his head. He was even able to enjoy the beautiful weather. . . .

"So what is it? Let's have the truth!"

Aaron saw his father-in-law standing next to him. The old man was paler than usual, and his lips were twitching slightly.

"I heard what you said to that Bender, I followed the two of you from the dining room because all through breakfast I had my suspicions that something wasn't kosher. So tell me the truth, please!"

"If you heard us for yourself—"

Already, as he said these words, Aaron could feel his stomach beginning to ache again. He had felt this way the first time he ever met old Schwarzkopf—that terrible night when Sophie made him come for dinner and he had walked into the living room and started across the long Oriental

230

rug toward the fat man in evening clothes who stood with his back to the fireplace rocking gently on his heels. Like some film in which the poor wretch who's been sentenced to death has to walk across the courtyard where the hangman is waiting. More than twenty years ago that was, and still he couldn't keep that sick feeling from clutching his stomach.

"I heard you, but I didn't believe my ears," the old man was saying. "The Americans won't take us in? They're throwing us out like everyone else? *This* is what you found out this morning! You were lying to us at breakfast!"

"Please—everybody'll hear you if you don't keep your voice down—"

"You're telling *me* to keep my voice down? You're giving *me* orders? Listen to me—you're not fooling me with this big-shot act you've been putting on lately. I knew you from when you were a skinny, nearsighted little nobody without a penny to your name."

"It's just that the rest of the passengers mustn't find out—"

"Who says they mustn't find out? That's one of the brilliant decisions you made in your new executive capacity? In my opinion *everybody* ought to know what's going on so we can get together and *do* something. Raise money maybe, make an offer to those American officials—"

"It's no use trying to bribe them—"

"How do you know *what's* any use if you don't even try? That's the whole trouble so far; this matter has been in the hands of good-for-nothing dreamers. It's time some hard-headed businessmen who know something about the world took over the arrangements. At lunch today I'm going to tell everybody the truth, and then we'll have a vote on the question, we'll decide who should be running things on this ship!"

"You can't do that—don't you see what a panic there'd be? Until we're organized—"

"*You* organized? You couldn't organize a ladies' tea party! I'm telling everybody the truth—because this is no joke anymore, we'll be sent back to Germany if somebody doesn't do something! It's my life you're playing around with—it's my *life*—"

The old man started coughing. His face turned red, and he coughed and choked and spluttered, waving his fists in the air. And for a moment Aaron just stared at him, sick, horrified, knowing that it was all slipping out of his grasp, the worst was going to happen, and there was no way he could stop it. Knowing this and also wondering, way down deep, if he really *wanted* to stop it. What a relief it would be to get rid of the whole awful burden in one swoop—to let the old man take care of things—

And then suddenly he noticed that old Schwarzkopf had a black smudge on his left cheek. In waving his arms and thrashing around, he must have rubbed his hand against something sooty, and then he must have rubbed his cheek. All his life Bruno Schwarzkopf had prided himself on his elegant appearance, on being as well groomed as a show horse. A smudge on his cheek was worse than a mud bath on anyone else; it made him look like a grubby child.

And the next moment Aaron began to laugh. Not much of a laugh—soft and quick, more a sound of relief than of merriment. But it cleared his head, it drove away the helplessness and the horror, and the pain in his stomach went away, too. When he spoke he was able to bring out the words calmly, even with a kind of relish. "You won't say a word about this to anybody. At lunchtime you'll keep your mouth shut. For once in your life you'll think of somebody besides yourself."

"What—what—" The old man's mouth was working, and his eyes looked as if they were about to pop out of their sockets.

"You'll keep quiet for three reasons," Aaron said. "First, because if you open your mouth and somebody gets hurt, if somebody kills himself, maybe, I'll personally make sure that everyone on this ship knows who's responsible; whenever anyone looks at you, you'll see in their eyes that they're accusing you of murder. Second, you'll keep quiet because I'm telling you to, and as you just pointed out yourself, *I'm* running things now. I listened to you once too often in the past. If I hadn't listened to you we wouldn't be here now, we'd all be safe in America. But *you* gave orders, and I listened— Well, this time I don't make the same mistake. You're a stupid old man, and your days of giving orders are over. Third, you'll keep quiet because—because—"

Aaron hadn't really thought of a third reason. He had come out with the number three for rhetorical purposes, because it sounded better than two." But he hesitated only a split second now, and then the third reason came into his head. "—because you wouldn't want your wife and your daughter and your card-playing friends to find out what a reckless, irresponsible four-flusher you are—an idiot who was willing to risk everyone's life and the future of this whole voyage so that you could smuggle a hundred marks in your hat. Oh yes, I know all about that, and the story becomes public property if you don't keep your mouth shut at lunchtime."

The old man was gasping for air, but no sound was coming out of him. A natural reaction, Aaron thought. Nothing could be more shocking to a man like Schwarzkopf than the spectacle of a worm turning.

Aaron's instinct told him that having won his victory, he now ought to leave the field. "I'm sorry I had to tell you these things," he said. "You behave yourself at lunch, and we'll never talk about this again."

He gave the old man a pat on his shoulder—the encouraging pat that an elder will give to a confused and tearful younger—and he stepped around him and walked briskly down the deck.

He reached the main lounge a few minutes later. Then he realized how hard he was breathing. He felt as if he had just been running twenty laps around the deck. He lowered himself into a chair to catch his breath, to shake the ringing out of his ears. But his stomach wasn't hurting. That was the big thing. After what he had just done, he didn't see how he could ever be plagued by stomachaches again.

You ought to be ashamed of yourself, he thought. A nice person doesn't talk to *anyone* like that. Maybe you're finally learning the truth about yourself after all these years. Maybe you're not a nice person and never have been. Maybe you were meant to be a bastard all along.

This thought, instead of upsetting him, made him laugh. So this, he told himself, is what the feeling of power is like. Yes, he could understand why people yearned for it so desperately. It was really a very *pleasant* feeling. So much pleasanter than its opposite, the feeling of helplessness.

No more helplessness for me, he told himself. I can do things now. I can do *anything* now. Yes, I can even get us off this ship. . . .

* * *

Stupid old man? thought Schwarzkopf. So that's the way it is. Stupid old man—after all I did for him and his no-good family. After I picked him up from the gutter and gave him my daughter's hand in marriage. My beautiful little Sophie, my only child, the sweetest thing in my life—and I threw her into the arms of that jellyfish—and this is how he pays me back. Stupid old man! And now look at him, shoveling food into his mouth, looking so cool and collected. If these poor dopes knew what he was hiding from them they'd tear him to pieces, they'd throw him overboard. My God, I've got half a mind—

No, I wouldn't do it, Schwarzkopf decided. I wouldn't play into his hands. People like him, little worms who suddenly get big heads, the worst thing you can do is treat them as if they were important to you.

"Bruno, that's your fifth potato pancake," Emma said. "You know what the doctor said about your weight."

"When I want to eat something, I'll eat it," Schwarzkopf said. "People don't give me orders. Especially you. And by the way, since we're talking about weight, who is it put on five pounds already on this ship?" He grunted and took three more potato pancakes from the platter in the center of the table.

"How long do you think it'll be before the Americans decide about us, Mr. Peyser?" It was that Buberman girl, the newlywed who sat at their table. She had a worried look on her face, and in her lap she was holding tight to her husband's hand. The amount of hand-holding that pair did!

"What Lisa means," said her husband, "if the Americans take too long to make a decision, isn't it possible the captain will get orders from Germany—" His mouth was trembling, like a baby on the verge of tears. He looked as if he was about twelve years old, and the measly little mustache he was trying to grow didn't help a bit. When *I* got married, Schwarzkopf thought, I already was working six years in my father's store—and if the truth were told, I was practically running things all by myself. And even though I was only twenty-four, people took me for ten years older.

"Don't worry," Aaron said. "I'm sure the Americans will make their decision very soon—long before the captain gets any orders."

With an absolutely straight face he said this. A liar, a

no-good—didn't I know it the first time I ever set eyes on him?

To this day Schwarzkopf could remember every detail of that first meeting. It was in the big drawing room of the old house on Petersplatz, the big house that they had had to move out of a few years ago. It was seven o'clock at night, and the nobody was coming for dinner—after all the talking Sophie did about him and all the time she spent at the university with him, Schwarzkopf had finally insisted on meeting him. And deliberately he had told Emma to make it a fancy formal affair—to show the nobody right from the start what kind of people he was dealing with and also to find out what kind of stuff he was made of, if he could stand up to the pressure. I've got my back to the fireplace, Schwarzkopf remembered, and the door opens way off across the room, and this fellow comes walking toward me—and right away I know what Sophie has picked for herself. Looking this way and that as if he's expecting somebody to jump out at him and tugging at his collar and his cuffs so it's obvious that evening clothes are about as natural to him as a suit of armor. And *this* is what wants to take my daughter away from me, to marry into my family?

It was later that night, he remembered, that the fight took place, up in Sophie's room. That was his big mistake, he realized later. Never have a showdown with a woman on her own ground—with her bed right there so she can throw herself on it and sob into the pillow; with little handkerchiefs all over the place for her to clutch at, and all those lacy frilly feminine-type decorations to remind you how weak and fragile she is, and her mother screaming in the corner, as if the house were falling down. Screaming women—a man has to give in to them, or they'll drive him crazy.

Lunch was over. Schwarzkopf excused himself and left the table, ignoring the questions that Emma was calling after him. Stupid old man, am I? Wait till that no-good sees what the stupid old man is still able to pull off. Yes, I've waited long enough, Schwarzkopf was thinking as he climbed the stairs. The time had come to tackle Stieffel, to ask him straight out for that business loan once they got to New York. A smart man softens up the prospect before he tries to make the sale—but he also knows that you can't keep on softening forever. A moment comes when you have to take your courage in your hands and make your move. And Schwarzkopf's instinct told him that *this* was the moment—his famous instinct which had never once let him down after forty-five years in the business world.

He tried to figure out where Stieffel could be. Usually he left lunch early without his dessert and took his walk on deck, three or four times around, to help the food settle and firm up his waistline. Very careful about his health, Stieffel was—practically a hypochondriac. I'll find him out on deck, Schwarzkopf thought, and I'll settle this business once and for all.

Halfway across the lounge he stopped. He stared around, like a man who suddenly realizes that he's lost his way. What the hell am I doing? he asked himself. *What* business am I going to settle? He'll give me a loan so I can set myself up in New York? Who's going to New York? Not me. Not Stieffel. Nobody on this ship is going to New York. We're all going back where we came from. The bums in uniform with the swastikas on their arms will be waiting for us on the dock.

Schwarzkopf sank into the nearest chair. He lifted his fist to his cheek, ground it into his cheek while he shook his head back and forth. A crazy thing for him to do. It was what his mother used to do whenever she wanted to say how hopeless everything was. His poor mother—an ignorant village woman, a postman's daughter right up to the end, even after he was able to set her up in a beautiful apartment and give her a fur coat to wear.

We're finished, the family is finished, he told himself, pressing his fist into his cheek. And it's my fault, just like *he* said. I gave the orders, I made the decision. . . .

Slowly Schwarzkopf became aware of the people sitting near him, an old lady and a boy of fourteen or so. They were staring at him in a funny way, as if he were a freak.

He stood up and strode out of the lounge. On deck he went to the railing and began to breathe in the salty air. He could feel his face tingling. What's the matter with you, Schwarzkopf? My God, since when are you a man to blame yourself for things? Some people are whiners, and some people are doers. All your life you've been a doer, and you damn well aren't going to stop now.

Stieffel wasn't out on deck, so Schwarzkopf returned to the lounge. At last, in the small writing room, he saw him. Stieffel was alone—good. He was sitting on a sofa reading a book.

When he wasn't playing bridge or walking around the deck, Stieffel always had his nose in a book. An educated man, a cultured type. He had inherited his money, of course.

Schwarzkopf threw back his shoulders, opened the door of the writing room, and stepped inside. . . .

The private detective was just beginning to question the nightclub singer when the door of the writing room opened and old Schwarzkopf came stamping in. Loud and overbearing, as usual—an odious and familiar type. Arthur Stieffel shut the book he was reading, but he kept his finger between the pages. He didn't want to lose his place. Hopefully this unwelcome intrusion would be over soon, and he would be able to get back to reality.

"So here you are, Stieffel. I've been looking for you."

"Well, you found me," Stieffel said, smiling politely despite his feelings. His good manners, he sometimes thought, were the deepest part of his nature. Long after everything else had gone they would remain.

"There's a matter I'd like to discuss with you. A certain idea I've got for when we get to New York." Schwarzkopf pulled up a chair, far too close for Stieffel's comfort. "You're a businessman, Stieffel, and I'm a businessman—and New York is a city where lots of business gets done. So I've been thinking, maybe you and I can do some business together."

The man's settling in for the afternoon, Stieffel thought. And all the time the private detective doesn't know that the nightclub singer's gangster boyfriend is hiding in the closet. "What kind of business?" Stieffel said.

"A big brokerage firm like Stieffel, Weissberger, and Harris, a big Wall Street outfit that's always making investments in new enterprises—why shouldn't I throw an opportunity your way. And why shouldn't you throw an opportunity my way? Since we're both in the same boat—that's a joke!—why shouldn't we scratch each other's back?"

"I'm not sure I understand what you're suggesting."

"What I'm suggesting is a loan—no, more like a merger. In New York there's still plenty of room for a first-rate retail house. Like Schwarzkopf's in Berlin—the Schwarzkopf quality and stylishness applied to American conditions. There's a definite need for something like that, all my connections in New York have told me so. A small operation at first, naturally—maybe just a couple of floors—but with possibilities for growth. Now you have to admit, that's just the kind of operation I could turn into a big success. I mean, it isn't as if I'm an unknown quantity. Thirty years in the business, and nobody can say I haven't proven myself."

"No doubt of it, Schwarzkopf. You've more than proven yourself."

"But the point is, a deal like this needs capital. If it doesn't start off on a solid foundation, if it can't keep going for a year or two without worrying about profits—well, the point is, capital is exactly what I'm short of at the moment. Experience, connections, prestige, all these things I've got, and in abundance, if I say so myself, but capital is the one thing—so what I'm getting at, if you were willing to make a preliminary loan at maybe eight percent, or whatever the going rate is in America, I'm certainly not going to quibble over details—"

"Wait, Schwarzkopf, wait. It's true that my ex-wife's charming relatives generously arranged it so that I could leave Germany with more than the legal allowance. I don't know how you found out about that, but I'm certainly not going to deny it. However, I assure you that I'm carrying just about enough to keep me afloat in New York for a few months—not nearly enough to give you the kind of money you'll need."

"Well, not you personally. Stieffel, Weissberger, and Harris—on Wall Street—"

"But the Stieffel in that firm isn't me. It's my brother Anton."

"Sure, absolutely, I knew that already. But it's a well-known fact, when he came to America and started the firm, it was your personal financing—"

The situation was amusing, Stieffel thought. Schwarzkopf, the great tycoon, trying to borrow money from *him*. It was really quite a good joke. "Believe me, Schwarzkopf, my brother has paid me back for that investment many times over."

"I'm not surprised to hear it, not at all. But your continuing interest in the firm—"

"Continuing—?"

Yes, the joke was good, Stieffel thought, but it *could* be so much better. Suppose he told poor old Schwarzkopf the whole truth? It would be cruel, of course, a cruel trick. And there would be a certain loss of dignity, too. To discuss one's private affairs with a stranger, and such a crude, repulsive stranger, at that—there was a time when Stieffel couldn't possibly have considered such a thing. But that time was long, long ago, wasn't it? Pre-Hitler. Pre-Vera. Positively prehistoric. And good jokes had become so scarce these days. "My dear fellow," Stieffel said, "don't you know who I am?"

"You're Arthur Stieffel—Stieffel and Bauer—"

"I *used* to be Arthur Stieffel. Today I'm the pariah, the outcast. Today my name is Cain, and I've got the mark on me—the man who killed his brother."

"But your brother is alive in New York."

"How literal-minded you are. Yes, my brother is in New York, but how alive does that make him from *my* point of view? Finance a business deal for me? I rather doubt if he'll even let me inside his office. If he could keep me out of the same city as himself— Failing that, he'll do the next best thing. He'll make sure that he never has to set eyes on me as long as he lives."

"But you're on the United States quota. That means he had to vouch for you, sign your papers—"

"And so he did. Feeling at every moment, I'm sure, as if the pen were burning his fingers. But that ordeal, at least, was endured at a distance. Yes, he vouched for me, he's rented a room for me, and every week there'll be a check for me—one hundred dollars, to cover my expenses for the first year—and after that—'

Schwarzkopf's face was quite pale and puffy now. He was beginning to look a bit sick. "You can't tell me—a man's own brother— When you get to New York he'll change his mind!"

"No, I don't think we'd better count on that," Stieffel said. "If I had some of Anton's letters here—the one he wrote me when I married Vera, for instance. A masterpiece, in its way—I never suspected that my sweet, docile baby brother was capable of such invective. He didn't like my new second cousin, Julius Streicher, among other things. Have you ever read any of Streicher's writings about the Jews? An intemperate man, my cousin Julius. To tell the truth, my wife's family never used to think he'd amount to anything. And another one of my brother's letters that you ought to read—"

Stieffel broke off. Even for the sake of the jest, there were things he couldn't— But no, he had no right to be scrupulous. He had forfeited his scruples long ago. Now that he had started this, he must push on to the end. It was a matter of honor. "I'm referring to the letter Anton wrote me around the time of the synagogue-burnings. How long ago was that—two years, three years? He saw a copy of a Berlin newspaper with a report of the big party gala at the opera. He saw my name there among the guests. He felt called upon to drop me a line about that." Stieffel smiled. "I remember the postscript especially. He said he was contributing five thousand dollars to the American Jewish Refugee Service in my name. I've often wondered if cousin Julius ever found out about that. There's a rumor that he's on the subscription lists of all the big American Jewish organizations. Well, where was I? Oh yes, Anton's letters. That one turned out to be the last. I've written to him several times since then, but he hasn't chosen to answer. Even when he made arrangements for me in New York—I was informed of them in a business note from his chief accountant."

Schwarzkopf was the color of chalk. "Everything you did for him—*you* put him into business—such ingratitude—"

"Ingratitude? No. No, I wouldn't say such a thing about him, really. Gratitude is a noble virtue, but there comes a point, you know— You may owe a man a great deal, but what if he removes himself from the human race?"

And suddenly it came over Stieffel that the joke wasn't funny anymore. He didn't want to go on with it. He wanted to get back to the private detective and the nightclub singer. "That's what I've done, you know, my dear fellow. I don't belong to the human race any more. The mark is on me for the rest of my life."

He opened his book again. He could hear Schwarzkopf breathing heavily somewhere far away. Behind the private detective's back, the closet door was slowly opening. . . .

Schwarzkopf stood there for a while, gulped a little, tried to say something. But he knew it was no use talking. Stieffel wasn't even looking at him any more. Stieffel seemed to be in another world. So Schwarzkopf left the writing room quickly and moved across the lounge, heading for the deck.

No sooner did he step outside than he found himself face to face with Monsky and that Tannenbaum girl. They were arm in arm and laughing together over something.

"Greetings, Schwarzkopf," Monsky said. "Did you recover yet from last night?"

Last night Schwarzkopf had played bridge with Stieffel

and with Gottlieb, the lawyer from Munich. And Monsky, as happened too often, had been the fourth. Schwarzkopf hadn't done well at all, lousy cards all night long. Monsky, of course, had been the big winner.

"Poor Schwarzkopf," Monsky said, turning to the Tannenbaum girl. "He must have a wonderful relationship with his wife, because in cards he certainly isn't lucky. It's a good thing we haven't been playing for money. By this time he would've lost a couple of floors of his department store."

Monsky's laugh was a physical pain—like somebody scraping a file across Schwarzkopf's nerves. "What are you doing with this fellow?" he said, turning to the girl. "In your condition, a baby coming soon, and you're spending your time with this lazy, ignorant foreigner—"

"Now just a minute," he heard Monsky say, and he saw the shock in the girl's eyes, but he couldn't have stopped himself now even if he had wanted to. "What would your husband think if he knew about this? Can't you imagine the shame he'd feel? To see you making a fool of yourself with this—this stupid old man!"

Then Schwarzkopf stamped right past them and kept walking until he was sure they were out of sight.

He went to the railing and gripped it hard and stared down at the glaring blue water. Who's stupid, who's stupid? he kept saying to himself. All I have to do is think, figure things out. Sooner or later I'll come up with a plan. Bruno Schwarzkopf always comes up with a plan.

*   *   *

Bender was careful, after Aaron had finished telling him the news, to give no outward indication of what it meant to him. But a switch went click in his head, and a logical sequence of thought was instantly set in motion: A) I decided yesterday that I would carry out my plan if the news from New York was bad. B) The news has now come from New York, and it *is* bad. C) I must therefore take the first step in my plan; further debate with myself can only be irrelevant and degrading.

Nevertheless, that first step couldn't be taken immediately. Julia invariably spent her days in furious activity, social and athletic, and except for lunchtime he seldom saw her until they met in the lounge for afternoon coffee. This, unfortunately, would be his first chance to talk with her alone. It was necessary, therefore, to occupy his mind until then; by some means or other he must prevent himself from engaging, against his own will, in that fruitless and possibly dangerous debate.

The means might lie, Bender realized, in the problem that Aaron had just presented to him. To keep his mind busy for the next six or seven hours nothing was likely to be more effective than an intriguing problem of a professional nature. And so after leaving Aaron, he settled himself in his deck chair near the swimming pool, took out his notebook, and began to consider the suicidal potentialities of his fellow passengers. He hardly knew any of these people, of course, and the risk of making a wrong decision was overwhelming. But this risk had to be run—calmly and cold-bloodedly, as if the odds weren't impossible.

First he had to recognize one serious limitation on the value of his conclusions, no matter how skillfully he arrived at them. Out of a thousand passengers there were undoubtedly a great many who would be excellent choices for Aaron's suicide patrol—but Bender hadn't had any contact with them. He was a gregarious person and made a point of entering into conversations with strangers, but he could hardly claim to have talked with more than fifty or sixty of his fellow passengers.

Out of those fifty or sixty, the women and children must be eliminated at once, and also those men who were too old or infirm to prevent potential suicides from carrying out their intentions. Aaron Peyser's father-in-law, Bruno Schwarzkopf, clearly hadn't engaged in any kind of physical exertion in years. Karlweis the conductor seemed to be in excellent condition—Bender had noticed him walking determinedly around the deck several times each day—but his demeanor made it clear that he was unlikely to involve himself in any cooperative effort for the benefit of the other passengers. Ehrlich, the ex-soldier with only one arm, couldn't hope to do much against a really determined opponent. Rabbi Einhorn, though he would no doubt be eager to help, was far too frail and gentle.

And so the field was narrowed considerably. Among Bender's acquaintances there were perhaps only a dozen possibilities. These he now considered, one by one, from the psychological point of view.

Gottlieb, the lawyer from Munich? Small, plump, nearly fifty, yet he gave a definite impression of toughness. He was energetic enough to hold on to the bitter end rather than kill himself, and he was unimaginative enough to feel no qualms about stopping somebody else from killing himself. Yes, he had to be on the list.

The young newlywed—what was his name?—Buberman, who sat at Aaron's dining room table. In Berlin he had been a licensed pharmacist—a solid profession requiring a cool head and steady nerves. And yet—something troubled Bender about young Buberman. A bride, of course, is supposed to cling to her husband for support, but Bender sometimes wondered, when he saw those two holding hands, just who was clinging to whom. The first few months of marriage, he decided, are an unstable period at best. No man is entirely in his right mind during that period. Young Buberman had better not go on the list.

Now Bender remembered another young man, the one he had talked to in the lounge for half an hour the night of their departure from Cuba. Altdorf was his name, Franz Altdorf. Bender hadn't run into him before or since, but that brief talk had impressed him favorably. A serious, mature young man, though he wasn't twenty yet. And he came from an Orthodox family and was devoutly religious. Bender had to smile at himself. With *his* views on organized religion, how perverse to assume that a pious boy was less likely to be suicidal than an unbeliever. Nevertheless, he made this assumption. Altdorf must go on his list.

And the rabbi's son, Peter? He was the same age as Altdorf and clearly a leader, one whom other boys looked up to. Yet Bender was worried about a certain hotheaded streak in the boy. But surely the last thing that streak would lead him to was suicide. Peter Einhorn was a life-lover, he wanted to go out into the world and do battle. He might be guilty of bad judgment, but never of despair. So Bender told himself that he was hesitating out of prejudice. Being the very opposite of hotheaded himself, he had a totally unscientific suspicion of hotheaded people. After another moment's thought he added Peter Einhorn to his list—and put a question mark after his name.

He must now consider David Peyser, Aaron's older boy. If his name didn't appear on the list, would Aaron be hurt or angry? Such a consideration, Bender told himself, mustn't be allowed to carry any weight at all. There was no question in his mind that David Peyser would be a poor choice for this patrol. Though he wasn't sure he could give his reasons. . . .

The next name he considered was Arthur Stieffel. A strange man. Unfailingly polite, reasonably sociable, always in perfect control of himself. Yet somehow he seemed to be locked up in himself, cut off from the world around him. A perfect illustration of the strange fact that a man can be a hermit without going off to live in a cave. Could Stieffel be nursing, in his well-bred isolation, a deep-seated urge toward self-destruction? Bender didn't think so, really. He put Stieffel on his list.

He turned to Arthur Stieffel's cabin mate, Leon Monsky. At this fantastic idea Bender nearly laughed out loud. But then he began to wonder. Was anybody on this ship less likely to kill himself than Monsky? First of all, he had never succeeded in finishing *any* project that he began. Secondly, he was thoroughly fond of himself and completely convinced of the importance of his own existence. Especially now, when he seemed to have established a relationship with the Tannenbaum girl. The nature of this relationship wasn't clear to Bender—he would never believe that they were *sleeping* together—but obviously Monsky had persuaded himself that he was essential to her. He would welcome a stint on the suicide patrol, not as an opportunity to kill himself but as an opportunity to play the hero for Mrs. Tannenbaum.

On the other hand, how long could Monsky be expected to go *on* enjoying this glorious role? He would soon grow tired of it, as he had grown tired of every other job he had held. He was quite capable, in fact, of quitting the patrol in the middle of his rounds. On balance, then, Bender decided that Monsky wasn't a good enough risk.

He moved on to another name and then another, and by the time the lunch gong sounded his list was complete. Eight names, plus one question mark—but to tell the truth, he had absolutely no confidence in any of them. Aaron had chosen him for this job because he was supposed to be a scientist—and here he was, engaging in speculations and intuitions which were about as scientific as crystal-gazing.

After lunch he returned with Aaron to that same place on deck, very far forward, where they had talked in the morning. They exchanged lists.

On top of Aaron's list Bender saw Peter Einhorn's name.

"You've put a question mark after the Einhorn boy," Aaron said. "He's a very capable boy, you know. Very resourceful and responsible."

Bender was about to argue, but then he held his tongue, puzzled by a certain intensity in Aaron's voice.

The final list had fourteen names on it. It was decided to approach each of these men this afternoon, swearing them to silence and inviting them to a meeting just before dinner. Here they would be briefed on their duties and assigned to watches throughout the night and early morning. Everything must be ready before Aaron hurled his thunderbolt at dinner tonight.

They divided the list in half—Aaron would spend the afternoon contacting seven of the men, Bender would contact the other seven. Very casually Bender took the half with Arthur Stieffel's name on it. The truth was that he had a special reason for talking to Stieffel, one that had nothing to do with the suicide patrol.

It was only after he had separated from Aaron that Bender realized something. David Peyser's name hadn't appeared on Aaron's list, either.

A little later Bender found Stieffel in the small writing room off the main lounge. He was sitting on the sofa, absorbed in a book.

"Excuse me for disturbing you, Mr. Stieffel. If I could have a word with you—"

"Please, doctor. Sit down." As Bender took his place in a chair near the sofa, Stieffel closed his book, carefully putting his finger in his place. "What can I do for you, doctor? A matter of business? This seems to be my day for talking business."

"This isn't precisely business," Bender said. Then he told Stieffel what Aaron had heard from New York and was quiet while Stieffel had his reaction—a shake of his head, a slight loss of color from his cheeks. Then Bender explained about the suicide patrol and asked for Stieffel's help—and of course Stieffel agreed to give it. A man never feels a greater need to "do" something than when he knows there's nothing he can do.

Now Bender was coming to the difficult part, the unofficial part, of this interview. "There's something else I wanted to ask you, Mr. Stieffel—" It was absurd of him to feel so ill

245

at ease. After twenty years as a practicing psychoanalyst. How could he still have qualms about prying into people's personal affairs?

"It's presumptuous of me to ask this question. Under ordinary circumstances I wouldn't think of—"

"Please ask whatever you wish. When two people are sharing the same deathtrap, I think they might dispense with some of the amenities."

"In that case—your wife, I'm told, is a Christian?"

"Was. That is, she's still a Christian, but our marriage has been legally dissolved."

"I'm also married to a Christian. And as it appears that we're about to return to Germany, I'm very much interested in the procedure by which such a wife might separate herself from a Jewish husband—without jeopardizing her own security."

Stieffel was looking at him, not rudely but with a steadiness that was disconcerting. "Excuse me, doctor, but your wife has asked you to obtain this information?"

"My wife knows nothing about this." Illogically Bender was aware of a certain sharpness in his voice. "After I've learned the facts, I shall present them to her for her consideration." He pushed on, in the face of Stieffel's quiet gaze. "The element of security is of particular concern to me. How can a woman—who, I might add, is impeccably Aryan in every respect—extricate herself from a connection which has now become highly compromising? Is the Nazi government likely to administer punishment or reprisal? You seem to have been placed in a similar situation, and so I was hoping you might give me the benefit of your experience."

Bender stopped talking. He flattered himself that his face betrayed no sign of anxiety.

"You understand, doctor," Stieffel said, "my former wife is a rather special case. She has family connections among high party officials. This no doubt saved her from much inconvenience. And she has independent wealth, which counts for a good deal even among the incorruptible leaders of the new Germany."

"My wife has an independent income, too."

"I'm glad to hear it. Well then—it's impossible, of course, to give any absolute guarantees where our Nazi friends are concerned. They are most unpredictable. I hope you won't think I'm overstating the case if I suggest that they are sometimes irrational. Even so, if I were in your wife's situation, I think I might be optimistic. The marriage took place, I assume, before the passage of the laws which made such unions illegal? In that event, I'm sure she need only repent her error, cast off the monster who seduced her, and return humbly to the fold. To Nazis, as to most men, there is something peculiarly flattering about welcoming back the prodigal."

"Do you think she should announce her intentions immediately, while she's still aboard—or could she wait and do it as soon as she gets off the ship?"

"I would advise her to keep her intentions to herself until she steps ashore in Germany. The Nazis can hardly blame a good German girl for not exposing herself to contempt, anger, and possibly physical harm while she was trapped among the Jews. And who knows, something might come up at the last moment, we might land somewhere else after all—"

Bender looked for a moment into Stieffel's even smile, then gave a nod and rose to his feet. "Thank you, Mr. Stieffel, I'm grateful for your help. You've confirmed my own opinion. I can now go ahead with confidence."

"Dr. Bender—may I ask *you* a presumptuous question? You owe me one, I think."

Bender nodded.

"Are you quite sure that your wife *wants* to—to be extricated from this compromising connection?"

"Yours did, didn't she?"

"Oh, yes, she most certainly did."

"Nothing could be more natural. That's why I have no doubt that mine feels exactly the same."

He turned and left the writing room. As he shut the door, he could see Stieffel opening his book.

It was two o'clock. Bender used the next two hours to find the other six men on his list, to break the bad news to them and ask their help for the suicide patrol. As he expected, nobody turned him down. At last it was four, and he went to the lounge to meet Julia. He was feeling rather pleased with himself. Not the smallest twitch of doubt or fear had disturbed him. His resolution was as firm as ever.

The band was gathered at one end of the lounge, warming up for its coffee-hour concert. According to the ship's bulletin, excerpts from *Die Fledermaus* would be repeated "by popular demand." He found Julia in her usual corner, as far from the band as possible. Early in the voyage she had remarked that "the coffee and pastry are excellent, but the price is exorbitant." Eva wasn't with her—the child was off at the afternoon film, no doubt—but Claire Halevy was there, smiling at something Julia had just said. This strange, troubled woman, with her intense, rather unlikable son, was the sort of person Julia invariably attached herself to—intelligent, withdrawn, not too friendly with anyone else. Bender had nothing against her and would never have been deliberately rude to her, but his need was urgent now.

"Julia my dear," he said, "there's a matter I must discuss with you. You'll excuse us, won't you, Mrs. Halevy?"

"Can't we discuss it after I've had my coffee?" Julia said. "Neither of us is planning to leave this ship in the next hour, I imagine."

That was just like her, of course. If he pushed too hard, she instinctively pulled back. She couldn't bear any suggestion that she was being dominated. So he softened his tone. "It *is* important. You'd be doing me a great favor."

Sometimes she was willing to grant as a favor what she refused as a demand. And luckily she allowed herself to melt this time. "What a bore!" she said. "But how can I resist that hangdog look? We'll be back, Claire. Do snatch some of those little *schnecken* for me, will you, before they're all gone."

They went out on deck together. Bender took Julia's arm, and they began to walk. The sun was still high, and the glare made him blink and turn his face away.

"You should have come along sooner, darling," Julia said. "You missed a great comic performance. Monsky sat down with us and belabored us with one of his fantastic tales. How he used to play hopscotch with Hermann Göring as a child—"

"My dear Julia, I'm sure Monsky never claimed that he played hopscotch with Hermann Göring as a child."

"Well, if it wasn't that, it was something equally fantastic. The man's infuriating, but he *is* the only bright spot in this otherwise dreary voyage. He's quite impervious to hints or insults. Do you know what I did when he finished his Hermann Göring story? I asked him if he had ever met the Baroness von Krakenau, my dearest childhood friend. Right away he told me all about a dinner party he attended with her ten years ago and the discussion they had about child-raising till the early hours of the morning. Then I broke it to him that there *is* no such person as the Baroness von

Krakenau, that I made her up on the spur of the moment. Did he blush? Did he stammer? Did he retreat in confusion? Not a bit of it. He laughed merrily and said what a marvelous coincidence it was that the name I made up should be identical with the name of this real woman he met ten years ago —and without even pausing for a breath, he went right on piling up details about that dinner party."

Bender joined in her laughter. This story gave him confidence. Only Julia could take pleasure, at a time like this, in baiting poor absurd little Monsky. She was hard, resilient, imperturbable. She attached herself to people, but when the chips were down she looked after herself. She would think about his plan, and perhaps she would balk at it at first, but in the end she would agree.

"Something serious has happened," he said. "You'll hear about it at dinner, but I wanted to discuss it with you first—"

He told her Aaron's news, and her reaction was what he expected. She looked frightened and upset. She tightened her grip on his arm. "Is that the end of it then? For everyone?" Her meaning was clear, though she might not quite realize it herself. By "everyone" she meant "even those of us who aren't Jews."

"I've given this a lot of thought," he said. "When we return to Germany—as we certainly will—my position will be extremely dangerous. I shall most likely be arrested and sent to a concentration camp. So shall most of the other people on this ship. We've had our lucky chance, and somehow it's slipped away from us. We can't expect to get another. But for you—for Eva and you—this misfortune needn't occur. You're in a unique position to save yourself and your daughter."

Then he told her—several times, to make sure she understood—how she must avoid his company as much as possible while they were still on the ship, how she must demand to see an official of the government as soon as the ship docked, how she must declare her intention of immediately divorcing her Jewish husband. If she made her change of heart convincing —as he knew she was capable of doing—she would not only be believed, she would elicit great sympathy. After that the legal procedure would be merely routine. Once she was off the ship, in fact, she would probably never have to see him again.

"Now, I realize this suggestion comes as a shock to you,"

he said. "You can't possibly understand all the implications at once. You need to think about it, consider all its advantages to you. And to Eva—above all you must consider Eva. Her safety is more important than mine or yours. Furthermore, don't ignore one vital factor—my fate will be the same no matter what you do. You can't do me a bit of good by endangering yourself. You'll only make it worse for me by depriving me of the satisfaction of knowing that you and Eva are safe. In short, you have no rational excuse for rejecting this plan. But I don't want you to give me your answer yet." He raised his hand quickly. "Please don't say anything which you might regret later on. Think about it very carefully. Give yourself a week—even longer. As soon as you've made a decision, come to me, and we'll talk about this again."

"But Carl—"

"A decision, I said. Not a hasty emotional reaction. Please —we won't discuss it any further."

He took her hands in his, then he kissed her gently on the cheek. Then he turned quickly and marched down the deck.

She'll say yes, he thought. No question about it. She can't possibly say anything else. And what a relief that will be! No more need to feel this terrible guilt at dragging her down to destruction with me. For why did I marry her, after all? Because she was rich and beautiful, because she moved in the best social circles, because she was a Gentile, because it flattered my ego to have this valuable prize, this highly desirable *shiksa*, hanging from my arm. For such a reason no woman should be required to give up her life.

He stopped at the railing and blinked out at the blinding sun. From somewhere behind him he heard the muffled thumping of the waltz from *Die Fledermaus*. Suddenly his eyes filled with tears. Julia, he thought.

Then he began to laugh. Very softly, so that nobody but himself could hear. Amazing, he told himself—the power which a conventional situation can exert to produce a conventional response. One finds oneself in a position where one is expected to shed tears, and so one sheds tears—even if they have no connection whatever with one's real feelings.

Well, the lapse was over now. Momentary weaknesses are permissible—as long as they remain momentary. His circumstances from now on would be such that he couldn't afford any weakness at all.

He wondered how long it would take her to make up her mind. . . .

*　　*　　*

In the middle of dinner Papa stood up and made a speech to all the passengers. He told them that he had just heard from New York, that the United States wasn't going to let them in, that the ship would be starting back across the ocean. He told them that there was still hope, that they *wouldn't* be returning to Germany, and nobody should let his disappointment lead him to do anything foolish. He told them about the volunteer patrols that would be walking the decks every night from now on, "as extra insurance for our safety." David knew what that meant, of course, and he supposed that everyone else knew, too.

He wondered why Papa hadn't chosen *him* for one of the patrols. Was he being punished on account of last night?

Papa stopped talking and sat down. Mama was staring at him in a funny, puzzled way, as if she had never seen him before. "You've known this all day," she said, "and you never told me?"

Papa should've let us go last night, David thought. We could be safe now, if it wasn't for Papa. And then David thought of Peter and Altdorf and Kurt Halevy and the others. All day long he had been keeping out of their way, turning in the opposite direction if he saw one of them coming toward him, because he knew what they must be thinking of him. His only hope had been that good news would finally come from New York. But now—the best friends he had ever had would shut him out for good, the way he had always been shut out. Contaminating the class . . .

He hated Papa. He hated him so much that he could hardly bring himself to look at him, to say a word to him.

Several times today, when he was alone, he had shut his eyes and forced himself through that terrible daydream. In the past that daydream had come over him against his will, and he used to put up a fight against it, but now he plunged himself into it on purpose. He would take the gun in his hand, open the door to the cabin where Papa and Mama were sleeping, tiptoe up to their beds and lift the gun and pull the trigger—again and again, squeezing bullets into their bodies. And for just a moment Papa would wake up and realize what was happening. He would know, in that moment of horror and pain, that he was paying for what he had done to this boy, this innocent boy he had snatched away from his own kind and passed off as his son— Halfway through the daydream David felt horribly sick, but he made himself go on to the very end.

"Don't you want your ice cream?" Joshua said. "Could I have it?"

Without looking at Joshua he pushed the dish across the table. He hated Joshua, too, almost as much as he hated Papa. As if he couldn't figure out who had told Papa about last night's plans!

Dinner was over. They all started out of the dining room. On the way they had to pass the table where Peter and Naomi were sitting. David watched Papa stopping at Peter's place and saying, "Your watch is at midnight, isn't it? Would you like me to wake you up?"

The rabbi answered. "I'll wake him. I've been sleeping rather lightly these last few nights."

Then Papa moved on, and they were out of the dining room, and David could feel himself choking—yes, really choking. Peter had been chosen to patrol the deck tonight. Even though he had been the *leader* last night, even though nobody was more to blame than *he* was. "Why not me?" David thought "What's Papa got against me?"

But in his heart he knew the answer. He had betrayed the secret. He had talked too much, and that's what gave the plan away. And even though Papa had taken advantage of that betrayal, he couldn't feel anything but contempt for the traitor.

Then David thought of Naomi. She must know about the patrol, she must know that Peter was in it and *he* wasn't. She must be feeling contempt for him, too.

Joshua came past him, heading for the stairs. David held out his arm. "I want to talk to you."

Joshua's eyes were wide. "There's a bingo game; I have to hurry." His voice was too loud. He was scared.

David made his voice as friendly as he could. "It's awfully important, really it is. It's about Mama's birthday."

"What about Mama's birthday?"

"It's in a week, you know, and we'll still be on this ship. So I think we should decide what kind of present to get her."

David could see the fear fading from Joshua's face. "How can we buy a present while we're on this ship?"

"Well, maybe we could make something. Come on, let's go where people can't hear us. We want this to be a surprise."

Joshua's suspicions were gone now. He let David lead him to the upper deck. They went to the section that was just outside the nightclub, where you could watch the dancers through the windows. But the nightclub wasn't open now. Nobody was around.

"What kind of thing can we make?" Joshua said.

Before David could answer, a loud roaring noise filled the air, and the railing began to shake and rattle. The anchor chain was being pulled up. For five minutes you couldn't hear yourself think, you couldn't do anything except stand still and wait.

At last the roaring stopped, and then a couple of blasts came out of the whistle in the smokestacks. David noticed for the first time that smoke was pouring from those stacks, gray and dirty like the twilight sky. Then the deck gave a tremor, soft at first but growing stronger. And Joshua, looking over the railing, said, "We're moving."

David stood behind him. Both hands under his armpits, one quick lift, and he'd go hurtling through the air, landing in the water below. They were pretty high up—the fall might break his neck.

But it wasn't right yet, David thought. The little pig had to know first what was happening to him. He had to understand why.

"I guess we really *are* going," Joshua said.

"Brilliant deduction," David said.

Joshua turned to him. A half-smile flickered on his lips. "I think I'd like to go down now."

"We haven't talked about Mama's birthday present."

"I think I'd rather talk about it tomorrow."

There was fear in Joshua's eyes again. It must be something in my face, David thought.

"You had to tell Papa about me, didn't you?" David said. "You had to open your big mouth."

"I didn't—"

"You're a liar. You're a liar and a sneak and a spy."

"You stay away from me, David—"

He was very close to Joshua now, forcing him back against the railing. He could feel Joshua's breath on his face. "Spies get executed," he said, taking hold of Joshua's wrist, gripping it hard. "Without a trial—"

"You stop it, or I'll tell Papa!"

"It doesn't do a spy any good to tell anybody. If he's caught, the government that hired him will pretend they never heard of him. *Nobody* cares what happens to spies and informers." He gave Joshua's arm a tug, swinging him around sharply so that his stomach was against the railing now. He twisted Joshua's arm behind his back.

"Let go of me, David! Help!"

He brought his other arm across Joshua's chest and wedged it up against his windpipe. Out of Joshua's mouth came squeaks and squeals. Like some small animal, a dog or a bird or something, who's in pain.

And then David saw somebody turning the corner at the other end of the deck. Darkness was settling quickly; it was hard to make out this person's face at such a distance. But a moment later, he saw that it was Naomi coming toward them.

He let go of Joshua. "All right, you've had a last-minute reprieve. But you better not go telling things to Papa again."

Joshua darted across the deck to the door. There he turned, his face terribly pale, his lips white. But his eyes were bright, blazing. "I'm not scared of you!" he cried. "If you ever do that to me again, I'll—I'll—I'm not one bit scared of you!" And he darted inside.

A few seconds later Naomi drew close. "Was that your brother? He sounded upset."

It took David a moment to meet her eyes. "He's a big baby, that's all."

"Well, what *else* can anyone be at a time like this?"

She came up next to him and stood at the railing. Her face half turned away from him, she gazed out at the water. "We *are* moving," she said. "I kept telling myself it wasn't true. Even after your father's speech. How can you be a bigger baby than *that?*"

The sound that came out of her was supposed to be a laugh, he guessed.

"What was it your brother said? I couldn't hear it too well. Did he say he wasn't one bit scared?"

"Something like that."

"I wish *I* could be that way." The laugh came out of her again and suddenly she faced him and put her hands on his shoulders. "David, I'm awfully scared—"

In a second she'll start crying, he thought. Crying in his arms—no girl had ever done that before. He wanted to break loose from her and run away.

But instead of crying she laughed again and let go of him. She turned her head away and stared out at the water. The sky was growing darker and murkier every minute. There were no stars, and the moon was hidden behind a clump of clouds that looked like huge bruises. A crazy thought came into David's head. "What are you doing up here, Naomi?"

"I was looking for you," she said, still keeping her face turned away. "Your mother told me she saw you going up the stairs."

The crazy thought suddenly wasn't so crazy any more. She had been feeling scared, and she had to talk to somebody, and *he* was the one she went looking for.

"I'm glad you found me," he said. He had trouble bringing out the words. His voice seemed to have gone hoarse on him. "It's good to have someone to talk to. The truth is—I'm scared, too."

She looked at him now.

"I know I shouldn't be," he said. "I'm a terrible coward. I've been scared for years now, most of the time."

"It's been like that for everybody."

"I know that. But it's much worse with me."

"I can't believe—"

"That's because you don't know the things I've been thinking—for years now. I'm so scared about what might happen to me, because I'm a Jew and all, that sometimes I wish—well, sometimes I have this daydream—"

He stopped himself sharply with a shudder. If she heard about his daydream, she'd know he was insane. She'd have to tell her father and Peter—and Papa would find out, *everyone* would find out. He wouldn't be able to stand it, he couldn't go on living.

"What is it, David? What kind of daydream do you have?"

Her voice was so soft, so tender. It was a trap, that voice. He had to be careful every minute. "I imagine that the whole world is completely different," he said. "There *is* no Hitler, and no Jews or gentiles. Everything is happy and peaceful, and nobody wants to hurt anybody else."

"What's wrong with that? Lots of people have daydreams like that."

"But don't you see, while I'm having it, I really think there *is* such a world. I can see the buildings, I give names to the streets, I can taste the food—you see how stupid it is? And beautiful music is playing, and there are plenty of movies, just the kind I like—I mean, I lose touch with reality. Like people in insane asylums who think they're God or Napoleon."

She laughed, a real laugh this time. "I don't think you have to worry about insane asylums. Maybe what you're doing is the sanest thing anybody could do. I have daydreams, too—sometimes I think I spend more time daydreaming than *doing* things. I wish I *could* believe in them—"

"There's something else," he said, realizing that he was getting excited now. He was beginning to *like* this daydream, even though he was making it up as he went along. "I'm not alone in this world. I always imagine that there's somebody in it with me, somebody I'm sharing it with."

"Who is it? Anybody in particular?"

The eagerness in her voice excited him even more. "It's a girl," he said. "She's almost the same age as I am, and she feels as lonely and scared as I do. I don't even know her name, I don't ever get around to asking, it doesn't seem to matter—but she's dark, and a little taller than average, and—and she's really beautiful."

"She's beautiful?" The light in Naomi's eyes dimmed a little.

"Maybe not like a movie star or anything," he went on quickly, "but *I* think she's beautiful—in the dream, that is—because she's so full of life, and she loves poetry, and she's so kind and sympathetic. I'm in love with her, I really am—in the dream, that is—"

"Do you ever tell her so?"

"No—I just can't seem to do it. I keep wanting to, but then I remember what a coward I am, and what terrible things I've got in me, and I know a girl like this just couldn't feel anything for me, so I keep my mouth shut—and that's where the dream always ends."

"The next time you have it," she said, "you should tell her how you feel. You might be surprised at what she says."

Her voice was very quiet. He peered at her through his glasses, barely able to make out her features in the darkness. He told himself that her words could mean only one thing.

His mouth was dry, and he could feel his heart begin to throb. He mustn't let this throbbing grow into a pounding, or he would lose the power to do what he suddenly ached to do.

He took hold of her, knowing he was being rough and clumsy. He kissed her. He shoved his mouth against hers as if he wanted to hurt her. And suddenly, for one moment, he could feel her mouth working under his, her teeth biting at his lips, her tongue pushing between them. What was happening to her? This wasn't Naomi anymore!

He pulled away, horrified. At himself or at her? "I'm sorry, I'm sorry," he kept saying. Over and over he kept telling her how sorry he was. . . .

And Naomi heard herself answering him, "It's all right, David—please—it's all right." As if she had something to forgive him for, though she knew that *she* had done all the maneuvering and manipulating. She had practically *forced* him to kiss her; she was much more the attacker than he was. Yes, she had looked at him, and suddenly she had thought what a beautiful mouth he had, what soft, pale skin, how much she wanted to taste that mouth and to feel that skin under her fingers, to feel his hands on her body. She had read about this kind of feeling many times and had talked about it with other girls, and once or twice—even in the sacred precincts of Father's living room—boys had tried to do certain things, though they had never actually got very far (it made them nervous, she supposed, to know that a rabbi was sleeping in the next room). But she had never really *felt* it before now, this unbearable urge suddenly sweeping over her.

She was shocked at herself. Not because of what she had done, but because she didn't feel ashamed. It wasn't shame that filled her now, it was more like bewilderment. She couldn't understand why this had happened to her. At this moment of all moments—the last thing on earth that any normal person ought to be thinking about.

And she couldn't understand why it had happened to her with this boy. She had nothing against him, she liked him, she felt sorry for him because of his shyness and his loneliness. He was suffering, and she never *could* be indifferent to somebody who was suffering. But it's one thing to feel sorry for somebody, it's something else to give yourself up to him, to let yourself care so much about him that his suffering becomes a part of *you*. She didn't *want* to care for David Peyser in that way. She didn't *want* to take on his burdens. She wanted to fall in love—she wanted that more than anything—but falling in love was supposed to make you happier, lighter, freer. The man she fell in love with should be able to lift everything off her shoulders. Especially now, when so many frightening things were happening— Love wasn't supposed to be an *extra* burden.

That's what it would be with David, she knew. He was just the opposite of the man she'd been dreaming about, waiting for. He was a boy, a baby—just as wretched and confused as she was. How could *he* stop this panic from rising up in her?

He was talking to her. He'd been talking all this time, and she hadn't heard a word. "Naomi, please—is there any chance that you *could?*"

"Could what, David?"

"What I just asked you—forget what happened, forget what I did? It was terrible, and I *am* sorry, but I don't want everything to change between us. I don't know what I'd do if I had to stop being friends with you. You *will* forget what happened, won't you?"

That tone in his voice—pleading with her, like a child pleading with his mother. *Please* don't make me go to bed. *Please* let me have another cookie. It reminded her of something, that pleading tone. Yes—she had heard it earlier tonight, at dinnertime, after Mr. Peyser told everybody the news. For a while nobody at the table spoke except Mr. Monsky—"Americans! They're as bad as the Nazis, didn't I always say it? What do they care about people's lives? All they care about is polishing their automobiles!" And then she had felt Father's hand on her arm, and she had heard him say, "Naomi, darling—Peter, my boy—it's important that you shouldn't lose hope. God isn't going to forsake us—" In her father's voice was that pleading tone, and it told her, in spite of his words, that he wasn't sure anymore.

And now it came over her in a rush—there *wasn't* any hope. It was only a matter of weeks, maybe days, then Germany would gobble them all up again. Everything would be over for her then. How stupid she was being, how senseless to insist on her scruples, her doubts, her high standard in heroes! When your life is almost over, you can't afford to be choosy. If she wanted a love affair—and she *did,* she just couldn't die without ever having had one—she'd better take it while she could, where she could. It was David or nobody —nobody at all, while the weeks rushed by, and then she'd be dead forever. *When two part from each other, hand*

258

reaches out to hand, and then begins the weeping, the sighing without end. . . .

"I *won't* forget what just happened," she said, putting all the feeling she could into her voice. "I want it to happen again. I love you. I *do* love you.

He opened his mouth. She could see he was going to stammer out another one of his apologies. She didn't want him to start pleading with her again. "Isn't there anywhere we can go?" she said. "So we can be alone?"

"There's my cabin," he said, and his voice was terribly hoarse. "It'll be empty—my brother's at the bingo game—"

She took him by the hand. He was trembling hard—or was that her? I feel like one of those women, she thought. What would Mother think of me if she could see me now?

For a moment she blushed, and then she shook her head and drove the blush away. Mother was dead. Dead people don't have any right to interfere. You have to live your life while you can. . . .

It seemed to David for a moment that he was going to faint. She had said she loved him. Nobody could love him, he was much too loathsome and disgusting, but *she* loved him, she had told him so.

She was a goddess. She was meant to be worshiped. That's what he ought to be doing, worshiping her, instead of— Her love would change him, her love would save him from himself. He would be grateful to her for the rest of his life. He *wasn't* going to pay her back with loathsome, disgusting feelings.

They were walking down the stairs. He knew what he ought to do. The words were on his lips. Then he felt weak, and the words wouldn't come out. He knew what he *wanted* to do. It filled his mind; he couldn't think about anything else. He saw her with her clothes off, felt her lying under him, felt himself putting his hands over her. His body was racked with pain, with yearning. Goddess, sacred object of worship—but all he wanted to do was—

No, that *wasn't* what he wanted. He wanted something else, something fine and beautiful and pure. Why must he always spoil things with horrible thoughts? This crazy violence always had to rise up in him, just when he most wanted to be tender and gentle.

They came to the door of his cabin. His hand trembled as he opened it. The cabin was empty. He followed her inside.

Please God, he thought, as he shut the door, don't let me make a fool of myself. For once in my life, let me do *one* thing right. . . .

An hour later they were on deck again, standing at the railing. A wind had come up, and it whipped against their faces. She didn't know whether to look at him or avoid looking at him, she didn't know which would hurt him more. For fifteen minutes he hadn't said a word.

She put her hand on his arm. "It doesn't matter," she said. "It'll be all right—"

She could feel his arm stiffening under her hand. Yes, she felt sorry for him, she knew what he must be feeling. But did he care at all what *she* was feeling? Did he care about the ache inside her, so much deeper than shame or disgust? For so long she had wanted this to happen, and now it had happened all wrong. And it didn't matter, that was the worst of it. Because now she was caught forever. There was no way for her to go back.

* * *

Peter's watch said a quarter to twelve. He leaned over to look at Father in the lower bunk. Father was fast asleep. He was breathing softly, sleeping like a baby. Peter smiled, remembering Father's resolution to wake him up for his midnight patrol duty.

He settled back on his pillow again. He could afford another five minutes—he had his clothes on already, all except his shoes and his overcoat. Not that he was tired. He hadn't shut his eyes all night. But he wanted to do some more thinking.

He was puzzled by his feelings. Last night, after everything blew up in his face, he had been all churned up. Angry, humiliated, frustrated, on the verge of tears almost. What puzzled him was how quickly it had all gone away. A few hours' sleep, and in the morning not a spark of anger seemed to be left in him, no matter how furiously he fanned away at it.

Not even this afternoon when David's father took him aside and told him the bad news from New York. He would've been within his rights to give Mr. Peyser the tongue-lashing of the century. And he had even had the feeling that Mr. Peyser was expecting something like that. Mr. Peyser didn't apologize about last night—he didn't say one word to suggest that last night had ever happened—but he seemed to be tensing himself for the explosion. And all Peter could do, after he had absorbed the first shock, was give a grin. The whole thing had suddenly struck him as funny. The thought that had come into his head was, "With our luck, even if we *had* got away in that lifeboat it probably would have sprung a leak and sunk!"

A little later he had realized something else—the reason why he had been asked to join this special patrol. This was Mr. Peyser's way of making up to him for last night. What Mr. Peyser was telling him was, "I don't think you're a *completely* irresponsible lunatic." And when he realized this, Peter had grinned again—and instead of gnashing his teeth with resentment, he had felt flattered.

Kurt Halevy had come up to him after dinner tonight. He had been boiling with rage, and all of it was directed at David's father. "He's not so bad," Peter had said, and Kurt had stared at him in amazement. "How can you defend him after what happened?"

"He did what he thought was right," Peter had said. "And he put up a fight for it, too. You don't see that very much—in people his age."

"Well, I'll *never* stop holding it against him," Kurt had said.

And how is that going to get us off this ship?—this was what Peter felt like saying. Some constructive ideas were needed. A brilliant, daring new plan. And tonight, lying on this bed for the last couple of hours, he thought he had the glimmering of one. It would be a lot riskier than the first plan, would put a much bigger strain on their nerves and their courage. How tough could they be when their lives were at stake? Would they be able to do certain things . . . ?

"Will *I* be able to do them?" Peter asked himself. He thought that he would. The feelings which had been puzzling him today, his strange calm reaction to Mr. Peyser's news—didn't this mean that he was finally learning how to follow Wilhelm's advice? "The more you care, the colder you must be."

He looked at his watch. His five minutes were up. The details of the new plan still had to be worked out. Maybe he could make a start at them tonight. What else would there be to do, pacing up and down the deck for the next four hours?

Somehow he didn't think that people would be rushing up to the railing and trying to jump over it every ten minutes.

He climbed down from the upper bunk, making as little noise as he could. He slipped into his shoes and his overcoat. Father stirred slightly in his bed.

Peter stood over him, staring down. Father had been looking so tired lately. To Peter it had seemed that his face had more wrinkles on it than when he came aboard this ship. That was probably his imagination, though. . . . But the funny thing was, stretched out on his bunk now, Father seemed to have lost most of those wrinkles. His face was almost the face that Peter remembered from his childhood. Looking up into that face when he was a little boy, he never felt quite as bad about his problems and his fears as he had a moment before. Father would frown in that thoughtful way of his and tug at his lower lip and shake his head solemnly a few times, and then in his slow deep voice he would begin to speak— and a moment later relief and happiness would come flooding over Peter. . . .

He wished he could talk to Father about his new plan. He wished he could pour it all out to him now, all his doubts and his fears, and the things he might have to do when he put this plan into effect, and all the reasons why those things *had* to be done, no matter how much they made him shudder. And Father would frown and tug his lip and shake his head and then say with great deliberation, "You've got no choice, my boy. It's hard for you, I know, but you've got my blessing."

He *could* make Father understand. If they just had a chance to talk, to sit down together and talk— What if he woke Father up right now?

But as soon as he had said this to himself, he knew that he wouldn't do it. He just couldn't take the chance. You have to be cold. The more you care . . .

Father's eyelids fluttered, and then his eyes opened slowly. For a few seconds he blinked up at Peter. His voice came, weak and drowsy. "Peter—my boy—good heavens, your patrol duty—"

"It's all right, Father. I'm on my way."

"But I was going to wake you—I must have dozed off. I'm sorry."

"No harm done. Why don't you go back to sleep?"

"Yes—yes, I believe I—" His voice grew drowsier still.

"You're wrapped up warmly enough? It's become quite cold outside—"

Peter smiled down at him. "Who says I don't have a mother?"

It was a long time since he had made this joke to Father. He saw Father smiling, too, very faintly. Then his head sank into the pillow, and his eyelids started fluttering again.

Peter stood there in silence until Father was asleep.

Someday, Peter thought, you'll know that I did the right thing. When we're finally out of this. When we're all together in the homeland.

*   *   *

Twenty minutes before midnight Gottlieb climbed down from his upper berth and started to get dressed. Actually, he hadn't slept at all, though Sarah and he had gone to bed before ten.

He was putting on his shoes when her voice came to him out of the darkness. "It's raining, Meyer. Don't forget your rubbers."

"Rubbers? How did you manage to find room for rubbers in that little suitcase of mine?"

"I packed them in *my* suitcase. Your rainhat, too—it's in the bottom drawer."

"And to fit in my rubbers and my rainhat, sweetheart, which of your own things did you have to leave behind? Your favorite dress? Your one and only pair of walking shoes?"

"As a matter of fact, it was *my* rubbers I left."

"Is that so? Very interesting. In your opinion your feet are waterproof and mine aren't?"

"It isn't that. It's just that I asked myself, 'If it rains, who's going to run down the street for taxicabs, and who's going to wait nice and dry under the awning?' So in self-defense, I decided you'd better have the rubbers." He couldn't see her face, but he knew she was blushing. It always embarrassed her when she was caught out in an act of self-sacrifice.

"While we're on the subject," he said, "who told you we'd be able to afford all those taxicabs?"

"That doesn't worry me a bit. Once you're a big success in the hardware business, we'll be eating caviar for breakfast."

He was all dressed now. His watch said ten minutes before midnight. He sat down on the lower bunk and took Sarah's

263

hand. "You want to make a last-minute inspection? See if my teeth are brushed and I'm clean behind the ears?"

"Four hours, Meyer. It's such a long time to be on your feet."

"What can we do? The decks have to be patrolled all night long, and there aren't enough men to make the watches shorter. Don't you worry, though. In the navy I used to stand six-hour watches, and my feet didn't even hurt at the end of them."

"Your feet were only twenty-three years old then."

"And what's that supposed to mean? You think I'm an old man today? You think my creaking joints can't stand the strain? That's a fine attitude for a wife to take! I notice you didn't think I was so old and decrepit last Monday night!"

"Excuse me, but last Monday night you weren't on your *feet*."

"Jokes! Now she's making fun of me! I'll be back at four o'clock this morning, and you'll see how much energy I've got after a four-hour watch."

Sarah giggled. Then her hand was against his cheek. "All right, you're younger than you ever were. Just the same, don't let yourself get too wet and cold. And be careful about—" She paused.

"Be careful about what?"

"If anybody comes along who—" She gave a shake of her head. "It isn't going to happen. I just don't believe that anybody will be so foolish."

"Of course they won't. We're smart German Jews on this ship. We're not a bunch of stupid Aryans."

But now it was time for him to go. He couldn't dawdle any longer.

On the way up the stairs to the main deck he told himself again what a lucky man he was. People who didn't really know Sarah probably thought she was a typical *hausfrau*— pleasant features but not exactly a beauty, putting on weight, turning gray. These people never saw what was underneath —the joy she got out of life, the kindness and generosity for everything weaker than herself, the passion. Yes, passion, a young girl's passion—improbable as it might seem to anyone who looked at the two of them. This fat, middle-aged couple were actually Romeo and Juliet? The mere idea of it was laughable. As a matter of fact, Sarah and he often laughed about it themselves, afterward.

264

We've had a good life together, he thought. Only one big sorrow really—that they never could have any children. Not after little Anna, who died so quickly. . . . What a mother Sarah would have been! But there had been plenty of happiness to make up for this. And to make up, maybe, for the way it was going to end. . . .

On the main deck he relieved Professor Weissbrod, who had been on the eight-to-midnight watch. Professor Weissbrod used to teach economics at the university in Munich and was the author of several well-known textbooks. (One of them was still widely used in Germany, though his name had been removed from the cover and the title page.) He was a little man with a goatee, always very neatly trimmed, and a serious, dignified manner even when he was just making small talk. But right now he didn't look so dignified—his hair was rumpled, his suit was wringing wet, his goatee was soggy.

"Did you have trouble?" Gottlieb asked. "Did someone try to—"

"No trouble—no, not really." The professor's voice was hoarse, and he interrupted himself to give a sneeze. "My own fault, really. Nerves, I'm afraid. Three times in the last hour I saw somebody at the stern of the ship. I could have sworn he was climbing over the railing. I ran to him as fast as I could—that's how I got soaked to the skin."

"Who did it turn out to be?"

"The first time it was the boy who assists the cook. He came up from the kitchen to throw out the garbage. I grabbed hold of him, and we—we struggled. It was really most embarrassing."

"And who was it the other two times?"

"The same boy. He came up with two more loads of garbage, and each time I made the same mistake. Nerves—sheer nerves. Let me tell you, my dear Gottlieb, *nobody* on this ship has any intention of committing suicide. What you *really* have to worry about while you're on patrol is your own imagination."

The professor moved off, shaking his head and sneezing, and Gottlieb carefully kept himself from laughing out loud.

And as soon as he was alone, he wondered if the joke was really so funny. The deck was heaving under his feet, and the sea and sky merged together in one great blotch of blackness. The wind was so strong that even here, under the covered section of the deck, drops of rain were flung against his face. The deck lights were on, but they cast as much shadow as light, and Gottlieb knew that every shadow, as the hours crawled by, would have a way of turning into a stealthy human form, that every creaking noise would become a human whimper.

No, he couldn't laugh at the poor professor, for when you got down to it, how good was *he* in the darkness? He began to walk slowly up and down the deck, and as he walked he remembered those three years during the war when he had served in the navy. He remembered his enthusiasm when he joined up—how romantic and exciting it was to go to sea, especially after the dullness and dryness of the university. But the first night he had stood watch, all by himself in the darkness, with the sky lowering over him and the water stretching to infinite distances all around him—then he had known that the sailor's life was not for him, that he would take his father's advice and go to law school as soon as he was discharged. For there was something about the darkness and loneliness. They opened his mind to thoughts. . . .

He peered at his watch and saw that it wasn't even one o'clock yet. In a book once he had read that time is an illusion, that it doesn't exist outside people's heads. Every man, according to this book, lives by his own private inner clock that speeds up or slows down according to his feelings. What nonsense, he had thought after reading that book. . . .

He went to the railing. He leaned against it and gazed down at the black water. It made him dizzy, that blackness. A chill went through him, panic was leaping up in him. He held tight to the railing until the panic had subsided.

Why had that happened to him? What had frightened him so suddenly? He was glad Sarah wasn't with him now. She depended on him, she expected him to be strong. It wouldn't do for her to find out. . . .

The darkness was so thick. Gummy—you could almost feel it oozing over you. Quickly he turned his back to the railing. What if somebody came along now and felt the urge to— Could *he* ever feel such an urge? No, no, that was impossible. He was much too attached to his skin. He was a pretty good Jew, went to synagogue, believed in God—but when they read the prayer for the dead, he always shut his ears. Why did Judaism, and every other religion he had ever heard of, have to spend so much time reminding you about death?

He remembered old Rosenthal. Old Judge Otto Rosenthal, removed from the bench in 1935, stripped by Hitler of his honors and his position. And that night he went home, locked himself in his bathroom, and cut his throat. Gottlieb hadn't known the old man too well, had tried only a few cases before him—but the news had shocked him. How could a man give up his life—his *life*—just because people wouldn't be calling him "your Honor" any more?

And yet—it came to Gottlieb now, with this cold rain splashing against his face, stinging his eyes—old Rosenthal hadn't been a fool. An arrogant bastard, yes, but never a fool. Maybe he had been smarter than any of them. He had known that the loss of his robes was only the beginning. He had guessed what lay ahead. . . .

What lay ahead? You heard stories. Maybe they were exaggerated. Or maybe— Did you really want to find it? Wouldn't it be preferable—

But what would Sarah do afterward? How would she get along? Foolish questions. Her end would be the same whether or not he— Even if he didn't do it, how long could it be before she was torn away from him? Either way, the time was near when they'd never see each other again. . . .

What if he went down to the cabin now, woke her, asked her to come up with him?

He heard footsteps. He looked up, startled. They were coming toward him from the front of the ship. Two people were moving down the deck. They moved from the shadows into the light, and he recognized that young couple, the newlyweds.

They were holding hands as they walked. Their arms and shoulders were touching.

They stopped a few feet away from him. They looked surprised to see him. He thought he saw fear on their faces.

"Good evening," Gottlieb said. "Our luck was too good to last, wasn't it? We're finally getting some rough weather."

The young man blinked at him. "Luck—?" His voice was tight, like a rubber band stretched to the snapping point. "Excuse me—I don't understand—what are you doing out here?"

"I'm on patrol, believe it or not." Gottlieb laughed. "Playing boys' games, at my time of life. But there it is. I'm covering the port side of this deck, and somebody else is covering the starboard. And there are people on the upper deck, too."

He went on smiling into those white faces. Then he reached out and put his hand on the young man's arm. He tried to make his touch firm but not insistent. "It really *is* a dreadful night, you know. Don't you think you'd be more comfortable inside?"

The deck lifted high, shuddered, then dropped again. The wind slapped and whistled against the side of the ship. The boy let go of the girl's hand. "No—we don't want to go inside—" He raised his arm slowly—and Gottlieb was suddenly conscious of just who he was. Meyer Gottlieb, forty-eight years old, below average in height, above average in weight—let's face it, fat. And how long had it been since he had fought anyone with any weapon except his voice? Even as a schoolboy, he was usually the one who ended up with a bloody nose. As for being a match for this tall, healthy young man— The situation was almost comical, he thought. He felt a definite temptation to laugh.

He laughed. "Listen to me—giving orders, like I thought I was the captain. You can see what this night patrol does to a man's nerves. Please forgive me—I was rude, and I apologize." He grinned and spread his hands. "It's a good object lesson, isn't it? A man should keep his head, no matter what. He should hold on to his courage and his good sense, because giving up hope while there still *is* hope—this isn't how a *man* acts, a married man with responsibilities; this is how a *baby* acts."

He stopped talking. Still grinning, he looked steadily into those young frightened eyes.

A few seconds later the boy lowered his arm, and then his hand reached for the girl's hand. "It *is* dreadful out," he said. "I guess we'll go inside."

"That's the smartest thing you can do," Gottlieb said.

He watched them until they disappeared through the glass doors. Then he became aware of the tightness in his chest. He took a few deep breaths until his chest stopped hurting.

He began to shiver. Stop it, that's enough, he told himself. But he went on shivering. What he needed was to go to Sarah, to listen to her voice and feel her hand on his cheek until the shivering stopped. And then to tell her—no, he couldn't tell her about the thoughts that had come to him in the darkness. Thoughts like that he could never confess to her. If they ever came to him again, he would just have to handle them by himself.

He looked at his watch. Nearly two. I'll handle them all right, he thought, as the ship was scooped up by another wave. Old Rosenthal was a damned fool. . . .

And so the hours passed, the wind rose, the ship plunged and pitched head on into the rain. And Gottlieb paced up and down and hugged himself to keep warm until Aaron Peyser relieved him at the stroke of four.

NINE

IT seemed for a while as if the *Franz Joseph* had disappeared off the face of the earth. Early one night it sailed out of radio range, and from then on Morrie had no idea where it was or where it was going. In the next few days Al made cautious inquiries through his contact in the New York office of the Hamburg Line. He found out that the ship was heading in the direction of Europe, but nobody could say just what this meant. Had Aaron Peyser talked the captain into dropping anchor off the coast of France, or was the captain following orders to return to Germany?

Morrie sent two radiograms to Aaron Peyser, asking for further information. No answer came to either of them. He sent a third radiogram just before he and Al flew to Paris. He advised Aaron Peyser of their hotel address and of the plans AJDA had made, through certain friendly officials of the French Line, to set up direct radio contact with the *Franz Joseph* as soon as it came within range. He begged Aaron Peyser to respond to this message and felt sure that this response would be waiting for him at his hotel in Paris. But when he and Al reached the hotel, nothing was there.

A little while later his anxiety was temporarily driven out of his head. The desk clerk called up to announce that Abraham Weinstein was in the lobby and wanted to come up to see them. Morrie had the feeling that he was suddenly being plunged into a dream. All his life Weinstein had been more of a legend to him than a real person. Throughout his boyhood his father, a passionate Zionist as well as a passionate American, had invoked the name of Weinstein, along with Weizmann and Ben-Gurion, in the same tones that an Orthodox Jew might use to invoke Abraham, Isaac, and Jacob.

If Weinstein was less familiar to the general public than Weizmann or Ben-Gurion, that was because his services to

Zionism were scholarly rather than political. Born in Russia of wealthy parents, he had been brought to England when still a baby, had been educated at the best schools, and had graduated from Oxford. This kind of educational career wasn't common for a Jewish boy, even a wealthy one, in the 1890's. Doors had been opened for young Weinstein by his family connections. His father's firm, Weinstein Brothers Ltd., was the exclusive supplier of port, sherry, and fine French wines for some of the leading Tory noblemen, and on several occasions his father had advanced sums of money privately to the Conservative Party. As it happened, however, young Weinstein also turned out to be brilliant. At an early age he showed an extraordinary enthusiasm and talent for the study of history. After graduation he accepted a fellowship at one of the smaller Oxford colleges—less prestigious socially than some others, but highly prestigious academically —and he began work on his first and what was to be his best-known book, *Religious Tolerance and Persecution in Eighteenth-Century Europe*. He was particularly qualified to deal with this subject because of his extensive knowledge of the Continent. His mother had died when he was a boy, and his father often took him along on his business trips. By the age of eighteen the young man could do what few English historians have been able to do—he could speak five European languages fluently.

He could also speak Hebrew. His father, a devout Orthodox Jew, prided himself, in the manner of many Jewish merchants of his era, on his knowledge of Talmud and Torah. His son often heard him say, with a great sigh, "I should have been a scholar, a *rebbe*. That was my father's dream for me. But I was restless and ambitious, I wanted experience, excitement, material success. I was tempted by the world of men, and so I threw away my most precious jewel. Don't you ever do that, my boy. Never forget what's truly important in life."

Young Weinstein may have had that advice in mind, in the early 1900's, when he paid a visit to Vienna and met Theodore Herzl. His interest in Zionism began almost immediately and increased through the years. On the eve of the World War he published his monumental treatise, *The Zionist Ideal*, in which he used the methods of scientific historical scholarship to justify the establishment of a Jewish state in Palestine. *The Zionist Ideal* startled and dismayed the English academic world. It was felt that a young historian of such great promise ought not to waste his talents on such a narrow, parochial cause. Many critiques of the book, some of them extremely bitter and caustic, appeared in scholarly journals. Attempts were made to discredit the authenticity of his research, and while he was able to demolish them all and to uphold his reputation for reliability and integrity, it was nevertheless clear that his position in academic circles had been irreparably damaged. In some indefinable way he had been disloyal to the club. And so, a year after his book was published, he resigned his fellowship at Oxford.

Apparently this was no blow to him at all. By this time he had come to realize what was truly important in his life. Though the Zionists were a small group, poorly financed, condemned as cranks and troublemakers not only by those Christians who had heard of them but by most Jews, as well, Weinstein cast his lot with them. They hailed him joyously, of course. Since the days of Herzl himself no scholar of equal eminence had joined their ranks. He soon became Zionism's official intellectual, and through the next twenty-five years his immense learning and unimpeachable reputation were always available to lend weight to the cause. It was said, for example, that Weinstein's influence was more responsible than any other factor for England's promulgation of the Balfour Declaration.

Today, at seventy-two, Abraham Weinstein's prestige was still great. Officially AJDA was a non-Zionist organization (it had once been staunchly anti-Zionist, but recent events in Europe had caused it to modify its hostility), but everyone realized from the start that Weinstein was the only man who could possibly arrange this Paris conference. Nobody else was sufficiently respected by various European heads of state to persuade them to send representatives on such short notice. In fact, it had taken him only four days to make all the arrangements, a kind of miracle that filled Morrie with hope. If a dozen European governments were willing, under Weinstein's prodding, to attend this conference, they surely must intend to help the refugees.

There was a soft knock on the door, then Abraham Weinstein entered the room. Morrie had seen pictures of him, of course, and he was prepared for the long white beard, the hawklike nose, the shoulders as straight as a young man's. "The prophet Isaiah in a business suit," said Al, who had met Weinstein in New York a few years before. What Morrie wasn't prepared for was the relaxed, comfortable effect that this old man produced. The prophet Isaiah should have been awesome—but Weinstein, with his clipped English accent, his bright, almost boyish eyes, his long, delicate fingers clasped over the top of a walking stick, reduced the awesomeness to human proportions.

He shook hands, lowered himself into a chair, and apologized for calling on them so soon after their arrival. Then he turned his soft smile on Morrie. "And you're our liaison man with the ship? That's very good. Those people mustn't feel that the outside world has abandoned them. This is almost as important as saving their lives."

Al asked him what he meant by that, and Weinstein gave a gentle sigh. "We'll get them off that ship, I'm sure of that —but in what condition, in what frame of mind? An extended exposure to cruelty can do terrible things to a man. I've seen hundreds of refugees from Germany in the last few years. I'm now beginning to see Austrians and Czechs, too. Many of them have had their faith in their fellow men beaten out of them, and I assure you that the experience has left them empty, quite empty. Some are perpetually terrified in their emptiness; others try to fill it with arrogance, malice, or a cold cruelty matching the cruelty of their persecutors. Either way it amounts to the same thing, a kind of living death. That's why your job, Mr. Feldman, is invaluable. Of what use to save the bodies of those unfortunate people if their souls are lost?"

He frowned for a moment. Then he smiled again. "Which brings us to the purpose of your visit, tomorrow's conference. Our objective is to make Mr. Feldman's job superfluous as quickly as possible. To provide those people with something more substantial than mere hope—" And for the next hour he filled them in on details—what procedures would be followed tomorrow, what they ought to say and when they ought to be silent, by whom each government would be represented. He gave a thumbnail sketch of each representative—three or four sentences which impaled the man's habits, opinions, and personality for all time. It occurred to Morrie that kindliness and compassion weren't the only elements in Weinstein's character. He wouldn't be a good man to have for an enemy.

Then he touched on the one real disappointment that had occurred so far. It appeared that the Soviet Union, with whose ambassador Weinstein had been negotiating, wouldn't be represented at the conference. The ambassador had never given a positive refusal, but he kept making inconclusive and contradictory statements, alternately encouraging and discouraging. "We mustn't complain, I suppose," Weinstein said. "The British and French are having the same difficulty at the moment. One day Stalin hints that he's willing to work out an agreement with them to stop Fascist expansion, the next day he makes a speech accusing them of weakness, duplicity, and secret Fascist tendencies. Meanwhile, the rumors are rife that Ribbentrop may leave for Moscow any day now. I'm afraid we can't expect our Russian friends to—what's your American expression?—'play ball' with us until they decide which team they're on."

Nevertheless, Weinstein had high hopes for those countries who *would* be represented at the conference. "We simply have to be patient," he said. "It will be three or four days before any of these men are ready to commit themselves to an answer. They'll ask a great many questions first and demand a great deal of information about specific passengers —your radio contact with the ship may be crucial in this respect, Mr. Feldman. In the end each representative will insist that he must report back to his government for further instructions. Don't be misled, however. None of these men are mere flunkies. They carry real weight. We may feel reasonably certain that what they recommend will eventually be confirmed by their superiors."

"How long is eventually?" Al said. "If Hitler decides to order that ship back to Germany—"

"Understood, understood. We'll make that point over and over again and hope they'll take it to heart. Beyond that, we're in God's keeping." And Weinstein spread his hands in a gesture that reminded Morrie of neither an Old Testament prophet nor an Oxford scholar but of somebody's grandfather in the Bronx.

"What do you think our chances are?" Morrie said.

"It's difficult to evaluate, Mr. Feldman. Europeans are realists, above everything. In deciding what to do about the passengers on the *Franz Joseph*, each representative at tomorrow's conference will consider the practical advantages to his own government and act accordingly."

"But what practical advantages *could* they get from letting those people in?"

"I can think of several. With war looming on the horizon, the services of a large body of rabid anti-Nazis might be distinctly useful. These people speak German, understand German ways, are familiar with the German business, professional, and cultural worlds. They could translate German documents, interpret German military and diplomatic dispatches, write propaganda directed at various strata of German society. My point is that tomorrow's representatives will weigh this kind of asset against certain potential liabilities, and the resulting balance will determine their final decision."

"Do you think," Al said, "that anti-Semitism will influence that decision?"

"No—no, I really don't think so. In Europe today anti-Semitism is as pragmatic as anything else. Governments invoke it when Jews are a danger to them—in terms of economic competition, perhaps—and I rather doubt that those poor wretches on the *Franz Joseph* will look particularly dangerous to anybody. On the other hand, of course, one can never really—"

Weinstein broke off, and a glint of amusement appeared in his eyes. "It isn't really fair, you know, to bring anti-Semitism into this discussion. I *am* a Jew. Therefore, I'm bound to lose my head on that subject. I wonder if you gentlemen would care to be my guests for dinner."

They had dinner in a small pleasant restaurant with a garden in back. Then they dropped Weinstein off at the building owned by the World Zionist Organization—he was staying in the guest suite on the top floor—and decided to walk back to their hotel.

It was a mild, clear night, and as they crossed the bridge to the Left Bank Morrie suddenly realized that he was in Paris. On the horizon was the Eiffel Tower. Stretched below it was a network of funny, curved rooftops. In the large square at the other end of the bridge, the sidewalk cafés were all lighted up, and people filled the tables. This was Paris, the beautiful, romantic city that he had read so much about, that Ruth and he had always wanted to visit—"as soon as the kids are old enough to appreciate it."

Well, here he was in Paris, and till this moment he had hardly noticed it. And even now—he had to admit how little it meant to him. He felt no urge to do any of the things and see any of the places that Ruth and he had talked about so often. There was really only one place in the world right now.

That place was some unknown stretch of the Atlantic Ocean where the *Franz Joseph* was cutting through the waves.

When they got back to their hotel, Morrie and Al found a radiogram waiting for them. With trembling fingers Morrie opened it; he knew that it had to be from Aaron Peyser. He read the first few words to himself, and then he read the whole message out loud. The *Franz Joseph*, after a five-day cruise, had just dropped anchor fifteen miles off the coast of France, due west of Calais. The captain had promised to remain in this spot for the next ten days and perhaps longer if orders from Germany weren't forthcoming. Aaron Peyser believed that the captain would keep his promise.

* * *

The conference began on Monday morning and came to an end on Thursday morning. During these three days Al and Morrie held constant meetings. Large meetings with the entire group—eighteen or twenty people in all, plus stenographers and interpreters—took place in a conference room on the second floor of the World Zionist building. Small meetings, with individual representatives, took place almost anywhere —in hotel rooms, in elegant restaurants, at café tables.

At all these meetings, as Weinstein had predicted, the representatives expressed no definite opinions beyond a word or two of polite sympathy for refugees in general. They asked a great many questions, particularly about how the people on the *Franz Joseph* expected to keep themselves alive if they were admitted to a foreign country. In answer to this, Al and Weinstein were able to produce pledges of money and assistance from AJDA, the World Zionists, and other international organizations and from the local Jewish philanthropies of every country represented at the conference. And Morrie— in radio contact with Aaron Peyser from the wireless office of the French Line, located in a warehouse near the edge of Paris—got the names of all passengers who had relatives, friends, or business connections in any of those countries.

At the end of Wednesday afternoon's large session each representative declared that he would spend the evening examining the facts he had gathered and communicating his ideas to his superiors back home. And each representative was sure that he would be able to announce his final recommendation at tomorrow morning's session. Weinstein seemed pleased to hear this. It was a good sign, he said. It meant that everyone appreciated the urgency of the problem.

Weinstein's confidence affected Morrie, and he decided that he was justified in expressing some of it to Aaron Peyser when he talked to him on Wednesday night.

"I don't want to raise any false hopes," Morrie said, "but I think you *can* be optimistic—" He broke off, feeling uneasily that he had used the word "optimistic" too many times during these conversations.

On Thursday morning the proceedings began at nine o'clock sharp. A stenographer was present, as he had been regularly. He took verbatim notes of the discussion, translated it into English whenever necessary, and prepared this transcript for AJDA's records.

ABRAHAM WEINSTEIN (presiding): Gentlemen, are there any more questions you would care to put? Any more information you need concerning the people aboard the German liner *Franz Joseph?* (Silence.) In that case, may I hope that some of you gentlemen are prepared, in the name of your respective governments, to offer refuge to at least some of these people—temporarily perhaps, until their United States quota numbers become activated? (Silence.) May I remind you, gentlemen, that over a week has elapsed since the *Franz Joseph* left American waters. Any day now it is entirely possible that the German government may order the ship back to Hamburg, in which case it will be too late to do those people any good. Under the circumstances, if any of you can possibly—Yes, thank you, Sir Douglas Grainger.

SIR DOUGLAS GRAINGER (Director of the BBC, Member of Parliament from Cambridge, former Ambassador of Great Britain to Austria): My position at this conference, as you know, is entirely without official status. I have retired from the Foreign Office and am here simply as an observer because of the sympathetic interest which His Majesty and the Prime Minister, my old friend, take in this grave problem. I will convey my personal impressions directly back to Mr. Chamberlain, but these impressions will carry no official sanction whatever. Final recommendations will be made by Mr. Horatio Parsons of the Foreign Office, who will express his views in a moment. Though Mr. Parsons has been kind enough to consult with me from time to time, it must be clearly understood that he has formed his opinion entirely on his own, and my agreement or disagreement is quite irrelevant. This is as it should be. Mr. Parsons is a most efficient and sensible man, far more capable of forming a judgment in this matter than a superannuated old relic like myself.

(As he listened to these words, Morrie had fervently hoped that Parsons *would* be using his own judgment. Sir Douglas, an old man with a white mustache and a cold, fishy stare, had been a Mosleyite in the early thirties, and though he had broken with Mosley on the pro-German issue, his cast of mind was clearly reactionary and probably anti-Semitic.)

HORATIO PARSONS: Thank you, Sir Douglas. I must, however, correct a certain false impression which you have given, no doubt unintentionally. While I *am* the British government's official representative to this conference, and while I *have* formed certain views on the matters we have been discussing, the government certainly will not rely on my judgment alone in reaching its conclusions. What I say now is merely the essence of the detailed report which I shall submit to the Prime Minister when I return to London this afternoon. Whether or not he chooses to act on my recommendations is, of course, entirely out of my province. He may very well ignore those recommendations—that would be within his rights.

(Pause. Mr. Parsons consults papers, polishes glasses.)

It is my considered opinion, gentlemen, after careful examination of all the circumstances, that His Majesty's government would be ill-advised at this time to permit either all or a portion of the German nationals aboard the liner *Franz Joseph* to enter British territory. The dangers of war in Europe, as none of us need be reminded, are considerable. The chance of maintaining the peace is slim. Communication between Mr. Chamberlain and Chancellor Hitler has not yet broken down, but it could very easily do so as a result of a provocative act on our part, or even of some act which Chancellor Hitler might interpret as provocative. In my judgment, if His Majesty's government were to take these German nationals into British territory at this time, we should be performing just such a provocative act. We should, in point of fact, be endangering whatever hope remains to avert the war. One sympathizes deeply with the plight of these unfortunate people, of course, but one also recognizes that the cause of world peace is worth any sacrifice. Thank you, gentlemen.

(Silence.)

WEINSTEIN: Isn't it a fact, Mr. Parsons, that Parliament only last week passed a bill to increase the strength of the Royal Air Force, that a Ministry for Home Defense has been formed, that barrage balloons are being tested over several of our large cities? Wouldn't you imagine that Hitler would find these acts a good deal more provocative than the granting of a temporary refuge to a thousand wretched people whom he's expelled from his country anyway?

PARSONS: Excuse me, Mr. Weinstein, but the acts you mention don't fall within my province, and so I cannot be expected to answer for them officially. Nevertheless, it does seem to me that they are all essential measures for our national defense, and therefore the responsible authorities may well consider the element of risk to be justified in those specific cases. That justification can hardly apply, however, to the admission of these refugees into our country. Do you contend that *they* are essential to our national defense?

WEINSTEIN: They may be essential to our illusion of being human.

PARSONS: That, of course, is a metaphysical question which doesn't fall within my province.

(Silence.)
279

WEINSTEIN: Are any of you other gentlemen prepared to make a statement on this matter? Yes, Monsieur Schmitt?

ANDREAS SCHMITT (Representative of the Republic of Switzerland): Switzerland has been a traditional haven for political refugees from all countries. However, we are not in any sense a military power. Our chief asset and protection in the world today is our neutrality. There is a real question in my mind whether our acceptance of the people from the *Franz Joseph* might not be considered by the German government as a violation of that neutrality. In any event it won't be necessary for me to examine that question in detail, because the latest government regulations clearly state that any individual seeking to immigrate into Switzerland is required to establish a certain minimum balance in one of our national banks. As I understand it, none of the people aboard this ship would be in a position at present to fulfill that requirement.

(Silence.)

WEINSTEIN: Monsieur Binet, do you wish to speak?

LUCIEN BINET (Permanent Secretary to the French Foreign Office): Thank you, Mr. Weinstein. And let me begin by saying how delighted the government of France has been to have such a group of distinguished gentlemen in our midst during the week. We have been unable to entertain you as we would have liked to do had your visit been of an official nature, but we certainly hope that your stay in Paris has been enjoyable and that you have found time, in moments of rest from your serious affairs, to sample the splendid cultural and gastronomic resources which this city offers.

(Pause. Expressions of appreciation, thanks, etc.)

BINET: To proceed now with the more serious remarks I am obliged to make. I have, of course, been in a most advantageous situation throughout this conference, compared with the rest of you. My ministry is here, my superiors occupy offices only a few blocks away. I have been able to maintain constant communication with them as these proceedings developed. What I say now, therefore, expresses not only my own views but the views of those in authority above me. The conclusion we have reached—reluctantly, sadly, but also, I fear, irrevocably —is that France can do nothing for the passengers of the *Franz Joseph*. Our reasons are rather different from those of our great ally across the Channel. Our government does not, in all candor, put much faith in the possibility that peace can still be maintained. We fully expect war to come, and we don't deceive ourselves that Herr Hitler's plans will for one moment be influenced by anybody's actions regarding those poor, benighted people on that ship. Our concern, therefore, is entirely with the question of national security.

(Pause. Monsieur Binet takes drink of water.)

Gentlemen, when the war inevitably comes, France must be in the strongest possible position. Above all, she must not be weakened by internal dissension. We have here our party of the right, our pro-Fascist, pro-Hitler party. They are not numerous in themselves, but they could under certain conditions form alliances with the more traditional conservative parties and even with some who are more moderate. The one issue around which the extreme right might rally support from these other factions is the Jewish issue—that is, their common dislike and distrust of the Jews. Yes, I am sorry to say that there is still a strong anti-Semitic strain among many Frenchmen, especially those in the provinces who are less sophisticated, less attuned to the modern world. In the past five or six years many Jewish refugees have come to France, and though they present, by and large, no real problems—for their own organizations take care of them quite efficiently—their presence is nonetheless resented in certain quarters. The present French government, the anti-Fascist center, maintains a precarious balance of power. If it were to admit any sizable number of foreign Jews just now, the right might well pounce upon this as just the pretext they need to stir up trouble, to alienate certain conservative elements essential to our coalition. The balance could be upset, the government could fall. Gentlemen, the security and freedom of Europe depend on the strength and stability of the anti-Fascist center in France. We cannot jeopardize that for the sake of a thousand people. Thank you, gentlemen—thank you, Mr. Weinstein—for your indulgence.

WEINSTEIN: M. Binet, the French government has privileged access to all media of communications. Couldn't you use government newspapers and radio stations to dramatize the terrible plight of these refugees, to present their admission into France as a humanitarian gesture that even the most conservative wouldn't care to oppose?

BINET: We could try. But it is a risk we dare not run.

WEINSTEIN: Aren't you underestimating the natural inborn sympathy and generosity of your fellow countrymen?

BINET: It is a risk we dare not run.

(Silence.)

WEINSTEIN: May we hear from some of the other gentlemen?

COUNT AXEL FJELDSTROM (Representative of Sweden): We are a small, weak country, gentlemen. I will not mince words with you. We are terrified of the Germans. One look at the map of Europe should explain why. Nevertheless, we are not monsters. We sympathize with these people, and we would like to help them. We would gladly take in every one of them, if we could. But gentlemen, how can we act alone in this matter? If the big powers of France and Great Britain and the United States, with all their resources, feel that they are unable to accommodate even a small number of these people, how can Sweden possibly take the initiative? Isn't it obvious what the public outcry would be, how the government would be accused of putting the life of every Swedish citizen in jeopardy? And this accusation would be unanswerable. What justification could we find for exposing our little country to a danger from which even the most powerful nations on earth have shrunk?

(At this point the transcript runs for twenty-two pages, as the representatives from Belgium, Norway, Denmark, Holland, Hungary, Greece, Rumania, and Yugoslavia are heard from. There is considerable variation in the length of their speeches, but all express much the same view as the representative from Sweden.)

WEINSTEIN: Gentlemen, none of you have offered to take in even a handful of these people. Is there any possibility that you might reconsider your decisions?

PARSONS: May I remind you that His Majesty's government have made no decision as yet. I have simply outlined what my personal recommendation shall be—

WEINSTEIN: Is there any possibility that you might reconsider your recommendations?

(Long silence.)

WEINSTEIN: One person here hasn't spoken yet. He represents no government in the usual sense, but the moral authority of his superior might, I think, exert some influence on you. Monsignor Vacelli, you've been present throughout these proceedings. Have you had the opportunity to make a report to the Vatican? Could His Holiness be induced to express his concern for the people on the *Franz Joseph*?

MONSIGNOR VACELLI: His Holiness does express his concern. The fate of every soul on earth concerns him, and in his prayers every night he includes his children on the liner *Franz Joseph*, though they neither profess the Christian faith nor recognize the supremacy of the Church. His Holiness must stop short, however, of directing any specific pleas to any of the nations of the world on the question of allowing these people to cross their frontiers. This would amount to interfering in the internal political affairs of these nations, which of course the Vatican will never do. But even more important, the people of Germany are also God's creatures, whose souls must be considered in His Holiness' prayers. If the German government eventually decides that these thousand refugees are to return to their homeland, how can His Holiness speak out against this without implying that the German government intends, in some manner, to mistreat the returning exiles?

WEINSTEIN: But it *does* intend—

VACELLI: Perhaps so. But this is something of which His Holiness cannot possibly be certain. The assumption that a man will commit a sin cannot be made before the fact. The human will is free, and therefore a man's actions cannot be condemned until after he has performed them. Just as every man may, through sincere repentance, find absolution even in the last moment of his life, so it must be assumed that every man, right up to the very moment of action, will see what is right and refrain from doing evil. Therefore, though his sympathy for the Jews is boundless, His Holiness will not fall into the grievous error of prejudging his children the Germans—and so he cannot express any official views concerning the liner *Franz Joseph*.

(Silence.)

WEINSTEIN: Then those people are doomed. Thank you, gentlemen, for your valuable time and for your generous expressions of sympathy.

(The meeting is adjourned.)

* * *

Morrie hadn't intended to lose his temper. Certainly not in front of Abraham Weinstein. But in the cab going back to their hotel Al and Weinstein started talking about plans for another conference, about contacts in South America and Africa and China, about several important men whose help might be enlisted—and Morrie was tired, and his head was aching, and before he could stop himself he was waving his arms and talking at the top of his voice.

Mostly he repeated what he had said two weeks ago in Washington. Behind-the-scenes negotiations, bowing and scraping to important men, appeals to the consciences of world leaders—all these techniques that AJDA was so proud of simply weren't going to work. With a few exceptions— FDR, if anybody could ever *get* to him, and maybe a handful of others—world leaders have power and parasites and love applause but won't respond to a human appeal. The only hope for the people on the *Franz Joseph* was to give the story to the newspapers, let the ordinary man know what was happening. Nobody was going to help those poor bastards except their fellow human beings.

All right, Morrie knew what Al would say to this. He could imagine the words already—"It's against AJDA's policy!" What he wanted to hear was Weinstein's opinion.

And after a moment Weinstein gave his soft smile. "When you say that Jews can't depend on important men, Mr. Feldman, how could I possibly disagree with you? I've seen too many of the breed myself. But when you suggest that we take our grievances to the ordinary man, to our fellow human beings—that, I'm afraid, is when you show how young you really are. By the time you're as old as I am, you'll understand that people get the leaders they deserve. Important men are no more than magnified images of unimportant men. If the leaders don't give a damn about us, why suppose that the followers feel any differently? Are you under the impression that pogroms through the ages have been esoteric activities indulged in by an elite minority? Read a bit of history, Mr. Feldman. You'll discover that the persecution of Jews is one of the most *popular* sports ever invented by Western man."

The cab pulled up to the hotel. Morrie and Al got out, but Weinstein was going on to the World Zionist building. So he leaned forward on his walking stick and spoke to them through the open door. "Among Zionists, you know, there are those who welcome the coming holocaust. Yes, they welcome it, even though they know it will mean the destruction of hundreds of thousands, perhaps even millions, of European Jews. This sacrifice may be necessary, they think, so that the survivors should learn the vital lesson once and for all: Jews can't depend on their fellow human beings. Jews don't *have* fellow human beings. Jews can't depend on anybody but themselves."

"But *you* don't believe that?" Morrie said.

"Me?" Weariness was in Weinstein's eyes. "I'm a very old man. You can't imagine how old I am. I'm so old that I have grandchildren who no longer look young to me. Whatever happens, I won't be a survivor for many more years. I wonder, then—am I entitled to an opinion?"

Another soft smile, then he shut the door and leaned back in his seat, and the cab moved away from the curb. . . .

Al and Morrie went into the hotel and rode up in the elevator in silence. As they opened the door of their room the phone started ringing.

Al answered the phone. He talked into it for nearly twenty minutes, but Morrie couldn't make out much about the conversation. Mostly monosyllables from Al. Finally he hung up the phone and looked up at Morrie with a sour grin. But all of Al's grins were sour—there was no way of knowing whether this one expressed satisfaction or disgust.

"Somebody's made an offer for our cargo," Al said.

For a second Morrie couldn't absorb this. "What cargo?"

"Well, for *one* piece of the cargo, to be exact. That was the representative from Holland—what's his name? Van der Hoeft? Van der Hoeven?"

"Van der Hoeft. What did he *say?*"

"The Netherlands Radio Symphony Orchestra—a government-financed organization—has been looking for a permanent conductor for three years, ever since its old one died. They offered the job to Emil Karlweis three years ago, and he turned it down. Now that they've found out he's on the *Franz Joseph*, they want to renew the offer. If he'll accept the conductorship of their orchestra, they'll give him a visa to enter the country."

"Just Karlweis? Nobody else?"

"How many conductors do you think this orchestra needs?"

Morrie could feel the excitement dying away inside of him. "One out of a thousand," he said. "Well, I guess it's better than nothing."

"Better than nothing! Is that all you can say?" Morrie couldn't understand why Al's face was suddenly so flushed. "This is what we've been waiting for, don't you get it? The wedge in the door—the leverage—the straw that broke the camel's back."

"You mean, when the other countries hear about Karlweis going to Holland, they might change their minds—"

"When they hear about Karlweis *not* going to Holland. When he *refuses* the Dutch government's offer. Imagine the headlines, will you—in every newspaper in the world, outside of the Fascist countries. 'World-Famous Conductor Refuses to Leave Doomed Ship. Won't Desert His People, Karlweis Declares.' My God, you keep talking about appeals to the conscience of humanity. Can you imagine a more irresistible appeal than that one?"

The excitement was stirring in Morrie again. But he had to keep shaking his head. "How can you be sure that Emil Karlweis will go along with this?"

"He damn well has to. We'll cancel our plane tickets this afternoon, we'll stay in Paris a few more days—you'll get on the radio to Aaron Peyser and explain the situation to him and tell him that it's up to him to *make* Karlweis refuse that offer."

Before Morrie could raise another objection, Al was on the phone, demanding numbers from the operator, barking orders, giving Morrie instructions out of the side of his mouth.

An hour later they were in a cab on their way to the French Line warehouse where the radio set was located. For the first time Morrie realized what had been nagging at him subconsciously. "This idea depends on publicity, lots of publicity," he said. "So what about AJDA's sacred behind-the-scenes negotiations? What about not calling attention to ourselves, not making ourselves conspicuous, not arousing latent anti-Semitism by raising a fuss? What about all those policies you've been defending lately?"

"Have you heard me stop defending them? They're wonderful policies. Wonderful. As an AJDA employee in good standing, I'm behind them a hundred percent. But who has to know what I'm doing on my own time?"

"You think Dan won't find out eventually?"

Al leaned back in his seat, and Morrie had never seen such a contented smile on his face. "What's he going to do, fire me? I doubt it, somehow. Once the war starts and the USA is in it, AJDA will be begging on bended knees for good over-age men."

TEN

IT was bitter cold on deck, though it was only two o'clock in the afternoon. The water was gashed with foam, and the sky was clogged by those thick gray clouds which came swarming in early every morning to smother the first faint flickers of the sun. I can't *stand* it here, Julia Bender told herself. What had become of that glorious midocean feeling of space stretching away in every direction? Here in this Godforsaken spot, this pocket of gloom in the middle of nowhere, space seemed to be pushing closer all around them every day. How long would it be before the ship was squeezed to a pulp?

Julia was sitting in a deck chair by the swimming pool. It was deserted now, drained of its water and covered with stretched canvas that flapped at the edges. She was bundled up in blankets, but even so, her lips were trembling. I must be crazy to stay out here in this miserable weather, she thought. I'd go back inside like a shot, if I could just decide what drove me outside in the first place.

Could it be what she and Claire Halevy had been talking about at breakfast this morning?

"Ever since we anchored in this dismal place," Claire had said, "it isn't Hitler and the Nazis I've been hating. It's the inside of this ship. That cabin of mine with the chipped paint above the porthole—this dining room with that mirror over there sending me back my own image three times a day while I shovel food into my mouth—that lounge upstairs with its dreadful resort-hotel murals and those ugly overstuffed armchairs!"

Julia had the same feelings—not about the furniture but about the walls. It seemed to her lately that every crack and every bump on every wall on this ship had been familiar to her since childhood. She found herself wandering desperately from room to room, searching for one square inch of wall that she hadn't seen a hundred times before.

"Do you suppose we're the only ones?" Claire had said. "Is anybody else as sick of this ship as we are?"

Julia didn't know the answer. It was a matter of temperament, she supposed. Carl had told her once that some men in prison become so attached to their cells that they can hardly bring themselves to leave them once they're set free. She didn't think she would enjoy their company very much. She preferred restless, unstable, neurotic types like Claire Halevy. She had spent a good deal of her adult life trying to surround herself with such types, trying to break free of the stuffy, predictable, upper-bourgeois world into which she'd been born. "Some of my best friends are lunatics"—that was one of her remarks that used to infuriate Gunther. Poor hidebound Gunther with his Prussian-officer mind, as old-fashioned and overstuffed and ugly as those armchairs that Claire despised. Carl, of course, would never let such a remark faze him in the least. Rather he would greet it with one of his ironic smiles, instantly revealing it in all its puerility—

She shivered and hugged her blanket closer. Stop thinking about Carl, she told herself. Don't let him push himself into your mind. Tactful, disciplined, undemonstrative Carl—who ever would have supposed he could be so pushy? "Just another one of those pushy Jews!" Her uncle Ernest had said that when she told him that she and Carl were planning to get married. And she had laughed and teased him about his out-of-date prejudices. Who could have guessed how very up-to-date these prejudices would become only two years later?

And if I *had* guessed how the world was going to change in two years?

A thoroughly futile question, of course. Yet it had been in Julia's head more and more these last weeks. Since that afternoon when Carl told her about his plan. . . . She wished she could forget that afternoon. They had been playing the waltz from *Die Fledermaus* in the lounge; you could hear it through the open doors, thumping away in time to Carl's words. For the rest of her life she would never be able to listen to that waltz again.

How could he have said such terrible things to her? How could he have asked her such a question—and worse, still worse, shown so clearly what he expected her answer to be? If that was the kind of person he thought she was—if he had so little respect for her, so little faith in her—my God, how she wanted to fling her answer back in his face!

She smiled to herself and shivered and began to hum the waltz from *Die Fledermaus*. Deliberately she forced the whole long, insipid melody through her head. For she *hadn't* flung her answer back in his face. A week had passed since that terrible afternoon—more than a week—and she still hadn't opened her mouth. Carl never pressed her, never mentioned the offer he had made. They ate together, went to films and concerts together, strolled together on the deck—and at night he saw her dutifully to her cabin and kissed her at the door —and not once did he refer to the awful question that hung between them. And not once did she refer to it, either. All she had to do was lift her chin indignantly, in the manner of an "insulted" movie heroine, and inform him, "I'm not the sort of person you took me for!" So easy—but the days slipped by, and she didn't do it.

What was she waiting for? A miracle, a stroke of lightning, a God swooping down in a machine—the sudden announcement that the ship was saved, that France or England or some other benevolent nation had decided to take in all the passengers, that no more horrors lay before them? Because the longer she could pretend that no decision was being asked of her, the better chance there was that no decision *would* be asked of her? Why else had she kept herself so busy these last days, done so much swimming, played so much deck tennis, ploughed through so many boring books?

A violent fit of shivering came over her. She stood up, rubbed her hands together, walked to the railing. She stared out at the choppy water and the scowling clouds. All this grayness, this dreariness—it made her see how hopeless her stupid delaying tactics were. Waiting for a miracle that couldn't happen—knowing all along what she would do eventually. And after all, why not? How could anybody blame her? As Carl himself had pointed out to her, she couldn't save *him* no matter what, so it was her duty to think about Eva, about her poor child who hadn't done anybody any harm—

She shook her head, feeling the sharp wind against her cheeks. No, I won't fool myself this time. If I accept Carl's offer, it'll be for nobody's sake but my own. I won't use my daughter to cover up my shame. I know perfectly well that I can save Eva without saving myself—I can send her to live with Gunther's parents, they're always saying what a scandal it is for her to be under my evil influence. They'll take good care of her, nobody will touch her, she hasn't got a drop of Jewish blood in her. If I *do* save myself, I won't be able to claim Eva as an excuse.

If I do? But I'm simply not going to. I'm not the sort of person Carl thinks I am. . . .

A figure rose up before her eyes—a tall white wraith that seemed to materialize from the shadows. She gave a little cry, quickly suppressed as she realized it was only another passenger moving into the light from the covered part of the deck.

It was the man with one arm, the man named Ehrlich. In the course of the whole trip she hadn't exchanged three words with him. On the first day her attention had been caught by his empty sleeve—because she hated deformities, always shuddered away from blind men or hunchbacks or people who were crippled in any way—but after that she had hardly noticed that he was around. Until a day or two after the ship left New York—then suddenly Ehrlich seemed to be forever before her eyes. She'd be sipping coffee in the lounge, and she'd see him passing by the window. She'd be dancing in the night-club, and over her partner's shoulder, through the doorway into the bar, she'd see him sitting up straight at a table, slowly raising and lowering a glass. Something was strange about the way he moved his arm and his legs, held his head in the air, stiff and mechanical like a badly manipulated puppet. And every day his face seemed to grow whiter, as if a few more drops of blood had been drained from him. It frightened her to see him. There was something about him. . . .

He crossed the deck. He was only a few feet away from her. She held her breath, shrank back against the railing. She couldn't bear it if he turned and looked at her.

He went right past her, picking his way among the deck chairs, and disappeared into the shadows at the other side of the ship. And Julia slowly let out her breath. She felt as if she had just seen a corpse. Yes, that was the thing about his eyes. They were dead. The man was dead. The strings that held him to life had snapped. He was a puppet who should have collapsed in a heap on the stage—only somehow, maybe out of sheer habit, he kept upright and in motion.

And now, at last, she knew the truth about herself. It could happen to me, too, she thought. It's fear that does such a thing to a person, fear that goes beyond ordinary everyday fear, terror that bursts the bonds of human feeling—and she knew that terror of that kind could come to *her*, and maybe she wasn't so far away from it right now. All her life she had been a coward. The air of boldness she had cultivated since girlhood, that look of careless defiance which she had worn for the benefit of her family, her social circle, her conventional world—all that was really nothing but an ingenious camouflage for the shameful cowardice that lay at the heart of her. A cheap form of camouflage, at that, for in creating the mythical figure of "that girl who isn't afraid to do absolutely *anything*" she had attacked only those without defenses. People like poor Monsky and little Betsy Tannenbaum—those were the targets of her wit, her sarcasm, her famous courage.

And her marriage to Carl—yes, no doubt of it, this had been one of her very cheapest gestures of bravado. He was a Jew, and on her level of society it "wasn't done" to marry a Jew. So she defied the world and married him—bravo for her. Except that she hadn't really lived on "her" level of society for years—not since her divorce from Gunther. Most of her friends came from quite a different level, from a fashionable Bohemian world in which Jews were quite happily tolerated, in which marrying one of them, though it may have been considered rather adventurous and "fast," couldn't have been safer. And then again, *what* a Jew she had married—handsome, brilliant, one of Berlin's leading psychiatrists, uninvolved in his religion, indifferent to the Jewish community, accepted for years in certain circles where few of his race had ever penetrated. She couldn't have found a more un-Jewish Jew if she had tried.

People had fawned over her in her set when she announced the engagement. They had flattered her for her "heroism," her "broadmindedness," her "advanced" ideas—and she had lapped up the flattery. But later, when the shadow fell, when a *real* test of her heroism presented itself—look what she did, look how she rose to the challenge. She showed what fine material she was made of by going to Santini's every week, pretending to be Mrs. Gunther von Helmuth, listening without a word of protest to the anti-Semitic filth that was spewed out all around her.

And now, right now, she was about to act the same way again. Fear would pulverize her, as it had always done— once a coward, always a coward. She intended to accept Carl's offer. She intended to go along with his plan, as he had known she would from the start—how exasperating of him to be always so right about her! She intended to go to him right now and tell him what she had decided.

She left the deck quickly and headed for the reading room off the main lounge. This was where he seemed to be spending his afternoons lately. Halfway across the lounge she saw him through the glass partition. He was alone, absorbed in his thoughts. He hasn't seen me, she thought. Still time to pull back. Why tell him my decision face to face after all? Why put both of us through such a painful and unnecessary ordeal? Much better, much *kinder*, to get it all down on paper, and seal it in an envelope, and ask a steward to deliver it to him. . . .

Furiously she rejected this thought. You're a coward, she told herself—you can't seem to do anything about that. But at least you can be an *honest* coward.

So she continued across the lounge until she got to the reading room, and without hesitation she opened the door and stepped inside. Carl looked up and saw her. A smile— one of his soft, ironic ones, of course—came to his face.

*   *   *

In spite of the static, Aaron could hear the excitement in Morris Feldman's voice. "There are no guarantees, of course, but if you *can* persuade Mr. Karlweis—"

"I'll speak to him," Aaron said. "I'll do what I can."

He tried to put some enthusiasm into his voice; he knew this was what Morris Feldman wanted. But mostly what he was feeling was a kind of wry amusement. So this was the pass they had all come to. Their lives might be saved if the great Karlweis could be persuaded to risk his own. Could anything more unlikely be imagined than the spectacle of Emil Karlweis sacrificing himself for his fellow men?

Morris Feldman was saying, "Get in touch with us as soon as you know anything—even if it's the middle of the night. So we can get the ball rolling."

The ball rolling, Aaron thought, as he turned away from the radio set. To Morris Feldman, with all his sympathy, with all his anxiety for their safety, this was still a kind of game. Aaron noted this without resentment or bitterness. It was simply a curious fact of human nature. Nobody believes, really believes, in somebody else's pain, in somebody else's death. Such things can't be experienced from the outside. He had been no different himself, he realized. How many times through the years had Sophie told him, when he came home from work, that so-and-so had just died—and after the first moment of shock, the first conventional expression of regret, he had managed to dismiss the tragedy from his mind and enjoy a hearty dinner.

He thanked the wireless operator and walked out of the radio room. As he moved down the corridor he began to notice something strange about his reaction to the news Morris Feldman had just given him. It was very bad news— the governments of Europe had refused to help them—yet he was feeling quite cool and dispassionate about it. He was deliberately detaching himself from it, deliberately keeping all emotion at a distance. He had made a promise to himself the night the ship weighed anchor outside of New York. He had promised himself that somehow he would lead these people to safety. There were many moments since then when it had seemed like a stupid, arrogant promise, but nevertheless he intended to keep it. Anger, hatred, despair— intense feelings of any sort—could only interfere with him in keeping his promise.

Above all, he had to protect himself against something which he could see happening to many others around him. The idleness, the frustration, the growing fear were making more and more of them feel the urge to do something, to do *anything,* even some wild act of violence that couldn't possibly achieve any practical results. Already there had been minor explosions—the Fischel woman blurting out her outrage back in Havana, David and Peter and those other boys with their escape attempt. How long could it be before a major explosion occurred? Look at how strangely his father-in-law had been acting lately. No long-winded speeches, no card playing with his cronies—more and more sitting alone scowling, muttering to himself. All his life he had been a man of action, a man who was used to controlling his own destiny—sooner or later wasn't he bound to explode into action here? And the ship was full of men like him, young ones as well as old ones.

From these people, smouldering with impatience, nothing could come but disaster. Somebody had to keep his head. Somebody had to think things through coolly and come up with a workable plan. It was up to him, Aaron knew.

Well, what about the plan that Morris Feldman had just suggested? Self-sacrifice from Emil Karlweis—talk about drowning men clutching at straws! All right, all right, but drowning men *do* clutch at straws if nothing else happens to be available. How foolish to dismiss Morris Feldman's plan out of hand without at least giving it a chance. And so as he started down the stairs from the bridge, Aaron asked himself what kind of pressure could be applied to this stubborn, egotistical, supremely self-reliant old man. Humanitarian pleas? Karlweis considered himself to be in a different class from the rest of humanity. Threats of ostracism? Karlweis had already ostracized himself from his fellow passengers, and it didn't seem to bother him one bit. Trickery? What if Aaron never told Karlweis about the Dutch government's offer and trumped up a refusal in his name? No, this wouldn't work. The Dutch representatives would insist on talking to Karlweis over the radio—

Aaron heard his name being called.

Muller was standing at the top of the stairs, looking down at him. "I was about to send someone to look for you. The captain has a message for you. Please come to my office."

"I've got some things to do—"

"They'll have to wait. This message is urgent."

Aaron looked up into that cold, yellowish face, those hard, unblinking eyes—just a bit bloodshot, with puffy circles under them. If Aaron's memory wasn't misleading him, Muller's eyes hadn't looked that way at the beginning of the voyage. Evidently the waiting was getting on *his* nerves, too—possibly the thought of Jewboy Peyser receiving regular messages from the captain was causing Muller to lose some sleep. Well, that was something anyway, one positive achievement, however small, in the midst of the debacle.

He followed Muller up the stairs. As he watched that stiff ramrod back, it occurred to him that he knew absolutely nothing about this young man. Was Muller married, did he have children, parents, girlfriends—or was he all alone in the world? Could someone like Muller be anything *but* alone in the world? People like them, Aaron had often thought, can't have anything in common with people like us.

They came to Muller's office. Muller sat down at his desk, and Aaron started to sit down, too—as usual, without being asked. Then he saw the faint smile twitching at Muller's lips, and he knew that something bad had happened. He remained standing. Suddenly he had lost his taste for Muller-baiting.

"The captain, Mr. Peyser, has just heard from Hamburg."

After a moment Aaron said, "Orders to go back to Germany?"

"In a sense. Last week Hamburg was contacted—not by the captain himself, I might add." Another twitch of Muller's smile. "The point was made that our original mission has failed, and each day at sea increases the likelihood of our situation attracting public notice and causing embarrassment to the Reich. Hamburg has now replied, expressing agreement but pointing out that it cannot rescind the captain's orders, as they were originally issued by a very high source—the highest possible source. Therefore Hamburg has put the matter in his hands and expects his response shortly. Having no doubt what it will be, Hamburg advises the captain to be prepared for sailing orders within a few days."

Aaron refused to let any reaction show on his face. "The captain promised us two full weeks," he said. "There are almost six days to go."

"You'll get your six days," Muller said. "That can't be prevented. Even if the orders should come tomorrow, the captain would be permitted a certain amount of time to check equipment and make repairs—"

"And afterward? If nobody has taken us in six days from now?"

Muller didn't say anything.

"What will the captain do?" Aaron said. "Now that he's fattened us up, will he turn us over to the butchers?"

Muller still didn't say a word.

"I want to see the captain," Aaron said. "I want to ask him—"

"I'll pass on your request to him. If he wishes to see you, he'll send for you."

"I've been through that already. He never even acknowledges my requests. I've got a right to—"

"Right?" Muller said the word softly. "The captain is supreme commander of this ship. He confers benefits. He doesn't recognize rights." Muller leaned back, contemplated Aaron in silence for a moment, then went on. "Let me give you a piece of advice, Mr. Peyser. Don't depend on the captain. He's gone as far for you as he can go."

"Not if he chooses to go further."

"What he chooses is no longer the issue. The captain is our supreme commander, but even he can't act with absolute freedom. His choices are limited, just like yours or mine."

"Limited by what? Does he have a family back home? Is he afraid of reprisals?"

"He has no family. He's quite alone in the world."

"What's frightening him, then?"

Muller's face darkened. "Is fear the only form of compulsion you can imagine? What an incredible people you are! Do you recognize no ideal, no loyalty, no unselfish goal outside of your own desires? No wonder the whole world has hated you throughout history—"

Muller stopped abruptly, seeming to regret that he had allowed himself to raise his voice. After a moment he spoke calmly again. "You've heard the captain's message. There's no more to say. Good afternoon, Mr. Peyser." And he got to his feet.

Aaron stared at him for just a second. Then he turned and left the room as quickly as he could.

No emotion, no emotion, he kept telling himself as he hurried along the corridor. Emotion must be kept at a distance. There's a problem to solve. Concentrate on the problem.

The problem was Karlweis. What was the best way to approach Karlweis? As he walked down the stairs, Aaron turned this over in his head, and by the time he reached the main deck he realized that the problem had only one possible solution. On this whole ship there was only one man who might conceivably have any influence over Karlweis.

What Aaron had to do now was find Rabbi Einhorn.

As he entered the main lounge, somebody passed him on the way out. Gray, stiff, cadaverlike—Ehrlich, the one-armed ghost. Aaron shivered.

*   *   *

"My God," Monsky said to himself, "such a face on the man! Death warmed over. Faces like that should be banned as public nuisances."

He gave a sigh of relief as that one-armed Ehrlich disappeared around the corner. Then Monsky started pacing the deck again. He was waiting for Betsy, for their regular afternoon constitutional. Four thirty sharp every afternoon, followed by hot coffee and schmaltzy music in the lounge. Two weeks ago he had had a private word with a certain connection of his who worked in the ship's hospital, and this connection had had a word with the ship's doctor—a dilapidated old man, he looked like he'd been senile since childhood, but still, he ought to know about pregnant women. Nothing could be healthier in the last two months, the doctor had said, than regular exercise within sensible limits. And no exercise is better for mother and child than walking. So Monsky had passed on the advice to Betsy—telling her he had heard it years ago from a cousin of his who was one of the biggest obstetricians in Prague (she was more likely to pay attention if he gave his story an air of authority)—and ever since, he had been devoting himself personally to making sure she stuck to it. Exercise wasn't exactly the most joyous thing he could imagine himself doing—in the old days the most exercise he ever got was from lighting his cigars or shuffling the cards—but if *he* had to exercise so as to get *her* to do it, all right, he'd make the supreme sacrifice.

Rain or shine, hot or cold, too. When this terrible weather hit them a few days ago, she wanted to give up the whole idea. He positively wouldn't let her. "Listen," he said, "if a defective specimen like me can expose himself to the elements, so can a healthy child-breeding animal like you."

This made her blush and giggle. His great power over her was that he could make her blush and giggle practically at the drop of a hat. He had never been able to do that to any woman before. Plenty of them had giggled at him—or indulged in other, more raucous forms of laughter—but not because they liked his sense of humor. "She thinks I'm witty," Monsky told himself. "Yes, thank you, Mrs. Fischel, Mrs. Dr. Bender, Mrs. Landlady Baumeister, Miss Albertine Freiberg with your high-class relatives, that anonymous whore in the green dress, and all you other harpies who have been sticking your needles in me most of my life—yes, there *is* somebody who finds Leon Monsky witty, who appreciates his jokes, who enjoys his sophisticated, mocking, penetrating view of life. All right, admittedly she hasn't got the brains of an Einstein, or even a Mrs. Einstein—but what about you, my fine, snotty bitches? When did any of *you* ever pass an examination to be geniuses?"

Monsky reached for a cigar. He was in a tremendous mood. He was in just the kind of mood that a cigar gives an edge to, transforms from pleasant euphoria into positive ecstasy. But no, he knew he'd better not light up. He was down to his last five cigars—and even this had been possible only by the most heroic exercise of his willpower. That is, he had rationed himself to one cigar every other night, and except for once or twice he had kept to his rations like a martyred saint. So he couldn't throw away the future just because of a random mood.

Besides, Betsy would be here any minute, and the smell of cigars upset her, a temporary disturbance of her system due to her pregnancy. He often imagined how pleasant it would be someday to settle back in an easychair and light up his cigar while Betsy hurried to put the ashtray within his reach. And little Leon came scampering up to him, demanding to be read to.

What would little Leon call him? "Uncle"? Much too ordinary—children call *everybody* uncle. "Grandpa"? That sounded better. Though God knows he planned to get a lot closer to this little boy than most grandfathers get. Most of them he had seen, they hand their grandchildren a little money from time to time, and that's all the interest they show.

"Not me," Monsky told himself. "That's positively not the kind of grandfather *I'm* going to be. When little Leon—or maybe little Leona, who can tell?—feels like sitting on my knee and expressing his opinions about life, this knee and these ears are going to be available."

He frowned. The flow of happy thoughts ground to a halt. What kind of foolishness was he thinking? Where—in what world exactly—was all this blissful domesticity going to take place? If this ship got to a safe port, then waiting for Betsy, somewhere along the line, would be Martin Tannenbaum and that house in Camden, New Jersey—that insipid little paradise for middle-class clods. What room was there in *that* world for self-appointed grandfathers?

And if this ship took them all back to Germany? To think of Betsy there was terrible. It was terrible. They would do things to her there—and to the baby after it was born. If they even *let* it be born. . . .

But that part would be all right, Monsky felt sure of that. Not because the Nazis weren't animals enough for anything— but because they were slow animals, they moved like bureaucrats all over the world. "I should know," Monsky told himself. "Didn't I work for eight months in a government shipping office? The most relaxing job I ever had!" So the chances were, when the ship docked in Hamburg, all the passengers would be sent back where they came from—back to their own cities, their "restricted" neighborhoods—and there they would wait, for months at least, maybe for years. They might starve a little while they were waiting, and a few unlucky ones—or lucky ones, maybe—might get picked up and hauled off to God knows where. But for most of them there'd be time—enough time for little Leon to get himself born, learn to walk maybe, even say a few words. Of which "Grandpa" would be among the first.

"Time—what else do you want?" Monsky asked himself. A month, a year, a couple of years. Him and Betsy. Somewhere he'd find a place for her to live, food to keep her in health till the big moment, a doctor when it finally happened, milk for the baby afterward. Somewhere, somehow he'd find these things. He had *always* lived from hand to mouth. Plenty of times in his life he had wondered where the next meal was coming from, but it always came from somewhere in the end. A man just has to have patience and a brain or two and a little experience at handling a deck of cards or spinning out a plausible-sounding story. That was the big advantage he had over everyone else on this ship. He knew what it was like to be up against it. He was already an expert at surviving.

And his expert knowledge could be used for Betsy's sake, for the baby's sake, as well as his own. She could depend on him, and he wouldn't let her down. When she said to him in the morning, "We need some soup for dinner tonight," she would know for a fact that soup would be forthcoming. Would Mrs. Aaron Peyser be able to feel so sure of her soup? Would Mrs. Bruno Schwarzkopf look so plump and healthy after a few weeks of the kind of diet *that* big fourflusher could provide? And what about Mrs. Dr. Carl Bender—how many mink coats and diamond bracelets would her brilliant psychoanalyst be able to dig up for her conducting his practice among the garbage cans?

But Mrs. Martin Tannenbaum won't have to worry, he thought. She'll have Leon Monsky taking care of her. He'll be father and husband to her both. Not in the nasty filthy-minded way that was being imagined, he knew, by vicious scandalmongers like that Fischel woman. He would be her protector, her proxy guardian. Her Martin couldn't be with her any more, but Leon Monsky would do the job.

He remembered something she had said to him a couple of nights ago. "What I worry about more than anything is that I might have the baby before I can be with Martin again. I don't know, it's hard to explain, but even if there are good doctors and nurses, and nothing at all to worry about—a woman wants her husband to be with her."

A spasm of pain had shot through him when he heard her say that. "You know what *I* worry about more than anything?" he had felt like snapping back at her. "I worry that this ship will come to port, that somebody will take us in, and your stupid Martin will be waiting there for you with his big shit-eating grin, as pleased as he can be because he's ruining my life!"

And then, while this thought was churning in his head, she had put her hand on his arm and smiled at him, that terribly earnest smile. "But *you'll* be there when it happens, Mr. Monsky. Even if Martin can't—I'll know that *you're* close by, and that'll be almost as good."

It was all he wanted from her, really. Crumbs from Martin's table, but what did he care? In his life he had got along with less than crumbs. "I'm a man in my forties, almost in my fifties," he told himself. "After all these years I'm entitled to some happiness. Even if it's for only a short time, a few months, a year or two. And after that—"

After that?

"All right, Monsky, how about it? What kind of a man *are* you? Do you really want her to go through that hell? For the sake of a few crumbs, a piddling handful of days, are you really willing to wish such a terrible ending on her?"

He was willing. That was the whole truth—he looked into himself, and he saw how hard he was wishing, praying, for exactly that.

He was what he was. He felt what he felt. Leon Monsky wasn't going to turn into Little Saint Leon in one night—or in *any* number of nights. The important thing was to keep his nastiness locked up inside him so that Betsy would never see it, never even suspect that it existed. If she ever found out what he was thinking—if she found out that he, of all

301

the people on this ship, was happy while there wasn't any news and was hoping only that the news shouldn't be good— she'd never talk to him again, she'd never be able to stand the sight of him again.

Fortunately, he had spent a lifetime hiding what he really felt from people. Let's face it, he was a natural-born liar, it was practically his only talent. He could sigh and pat Betsy's hand and join in the general gloom and stick out his jaw and face the worst nobly—he could play the part to the hilt and even get a kick out of playing it, and Betsy would never tumble to the truth. Poor lovable Betsy—thank God she was also, just a little bit, stupid Betsy.

Then he saw her coming along the deck. Right away he put a smile on his face and gave her a jaunty wave. And he noticed with satisfaction that already she was beginning to blush and giggle.

* * *

All the time Aaron Peyser was talking, Rabbi Einhorn managed to keep quite calm. "Yes, of course I'll go to Emil," he said. "Yes, I'll certainly do my best." Then Aaron Peyser left him, and the rabbi was alone on deck, and his heart started pounding.

He hadn't felt this way since the first time he stood up in front of a congregation over thirty years ago. Why should he be so afraid of asking Emil for help? What could Emil possibly say to him that would arouse this violent emotion? Surely, rather than falling into this state of agitation, he ought to be eager, full of hope. A new chance was opening up for all of them, a chance that their lives could be saved, and *he* was an essential part of it. He didn't have to wander aimlessly anymore, racked with his wretched sense of helplessness. At last there was something he could do.

He was cold. In the late afternoon just before sunset this grim gray mist was thicker than ever, it felt like icy needles against his face. He began to pace up and down to keep warm. For ages now, or so it seemed to him, the ship had been crouching in this shroud of mist. The end of the world, that's what this place was like. The plague of darkness was on them here. No wonder that one's mind became infested with gloomy thoughts.

Yes, he knew why he trembled with dread at asking

Emil for help. This was everybody's last great hope—and he had no hope for it, no hope at all. It was a cruel and tempting trap, carefully laid to lead them on, to cajole them into expecting the best—so that the pain, when the jaws of the trap snapped shut, would be that much more intense.

And who had laid this vicious trap?

For a week now the rabbi had been giving assurances to his children. "Trust in God," he had said to them. "God will not forsake us." How long had he known that this was a lie? How long had he been saying these empty, meaningless words while knowing in his heart that God had forsaken them already?

He had asked for a test—some way of testing his faith—in action, against real obstacles, because these endless debates with himself were as useless as chewing on air. Days and days ago he had prayed to the Lord for that test, but now his prayers seemed purely academic. The test had become irrelevant. While he had been praying so diligently, his faith had quietly deserted him. He was afraid of talking to Emil Karlweis because he knew that nothing could come of it. God, who didn't exist, would make sure that nothing came of it.

From the main lounge came the sounds of a waltz. A tuba, oomphing and bleating, nearly drowned out the melody. Emil certainly wouldn't be in there. When Edelmann and his orchestra gave a concert, Emil stationed himself as far away as possible.

The rabbi started down the deck towards the stern of the ship. He passed a figure by the railing, looking out at the sea. It was Ehrlich, the man with one arm. He was stiff and straight as a waxwork, this strange man to whom nobody on the ship could talk—for every conversation with him always came back to the same thing, to the arm he had given to the fatherland, to the "special category" it had put him in. Torn between guilt and anger, pride and shame—another one of the halfway people. How well the rabbi understood his predicament.

He increased his pace to get past Ehrlich as quickly as possible.

At the stern of the ship he climbed the outside staircase and made his way into the sun parlor. Here, as he had expected, he found Emil. This glassed-in room, with its wicker chairs and potted plants—and its murals of palm trees and jungle animals—was intended to create an atmosphere of tropical leisure and isolation. It was almost soundproof—Edelmann's hideous thumping couldn't reach in here.

Emil looked up from the chessboard on which he was working out a problem. "Max—what luck! Just time for a game before dinner."

It was a great temptation. They could settle into the game, the time would pass, his mind would clear itself of everything else—he could forget what Aaron Peyser had asked him to do.

"If the game could wait awhile, Emil. I have to talk to you about something important."

Emil leaned back in his chair. "I'm at your service, Max. What's important? A new argument that proves the existence of an exclusively Jewish God?"

The rabbi smiled nervously. This was an uneasy point with him. The boorish, presumptuous attempts he was always making to coax Emil back to Judaism—what right did he have to interfere with another man's beliefs? Who told him he was God's representative to the human race?

"It's hard for me to say this, Emil. When I was younger I was better at asking favors, making tactful requests—"

"When *I* was younger, I was better at turning them down. In my old age I've become softhearted, as you've no doubt observed. So fire away with your tactful request."

This speech made the rabbi more nervous than before. Emil's sense of humor always disconcerted him. To him Emil was invariably polite—but he had seen him turn his scorching sarcasm on other people. And in the back of his mind there was always the fear that Emil might at any moment turn it on him.

He mustn't think about that. He must simply do what he had to. So he took a deep breath and told Emil about the bad news from Europe. And then, before Emil could say anything, he told him about the Dutch government's offer.

He stopped there, as he saw the look that had come over Emil's face. The color had drained from his cheeks, and for a long time he didn't seem to be breathing. In his hand was a chessman—a white bishop—and he was pressing it so tightly between his fingers that the rabbi thought he would break it in two.

A moment later the breath came out of him slowly, and he lowered the white bishop to a square on the board. "Amazing," he finally said. "They're giving me back my life. I've

304

been telling myself they would, of course. They couldn't touch *me*, I've been telling myself. But you know, these last five or six days, I've been wondering just a little—" A kind of smile flickered over his face. "Well, my problems are over now, aren't they?"

"Over—?" The rabbi blinked at him. "No—I haven't finished yet—" He brought out the rest of it now, the plan that Emil was supposed to agree to. And when he was finished he lowered his eyes, almost as if he were ashamed of himself. He had no right to ask what he had just asked, no right to apply moral blackmail to another human being. This was what he had been doing all his life, he realized. This was what it meant to be a rabbi, to stand up in front of his equals and order them to be good. From the beginning, of course, he had justified himself. He was serving Judaism, he was serving God. How could he justify himself now? If there is no God, then all men aren't brothers.

He raised his eyes slowly and made himself look at Emil's face. It was like a plaster mask, empty and perfectly still; the least little twitch or blink, it seemed, would somehow smash the plaster to pieces. "Now let me understand you, Max," he said. "You're asking me to throw away my life all over again?"

"No—there's practically no chance of that. Aaron Peyser's American friend has assured him—"

"Aaron Peyser's American friend will be sleeping on dry land tonight. Aaron Peyser's American friend won't have to go back to Germany if the great gesture fails to impress the world."

"All right—I know that, Emil. There *is* a risk—"

"Thank you for admitting it. Now tell me, please—why should I run that risk?"

"There are a thousand people on this ship."

"A thousand people." Emil picked up the white bishop again and turned it between his fingers as he talked. He probably wasn't even aware that he was holding it. "Three weeks ago I had never set eyes on any of them. They didn't exist for me. Now you expect me to give up everything for them?"

"I know—I realize what I'm asking. If you say yes, and it turns out badly, don't you know what I'd be feeling—"

"Nothing like what *I'd* be feeling!"

The sarcasm made the rabbi wince. "All right, I understand

305

that. But a thousand people—could you have them on your conscience for the rest of your life?"

"On my conscience!" Emil stopped turning the white bishop between his fingers, but he still didn't let go of it. "It always amazes me, the ease with which some people can lay down the law for other people's consciences. What about these thousand consciences you're asking me to bleed for? How much bleeding will *they* do for me? If I offer to do what you want me to do, how many of these people, do you think, will come up to me and say, 'No, no, you mustn't take such a chance for us, I'd always have you on my conscience!'"

"Maybe none of them would—people are weak, I can't argue about that. But this is a case of a thousand against one—"

"Thank you for the lesson in mathematics." Emil was tightening his grip on that white bishop, and his face was getting tighter, too. "You'll excuse me, however, if I find it difficult to think of my life as a number in an accountant's ledger. According to *my* mathematics, this one life you're so willing to cancel out equals the value of a thousand, and another thousand, and another million if necessary. The only life I've *got* is my own!"

"But you just can't be so selfish—"

"Why can't I be? I've *earned* the right to be selfish. In sixty-six years have I ever taken help from any man? Everything I am, everything I ever accomplished—I did it by myself, with no favors asked or given. And in return, I might add, the world has received a certain amount from me. That was never part of my purpose, I won't deny it—I've made music for myself, and for myself alone—but the benefits have spilled over, haven't they? Are you going to say that the benefits haven't spilled over? And now—and now—" The plaster cracked—Emil's face became an explosion of wrinkles, splotches, veins standing out. His fist had closed around the white bishop, and he raised it in the air. "And now you ask me to throw all that away? You ask the impossible. You ask what doesn't make sense."

"You're right, of course you're right. Sense has nothing to do with it. It's instinct, Emil. It's the way any normal man would react—"

"Normal? You're accusing me of being a normal man?" Something like a laugh burst out of him, and he gave an

306

angry shake of his head. "Besides, I don't believe in this 'normal' instinct of yours. Do you really imagine that anybody else on this ship, if he found himself in my position, wouldn't do exactly as I'm doing?"

"I don't know," the rabbi said. "I can't answer for other people."

"Can you answer for yourself?"

Emil's gaze was fixed on him now, and his eyes were shining. "Yes, of course I can," the rabbi said quickly.

"Let me give you your opportunity, then." Some of the redness went out of Emil's face, and his fingers relaxed their grip on the bishop. "I'll tell the Dutch government that I accept their offer—on condition that they give you a visa, too. You and your son and your daughter. I'll say that you're on my staff, that you're my good-luck charms. It doesn't matter what I say—they're bound to agree, how else will that second-rate orchestra of theirs ever get a first-rate conductor? Well, what's your answer, Max? I know what you'd *like* to answer, I can see that on your face. Have you got the courage of your selfishness?"

Emil's smile was quivering before the rabbi's eyes. Freedom, he thought. Life. For Peter and Naomi, too. And nothing to stand in the way of it—except something that was only an illusion—of *course* he wanted to say yes. Of *course* he wanted to escape from this horror. Dear God, forgive me, he thought. God of Israel, forgive me. But you shouldn't have made it possible for me to doubt you. You should have made me *sure* of you.

And then suddenly he was in pain. He felt it deep inside him—but where was it? It was located nowhere—it was everywhere—and it was growing inside him, like the crescendo at the end of a Beethoven symphony. And it came to him, as the pain slowly built up inside him, that it didn't matter if he believed in God or not. Perhaps nobody *could* believe, perhaps nobody had *ever* believed, without any doubts, without any despair. Perhaps that was the test that he had been praying for. You were asked to believe in *life*, doubts and fears and all, to love it so fully that you could take it without guarantees.

The terrible pain was swelling into tears. The rabbi lifted himself unsteadily to his feet. "Thank you for your generous offer, Emil. I'm sorry I can't accept it."

"You *have* to accept it! Use your head!"

The rabbi found himself smiling. "After all these years?" he said. He left the room with Emil staring after him, crushing the white bishop in the palm of his hand.

*　　*　　*

It was over a week since they had had a meeting. Not since the night when Papa ruined everything. . . .

Even if they did have another meeting, David knew they wouldn't ask him to join them. So when Peter came up to him this afternoon and said, "The music room—six o'clock!" and then went away before he could answer, he couldn't believe it at first. They were really taking him back? They were going to be his friends again?

It was because of last night, David thought. He had been with Naomi every night for a week now, and it had been horrible, humiliating, and every time, after it was over, he told himself that he couldn't go on with it. But he wouldn't give up—a man doesn't give up—and finally, last night, a miracle had happened. It was as if he had spent his whole life shut up in a box, dark and cramped and stifling, and suddenly the box had sprung open and he had burst out into the light and the fresh air, into happiness and freedom. No wonder everything else was changing for him, too. From now on he would be living in a different world, a world in which he, David Peyser, would be somebody for once, in which he could finally get what *he* wanted. To begin with, tonight he would be seeing her again. . . .

He was the first one in the music room. He couldn't sit still while he waited for the others. He kept thinking about last night. He remembered Naomi lying on the bed—and the sound that came out of her, the soft sound that was partly a sigh and partly a groan. He remembered the joy and shock that had spread like fire through his whole body when it happened. And the moment before that, when he knew it was *going* to happen—finally, finally, after all his suffering and humiliation, everything was going to be right—*that* moment was better, almost, than what came after.

He had cried a little when it was over, though luckily Naomi didn't notice. It was stupid to cry, but he couldn't help himself. Then he had raised himself on his elbow and looked into Naomi's face and asked her if she was happy.

She hadn't said anything. Her eyes were half shut, and her face was almost empty; all the lines of worry and fear had been smoothed out of it. He had read once that for girls it was like being transported into a special private world of their own, that for a while afterwards they didn't seem to be on this earth at all.

He had kissed her on the cheek, and then he had settled back against the pillow. It was so comfortable here, so warm and peaceful. He hadn't felt this peaceful since he was a little boy and Mama used to come to him at night and tuck him under the covers. Nobody could hurt him while he was here.

He began to speak, looking up at the ceiling but really speaking to Naomi. "Thank you," he had said. "It's been so hard on you—I guess I know how it's been for you. Putting up with someone like me."

For the first time her voice came, low and muffled. "There's nothing to thank me for."

"I love you," he had said, still looking up at the ceiling. "Don't ever leave me. Everything's going to be good from now on—"

The door of the music room opened. Altdorf and Halevy came in. Halevy's face was dark with anger. With something else, too. He looked tired. His red hair was rumpled, as if he had tossed and turned in his bed all night. "So what's this all about?" he said. "If our leader thinks I'm rowing back to New York from *here*—"

Schlossberg arrived, out of breath. He looked bewildered—he asked each of them twice if they knew why Peter had called this meeting. A moment later the boy named Paul arrived. He was paler than ever, and he seemed to have lost weight since David had seen him last a few days ago. He nodded at the others and slumped into a chair without saying a word.

Finally Peter arrived. He told them all to sit down, then he stood in front of them. "You'll hear about this soon enough," he said, "so you might as well hear it from me. The big conference in Europe has been held, and it's a complete failure. None of those countries—not a single one—has offered to take us in."

They all started asking questions at once. How did Peter find out about this? How could he be sure? Maybe it was just another rumor—

"I found out from our old friend Strassvogel," Peter said.

309

"We've become very close, ever since the night I showed such an interest in his New York girlfriend. He talks to me about her at every possible opportunity—and drops useful bits of information, too. He was on duty on the bridge this afternoon, and he heard what went on in the radio room. He heard your father talking to his American, David."

"What happens now?" said Paul. "Is there anything else they can do for us?"

"Strassvogel didn't hear any more. But I think we know the answer to that, don't we?"

They stopped asking questions. Silence settled over them, gray and gloomy, like the clouds outside the ship. David made himself look gloomy, too. But it was funny—underneath, though he knew how bad this news was, he kept on thinking about tonight, about Naomi.

"So the question is, what are we going to do about it?" Peter said. He looked around at them all. Nobody had anything to say. Peter went on. "I don't know how much longer this ship is going to sit here. A few more days. Maybe a few more weeks. It doesn't really matter, because sooner or later the Führer will give a twitch on his line and haul us back to Germany. That's inevitable, you understand. There's no way out. We'll sit here like rats in a trap, waiting for the cat to pounce—unless we take matters into our own hands."

He was silent, staring around at them. It didn't matter how bad things looked, Peter could always start them hoping again. There's nobody like him, David thought. He *will* get us out of this.

"What we're going to do," Peter said at last, "is to take over this ship. That's right, you heard what I said. We'll deal with the captain and the crew, and run the ship ourselves—and then we'll send the news out by radio, and don't you think it won't be played up all over the world. And then we'll sail from port to port until somebody takes us in because it's too embarrassing *not* to take us in."

"Piracy on the high seas," Halevy said. "I always thought this would happen to you, Einhorn. You've been seeing too many trashy films, and they've finally scrambled your brains."

"Sarcasm isn't going to keep us out of Germany," Peter said quietly, "so unless you can think of something that *will*—"

"But how *could* we take over the ship?" Altdorf said. "Only six of us?"

"You have to start using your imagination, Franz. Sure, there are only six of us. But there are a thousand passengers, and every one as desperate as we are. If we once make a start, show the rest of them that it can be done— Do you think this crew of a hundred or so is going to be any match for a thousand desperate people?"

"But even to make a start, like you say—it just doesn't seem possible—"

"It's the easiest part, the easiest of all." Peter's eyes were bright now, and his arms began waving. "Did you know there are guns on this ship? That's right, there's a whole arsenal—rifles, pistols, dozens of them, and plenty of ammunition, too. You know where Muller's office is—on the top deck, just below the bridge? Well, the door next to his, the one that's always locked—that's the door to the arsenal. They practically never open it up, it's strictly for emergencies. But I know where the key is, and I know how to get hold of it. All we have to do is go in there late at night, stock up on arms and ammunition, overpower the captain and Muller and the other officers— All right, it's crazy, it's out of a trashy film, it's impossible—but *is* it impossible? This isn't a navy ship, and the officers and the crew, even the captain, aren't military men. They're trained to run a ship, not to fight. So why shouldn't they run the ship the way *we* order them to— if they've got guns pointed at their heads? And don't forget, it won't be long, no longer than an hour or two, before the rest of the passengers will be joining us. There are plenty of able-bodied men among them—once we give them guns, once everybody is armed who can possibly be any use—what's an unarmed crew going to do, risk their necks for no good reason? They'll know we don't want to hurt them, we just want to save our lives."

"Some of them might not be overpowered so easily," Halevy said. "A fanatic like Muller would jump at the chance of risking his neck for the glory of the fatherland."

"How many Mullers could there *be* on this ship? Three or four, if that many. The rest just want to get home safe and sound to their wives and their whores. All right, so if Muller or anyone else tries to make trouble—"

Peter stopped and stared around at them again. After a while he went on, in a quiet voice, "You said it yourself, Kurt. Not so long ago. We can't be squeamish. If that's the only way."

Halevy looked into Peter's eyes. His face had gone white. He wet his lips.

"It *is* the only way," Peter said, turning from Halevy to the rest of them. "That's what we have to recognize. It's too late now for kidding ourselves. We're at the end of our rope. We either have the guts to do this, or we just lie down and die."

He waited, his eyes bright again. He turned those eyes on each one of them.

Altdorf was the first to nod. "Let's do it, then," he said in a low voice. "God help us."

Schlossberg said, "We're not going to hurt anybody, Peter? You know, I've always had to be careful—being so strong and all—"

"I promise you, Ernst—we won't hurt anybody who doesn't try to hurt *us*."

Schlossberg hesitated, grinned a little, then nodded.

Halevy scowled more fiercely than before. "It's the craziest thing I ever heard of in my whole life. It doesn't have one chance in twenty million. Just to mention one *minor* objection —even if we do get our hands on those guns, which seems pretty unlikely to me, how many people on this ship have the slightest idea how to use one? You're not dealing with an SS elite—you're dealing with businessmen, housewives, students, babies. And Jews at that—Jews don't even like to go *hunting*. Put those guns in our hands, and we'll end up blowing each other's heads off."

"Will you go along with us, Kurt?" Peter said.

Halevy's scowl deepened. "Of course I'll go along with you. When did I claim to be any saner than the rest of you?"

Peter turned to David.

"I'll go along," David said. There was nothing he wouldn't have done for Peter. After last night they were practically brothers, weren't they?

Only Paul hadn't spoken yet. Peter turned to him.

Paul's eyes shifted away. After a long time he spoke in his thin, unsteady voice. "It's the wrong way to go about it. I've always said that—from the beginning—a mass suicide. All the Jews of Germany. All together, the same day, the same hour. There's the only action that can *really* help. Half measures are worse than none at all—"

"You won't go along with us?" Peter said.

Paul got to his feet. "No—I don't believe, I sincerely

312

don't—" He shook his head a few times, then lifted it suddenly, and his eyes were red. "It's all over, don't you see? We can't help ourselves any more! What's the use of trying?"

He turned and hurried to the door. But Halevy got there first, barring his way. "You'll keep your mouth shut about this?" he said.

Paul stared at him, and his eyes were getting wider. Halevy's going to hit him, David thought. He's going to smash his fist into his face.

Peter stepped up to them and put a hand on Paul's arm. "It's all right, Kurt," he said. "Paul isn't going to say anything. *That* wouldn't be any use, either."

He opened the door. Paul scurried through it and was gone. Coward, coward, David thought. Didn't he realize that you have to be bold in this world, you have to *take* what you want or you'll end up with nothing at all? The way *he* had taken what he wanted last night.

Peter shut the door and turned back to them. He began to fill them in on the details of the plan. They couldn't make their move, he said, till next Wednesday night, almost a week from now. His friend Strassvogel would be on duty then, in the corridor where the arsenal was located. For most of the night he would be sitting at the desk in Muller's office, emerging every hour to check the other offices on his patrol. The key to the arsenal was kept in a drawer in Muller's desk —this was one of those useful bits of information that Strassvogel had dropped. While the others waited at the end of the corridor, Peter would enter Muller's office by himself and come smiling up to Strassvogel, who trusted him completely. . . .

The planning went on until the gong sounded for dinner. David could feel his heart giving a jump. Soon he would be seeing Naomi again. Soon they would be going together to his cabin, as they had done last night.

War during the day, lovemaking at night. That was the proper life for a man. , , ,

And so as soon as they got to the cabin after dinner, David locked the door behind him. Naomi heard the click and watched him coming toward her, smiling at her. It's going to be like last night, she thought.

Last night— He had been so happy. She had tried to be happy, too, tried so hard to keep from showing what she felt.

313

She didn't want to spoil it for him. She knew how cruel that would have been.

Tonight would be the same, she thought. Tomorrow night, too. And every night from now on, as long as they stayed on this ship. How could she bear it? It wasn't fair. He had no right—

But he *did* have a right. She had to bear it, and there it was. Nobody else was to blame for this, she had done this to herself. Because of her fear, her crazy, desperate feelings. Yes, a kind of madness had come over her, and now she had to live with it, with him. "I love you. Don't ever leave me. . . ." And she couldn't leave him, no matter what she felt. She had to listen to him pleading with her, smile at him and kiss him, carry the burdens he loaded on her. . . .

He began to undress her. Slowly he undid the buttons of her blouse. She tried to think of something else. Dinner tonight. Father acting so strangely, as if the strain which had been growing in him steadily were suddenly gone. Very gentle, very calm. No distress at some of Peter's remarks. And he even laughed at Mr. Monsky's jokes— She had read about people who escaped from painful situations by pretending that they didn't exist. Had Father become one of those people? That would be terrible, wouldn't it? You can't shut your eyes to reality.

Why can't you shut your eyes to reality? Things can get *too* real sometimes. She didn't want things to be so real.

What she wanted was Wolfgang. Little Wolfgang Amadeus Mozart, the only cat she had ever cared for. She wanted him to cuddle in her lap again and purr and lick her fingers, just as he used to do. She wanted to stroke his neck, the soft warm fur on the back of his neck. Stroking, stroking, while in her mind an image took shape—the image of *him*—tall, handsome, with broad shoulders and white teeth, and such firmness on his brow, such sensitivity in his eyes. Someday he would come for her, tell her how much he loved her and how he would take care of her forever, all she had to do was lean on him and she wouldn't be afraid of anything again. And then he would murmur poetry in her ear through the long warm soft nights—soft as Wolfgang's fur. . . .

"Naomi," he said. "Help me. Please."

She stared. It was David who looked at her, his pleading look. His shirt was off, and he was having trouble with her buttons—

"No, not tonight," she said. "I'm too tired. I don't think I can—"

He reached out to her, the pleading words pouring out of him. Please, Naomi, please. She struck his hands away, she could feel her fingers smarting. She could hear her voice, so loud, so shrill, such an ugly voice. "I *don't* love you! I can't!"

"Naomi—you told me—"

"Let me go! Please, please, let me go!" She was fumbling with her dress, screaming and weeping at the same time. "I can't bear this, why won't you see? All I want is for you to leave me alone!"

She ran across the room, unlocked the door, ran out into the corridor. She couldn't hear him behind her, she knew he wasn't following her, but she kept running till she got to the top of the stairs. Somebody jostled her, moved past her down the stairs. That Mr. Ehrlich, the man with one arm. His face looked as if it were made of ashes. Any minute they might crumble away. Like the whole world, like the whole world.

She ran out on deck and up to the railing. What did I do to him, how could I do such a thing? The words kept rushing through her head. She had to make them stop. They weren't real. David wasn't real, what they did together wasn't real. Nothing was real except *him*. Smiling down at her, stroking her hair, telling her he would take care of her forever.

And poetry was real. Nothing was more real than poetry. And in a low voice, muffled by the pounding of the waves against the ship, she began to say the words she had known by heart since she was twelve years old.

"Do you know the land where the lemon trees bloom,
   Where the gold orange glows in the deep thicket's
   gloom,
   Where a wind ever soft from the blue heaven blows,
   And the groves are of laurel and myrtle and rose?"

Over and over she said these words, like a little girl saying her prayers when she's afraid of the dark. . . .

Darkness filled the cabin and swallowed up the patterns of flowers on the wall. David kept staring at those flowers, even though he couldn't see them any more. He lay on his back on the lower bunk. He didn't put on his shirt.

She had to be punished, this he knew. The Jewess had to pay for what she had done. Not for *his* sake, not to satisfy

315

his feelings, but because this was justice, because crimes mustn't go unpunished. Yes, her brother, too—his crimes were even worse than hers. Those who plot against the fatherland must be exposed. Those who attack the fatherland must be crushed.

What was the name of the first officer? His name was Muller, wasn't it? He was loyal. He was devoted to the Führer. He was hated by all the passengers. Muller—he was the man to see.

The time had come, David told himself. Now he would prove—once and for all, beyond any doubt—that he wasn't one of *them*.

*   *   *

Karlweis could eat no dinner. Roast pork and applesauce —from the day he had broken away from his strict Orthodox family, this had been one of his favorite dishes—but all he could do tonight was pick at it. Tonight of all nights, when he should have had the appetite of a lifetime.

He wondered if his appetite was being damaged by his sympathy for these people around him. What utter poppycock! The feelings and fate of other people—anonymous, faceless "other" people—hadn't he just got through telling Max Einhorn how little they meant to him? In the course of his life he had seen plenty of such people come and go. Occasionally he felt some dismay, but he never had any trouble getting on with what mattered. Music was what mattered to him. He had no talent for weeping and gnashing his teeth over miseries that he hadn't caused and couldn't cure. People shouldn't waste their time on activities for which they have no talent.

Yes, what he had said to Max was true—the passengers on this ship *were* faceless and anonymous to him. Or if their faces had managed to push into his line of vision, he had been quite unable to develop the least bit of interest in them. How sympathetic could he be with a face like that Fischel woman's—a jabbering, poking, gobbling, shrieking, sneering face? Why should he care about a face like that of his cabin mate, that one-armed freak Ehrlich who couldn't open his mouth without reciting the dreary details of his military career and complaining about the fatherland's ingratitude toward its heroes? A curious kind of logic, to expect compassion and justice from a government which has paid you to kill and maim. Surely it would be more dignified, as well as more realistic, if Ehrlich recognized that he and the German government were collaborators in blood and torture, if he accepted the sensible old Biblical reminder that he who sows the wind shall reap the whirlwind. But dignity, consistency, and fortitude are given to few on this planet. Most people are dreary, dispensable mediocrities.

Karlweis had seen this confirmed again and again. There was simply no reason for him to stop believing it now. Why then should he pretend to a "humanity" he didn't feel or deny a "selfishness" which brought him no pangs of guilt?

He remembered Max Einhorn.

Was Max responsible for his loss of appetite tonight? He could see Max right now, sitting at his table on the other side of the room, sitting between his son and his daughter. That long, melancholy face—even when he smiled, Max looked just a bit sad and older than he really was. "You look ten years older than I do," Karlweis had told him once, and Max had smiled and said, "I probably am." This afternoon he had told Max what he felt, with no expectation that Max would approve. Since when did Emil Karlweis hold his opinions subject to other people's approval?

One thing he would admit. He felt differently about Max than he did about the others on this ship. Leaving Max behind when he went free—this would be a source of regret to him, of genuine sorrow. Very well, but whose *fault* would it be? He had done his best for Max, hadn't he?

He stuffed a piece of meat into his mouth. As an aid to swallowing it, he made himself think about the future, about having an orchestra of his own again. There was no use hiding from himself any more how much this was going to mean to him. In these last years, since they had taken the opera away from him, it had become harder and harder to live with his restlessness, his urgent need. . . .

He *had* to be able to make music. He was like any other musician in this respect, any tenth-rate fiddler in the back row of the second section. The only difference is that the conductor's instrument is the whole orchestra, the whole galaxy of fiddles and winds and brasses and drums—an instrument much easier to take away from a man, as Adolf Hitler and his foul crew had proved. Yes, these last years had been torture for Karlweis. Only his pride, his stubbornness, his monumental powers of self-deception had kept him from putting an end to it long ago, from accepting the first offer that came along and getting out of the country.

And now the impossible was happening—the first offer that had come along was coming along again. And it *wasn't* such a second-rate orchestra, really, despite what he had just said to Max. The old man who used to be its conductor— now blessedly departed—had let it run down badly, but it had possibilities, it certainly wasn't hopeless. And the Dutch were well known for their generous budgets for cultural affairs. A strong hand at the helm, a few years of hard work —there was no reason why the Netherlands Radio Symphony couldn't become one of the best in Europe.

He was chewing and chewing, but his mouthful of pork just wouldn't go down. He took a glass of water and gulped until he had swallowed the meat by sheer force. Then he firmly placed his knife and fork on the plate before him. The mere idea of taking another mouthful made his stomach queasy.

It *is* these people, he thought, looking at the faces around him. Pale, drawn, heavy circles under their eyes—showing the strain more and more every day. Even the Fischel woman didn't seem to be talking as much or as loudly as usual. And beyond his own table he picked out other faces that he knew. Bender the psychoanalyst, the very epitome of urbanity and self-control till now—but look at him tonight, an expression that was practically haunted. It wasn't pleasant to imagine what these people would look like when Aaron Peyser finally told them the most recent news. The Dutch offer would certainly become known, and so would the fact of Karlweis' refusal. And then, no doubt, the howling mob would turn on the villain and tear him to pieces? No, on the whole, he thought that social ostracism was more like what he could expect. Nasty glances, pregnant sneers, insulting remarks made within his hearing.

Would he therefore spend his last few days aboard taking his meals in his cabin?

Absolutely not. Let them do their worst, let them persecute him to their hearts' content. He was damned if he'd hide from them. He was *entitled* to his life. He didn't have to apologize for that.

He excused himself from the table without touching his dessert. He went up to the small lounge on the sundeck, away from that nightly abomination, the bingo game. After everything that had happened in these last few weeks, hundreds of people on this ship still gathered every night, put stupid little counters on silly little cards, and called out, "Bingo!" And there was still a school of thought which refused to admit that the human race was composed largely of idiots!

Karlweis sat down in a wicker armchair, crossed his legs, recrossed them, began to drum on the end table. How was he going to pass the time tonight? What he craved was a chess game. The board and the pieces were all set up in this room. To concentrate on those beautiful carved men, to build a world out of them, to empty his mind of everything else—but there wouldn't be any chess tonight, he knew, or any other night while he was still on this ship. Between him and Max Einhorn the games were over.

A book was lying on the end table. He picked it up, glanced through it. Some sort of stupid detective story—American, no doubt. He started reading in the middle of a chapter. Later he shut it with a snap. He was ten pages farther on, and he didn't have the slightest idea what he'd been reading about. The words had rattled against his mind and fallen back again, like pebbles against a stone wall.

He started thinking about Bella. He seemed to be thinking about her a great deal lately. Only the other night he had dreamed about her—she was sitting in the front row at one of his concerts, and all the time he was conducting the Brahms First she was shaking her finger at him as a mother might do to a naughty child. Finally he had thrown down his baton and shouted at her, "It's your own fault, Bella! If you hadn't died when you did, I wouldn't be losing the beat!" She had started laughing then, and he had suddenly felt frightened, lonely, full of a terrible emptiness—feelings he never had when he wasn't asleep. Thank heavens before it could get any worse, he woke up.

What would Bella say if she were with him now? Would she shake her finger—or would she tell him he was doing the right thing? Foolish questions. He knew perfectly well what Bella would say. Nothing at all. She had given up a promising career for him—she was an excellent cellist—but in all the years they had lived together she had never once interfered with *his* career. Never a word of reproach from her—never so much as a hint or a suggestion, unless he specifically asked her for it. She was on his side no matter *what* he did. . . .

It was stifling in this room. He couldn't breathe. He stood up and went out on the sun deck. Dark, foggy—you could almost taste the air. He started to the outside stairs, when a figure loomed up in front of him. A big grin, a fat hand— there was no escape.

"Maestro, what a pleasure! I haven't talked to you for such a long time!"

"We'll have to talk tomorrow, Mr. Edelmann. I'm rather tired just now—"

"Of course, of course, only one question, Maestro. I had a discussion last night with the chief purser. He's an educated man, but he doesn't like music—no, that man is not a music-lover. 'Music has no use at all,' he said. 'It appeals to unreason, to unthinking emotion, to that part of man which connects him to the beasts.' He made me furious, Maestro. *Nothing* is of greater importance to mankind than music— this I know, of course—but how are we to explain our feelings to those who aren't able to understand?"

For a second or two Karlweis glared into that earnest, troubled smirk. Our feelings, he thought. *Our* feelings. And then he could do nothing but laugh. Here it was, standing before him—white dinner jacket, gold epaulettes, striped pants—grinning and smirking and bobbing its head obsequi-ously—the embodiment of German Culture, the living, breath-ing idol on whose altar Karlweis had worshiped all his life.

He couldn't even bother to give a caustic answer. The balloon wasn't worth deflating. Laughing and shaking his head, he walked past Edelmann. But then his laughter choked to a stop, and a terrible aching was in his head. "Our" feelings —perhaps it wasn't such a joke, after all. If *that* was the world that he really belonged to, if Edelmann had a right to claim kinship with him— What *other* world could he belong to? Did he belong anywhere at all?

His headache was unbearable; he had to lie down. He went inside and started down to his cabin. But a few feet away from it he heard a noise. Loud, sharp, then something heavy crashing to the floor.

He hurried his pace and opened his cabin door. At first he thought there was a bundle of blankets on the floor bunched up beside the bed, twisted in a peculiar way. And some kind of red liquid was oozing from one end of the bundle.

It was a moment before he realized that the liquid was blood. He wasn't used to such things except on the stage of the opera house, where everything was accompanied by beautiful music.

He took another step into the room. The bundle was no longer a bundle. He saw Ehrlich's brown jacket, his crumpled brown trousers, his thick, grayish hair spread out from his head like a fan. The blood was flowing from that hair, streaking that fan with red.

Karlweis had already started yelling—yelling at the top of his voice—when he noticed Ehrlich's hand, his fingers curved like claws against the carpet. And twitching—softly twitching. And a few inches away was a gun, small, black, with a piggish snout.

Somebody was by Karlweis' side now. Several people were standing behind him. He heard someone say, "My God, he killed himself!"

The person by his side was small, fat—the lawyer Gottlieb. "I'll call the doctor; he isn't dead yet!"

Gottlieb was gone, though people were still crowded beyond the doorway. "Look, he's trying to talk," someone said.

For the first time Karlweis made himself look at the face. The whole top half of it was covered with blood, smeared with it, even the eyes. Little strangled gasps were coming out of the mouth. It was trying to produce words. Karlweis could hardly make them out—slurred, choking words. He knew he ought to get on his knees and listen. A man's last words— there ought to be somebody listening. . . .

He had to clench his teeth. He forced himself to kneel and bring his head as close as he could. He shut his eyes. If he looked, he was going to be sick.

"Deserve it," the voice was saying. "Deserve to die—you hear? You hear me?"

Karlweis made himself nod and say, "Yes, I hear."

"Gun from the war. Souvenir—smuggled it on board. Won't let them take *that* away from me—"

The voice came grating to a stop, like a phonograph running down in the middle. Was he dead now? Karlweis felt a surge of panic, and he opened his eyes. The lips were moving again.

". . . special category. Saw what they did to others. Signs on the wall, people beaten. Dirty Jews— Kill the Jews— Saw what they did to friends. Old friends— Tried to pretend I wasn't—one of— Very funny—"

The lips, hideously white, began to curl. Ehrlich was trying to grin.

Karlweis couldn't bear to see what happened to that grin. He got to his feet and turned away, just as Gottlieb arrived with the doctor.

Karlweis pushed through the crowd in the corridor. They called out questions at him, but he didn't answer. He climbed the stairs and dropped into the first chair he saw.

For a long time he fought against his nausea. Finally it began to ebb. His breathing grew lighter, too, and later—he didn't know how much later—he found that he was calm again.

Quite calm, quite cool. In control of himself, as always, and knowing quite clearly what he now intended to do. Strange, most strange, because he couldn't remember having made the decision. The verdict was in, it seemed—the final, irreversible verdict—but when had the trial taken place?

He stood up and entered the main lounge. He started looking around for Aaron Peyser.

He found him fifteen minutes later out on deck at the front of the ship, standing at the railing.

"Mr. Peyser, excuse me," Karlweis said. "On careful consideration, I have decided to refuse the Dutch government's generous offer. Will you be in communication with them? Do you wish me to sign a statement or speak to someone over the radio? I'll do whatever you think necessary."

And so it was over now. The great sacrifice. The noble gesture. He ought to be feeling exalted, inspired, filled with a deep, ecstatic peace. He ought to be congratulating himself on what a beautiful character he was. All he felt was irritation, exasperation—yes, even anger. Idiot, idiot, he kept telling himself. Why did you do this, why? Compassion? Fellow feeling? For *these* people, these stupid mediocrities? Incredible, absolutely incredible. You're throwing away your life for them, and you despise them as much as ever.

"Mr. Karlweis," Aaron Peyser was saying, "none of us will ever be able to thank you!"

"Thank me!" Karlweis cried, pulling away from the hand that Peyser held out to him. "How *dare* you thank me! How dare you say one *word!*"

* * *

322

By ten o'clock that night, though no official announcement had been made yet, everybody knew what had happened. The general reaction should have been grim; the news wasn't really good, there was only a glimmer of a hope. Yet this glimmer seemed to drive away the surrounding gloom. Suddenly, after the endless days of lethargy, optimism returned to the ship. Eyes were brighter, voices stronger—even the eyes and voices of those who kept shaking their heads and saying, "We're not out of this yet, we mustn't count our chickens . . ."

Most of all, everybody was talking about Karlweis' "sacrifice." It was universally agreed that nothing quite so heroic had occurred in anybody's memory. All over the ship people were telling their friends and relations that they had recognized something in the great conductor "from the beginning." His integrity, his love of humanity, his grandeur of soul had shone right out of him, though he tried to conceal these qualities under a modest and retiring exterior. "But anybody with eyes in his head," said Mrs. Fischel to a group of ladies, "would have seen right away that this was a *big* man." And Mrs. Moritz nodded admiringly, quite forgetting that Mrs. Fischel had remarked only yesterday, "What a nasty little snob that Karlweis is, acting like he's too good to give the time of day to ordinary mortals!"

Karlweis himself appeared in the bar shortly before eleven for the nightly stein of beer with which he edged himself to sleep. Immediately a crowd of people descended on him, holding out their hands to be shaken, slapping him on the back, telling him what a great man he was. One lady burst into tears an inch away from his face. It was a long time before he could free himself from his tormentors and go flying down to his cabin, hoping that all traces of blood had been cleaned up by now and muttering to himself all the way, "That's what you get for behaving like an idiot. Only yourself to blame."

The optimism continued without him. It wasn't even dampened by the news about Ehrlich, the one-armed man—he had shot his head off and died instantly, said one version of the story; he had tried to hang himself from the light fixture in his cabin and was cut down in the nick of time, said another version. There were sighs, troubled shakes of the head, murmurs to the effect that "the poor fellow should have held out just a little longer"—then everybody went back to talking about Karlweis and about the future. . . .

At midnight Bender went out to the main deck, port side, to begin his patrol. The man he relieved was Arthur Stieffel. Even with a wool scarf wrapped around the lower half of his face covering his gray mustache, Stieffel managed to look calm and self-possessed.

"So it appears," Stieffel said, "that our marathon cruise may soon be coming to an end."

"It's possible," Bender said.

"I shall find it difficult to make the adjustment," Stieffel said. "I was beginning to think that I should spend the rest of my life on this ship, sailing the oceans forever, going eternally from port to port, always just about to land but never actually landing. Like the Flying Dutchman. Or more appropriately, the Wandering Jew. Whoever he was. Who *was* the Wandering Jew, doctor?"

"I'm not quite sure. But I gather he didn't much enjoy his life of wandering."

"Is that so? How curious. It sounds like the ideal life to me." Then Stieffel said good night, and Bender was left alone in the darkness.

There was a ceiling over him to stop the wind, yet the cold went through him like a thousand knives. His overcoat just couldn't seem to keep it out. It was in him to start with, perhaps, regardless of the weather outside. In the course of his life many people had told him that he had ice water in his veins.

It was hard to see anything beyond the railing. Fog had rolled in, as it had been doing every night since they anchored here, and only vague, massive shapes were visible. Still he stood there motionless, staring out at that blankness as if he hoped to find something in it. Some shaft of light, perhaps, that would pierce the blackness in his head? And again, for the hundredth time in the last eight hours, he remembered his talk with Julia.

For a week he had been prepared for this talk. He had known exactly what she would say to him. It couldn't possibly have taken him by surprise, or disappointed him, either, for even from the start he had entertained no false hopes. He had known also exactly what his reactions must be; indeed, he had carefully chosen what words to say to her and had even rehearsed the tone of voice in which he would say them.

And his performance had more than lived up to the

promise of the rehearsal. He was so calm, so understanding and gentle and tactful. Forgiving—yet not so forgiving as to make her feel that she had done something to be forgiven for. Having made up his mind that he wanted her to do this, he certainly didn't intend her to be miserable about it.

And he had achieved his object. He had convinced her, he was quite sure of this. She would never think she had deserted him—you can't desert someone who doesn't particularly care if you remain. She would never think she had betrayed him— you can't betray someone to whom you mean nothing.

And all the time, while he went through this well-rehearsed scene with her, he had known that she meant everything to him. It seemed to him that he was discovering this even as he smiled at her and hinted at his indifference. And when it was all over, it seemed that he must have known it all along —not just for a few minutes, not even since they stepped aboard this ship, but for years and years, since the first moment he ever set eyes on her. How could he have been so dense that he hadn't realized it before? These last ten days, as he waited for her to tell him her decision, had he really not recognized the fearful hope inside of him? And while she was talking to him this afternoon, faltering, smiling uneasily, repeating her words, was he really unaware of watching her every minute, against logic, against common sense, for signs that she didn't mean what she was saying?

Yes, logic and common sense seemed to be breaking down in him. They were the bulwarks of his whole life. Skeptical about everything else, he had always believed this one thing —that man can be rational, that a life built on reason is the only life with meaning. And now he was obliged to contemplate himself as the prime piece of evidence to disprove his own theory. Yet no other conclusion was possible when tonight, all through dinner, all through the hours since dinner, that futile childish daydream kept pulling him in. . . .

Such a simpleminded daydream, too, wish fulfillment of the crudest sort. If a man like him intended to deceive himself, you'd expect him to find a more subtle way of doing it. But no, the daydream consisted of nothing more than one brief, unvarnished scene—she comes through the door, she walks up to him with a smile on her face, she says to him, "I'm sorry, Carl, I don't know what came over me, I didn't know what I was saying. Of *course* I won't let you face this by yourself, my darling. I want to be with you till the end.

Whatever they do to you, to us, I'm never going to leave you." And they fall into each other's arms and confess that they've loved each other all along.

Here he was, doing it again right now, plunging into that daydream just as if it had never caught him in its snare before. This couldn't be happening to him. It simply wasn't possible. After Hannah's death he had sworn that he would never let it happen to him again.

He remembered it so well, the day of Hannah's death. He realized now that it had never been out of his mind for long. She had gone to the meeting in the afternoon, in spite of the rumors that those Nazi hoodlums were going to make trouble. She had gone to the meeting *because* of those rumors. Yes, that was Hannah all over. "At a time like this it's essential that we show our solidarity. How could I live with myself if I didn't have the courage to stand up and be counted?"

So she stood up and was counted, but she didn't have much longer to live with herself. He remembered waiting in the apartment while the time passed. Five o'clock—six o'clock—she should have been back long ago. He remembered staring at the plant on the windowsill, that hideous green crawler that she had brought back from America and tended as lovingly and conscientiously as if it were her child. Though it was Hannah, of course, who had insisted that they have no children. "How can anyone bring children into a world like this?"

Then the phone had rung, and he was told the news, which he had been expecting all along. The trouble had come, the hoodlums had poured into the hall, swinging bats and truncheons—the usual Fascist methods of political argument. And Hannah, of course, had been one of the first to jump to her feet and make a speech about oppression and injustice. Poor Hannah—thinking of herself, no doubt, as a tragic heroine, as Joan of Arc or Mary, Queen of Scots—never realizing that she was really a comic figure. To anybody, that is, who didn't happen to love her more than he loved his life.

"She's in the hospital now," said the voice over the phone, "but there's no point hurrying, she won't regain consciousness." And he remembered what he had said to that voice, his loud, incoherent speech about political nincompoops, spoiled adolescents with delusions of grandeur playing their games with the lives of innocent, misguided women. And he remembered that he had hardly been able to look at that wretched

326

plant of hers for weeks. He had stopped giving it water, and it had died.

Irrational. Hysterical. And the hysteria had lasted for quite some time indeed. Five or six months, at least, before he could imagine himself thinking and feeling like a human being again.

But then reason had taken over—as he had known all along it would. Slowly he had been able not only to endure his loss but to think about it, to ponder its causes, to arrive at sensible conclusions about the experience he had been through. At last he had been able to do what grown-up people must do, to learn from grief and despair. In teaching men a lesson, in helping them to guide their conduct for the future, the tragedies of life are saved from being totally useless. Out of chaos comes something meaningful, something productive.

Out of *his* chaos had come—he thought—a deep and final knowledge of himself. He was more susceptible than he should have been to the pain of loss. Involvement of the kind he had allowed himself to have with Hannah could be nothing but debilitating to him. And so when his head was completely above water at last, he had sworn that he would never get involved again.

And he had stuck to this, too. Yes, he *had* stuck to this. All these years of his marriage to Julia, more than seven years now, there had never been any of the anxiety or the anguish that he had felt with Hannah. Things that might have shattered him before, the very worst things that ever happened between Julia and him, had no power to do more than make him smile. Her parties, the silly Bohemian set she traveled with—they made him smile. Her rudeness, her whims, her deliberate exercises in neglect—they made him smile. Her affairs with other men, hardly affairs at all, absurd flirtations about which she was ironical herself—he simply smiled at them all.

Even later, when devastating things started happening to their world, a smile was still his characteristic expression. Yes, even when he came to realize how bitterly she regretted their union. Those visits she made to the hairdresser, for example, to that Italian harpy on the Boulevard. She was under the impression that she had concealed those visits from him, but of course he knew all about them. He knew why she went there, too, how she lied to the ladies under the dryers.

327

Once a week, he knew, it was important to her not to be "Jewish"—to bask for a while in the toadying admiration and share the vicious snobbery of those trashy people whom she herself knew to be lower than garbage. And yet even at this he smiled.

Why wasn't he smiling now? Dear God, why wasn't he smiling?

He clenched his fists on the railing. He forced his lips apart, forced the corners of his mouth to curl upward. Smile, damn you, smile. He finally succeeded in doing it. Because it really *was* an excellent joke, it deserved an appreciative audience. The great Dr. Bender, the brilliant authority on human motives, couldn't even keep himself from making the same mistake twice.

He shivered in a sudden blast of cold air. He knew the answer now to that puzzle which had been nagging at him since he had first stepped aboard this ship. That very first night he had asked himself why he, with his highly developed instinct for survival, had stayed in Germany so much longer than many of his less perspicacious friends. Why had he waited till the last shreds of hope were gone?

It was not, as he had speculated on that first night aboard, because he had expected Julia's Aryan blood to protect him from the monsters. He had to give his intelligence more credit than that. He had stayed and stayed because he had been afraid that Julia wouldn't want to go, afraid that if he asked her to leave Germany with him she would turn him down flat, call him a "dirty Jew" and send him packing. He had stayed because he had loved her and couldn't bear to lose her.

Now he knew the truth about himself—and a stupid and humiliating truth it was. And even worse, it was no use to him, no possible use this side of the grave. The lesson had come too late. It could never be meaningful or productive now. For ahead of him now was—nothing. If he returned to Germany and died, or if the miracle happened and he was saved—either way Julia was lost to him, and there was nothing else.

He heard a door open behind him. He turned and saw Aaron Peyser framed in the light from the foyer. His shoulders were slumped, his eyes bloodshot. He looked like a man who hasn't slept in a week.

"I'm looking for the rabbi," Aaron said. "You haven't seen him?"

"Wouldn't he be in bed at this time of night?"

"He isn't in the cabin. He told the steward he was going out for air. Well, he has to be somewhere, I'll find him." But Aaron didn't move yet. After a moment he said, "I've just been down at the ship's hospital. Ehrlich died a few minutes ago."

"I'm sorry to hear it."

"Yes— The burial should be as soon as possible. First thing in the morning so it won't be on people's minds too long. That's why I'm looking for the rabbi." Aaron hesitated. Then abruptly he said, "Good night, Carl," and turned back into the foyer.

And Bender turned back to face the darkness. He remembered Ehrlich's face as it had looked at dinnertime, the last time Bender saw him. The caged lion finally petrified. White as a tombstone. White as the bones under a tombstone. His suicide, a few hours later, had been merely a technicality.

Suicide is stupid, Bender thought. It proves absolutely nothing. Any man can snuff out his life when he has no reason for living. The trick, after all, is to have no reason— and to go on living anyway.

ELEVEN

IT was after midnight when Aaron Peyser got back to Morrie with his good news. Al went into action immediately; he read Emil Karlweis' formal statement to the representative of the Dutch government and phoned it to the Paris offices of all the major news services and to every newspaperman that he happened to know personally on both sides of the Atlantic. Morrie had never realized before that Al knew so many newspapermen.

With breakfast the next morning they ordered the early edition of every paper in Paris and pored over them while they gulped down their coffee. Between the two of them they had just enough high school French to decipher most of what was written.

They soon realized that they had picked a good time to break the story. The world was on the brink of war, statesmen of all nationalities were issuing pessimistic or optimistic predictions, frantic preparations were going on behind the scenes—but for weeks, since Munich, in fact, there had been a shortage of the kind of news that could capture the public's imagination. For this reason most of the papers gave the voyage of the *Franz Joseph* large headlines and plenty of space. Pictures of the ship, of its captain, of Emil Karlweis were all over the front pages. And every paper ran some kind of comment on the editorial page.

All but one of these editorials expressed sympathy with the passengers and distress at the unwillingness of any of the "free" nations to give them refuge. The degree of this distress varied, of course, with the political complexion of the individual newspaper, and so did the target of its moral indignation. Pro-Western papers castigated the Soviet Union, with its immense underpopulated areas, for its callous refusal even to examine the question. Pro-Communist papers failed to mention the Soviet Union at all but accused the "so-called democracies" of "thinly veiled Fascist leanings" and suggested that such a disgrace could never occur under leftist leadership. None of the papers had a good word to say for the United States. But every one of these editorials eventually reached the same conclusion—the passengers must be saved.

The one exception was the newspaper of the extreme right. It gave the *Franz Joseph* only a small story on one of its back pages. And it commented on the incident in a one-paragraph editorial:

When the absurd and completely unwarranted furor has finally died down, it will be seen that the Jewish musician Karlweis has made his decision not out of heroism—at any rate a most uncharacteristic virtue for one of his race—but, as we may have expected, out of the shrewdest and most practical estimate of his own interests. He knows, as do all fairminded individuals who are willing to think with their brains rather than their tear ducts, that he and his companions are far more likely to receive just treatment from the government of the Third Reich than from any of the Communist-dominated, Wall Street-controlled "democracies." These people know that if all else fails, Chancellor Hitler at least offers them a home. They must be strictly supervised, of course, for they cannot be permitted to endanger the health of the German body politic—but how much more is being offered them by the loud, self-righteous "democracies"? Who are the savages after all?

It was an open secret that this newspaper was financed by funds from the German government.

All in all, then, the initial response was encouraging, and Morrie cautiously let his spirits lift a little. It helped to see how pleased Al was. "And wait till tomorrow," Al said, "when the public starts being heard from!"

Their phone rang. It was a transatlantic call from Bernie Kramer in New York. His first words were, "My God, what have you fellows been *doing* over there?"

"What kind of coverage are we getting?" Al said.

"Coverage! The damn thing is smeared all over the front pages. Ben Zuckerman is having a fit. Look—Dan wants you to get back here as quick as you can. He can't talk to you himself right now because he's too busy answering phone calls, but I imagine he'll have plenty to say to you later."

"We're looking forward to it," Al said. "We've got seats on the one o'clock plane."

Their flight got to New York early on Saturday morning. Bernie was at the ramp to meet them. His face had doom written all over it. Without a word he handed them a batch of newspapers.

In the cab riding in to the city, Al and Morrie read two days' accumulation of stories about the *Franz Joseph*—not only the seven New York papers but several from Newark, Philadelphia, Boston, and most important of all, Washington, D.C. The story was being played up in a big way, even bigger than it had been in Paris. Many of the inside pages had human interest material about passengers with American relatives. The editorials were full of pleas to "the civilized nations of the world" to help the poor refugees. Already there were letters to the editor expressing the same feelings—and most of them, Morrie noticed, were signed by non-Jewish names.

While he and Al read, Bernie talked. "My God, have you two stirred up a hornet's nest! Ever since the story broke—I don't think there's an AJDA member around the country who hasn't called Dan up. Not to mention the board."

Al said, "How's the vote running, for or against?"

"Most people sympathize with the passengers, of course— but that's not the point at all. Do you realize there isn't a single paper that doesn't mention AJDA? How *we've* been working behind the scenes, how *we* brought the story out in the open. We haven't had this much publicity in forty years. You should hear what Ben Zuckerman is saying. He was closeted with Dan for over an hour last night. What got *into* you fellows anyway? What possessed you to pull a stunt like this?"

"What stunt?" said Al. "When we read the papers yesterday we were as shocked as anybody else. After all our efforts to avoid undue attention—"

"Okay, okay," said Bernie with a wave of his hand, "but Dan wants to see both of you just as soon as he can open the office this morning, and I have a feeling he won't be in the mood for jokes. And there's talk about calling an emergency board meeting just to haul you two on the carpet."

"When?"

"Early next week, I think. No later than Monday or Tuesday."

Al eased back in his seat. "By Monday or Tuesday half a dozen countries will be making offers for those passengers. Instead of hauling us on the carpet, the board'll have to pin medals on us."

At this moment the taxicab radio went on, and a newscaster with a march-of-time voice began to tell the story of the *Franz Joseph*. Bernie groaned.

It was eight o'clock when Morrie got to his apartment. Just time for a shower, a shave, and some breakfast before he had to run downtown and face Dan. While he did these things he managed, over the noise of his kids, to fill Ruth in on the latest developments. And she told him about her phone conversation last night with her father, who was a doctor in New Haven. "You know how conservative Daddy can be about some things," she said. "But this *Franz Joseph* story really seems to have gotten to him. Once or twice he almost sounded as if he were in tears."

"He wants the United States to take those people in?"

"Absolutely. What he says is, 'If AJDA is in favor of it, so am I.' You know how he swears by AJDA."

Morrie knew, all right, and for a moment it put a damper on his spirits. How many other Jews in America, he wondered, were just like Dr. Weintraub? How many of them were willing to decide that a cause was good only after it got the seal of approval from AJDA—or from B'nai Brith or Federation or some other official Jewish organization? According to a lot of people, that was the strength of American Jewish life. It was so beautifully and efficiently organized that nobody ever had to make up his mind for himself anymore.

To build up his optimism again, Morrie picked up the New York *Times,* which was lying open next to his plate. He read the leading editorial, though he had already been through it twice:

It is hard to imagine the bitterness of exile when it takes place over a faraway frontier. Helpless families driven from their homes to a barren island in the Danube, thrust over the Polish frontier, escaping in terror of their lives to Switzerland or France, are hard for us in a free country to visualize. But those exiles floated by our own shores. They are on American quota lists and can be admitted here. What is to happen to them in the interval has remained uncertain from hour to hour. We can only hope that some hearts will soften somewhere and some refuge be found. The cruise of the *Franz Joseph* cries to high heaven of man's inhumanity to man.

The first two times he read it this editorial had moved and excited Morrie. But now, the third time through, he noticed something peculiar about it. Nowhere, in the whole course of it, did the *Times* writer recommend that the passengers be given shelter in the United States. Nowhere did he suggest that their ordeal and the rest of the world's indifference imposed any responsibility at all on the American people. He might have been sitting in a movie theater, Morrie thought, reacting with appropriate emotions to something that was happening up on the screen.

Morrie pushed the paper away from him, finished his coffee, and kissed his wife. Then he headed downtown to accept his bawling-out.

* * *

Three days later, first thing Tuesday morning, the emergency meeting of the AJDA board took place. Right up to the last minute the staff waited for some word—from Europe, from Washington, from South America, from anywhere. The office switchboard had been kept open twenty-fours a day since last Friday. All weekend Dan and Al and Morrie had taken turns on a cot in the office at night, just in case a cablegram or a transatlantic phone call should come in.

Nothing came. Nobody had anything more to say about the *Franz Joseph*. Congressman Lascoff prodded, but Washington didn't change its position; it didn't even bother to reiterate it. It simply maintained an absolute silence, as if none of the headlines of the last five days had ever appeared. There was the same silence from Europe, from Latin America. Cablegrams arrived from AJDA representatives, but they had nothing to offer.

"INTERVENTION COLUMBIA WITHOUT PROSPECTS. IMMIGRATION CLOSED."

"CHILE NOTHING DOING ACCOUNT POLITICAL SITUATION."

"PARAGUAY YET UNDECIDED."

In a long phone call Abraham Weinstein described his efforts to discuss the *Franz Joseph* with the English Prime Minister. So far he had failed even to get an appointment. The Dutch government had made no comment on Karlweis' refusal of its offer.

By Monday night Morrie could no longer shut his eyes to the truth. Public opinion may have been on the side of the people aboard the *Franz Joseph,* but public opinion was making no dent on the powers that be. All they had to do was go about their business calmly, as if that ship and its thousand passengers didn't even exist—and the uproar would die down all by itself. Already, in today's *Times,* the *Franz Joseph* had become a small item in the second section.

"I miscalculated," Al said, slumping back at his desk late Monday night. "I fell into the trap of expecting the best from human nature. I forgot that we're living in the age of publicity. Everything is a nine-day wonder. Every horror is nothing but a story in the morning paper—you read it over your coffee, weep about it for a while, and go on to the next story. It's getting harder all the time to make people believe that anything is real."

Early Tuesday morning the meeting was called to order in the AJDA boardroom.

Everybody was there—all the key men on the professional staff, all the members of the board, all the big givers who had come across with money for Cuba three weeks ago. Everybody looked tired and worried. And Morrie noticed how many of them were careful to avoid looking Al and him in the eye.

Not little Reuben Levinson, though. He came bustling up to Morrie and Al and shook hands with them vigorously so that nobody could possibly fail to see what he was doing. "I want to give you two my heartiest congratulations," he said in a loud voice. "You don't find too many people nowadays who not only *talk* about humanitarian principles but are also willing to *do* something about them. Even if it means risking their own necks!"

Senator Friedkin opened the meeting. Instead of making his usual speech of welcome, he simply cleared his throat and said, "Let's get started, ladies and gentlemen," then he turned the proceedings over to Dan. The senator must be feeling pretty low, Morrie thought, if he could sacrifice his speech of welcome.

"Ladies and gentlemen," Dan began, "we've called this meeting in order to discuss a very important question of policy. Before we get to that, however, I'd like to dispose of another less vital matter. I'm referring to the recent action taken by Mr. Margolinski and Mr. Feldman of our Department of Refugee Affairs in connection with the passengers on the liner *Franz Joseph*——"

And then, as Morrie's amazement grew, Dan laid out the facts of the case without a word or even an undertone of disappointment for what they had done. By the time he finished his speech, he had not only exonerated them but had strongly suggested that their actions had been performed with his permission. But what about the lecture he had given them last Saturday morning in his office? Whatever Dan might say to his subordinates in private, Morrie realized, he was scrupulous about standing up for them in public.

Dan sat down. Ben Zuckerman started signaling for the floor. In a moment, Morrie thought, the vultures would swoop.

Zuckerman turned toward Al and Morrie with his steelplate gaze. "I'm frank to admit that I was one of those who felt extremely disturbed when the unprecedented action of these gentlemen first came to my attention. I felt, and still feel, that employees and agents of this organization must avoid attracting excessive public attention to our activities. Any contemplated move which might lead to a violation of this principle ought to be preceded by serious discussion with the proper body of authority, that is, the board."

"Very true," said Sigmund Wolff.

"Nevertheless," Zuckerman went on, with no change in his tone, "I am aware that situations occasionally arise when quick action is essential. I am willing to take Dan's word that this was one of those situations. I myself, in the same position as Mr. Margolinski and Mr. Feldman, might have chosen to approach the problem in a different way, but I don't think that any real blame can be attached to them. I should like to propose that we drop the whole incident once and for all."

"I second the motion," Sigmund Wolff said.

Willie Levy grinned softly from his end of the table. "Pat them on the back and give them a second chance—yes, that's the right way to handle first offenders. You won't get any arguments from *me*."

"In that case," Dan said, "suppose we move on to the main business of this meeting."

Morrie stopped listening for a while. He was still a little dazed. He had been all tensed up expecting brickbats, and he had been pelted with roses instead. Only somehow they seemed to pack as hard a wallop as the brickbats might have done. He couldn't understand his feelings exactly. He stole a glance at Al—but Al was hiding his face with his hand, there was no way of knowing what he was thinking.

Morrie forced himself to pay attention to Dan's words. ". . . must unfortunately face the fact that the gamble hasn't paid off so far and apparently isn't going to."

What gamble? What was Dan talking about? It took Morrie a moment or two to grasp it. Karlweis' gesture, the publicity it was getting, the appeal to the conscience of the world—Dan was writing it off as a failure.

"Under the circumstances," Dan was saying, "and in view of what we've learned from this incident as to the nature of world opinion at this time, several members of our board have suggested that AJDA ought to reconsider its basic policy regarding the refugee problem. In this connection Ben Zuckerman would like to present a certain idea to you."

Zuckerman stood up, cleared his throat, and started reading from a pile of notes in front of him. ". . . not, I must emphasize, a formal plan worked out in any sort of detail, but simply a tentative suggestion along general lines . . ." Slowly, as Zuckerman droned on, Morrie realized that he was hearing about the "African idea" again—an idea which had been traveling around the American Jewish community for three or four years now. Every so often a lot of people, in a lot of different organizations, would suddenly be talking about it, and then just as suddenly it would dive under the surface again.

". . . some carefully selected area of land," Zuckerman was saying, "somewhere on the African coast—the exact location can be determined later, all that matters is that it should be relatively unpopulated so that no conflict may develop with entrenched native groups. It would then be the responsibility of Jewish communities like ours in the wealthier nations of the world to provide for the establishment of our unfortunate fellow Jews who have been forced out of their homelands in Europe. . . ."

Why hadn't the African idea shriveled up and died long

337

ago? It had been discredited any number of times with unanswerable facts and figures, but its staying power was amazing. A few people went on believing in it, Morrie supposed, because it provided such a simple, comforting solution to a complicated, upsetting problem. Send the refugees off to Africa, where money can be pumped out to them but they won't be constantly underfoot. Sweep the dirt under the carpet.

". . . what we must recognize," Zuckerman was saying, "is that the civilized countries of the world don't *want* these people. Further efforts on the part of organizations like ours to force them down the throats of friendly nations can only arouse resentment and hostility and add to the difficulties which all Jews—"

"And what about the people on that ship?" Reuben Levinson broke in.. "They haven't gone away overnight. They're still floating on the ocean, looking to us for help because nobody else is offering it to them. So what are you going to tell them, Mr. Zuckerman? That they should wait a year or two until we've got this nice piece of property in Africa ready for them?"

Zuckerman sighed. "What can *you* tell them, Mr. Levinson? Those people weigh on my spirits as heavily as they do on yours—but what more can either of us do for them? We've tried everything, we've pushed our resources to the limit— and we've failed. The situation of those people is hopeless."

"No—" Morrie heard himself speaking up. His voice sounded terribly tired in his ears. "No, it isn't hopeless—"

Zuckerman turned to him, and instead of the cold disdain that Morrie had expected there was something almost like sympathy in his eyes. "If you *can* come up with something, Mr. Feldman—"

This mildness confused Morrie, made him feel suddenly sort of foolish. But he managed to push on. "The trouble is we're still leaving it up to the bureaucrats—to the people who don't give a damn. Why don't we cut through all of them, take our case to someone who *can* help and *will* help— directly to the President."

Sigmund Wolff gave his high-pitched little laugh. "Are you under the impression, young man, that F.D.R. doesn't read the newspapers?"

"He has to hear about this *directly*—not from newspapers, not from official reports, not through intermediaries. Somebody who *cares* about those people has to tell him—make him see what they're going through—"

But it was no use. Morrie could see it from the way they were all looking at him. Politely enough, not antagonistically —but not really listening, not really letting themselves get interested. He saw what it was, now—these people were worn out. They had lost their spirit for thinking up plans, for taking action, for hoping. They had reached the limit beyond which they could absorb no more disappointment. They were turning their heads toward Dan—questioningly, almost imploringly—because all they really wanted now was somebody to tell them they didn't have to worry anymore.

Judge Goodfreund finally said what everyone else was thinking. "So what's your opinion, Dan? Is this African idea worth looking into?"

Dan creased his forehead and put on his most judicious frown. "This African idea has been talked about before," he said. "Many of you know that I've had my reservations about it. I still have those reservations. At the same time—how can we pretend that certain things haven't occurred? Perhaps the time *has* come to reexamine our present policies. No harm can come from *exploring* Ben's suggestion—even if we can't accept it in the end. What I advocate is that we set up a committee—"

Morrie could almost hear the sigh of relief around the room. He lowered his head so that he wouldn't have to meet Dan's eye. Because he finally understood what had happened, why Ben Zuckerman had taken such a kindly attitude toward what he and Al had done, why nobody had demanded their resignations. Dan had made a horse trade. My boys for your African idea—their necks for your peace of mind. It was that simple.

But Dan never traded unless he had to. Dan never backed down from a fight—unless he thought he had no chance of winning.

At that moment it occurred to Morrie for the first time that he would resign from AJDA. Organizations, even the best of them, are still only organizations. They're never any stronger or any better than their weaklings and their cowards—and sooner or later they all become riddled with weaklings and cowards. If you want to do anything that means a damn, you have to do it on your own.

I'll talk it over with Al after the meeting, he thought. But then he decided he'd better wait. Until he was sure that Al hadn't known about the horse trade ahead of time. . . .

The meeting broke up, and Morrie went back to his office. Ten minutes later there was a knock on his door.

He didn't expect to see Willie Levy there. His surprise must have shown on his face, because Willie Levy came out with one of his deep, appreciative chuckles; nothing gave him more pleasure than disconcerting people. "Do I get to come in," he said, "or have you got a girl in there?"

Morrie stepped aside for him, and Willie Levy arranged himself in the armchair across from the desk. His bulk seemed to overflow the sides. You never saw him in a chair that didn't look too small for him.

He tugged at his collar, loosening his tie. "Pretty hot today. When are you fellows going to start agitating for air conditioning in this office? Or are you all such idealists that you hate to see AJDA's money spent on anything except noble causes?"

Willie Levy chuckled again at the ridiculous notion that anybody could be that much of an idealist—though in fact he had put his finger on precisely the reason why the AJDA staff had never asked for air conditioning. "I better get to the point of this visit before I start melting away on your carpet." He rubbed his hand over the top of his head, as if he were afraid his hair wasn't messy enough already, and said, "You really want to see F.D.R.?"

Morrie just stared at him for a moment. "Yes—I would—"

"Cut through the bureaucrats and tell your story to the great man himself—was that what you said?"

"Yes—I think it might work. If *anybody* could understand and sympathize—"

"Okay, young fellow, I'll fix it up for you. F.D.R. owes me a favor or two. I've done some work, professionally speaking, for some of the people who back him. I'll give him a ring as soon as I get to my office. Stay here till you hear from me— say in an hour or so. Oh yes, he'll probably have to squeeze you in at some odd time, so you'd better be prepared to leave for Washington on a few hours' notice."

Before Morrie had much of a chance to thank him, Willie Levy lumbered to his feet, made another remark about the heat, and walked out the door.

An hour later he called Morrie and told him he was expected at the White House at eight o'clock that night.

* * *

It's a dream, Morrie thought. He passed through the iron gates, between the tall white pillars, through the heavy carved doorway. This isn't happening to me at all, he thought.

He was ushered down a long oak-paneled corridor and into a room with a high ceiling, graceful arches, tall windows with the lights of the city sparkling beyond them. It had a clean, fresh feeling, like something out of another age. Wigs—minuets—how *could* it be real?

Then he saw the man behind the desk. At first he looked smaller than Morrie had expected, but when he approached the desk, the man began to grow. Soon all the familiar details—the jutting jaw, the twinkling eyes, the long cigarette holder—loomed as large as they ever had in Morrie's imagination. Poor Papa, he thought. In his last year, tied to his bed most of the time, unable to move half his body, he had decided that his life hadn't been worth living. He'd change his mind, Morrie thought, if he could see his son right now.

"Sit down, sit down," said the man behind the desk. "Well now—my friend Willie Levy has some very nice things to say about you, young man. He assures me that I'll be impressed by what you've got to say for yourself. Let's hear it, then. You have my full attention."

He leaned forward in his chair and rested his chin in his hand. The famous frown was on his face.

Morrie began to speak. On the plane to Washington this evening he had gone over these words a dozen times in his head. Now, as he brought them out carefully and seriously, a part of him was watching his own performance, being amazed at how well he was doing.

And then he was silent, trying to keep from breathing too hard.

The man behind the desk looked grave. Compassion and indignation vied with each other on his face. "Thank you," he said, and the voice was like the voice Morrie had heard so many times over the radio—powerful, resonant, suggesting boundless depths of feeling. "I'm glad you came to me. Your instincts were absolutely correct. I had to hear about this directly."

He took a puff from the cigarette holder. Slowly the smoke rose to the ceiling.

The voice went on. "I heard about this ship before you came, of course. I've been reading the official reports. But you know what official reports are. It's beyond me how they do it—they take the most dramatic, the most human material and turn it into statistics. What you've done for me, young man, is turn the statistics back into flesh and blood again. I'm grateful to you for that."

Now the lines deepened on that face. Morrie remembered what Ruth's mother was always saying—"Every year he looks so much older!"

"Don't ever envy any man this job," said the voice. "Every day I have to make decisions that must seem cruel and inhuman to anyone outside. Often they seem cruel and inhuman to me. But the cruelty is built into this job. Too many people depend on what I decide. Whatever it is, somebody's hopes are sure to be shattered."

He looked up at Morrie, smiling. Not the big, hearty smile that the whole world knew. A sad sort of smile. "I sympathize with the people on that ship," he said. "That's not much use to them, I'm well aware of it. But there it is, sympathy is just about all I can give them."

Morrie didn't say anything. He watched the lights of the city sparkling behind that large head.

"Perfect justice," said the man at the desk, "demands that those people be admitted into our country. If this were a world in which perfect justice always prevailed—" He paused, and a small sigh came out of him. "I want you to understand something, young man. In my position you don't make any decision about anything without considering not only the rights and wrongs of the case but also the long-range consequences. What's likely to happen if I direct the Attorney General to activate those people's visas? Congress meets in a few weeks, and I've got a lot of legislation that I want to push through. Progressive legislation to promote the welfare and happiness of millions of Americans. Have you been in favor of my legislative program so far?"

"Yes, I have—"

"Then you know it's been a tight squeeze sometimes. How do you think I've managed it up to now? The same way

Washington managed it, the same way Lincoln managed it, the same way they all managed it—coalitions, compromises, promises in return for votes. It's a tricky game, and you don't win it by wantonly defying the people whose support you need most badly. My expanded relief bill will be coming to the floor this next session—at least five Midwest senators have threatened to vote against it if I don't soft-pedal my internationalist tendencies between now and the 1940 election. Seems as if I'm hurting their chances with their isolationist constituents. How do you think they'll react if I make a public gesture that looks like a slap in the face to the German government? What chance will my relief bill have after that?"

The voice grew stronger, more like the radio voice again. "And what about the next election? There's a chance I'll be running in that election. Haven't made up my mind yet, but I'm giving it serious consideration. If I run, there's going to be one hell of a furor. First President ever to try for a third term—wait till you hear the howls about dictatorship. I'll need all the support I can get; I can't afford to antagonize any element of the American electorate. Do you want me to lose that election? The fight against Fascism is going to be *the* issue in the next few years—you know that as well as I do. Who do you think is better equipped to carry on that fight, me and my party or some isolationist Republican and *his* party?"

He paused, then he lowered his voice. "The point is, young man, if you want to gain certain objectives in this life, you sometimes have to give up other objectives."

Another long puff from the cigarette holder. Morrie followed the smoke as it curled lazily up and up. His mouth was very dry.

"The only thing is," Morrie said, "this is just a thousand people. A drop in the bucket. It's hard to believe that the electorate would hold it against you——"

A laugh interrupted him. Not the famous laugh, rich and booming, but a quiet, ironical laugh. "I'm afraid you don't know much about politics. My enemies aren't all damned fools. If they saw me flying in the face of one of the most deep-seated emotions in the American heartland, you can bet they'd take full advantage of my mistake."

"What deep-seated emotion——"

"Anti-Semitism, I'm sorry to say. There's a good deal of that ugly disease rampant in this country just now. That's why your thousand people, your drop in the bucket, would be exploited with such enthusiasm by my political enemies. Your people are all Jews, and I'm already too closely linked with Jews for the comfort of my advisers. To hell with that sort of advice is what I've always said. I'll choose my friends and my associates from among those who are most congenial to me—that's nobody's business but my own. But I won't be unrealistic. I won't involve myself in self-defeating causes."

"All right, I see that—but even on realistic grounds—"

The lights sparkled, the smoke clung to the ceiling, the big broad smile seemed for a moment to be painted on the famous face. And suddenly Morrie heard himself saying things in a low tight voice that it wasn't possible for him to be saying. "You talk about the election, how important it is that you shouldn't antagonize any element. Jews are voters, too. We're only three percent of the population, but we go to the polls more regularly than any other group. If you lost the Jewish vote in New York City, you'd probably lose the whole state. And you could lose some other states too, if the election was close enough—"

"Pardon me, young man"—the head was cocked forward—"are you suggesting that I'll lose the Jewish vote if I don't let those people into the country?"

"I think there's a good chance of it. When the American Jewish community finds out—when our organization lets them know—"

The head lifted, and the big laugh boomed out at last. "Young man—the Jewish vote is one of my most precious political assets, you're absolutely right about that. I got nearly eighty percent of it in 1936, and there's every indication that I could do even better next time. Jews like me. They like what I stand for. I know it, and I assure you I'm grateful for it. But that's the extraordinary thing about Jews—you're genuine altruists, maybe the only ones left in this corrupt world. You believe in your principles, you vote for the man who shares them—and you never let your selfish personal interests sway you. I believe in helping the poor, the Jews believe in helping the poor—and so Jews vote for me, even when they're rich. Take my word for it, I don't get that sort of altruistic support from rich Episcopalians and rich Catholics. And the same thing applies to this present situation. You're annoyed at me because I can't let those people into the country—you feel I'm going against your interests. But when election time

344

comes, when you're actually inside that voting booth, will you violate your *principles* in order to serve your *interests?* I doubt it. I don't know too many Jews who would."

"In other words, you might as well ignore us, because you'll get our vote no matter *what* you do?"

"That's a cynical way of putting it. What I'm saying is that the Jews of America can be counted on to listen to the voice of conscience, as they've always done in the past."

A buzzer rasped on the desk.

"I *am* sorry, young man, but that's my secretary telling me that my next appointment is here. You'll have to excuse me for not rising—"

The jaw jutted out, the teeth flashed, and then the face disappeared behind a cloud of smoke.

Morrie left the beautiful room with its high ceiling, its graceful arches, its view of the lights of the city. He walked down the long oak-paneled corridor. He went out the heavy carved doorway, between the tall white pillars, through the iron gates. The conversation he had just had kept going through his head. He asked himself what Papa would say about it if he were still alive. He decided that Papa would simply refuse to believe it. "It never happened," Papa would say. "You dreamed the whole thing."

In a day or so, Morrie told himself, I'll begin to wonder if I did.

* * *

On the ten o'clock plane back to New York he thought again about quitting his job with AJDA.

He still knew that he had to do it, but for different reasons from those he had given himself this morning. He had been full of bitterness against AJDA this morning, but he saw now that his bitterness wasn't justified. It wasn't that AJDA was bad, nor even that organizations were bad. The whole game of altruism was an illusion, a corny joke, a fraud that could only take in children. The world is what it is, he saw, because it *has* to be. Nothing can ever be changed. People can never be helped or made to help others. The cesspool is too filthy, the muck goes too deep, for anybody ever to clean it up.

Ruth's mother had been right about him all along. He did get too emotionally involved in his work. Well, she'd be happy to hear that he had finally learned his lesson. Only a damn fool gets emotionally involved in hitting his head against stone walls. First thing tomorrow morning he would hand in his resignation, and second thing tomorrow morning he would start looking for a new job with some rich, successful business firm that could offer him a future. Ruth might fret a little because he would no longer be making his "contribution," but he imagined that a washing machine and a bigger apartment would console her nicely.

And what about the *Franz Joseph?*

What about it, for God's sake? Was he still so childish and self-destructive that he couldn't face the truth? There *was* no *Franz Joseph* any more. Those people were dead already. If nobody else in the world, either Jew or Gentile, was willing or able to help them, where did he get the arrogance to think that it was up to *him?*

In a little while, anyway, the fate of a thousand people wouldn't seem particularly important. The holocaust was coming. Millions of people would be killed before the carnage was over. The *Franz Joseph,* to use the words of a well-known ex-do-gooder, was just a drop in the bucket.

And what are you going to say to Aaron Peyser? he asked himself.

For a moment this question brought a lump to his throat. But then he realized that his distress was purely academic. Aaron Peyser was a couple of thousand miles away. Morrie couldn't talk to him now even if he had wanted to. It wasn't likely that Aaron Peyser and he would ever talk to each other again.

And deep down inside him somewhere—he couldn't pretend otherwise—he was feeling a kind of relief.

TWELVE

FOR a week the passengers on the *Franz Joseph* waited for the news they knew must come. Could the outside world fail to be moved by what Emil Karlweis had done for them? Could his unselfishness fail to melt the hardest heart? Within a day—two days at most—the message would come from Aaron Peyser's American friend. By radiogram or wireless it would come—it was expected hourly—and then their ordeal would be over.

The day passed. Then two days passed. A week passed, and hope seemed to drop away, grain by grain, like sand slipping through an hourglass. In the blackness of Tuesday night, as the passengers crawled into their beds, there was only a grain or two left.

Then they had their dreams—especially one particular dream, which had been coming to more and more of them lately, though in each case the details were different. They dreamed that they were landing in New York. The gangway was lowered, the ropes were lifted, and they were permitted to move out single file to their new lives of freedom and safety. . . .

Meyer Gottlieb saw himself behind the counter in his brother-in-law's hardware store—a model salesman, polite, friendly, knowing the stock inside out, enjoying the job as if he had been trained for it from birth. To tell the truth, he couldn't imagine any job that he wouldn't have enjoyed, as long as it was in the United States of America. . . .

His wife, Sarah, saw herself in their little flat making dinner for Meyer when he got home that night. Two rooms and a mousehole of a kitchen, that's all the flat was, and absolutely no help. It wasn't what she was used to, God knows—but it was certainly better than the last two years. In fact, living like this at the age of forty-seven, Sarah was reminded of the old days, right after Meyer and she were married, when he was just out of the university and nobody knew yet what a good lawyer he was. Those days hadn't been so terrible, had they? In some ways they had been the happiest of her life. If the end was going to be like that beginning, what did she have to complain about? . . .

Gertrude Fischel was in the office of Wurtzberger Fine Footwear, who used to be one of her husband's biggest American customers, and old Wurtzberger himself—the father, *not* the son—was smiling and bowing at her, very respectful, very deferential, like he used to be in the old days. "Well, if these financial arrangements suit you," he was saying, "we'll consider the matter settled. Now suppose you take a few weeks before you start work. You'll need to find an apartment, get settled in, buy a little furniture. My wife would be delighted to help you with your shopping, I'm sure." Mrs. Fischel thanked him graciously, but she remembered Wurtzberger's wife, that fat, stupid blond woman with her awful taste in clothes, and she made up her mind that she would do her own shopping. . . .

Emil Karlweis, having acknowledged the applause, turned abruptly to face the enemy. Yes, they were always the enemy, every single one of them, and from this came much of the excitement, the stimulation—to subdue them, to bend them to one's will, to transform their natural apathy and slovenliness and hostility into obedience, into beauty. Karlweis gave one sharp tap of his baton against the side of the score, then raised his hands in the air. "Those beautiful hands," one critic had written, "which seem to embody, down to their fingertips, the very spirit of music!" . . .

Rosa Moritz threw herself into the arms of her sister Elsa, who was waiting for her at the dock, and they hugged and kissed and cried on each other's shoulders. And for the next three days they practically never stopped crying, and Rosa couldn't remember when she had had such a lovely time. . . .

Rudy Buberman was in bed with Lisa, holding her in his arms, feeling her sighs of contentment, her shivers of delight. Everything was going well between them again. Thank God, thank God! He had been so afraid she would blame him for those last weeks on the ship, when he hadn't been able to make love.

Betsy Tannenbaum carefully smoothed down the bedspread in the upstairs guestroom of her house in Camden, New

Jersey. Mr. Monsky was coming for the weekend, and she wanted everything to be nice for him. The room was on the other side of the house from little Martin, so the crying wouldn't keep Mr. Monsky from sleeping as late as he pleased. . . .

Joshua Peyser was starting his first day of school in New York City. The other boys weren't too friendly at first. They told him that his clothes were funny, and they pronounced his name wrong, but before the end of the day he had won them over, and they were calling him "Peyser" and offering to teach him how to play baseball. . . .

And then morning came. The dingy rays of what passed for sunlight seeped through windows and portholes, and one by one the passengers groaned, shook their heads, and were jarred out of their dreams. Then they looked around and realized where they were and knew that the hourglass had run out.

*　　*　　*

Aaron Peyser had no time for dreaming.

It was the middle of the morning, and he was lying back in his deck chair with his eyes shut, but he was only pretending to be asleep. Otherwise a dozen different people would be sure to come up to him and ask him if there was any news, and when he told them that he didn't know any more than they did, they would look at him as if they thought he were deliberately hiding something from them. He had learned how to deal with this kind of thing by now, but this morning he needed time to think.

It was no good going to his cabin, either. Sophie was liable to come to him there, and her intrusions were more distracting than anybody else's. She looked very bad these days. She had started having headaches again, those massive migraines that clamped down on her head without warning and kept her in agony for hours. It was years since she had had her migraines—not since the first month she was pregnant with David.

If he could have said anything that would take her headaches away—but there was nothing he could say, and sometimes, seeing the bewildered pleading in her eyes, he felt furious with her for making such a demand on him. He felt almost like hitting her. In his whole married life he had never hit her. Maybe that's what was wrong with his whole married life. . . .

It annoyed him that he should have this thought. Nothing was to be gained by venting his frustrations on poor, unoffending Sophie. This was just a trick his mind was playing on him to avoid the hard thinking he knew he had to do—and the terrible truth he might have to face—

Because the plain fact was, almost two weeks had passed since he had promised himself that he would save the people on this ship somehow. In these weeks he had poured his energy into one plan after another. He had worked night and day, had made a nuisance of himself with practically every adult passenger, so that Morris Feldman could be supplied with information for his conference of European nations—but the conference came and went, and nothing to show for it at all. Then he had maneuvered the rabbi and Emil Karlweis into cooperating with Morris Feldman's next scheme—and that was turning into another fiasco. Days ago it had become clear—to anyone who wasn't an incurable dreamer—that Karlweis' great gesture wasn't going to change a thing.

So Aaron had racked his brains to come up with yet another plan. This time he would have no help from the outside world, nothing to fall back on but his own determination and ingenuity. He began to ask himself if there was any way of *forcing* this ship to stay right here on this spot, *physically* preventing it from sailing back to Germany. Could it be sabotaged, damaged seriously enough so that it would have to limp into the nearest French port for repairs and sit there for a long period of time? Could it be run aground, maybe even sunk—but slowly, so that other ships could take the passengers off? Any delay, even a short one, might be crucial—because in that time, even if it was only a week, even less, the United States or one of the European nations might change its mind and decide to help them after all.

For the last two days this idea had held Aaron in its grip. Cause a delay, *some* kind of a delay—at any cost, at any cost. These words had practically obsessed him. How could he find out if it was feasible? In the library he came across a book on ship construction and pored over it intently for hours. It was full of long technical descriptions and incomprehensible diagrams. In the end he had to put it away in exasperation.

Then he had gone to Meyer Gottlieb, remembering that

he used to be in the navy when he was a young man. Without saying in so many words what he had in mind, Aaron had asked Gottlieb about the workings of a ship like this, its weak points, its vital spots. But Gottlieb had admitted cheerfully that he knew no more about ships than an Arab who spent his whole life in the desert. He rather thought that a big ship of this kind could be rendered helpless only if something serious was done to its engines—but he couldn't really be sure about that.

Nevertheless, this was enough for Aaron. He had asked Dietrich, the second officer, if he wouldn't give him a tour of the engine rooms, and Dietrich had been delighted to satisfy his curiosity. Dietrich always made a point of being nice to the passengers—in the same way, Aaron supposed, that hospital nurses make a point of being nice to patients who are dying. So last night after dinner Dietrich had taken Aaron down to the bowels of the ship, and he had seen the huge boilers and pumps and generators belching smoke and spitting fire, and he had seen the men who tended them, brawny, blackened, dripping with sweat. And he had realized the hopelessness of launching an attack against these monstrous machines and their giant guardians. No effort on his part, no matter how desperate, was likely to put so much as a scratch on any of them.

And so late last night when he had emerged into the fresh air, his obsession had finally loosened its grip on him. It had left him feeling foolish—as if, in a sudden fit of a second-childishness, he had started playing cowboys and Indians again.

Last night he had laughed at himself and by this means had turned away from the terrible truth which he didn't want to think about. But this morning, stretched out on his deck chair, he was making himself think about it. You solve no problems, you win no battles, if you're afraid to think about the unthinkable—what *else* had he learned in these last weeks?

The truth was simply this: As he eliminated one by one each new idea for escape, how long would it be before he ran out of ideas completely? Wasn't he close to the bone right now? Wouldn't he be forced pretty soon to admit to himself that there simply wasn't anything more he could do? It's all over now, he would have to say to himself. There's no more hope for any of us. We're dead.

Dead? What was this, anyway? Was his stomach beginning

to ache? It was weeks since his stomach had bothered him. No, he couldn't afford to let himself be frightened. Fear dulled his senses, spoiled his judgment. There *were* other ideas, other means of escape—if he could only think of them. . . .

So he stopped thinking about his stomach and fastened his attention on the immediate problem. Yes, there was one more means of escape, one more plan he could try. It had been in the back of his mind for quite a while, he realized, only somehow he had always preferred to try something else first. For some reason this plan seemed like the last resort—

"Mr. Peyser! Please, Mr. Peyser!"

He opened his eyes and saw the chief steward, Hochschwender, standing over him. Amiable, red-cheeked, rolypoly Hochschwender—looking as always like the fat comic of a Viennese operetta. There were times, Aaron thought, when this whole ship, this whole voyage was like something out of an operetta—Franz Lehar rewritten by a madman.

"First Officer Muller wishes to see you in his office immediately," Hochschwender said. "It's a matter of the greatest urgency."

"And if I don't come, will First Officer Muller have me hung from the yardarm?"

"Mr. Peyser!" Hochschwender's eyes bulged, he looked genuinely distressed. "I assure you, the personnel of the *Franz Joseph* have all been doing their best—"

Aaron had to take pity on him. "It's all right, it's all right," he said, getting to his feet. "I'll be happy to talk to First Officer Muller. I can't think of a pleasanter way to break up the morning."

Aaron climbed the stairs, and a few minutes later he was knocking at Muller's door. The familiar voice, cold as a knife, told him to come in.

"Sit down, Mr. Peyser," Muller said from across the desk.

An unprecedented offer! An incredible act of generosity! All of a sudden it was clear to Aaron why Muller had sent for him.

With this realization came a wave of exhaustion. He did want to sit down, he had never wanted anything more in his life. But he knew he mustn't give in to this temptation. He couldn't let Muller have the satisfaction.

"The captain wishes me to tell you," Muller said, "that his orders have just arrived from Hamburg. If no arrangements have been made by Friday morning—two days from now—to admit our passengers into some foreign port, we are to weigh anchor and return home at once. This order has been signed by the Führer himself. It therefore has the force of law."

Muller stopped talking. In the long silence that followed Aaron refused to take his eyes from Muller's face. How pale, how nearly bloodless that face was—Aaron had never been so struck by this before. The eyes were shining, and a vein in the forehead was throbbing.

Aaron finally decided that he could trust himself to speak. "The captain might disobey that order."

"I think not, Mr. Peyser. One doesn't disobey a direct order from the Führer."

"Still, it *can* be done. Your Führer isn't God."

"God?" Muller gave a short unsmiling laugh. "Who knows what God is? Are you sure that God isn't the most powerful human being on earth at any given moment? Are you sure that God isn't the force that moves the world, flowing first through one man, then through another, from generation to generation? Today that force flows through the Führer. This generation is *his*."

"I want to see the captain."

Muller's voice became flat and mechanical again. "If he wishes to see you, he will no doubt issue the appropriate instructions. Now I suggest you pass on this latest news to your fellow passengers as soon as you can. If you'll make an announcement at lunchtime—"

"I don't believe this *is* the captain's decision," Aaron said, keeping his voice steady. "I believe that he wants to save our lives. I believe that he might disregard these orders if I could just talk to him face to face. And that's what I'm going to do—"

"That's enough!" Muller's face was paler than ever. "Please don't attempt to engage in any unauthorized actions. One of my duties is to enforce the laws of this ship—to perform this duty I'm prepared to take the most serious measures."

Aaron met his gaze a moment longer. Then he turned and left the office. He didn't shut the door behind him.

He went through the door marked "Keep Out" and walked down the stairs. He headed for the deck, for fresh air. Instinctively, almost, as wounded animals head for water. He wished he knew how badly wounded he was. He remembered something Carl Bender had said to him once. In times of crisis there turn out to be two kinds of people, those who fight and those who hide. But what about those, Aaron thought, who fight for as long as they can, who try their hardest to keep on fighting until they just can't go on with it any more—and then they drop in their tracks, they don't even try to find a hiding place? Because they've done everything they could, they've earned the right to lie down and rest—

But then, with a shake of his head, Aaron told himself that he hadn't reached that moment yet. I haven't used up all the ways, he told himself. There's still my last-resort idea. I'll get to the captain. I'll have this out with him face to face. The captain will do what's right.

*　　*　　*

At three in the afternoon Schwarzkopf went to the bar. He had to do something to keep himself from dragging around with his face down to his feet like everyone else on this ship. Since Aaron's announcement at lunch, this looked to Schwarzkopf like a ship full of zombies. This was how most people handled trouble. They stretched out on the ground and waited for the steamroller—instead of making a plan, the way *he* had.

The first person he saw in the bar was Monsky, sitting at a table with the Tannenbaum girl, drinking a beer, talking to her in whispers with his head close to hers. It was a shame what was going on between those two. A married woman with a baby coming, to throw herself away on such a bum!

He walked past Monsky and the girl to a table in the corner, where Gottlieb, the lawyer, was sitting. With him were the Fischel woman and that little Moritz. The Siamese widows, Schwarzkopf called them.

"This isn't a private party, is it?" Schwarzkopf said.

"Positively not," Gottlieb said. "This wake is open to everybody. We're all just as closely related to the corpse."

"Some people," said Schwarzkopf, taking a seat, "don't believe in digging their graves and jumping into them until they're actually dead. Feeling sorry for yourself instead of doing something to help yourself is strictly for jellyfish."

"You don't say so?" Fischel lifted her chin and gave one of her snorts through her nose. "Well, if *you're* in the mood to stick your head in the sand like an ostrich, that's fine with me. But please don't get snotty with people who refuse to share your delusions."

"Snotty?" Schwarzkopf turned to her sharply. "Now that's a subject you should be an expert on. Snottiness is definitely one of the things you're best at—"

"And a lucky thing, too, considering some of the vulgar, boorish types I've had to meet on this ship—"

"Gertrude, don't fight," Moritz broke in, her voice high and shaky. "There's so much fighting—people are so unkind—"

Her eyes were red and wet, and her mouth was twitching a little. Any minute now she's going to fall to pieces, Schwarzkopf thought.

Gottlieb spoke up quickly, "Mrs. Moritz is right. We're all under a strain—how could we help ourselves?—but there's nothing to be gained by taking it out on one another. We're not responsible for one another's troubles. The enemy isn't a passenger on this ship."

Fischel grunted. "All right, I'll apologize. Excuse me, Mr. Schwarzkopf, I shouldn't have let my feelings get the better of my judgment." Her words were addressed to Schwarzkopf, but he could see that her eyes were on Moritz while she said them. A moment later she said, "So are you feeling better, Rosa?"

Moritz gave a sniffle and nodded her head.

Fischel was pulling the humility act, Schwarzkopf thought. How many times had salesmen and employees tried to use it on him, tried to get the upper hand by making him feel ashamed of himself. He certainly wasn't going to let this old harpy outhumble *him*. "Apologies accepted and returned," he said. "And to show you there are no hard feelings, how about a friendly drink—on me, naturally." He snapped his fingers, and the waiter came scurrying over. "Let's have a bottle of champagne here. And make it the genuine imported French stuff."

The waiter gaped at him as if he'd been talking in a foreign language.

"What's holding you up? Didn't I make myself clear enough?"

The waiter muttered something and scurried away. And Schwarzkopf leaned back and enjoyed the stares of amazement from his companions.

"Excuse me," Fischel said, "but since when did they start offering free champagne on this ship?"

"What's free? A woman with your experience in business—didn't you tell me once that you were practically your husband's right-hand man?—you must've learned by now that nothing in this world comes for nothing. I'm *paying* for this little treat."

"If you don't mind my curiosity," Gottlieb said, "were you planning to use *money?* A bottle of French champagne must come to at least seventy-five marks."

"A hundred and ten would be more like it," Schwarzkopf said. Then he pulled the two notes from his pocket and waved them in the air. "What I always say is, what's money for if you're not willing to spend it on your friends?"

He watched the three of them fixing their eyes on the notes as if they were the kind of shiny objects that hypnotists use to put people in a trance. But he was in no hurry to clear up the mystery for them. He waited till the champagne arrived, tasted it, smacked his lips, and announced that it was satisfactory, not the absolute best but reasonably good. And only then did he explain to them how he had smuggled these two hundred-mark notes out of Germany.

Moritz's red eyes were bulging. "But Mr. Schwarzkopf, if they had *caught* you—"

"They didn't catch me, did they? In this world nobody hands you anything on a platter. If you want something, you have to take it for yourself—even if this means running a few risks along the way." He raised his glass in front of him. "A toast—to the future! To getting out of this in one piece. To having the guts to fight and win when your back is to the wall!"

He almost added, "To the success of my plan, which I'm going to put into effect as soon as the opportunity comes along." But naturally he didn't make such a stupid mistake.

Everybody drank.

"Oh, it's very nice," Moritz said. And Gottlieb beamed appreciatively. And Fischel gave a shrug and said, "Not bad—but you'll never convince me it's genuine imported French."

They were all silent for a while, drinking the champagne. Then Gottlieb looked sort of thoughtful and said, "It's interesting, what you said a minute ago, Schwarzkopf. The guts to fight and win—I wonder if that's really possible for us."

"Why shouldn't it be?" said Schwarzkopf, refilling his glass.

"We're Germans," Gottlieb said. "Have you ever thought of that, Schwarzkopf? Have you given that fact your careful attention, ladies? We're good, docile, obedient Germans, just like the people who want to destroy us."

Fischel snorted. *"Obviously* we're Germans—"

"Let me tell you what happened to me some years ago," Gottlieb said. "When our child was born, our Anna—nearly eighteen years ago. She died a few days later, but she'd be eighteen next March if she had lived. Sarah started feeling the labor pains in the middle of the afternoon. I bundled her into the car and drove her across the city to the hospital. The traffic was so heavy—by the time we got there her pains were coming at four-minute intervals. And the only parking space near the hospital entrance had a big sign on it saying 'Positively No Parking Here.' So what did I do? What could a good German possibly do? After all, the sign said 'positively.' I drove around the block until I found a legal parking space, and I walked poor Sarah all the way back to the hospital."

"So what's the point?" said Schwarzkopf, gulping some more champagne.

"The point is, we're all such *Germans.* It's in our blood, our good Aryan blood that Hitler keeps assuring us we don't have." Gottlieb took a sip of his champagne. "Don't you ever say to yourself, Schwarzkopf—what a good Nazi you would've made, if only they'd let you?"

"No—I don't believe that!" Moritz's head was shaking back and forth. "My husband used to tell me—Jacob, my late husband—there's a Jewish ethical tradition, and that's why Hitler hates us and has to persecute us. Because he knows he can never win us over to his side!"

"Your husband died in 'thirty-six," Fischel said. "Things have got worse since then."

"I know it—but even so"—Moritz's eyes were filling with tears—"Jacob could never have been one of *them.* . . ." The tears began to roll down her cheeks.

Another silence settled on the table. Moritz's tears and Gottlieb's stories were spoiling the party. This made Schwarzkopf sore. A hundred and twenty marks this champagne cost.

The door to the bar opened, and Schwarzkopf saw Stieffel coming in. Stieffel got as far as Monsky's table, then he stopped, said a few words to Monsky and the Tannenbaum girl, and sat down with them.

Right away Schwarzkopf forgot all about the champagne,

though there was still a quarter of the bottle left. Stieffel and Monsky coming together in the same place, settling down together for a sizable length of time—this was the opportunity Schwarzkopf had been waiting for. It had come suddenly, without warning—the way all opportunities come, didn't he know from experience? And you can't waste time worrying over them, you have to grab hold of them before they run away.

Schwarzkopf got to his feet. "Excuse me, ladies—Gottlieb —an urgent matter that I just remembered. Here's the money to pay for the bottle. You can give me the change later. And leave something for the waiter, will you, Gottlieb? Don't be stingy with him—how many tips is he getting this trip?"

Schwarzkopf left the bar—giving a quick nod to Stieffel as he passed by—and headed straight for the stairs.

As he walked down to A deck he went over the plan in his mind again. The important thing to remember was that it was necessary, there wasn't any other way. In a couple of days they'd be starting back to Germany, and once they got there nothing could help him except the one thing which always helps in the end, the basic, rock-bottom thing, money. Sooner or later this was what life boiled down to—do you have the money? And when they stepped ashore in Hamburg a few days from now—when he found himself facing those cold-fish Nazi officials across a desk again, as he had faced them so many times in the last six years—he knew that no skimpy hundred marks was going to do him any good. Real money would·be needed, and it would be needed right away, in cash, in a lump sum—before the wheels started turning, before the bureaucratic machinery caught him up and whirled him along and dragged him through the gates of the concentration camp. Though even there, if worse came to worst, money would talk, he was sure of that. . . .

Where could he find this solid lump sum? On this ship, full of people who had been squeezed dry long ago, there was only one answer. Stieffel had told him that he was carrying a pile of marks, a lot more than the legal amount—his influential in-laws had arranged for him to take it with him to America. How much did he say it came to? Enough to keep him afloat in New York for months. That must be a couple of thousand at least, maybe as much as five or ten thousand. And he had to keep it somewhere in his cabin—since he wasn't legally entitled to have it, he couldn't have put it in the ship's safe.

It wouldn't be stealing. This was what Schwarzkopf had to keep reminding himself. All his life he had been an honest man. He had a reputation for honesty in the mercantile world. When you deal with Schwarzkopf, you know where you stand. So what he was about to do wasn't stealing—it went way beyond that, it was a question of life or death. When it comes to keeping himself alive, a man doesn't split hairs. People like his son-in-law, Aaron, squeamish little people with no stomach for being realistic, split hairs maybe—but not grown-up men.

Besides, how badly did Stieffel need this money, when you got right down to it? He had plenty of other resources. Those same influential in-laws would be waiting for him on the dock, ready to shove more money into his hands and whisk him out of the country. He was the one person on this ship who *couldn't* use that money. It was no question of life or death for him. The dishonest thing would be for him to hold onto it when it could save somebody else's life.

Why not *my* life? thought Schwarzkopf. The first man to get to that money, to grab hold of the opportunity, that's the man who has a right to it. It's first come, first served in this world.

On the landing leading down to A deck he ran into Emma. Her face was white, and right away she clutched at him. She was always clutching at him these days. "Where's Sophie?" she cried. "I can't find that girl anywhere! Bruno, you have to help me find her!"

This was Emma's big worry—it had started growing on her last week. Where did Sophie go? Why wasn't she here, what had happened to her? You'd think Sophie was a little girl again who couldn't take care of herself unless her Mama was around. This was Emma's way of occupying her mind, keeping herself from thinking about other things. You cover up what really scares you by getting hysterical over something that isn't real at all.

"I can't help you now," he said. "I've got something important to take care of."

"But I haven't seen Sophie for an hour. She said she was going to the writing room, but she isn't there."

"Get away from me!" He pulled loose from her so hard

that she staggered back a step. Her mouth was wide open, her eyes blinking, as he left her on the landing.

She'll recover quick enough, he thought. She always did. It didn't matter what you said to her, how much contempt you showed for her; an hour later she was always whining at you or telling you some idiotic piece of gossip or wheedling you for money, just as if nothing had happened. Nothing ever *did* happen to her—not really. She had been the youngest and prettiest of four sisters, and her father, old Krauss—who had been a damned good salesman in his day—had spoiled her from the minute she was born. He had given her everything she ever wanted, seen to it that she never had to lift a finger for herself. Then at the age of eighteen she married Schwarzkopf, and things hadn't changed for her a bit; she went right on having charge accounts in all the best stores and plenty of servants to pick up after her. With all that cotton wool around her, how could real life ever get to her?

Schwarzkopf had known she was like this when he married her. It was *why* he had married her. If you've got a wife who has to be treated like a piece of priceless glassware, people know you can *afford* priceless glassware.

He was on the landing of B deck now. He went to the little room at the end of the corridor where the day steward sat. An old man with stupid, watery eyes—Schwarzkopf had already made a point of saying a friendly word to him whenever they met.

"I've got a favor to ask you, Oscar," he said. "I can't find the key to my cabin, and my wife is off somewhere, I can't find her, either, and there's something I have to get right away. Maybe you'd let me have your passkey for a few minutes."

"I'll open the door for you, Mr. Schwarzkopf," the steward said.

"Don't bother about that. You're enjoying your afternoon coffee, you don't want to be disturbed. Give me the key, and I'll give it back to you in a few minutes."

The steward didn't much like the idea, but Schwarzkopf just kept holding out his hand, and finally he had the key. People will almost always give you what you want if you show that you want it worse than they do.

He went down the corridor, turned a corner, and found himself at the door of Stieffel's cabin. He didn't hesitate. He ignored the slight sweating of his hands. If anybody came along, he had to look as if he was opening a door he had a right to open. How many times had he discovered, through the years, that what counts in this world isn't what you're entitled to but what you *look* as if you're entitled to.

He was in the cabin now. He shut the door behind him. He knew already which were Stieffel's dresser and Stieffel's bunk. He started going through Stieffel's things—very careful, putting everything back the way he found it. He didn't want Stieffel realizing right away that something was wrong. Not that he expected Stieffel to raise any alarms about his missing money. Stieffel wasn't going to ask the authorities to look for money that he wasn't legally supposed to have in the first place.

In the middle drawer of Stieffel's dresser he found a small leather pouch. Stieffel had shoved it inside one of his shirts—not much of a hiding place, Schwarzkopf thought. He took the pouch out of the drawer and started pulling it open. His fingers were trembling. Strictly a reflex, it didn't mean a thing—actually, he couldn't have been calmer.

Finally the pouch came open. He took out the pile of notes that was inside it. A thick pile—mostly tens and twenties, and some notes of a hundred, too. He riffled through it. It was as good as he had expected, four or five thousand at least. He would count it carefully later on—

The door opened behind him. He whirled around, his heart giving a jump that sent a stab of pain through him. He saw Monsky standing in the doorway.

For a second or two Schwarzkopf could feel that pain zigzagging through his chest. It kept him from saying anything.

"I came down for an aspirin tablet," Monsky said. "I've been getting a lot of headaches—since I ran out of cigars . . ."

Monsky's voice trailed off. Into Schwarzkopf's head came the thought that Monsky was as surprised as he was. The one who recovers first, Schwarzkopf thought, is the one who'll have the vital advantage. So get hold of yourself, take the initiative, hit him before he can get back on his feet.

"Did you know about this money?" Schwarzkopf said. "There's four thousand marks here, at least. Our friend Stieffel seems to have fixed himself up very nicely. The rest of us are stripped to the bone, and he's carrying this nice little nest egg—"

"Schwarzkopf—is it possible?" Monsky's voice was low,

with a funny kind of hoarseness in it. "You were stealing Stieffel's money?"

"Listen to me—we could use this money. When we get back to Germany—with this much money we could buy a lot for ourselves. It could make all the difference between— You and me, Monsky. Splitting it right down the middle—"

"You're a thief, Schwarzkopf?" Monsky said. "Stealing a man's money? Like any thief in a jail?"

"Listen to me, will you? Get some sense in your head for once in your life. This money could save your neck. Mrs. Tannenbaum's neck, too—if you wanted to use it that way—"

A sound came out of Monsky. A quick sharp sound like a squeak. It was a laugh. Monsky was laughing. "If the people on this ship found out—a thief, a fourflusher, the biggest bum of all—" Monsky's eyes were very bright. "Schwarzkopf, when I tell them—"

"You're not telling *anyone!*" Schwarzkopf put on the voice he used when he gave orders to his employees. Loud, angry, taking no backtalk from anyone—be tough with them or they'll walk all over you. "God damn it, you lazy good-for-nothing, you're going to keep your mouth shut!"

"Is that a fact?" Monsky's eyes were getting even brighter. "What a persuasive argument you're using. What thoughtful, well-reasoned points you're making, and in such a tactful, in-gratiating tone of voice. How could anybody in his right mind resist you?"

Monsky laughed again—soft enough, but to Schwarzkopf's ears that laugh filled the room, it echoed from wall to wall, it sliced through something in his head—and suddenly his heart was pounding, his legs were shaking, and he was crying out, "You *can't* tell anyone, Monsky! Look—I'm begging you—"

Begging? Was that the word that had just come out of him? Failures beg. No-goods beg. Bums at the end of their rope— jellyfish that a man like him would throw out of his office, if they ever managed to get through the door in the first place—

"Put the money back where you found it, Schwarzkopf," Monsky said.

"Yes—absolutely—"

"Close the drawer—nice and neat, please."

"Yes—it's closed—"

"Now get out of here before I call the steward."

Schwarzkopf moved to the door. But he had to turn in the

doorway, he couldn't leave without speaking again. "You're not going to tell anyone, are you? They're taking us back to Germany—we're all finished now, no matter what—what good will it do you to tell?"

Monsky was shaking his head. "Go away, will you, Schwarzkopf. I have to think this over. I'll let you know when I've decided what to do."

Schwarzkopf left the cabin and started walking. Where was he going? He didn't know. But his legs kept moving, and then they stopped and he was standing in front of a door. The door of his own cabin.

He went inside. Emma was there, stretched out on the bed. "I found Sophie," she said. "Out on deck—" She stopped short, and then she was on her feet, going up to him. "What's the matter? Are you sick? Oh, my God—"

He began to weep. His head was against Emma's chest, he was holding on to her tightly. He was holding on to *her?* As if she were somebody you could hold on to?

But even while he was cursing himself, he could hear the words pouring out of him. "We're all going to die—we're all going to be killed—"

And from a distance he could hear Emma's voice. "It's all right, Bruno. I'm here, I'm here—"

What was happening to him, anyway? This wasn't how Bruno Schwarzkopf handled trouble. Be a man, he told himself. Stand up like a man and fight.

But he knew that he didn't care anymore. What did it matter anymore, since everything was finished, anyway? Thank God he could finally stop fighting.

* * *

From Chief Steward Hochschwender—who loved to talk to passengers and seldom realized just what he was saying—Aaron found out that the captain always went to his office on the bridge after dinner and often stayed there till midnight. He also found out that Muller wasn't on duty tonight. Around ten tonight, then, would be the perfect time for him to see the captain. Except for Muller nobody on the ship was likely to stop him.

He left his family in the main lounge playing bingo. How strange this bingo game suddenly seemed to him. As he crossed the foyer and started up the stairs, he wasn't able to get it out of his mind. What was the secret of its strength, its stubborn ability to survive every misfortune that occurred on this ship? The closer many of his fellow passengers drew to their fate, the more eagerly they threw themselves into this game. As if Hochschwender's familiar monotonous roll call—"Twelve-B, twelve-one-I, forty-seven-G"—were some kind of religious incantation, a weird prayer to a pagan god.

But everything seemed strange to Aaron tonight. The simplest things, which he ordinarily took for granted, were turning upside down. All through dinner, for instance, his mother-in-law had kept saying to his father-in-law, "Eat your soup, Bruno, it's good for you—don't take another potato, Bruno, remember what the doctor said about your weight—" And the old man had finished his soup down to the last spoonful and had pulled his hand back from the potatoes with no sarcastic remark, no furious outburst, not so much as a grunt.

Aaron arrived at the "Keep Out" door. Instinctively, as he opened it, he began to move more cautiously. Though he knew that Muller wasn't around, he could feel his breathing getting faster as he went past the closed door of Muller's office. He continued through the glass door at the end of the corridor and up another small flight of steps, and he was in a white vestibule that reminded him of a hospital hallway. No carpet on the floor, no pictures on the wall, a black unmarked door at the end of it. Aaron knew that he had finally come to the captain's office.

He didn't take another step toward it. He wasn't sure why he was holding back. Fear of the unknown, he supposed. Until this moment he hadn't quite realized how little he knew of what was on the other side of that black door. Almost nothing would have surprised him. A blaze of light in the center of the room and the captain's disembodied voice rising out of it . . .

He made himself cross the vestibule. And then for the first time he noticed the music. It must have been playing all along, but his ears hadn't registered it till now. Thick, loud music, with strings, trumpets, kettledrums, a chorus of voices swelling up over the orchestra. The melody they were singing was familiar to him, the name of it tottered on the edge of his memory. Yes, it was Beethoven—Beethoven's Ninth Symphony—the "Ode to Joy."

It all came back to him now. This had been one of his father's favorite pieces, one of the records he used to play over and over on the phonograph in the old apartment, especially in the last years of his life when he hardly ever went out. Aaron was married then, of course, and he didn't have to hear that melody day in and day out, the way his mother did.

His father had always loved music. He had collected records almost from the time records began to be made, and he used to go to concerts and the opera often when he could afford to. And for a long time when he *couldn't* afford to. . . . Somehow Aaron had never caught his father's enthusiasm for music. He had even felt a little impatient at it. "If he gave as much time to his business affairs as he does to Beethoven and Mozart—" He remembered thinking this with a knot of resentment in his stomach—particularly during the years when he was holding jobs afternoons and weekends, tutoring, typing manuscripts, filing books in the library so that he could pay his way through the university. But now, as that melody sounded in his ears, it wasn't resentment that swept over him but pity. Poor Papa, beaten down, elbowed aside, trying to find some grandeur, some peace somewhere, if only in a scratchy old phonograph.

The words that the chorus was singing were suddenly in his mind. He had known them by heart once, hating every one of them. How strange that they should have been lurking in a corner of his mind all these years, waiting to jump into the light again.

> Joy, thou source of light immortal,
>   Daughter of Elysium,
> Touched with fire, to the portal
>   Of thy radiant shrine we come.
> Thy pure magic frees all others
>   Held in Custom's rigid rings;
> Men throughout the world are brothers
>   In the haven of thy wings. . . .

Aaron lifted his hand and knocked on the black door.

"Come in," said a voice from the other side of the door.

Aaron opened the door slowly and took a step into the room. It was almost completely dark. Only a few slivers of bleak moonlight shone through the window that formed most of the wall across from Aaron. In the grayish haze he could

365

see a desk and a man's form behind it. A large head, broad shoulders; but the face was turned away, nothing visible of it except the corner of a cheek. And the hair, the clothes, the desk itself had no color to them—everything was flattened into the same dull gray.

But most of all what Aaron was aware of in this room was the music. It seemed to be coming from a phonograph on the desk, a vague boxlike shape that revealed itself by being a little blacker than the surrounding blackness. From this shape the "Ode to Joy" thundered out and filled the room.

Abruptly the music grew softer, became a low throbbing in the background. The man at the desk had evidently turned a knob.

"Captain," Aaron began, "you must excuse this intrusion. I'm deeply sorry—but I had to see you. I'm Aaron Peyser. We've been in communication, but I had to see you."

He waited. No sound came from the man at the desk. No hint of permission to go on talking. No sharp command to leave the room, either.

Aaron took the silence as a signal to continue. "I want to thank you first," he said, "for the way you've treated us these last weeks. We're grateful for everything you've done for us."

He paused again. No acknowledgment came. There was nothing to do but continue. "But we have to know what you're planning to do with us, captain. After showing us so much kindness, are you going to turn us over to the Nazis now? Are you going to let them destroy us? You have to understand what we're feeling. It's not that we're ungrateful, but—you have to understand—

"Mr. Muller told me that you've received your orders from Germany, that we have to start back on Friday. If that's the truth, captain"—Aaron paused, but no sound came from across the desk—"I must ask you now—I must ask you respectfully but urgently—isn't there anything you can do? Can't you circumvent those orders somehow? You're the captain. You said it yourself, our first night aboard—you had Muller say it for you—the laws here are *your* laws. What would happen if you ignored those orders? If you just waited it out right here— Somebody has to take us in eventually. The longer we can hold out— Or maybe it would be better if we sailed from port to port, making our presence felt in as many places as possible, forcing them to notice us and remember us. The point is, why *couldn't* you do it?

366

"All right, I can think of certain objections you might raise. Sooner or later, won't we run out of food and water? I don't think that'll happen. I think we'll be taken in long before that. Or we could signal to other ships, friendly ships whose captains would be glad to share supplies with us. I'm sure we won't have trouble finding some. And even if we don't—we'll go on rations, your passengers will be glad to go on rations. My God, we'll starve ourselves first! And if the news got out that we were slowly starving, maybe that's just what we need to shame somebody into taking us in.

"I know, you're asking yourself what the German government will do if you disobey those orders. What *could* they do—send a warship to find us, shoot at us, sink us? On the eve of war I don't think Hitler will risk sinking or damaging a large ship like this. Germany is going to need every ship it's got.

"Then maybe you're concerned about your own crew. You're wondering how they'd react if you disobeyed orders. Will they be angry, will they rise up against you? There's no chance of it, Captain. The men on this ship aren't the kind who make mutinies. They don't have anything against us, they don't want to see us get hurt. All they want to do is obey orders and go about their work. There are a few fanatics like Muller, of course, but they're such a minority they couldn't give you any trouble.

"Then maybe you're hesitating, Captain, because you're afraid what will happen to *you* when you go back to Germany? You're afraid the Nazis will punish you if you disobey those orders. What can I say to that? If you take us to one of the free countries—to England or France or the United States—you could claim asylum, you'd be a hero in everyone's eyes. You know what Germany is like today. Not only for Jews, but for every decent man. And somebody like you, with your feelings, your conscience—sooner or later, even if you don't help us, you'll do something that the Nazis won't approve of. Sooner or later it'll be too much for you. . . .

"But even if it isn't, even if you never get into any trouble with the Nazis—there are a thousand people on this ship—three hundred of them are children. If you let them be killed —can you live with that? Will you ever be able to forget?"

He stopped talking. He waited, peering into the shadows, as if he could pierce them and see *something* on that hidden face.

He waited a long time, and then a voice came from behind the desk. It came in a whisper that for a moment sounded almost fierce. "I can't help you. Please go away."

"I don't *believe* you'll abandon us! You're the only hope we've got!"

"I can't help you," said the whisper. "Please go away."

And now there was something in that voice—Aaron had heard despair before, but he had never heard anything like this. It was total, absolute. There was no hope in it at all.

The music rose again, the hand had turned the knob. The "Ode to Joy" was building to its climax. The chorus was shouting, the trumpets were screeching—the volume rose and rose until Aaron thought his eardrums would burst. "Touched with fire, to the portal," the chorus thundered, "of thy radiant shrine we come!"

Suddenly Aaron didn't want to stay in this room anymore. There was a mystery here that he could never penetrate. He wasn't sure that anything waiting for him outside could possibly be worse.

He rushed out the door. He kept moving until he was down the stairs, through the glass door, standing in the corridor where Muller had his office. He let out his breath only when there wasn't the faintest wisp of music in his ears.

A few minutes later he was safe on deck again. And now what? The truth, it seemed, had to be faced at last. His career as a Leader of Men was over. He had done his job. He had led the lambs to the slaughter.

The slaughter? Sophie, the boys—the beasts clawing at them— Wait, wait, what was he doing? He was losing control, he wasn't thinking straight. But he *had* to think straight, he couldn't afford to give up yet. Because there's still a way of getting out of this, he told himself. There *has* to be a way—something new, a new idea you haven't thought of yet. You've got time—another day, at least, before the ship weighs anchor. You can go to bed, give yourself a chance to sleep on this. Maybe in the morning . . .

He turned from the railing and went down to his cabin. Sophie was lying in bed wide awake. She tried to talk to him, but he told her he had a bad headache and wanted to get to sleep.

Half an hour before midnight Muller left his cabin and went up to his office. He turned on only one light, the small shaded lamp on the desk. In the sallow orange glow he sat down and made himself be calm again. These spells of agitation wouldn't do. They came involuntarily—they had no connection with what he really felt—but still, they had to be dealt with.

Only a few minutes ago—stretched out on his bunk below, smoking a cigarette in the darkness—he had definitely decided what to do. But perhaps he had known from the start. Why else had he made up his mind this morning—as soon as he understood what the Peyser boy was trying to tell him —that he must handle this matter all by himself? He couldn't bring Dietrich or any of the other officers into this with him. Above all, he couldn't say anything about this to the captain. If nobody was by his side when the moment came, he would be free to take certain steps. . . .

What steps? No specific steps had been in his mind. Not until a few minutes ago.

Even now, sitting behind the desk in his office watching the minute hand of his watch as it slowly approached the number twelve, he didn't want to describe his intentions to himself. If he thought about them too much he might hesitate when the time came for action. He forced himself to think about other things.

He remembered the look of pleasure on poor old Strassvogel's face when he heard that he was to be relieved of his late watch, that he could sleep the whole night through. Life was so simple for the Strassvogels of this world. Whatever happened to them, they accepted it. No anger, no hatred—no joy, either. Necessary tools for the new order, of course. But leaders were required, too, and leaders were by nature more complicated.

He remembered the look on the face of Aaron Peyser's son —squirming in his chair, keeping his head down every minute he was talking because shame prevented him from meeting Muller's eye. Once this matter is settled, Muller wondered, shall I tell Peyser the truth about his son? To see the look on the face of the captain's darling favorite, his personal Jewboy . . . Muller had promised the boy not to reveal what he had done—this was something the boy had kept insisting on. But of what account are promises made to traitors and informers? In Muller's eyes such people had put themselves beyond consideration. There was a kind of satisfaction in discovering that the Jews could produce their traitors, too—the smug, self-righteous Jews with their airs of being better than other people.

How he hated them! As long as he could remember, he had hated them. Back in school there had been that little Jewboy in his class, the smart one who knew the answers to all the questions and finally won a scholarship to the university. Yet who had he been, after all? His father had been a waiter at the hotel, a pimpled, shabbily dressed little man who was even poorer, who stood even lower, than Muller's own father, a typesetter in the newspaper office. But it was the Jewboy who went to the university, and Muller had to go into the mercantile service because he didn't have the money or the influence to get an appointment to the Naval College.

He remembered these last weeks aboard this ship. Standing on the bridge that first day as the procession straggled up the gangway—the pang of fear that had shot through him— And every day since then disgust and anger had filled him whenever he looked at these people, listened to their loud voices, their shrill laughter. Joy had sprung up in him when the news came from Havana. Yes, joy—why not? Was it unnatural for a good German, a loyal Party member, to feel joy that the enemies of the state would soon receive their just punishment? And then, as this voyage went on and on, his suspense and anxiety grew more and more acute. Each new stop, each new message from the captain—would it mean that these people were going to slip away unpunished after all? Outwardly he kept himself calm, of course, but inwardly he was in agony—every day the pain grew worse.

And worst of all had been these last two weeks since he had sent the radiogram to Hamburg. Every day he waited, every day no answer came. The fools, he kept telling himself. They're going to let it go too long. By the time they decide, it will be too late.

But today at last the orders had come. Everything was going to turn out as he wanted it to. In a few days his anxiety would be at an end. Why then did he go on feeling this pain, this agitation? Yes, he was afraid that something could still go wrong, that these people could still escape. This fear wouldn't leave him until he made it leave by himself.

That, he realized, was why he had decided to do what he was about to do.

He opened the drawer of his desk and looked at what was there. He closed his hand over it to feel its hardness and coolness against his fingers, to assure himself that it was real. No, these people won't escape, he told himself. One of them won't, at least.

* * *

It was eleven o'clock when Father turned away from the railing. "It's time for me to turn in. Are you coming along, my boy?"

"No, I don't think so," Peter said. "I'm not feeling very tired."

"After a day like this? Oh, to be young again!" Father smiled. "Good night then, I'll see you in the morning."

But he didn't turn away. He just stood there, smiling into Peter's face. It came over Peter suddenly that Father was about to say something or ask something that ought to be kept quiet at any cost. It wasn't possible that Father suspected what was going to happen tonight. No, Father didn't notice things. His eyes were turned toward God, whatever that meant. The real world passed in front of him without making any impression at all.

"I don't think you're looking well," Father said. "You and Naomi—"

"This hasn't exactly been a health cruise for anybody," Peter said.

"No, it hasn't, of course. But"—Father wet his lips; Peter began to dread what he was going to say—"there's nothing else, is there, Peter? Nothing on your mind?"

For a moment Peter thought that Aaron Peyser had told Father about that night two weeks ago. But that couldn't be— Father would have mentioned it long before now. "My mind is an open book," Peter said. "Very little in it right now but abusive language."

"Well, that's healthy, I suppose—under the circumstances—" Father hesitated, looked as if he were going to turn away again. Then he said, *"I've* got something on my mind. For a week I've known I was going to tell you. I've been waiting for the best opportunity. My usual malingering tactics when a difficult job has to be done."

"What's so difficult to tell me, Father?"

"That I was wrong. All those arguments we've been having, all those things you've been saying. Yes, a man *does* have to fight for what he believes. It's no good believing in anything unless you can suffer for it—go through the fire for it."

Peter looked into Father's face more intently than he had ever done before. It was the same face he had known all his life—long, gray, gentle, a little sad. When had Father been through the fire? All these years could it be that he hadn't really known anything about Father at all?

"You were right, and I was wrong," Father said. "I hope you'll never turn away from that. I don't believe in your homeland, but I hope you'll always fight for it. I suspect that even God would want it that way. If you'll excuse me for bringing that worn-out, superstitious concept into this." The smile hovered on his lips another moment, and then Father was leaning forward, putting his hand on Peter's arm. "But listen to me about *one* thing, my boy. Don't turn away from kindness and gentleness, either. There's so much cruelty in this world already. It's right to fight when you have to—but don't ever fall in love with violence."

Father's voice was shaking. For a moment Peter wanted to put his arms around him, cry out to him, "I'm not that way, believe me! I don't *want* to be cruel! I *hate* it!" But he said nothing—it took the greatest effort he had ever made in his life, but he didn't say a word.

"Well, good night," Father said again. "I'll see you in the morning." He turned away finally, and Peter watched him moving down the deck, a tall, stooped figure in a shabby overcoat.

Later Peter went inside to the far corner of the main lounge, where he had arranged to meet the others. The lounge was deserted at this late hour—poorly lighted by a few lamps, so that the chairs and sofas cast long shadows across the floor.

He saw that he was the first to arrive. That was bad. He should have done what he usually did—waited on the deck outside, watched the door, kept out of sight until all the others had come. That was one of the first things Wilhelm had taught him—"a leader is never kept waiting"—so of course tonight, the big night, he had forgotten it. Cold because he cared? He could imagine Wilhelm's scorn.

Father's words were getting to him in spite of himself. He

could feel them undermining him. He must hold on to his memories of Wilhelm, strong, quiet, determined Wilhelm who never let anything ruffle him. He remembered Wilhelm sitting beside him at the table in the café, slowly sipping his brandy. It was always astonishing that Wilhelm could drink that cheap brandy with such calm, such elegance, never for a moment choking or wincing, though one taste of the stuff was enough to burn Peter's mouth. But that was Wilhelm—everything he did he did with style and confidence, such perfect confidence that he never had to raise his voice and call attention to himself. How Peter yearned to achieve such confidence. . . .

He remembered the first meeting between Wilhelm and his sister, Naomi. He had so much hoped they would like each other. Wilhelm was so good-looking, so forceful—how could she *help* but like him? He should have realized that a girl like Naomi, with her conventional female mind, could never understand someone like Wilhelm.

"What does he do, your friend Wilhelm Keitl?" she had said to him that night.

"He does what we all do these days—nothing. He had to leave the university, like any other Jew. He was a brilliant student of history."

"Oh, I'm sure of it. And he knows all about his own brilliance, doesn't he, your friend Wilhelm Keitl? Does he have a mother and father?"

"They're very poor people; they don't live here in Berlin. He's had a hard life, everything hasn't been given to him as it was to us. He's worked with his hands, and he's gone without food for days at a time. And when he was sixteen he ran away to Palestine and fought with the guerrillas. He'd be there now, but he can't get out of the country anymore."

"So he stays here and fills up little boys with pipe dreams. Yes, that sounds like your friend Wilhelm Keitl."

Then Peter had lost his temper. "Why do you keep calling him 'your friend Wilhelm Keitl'? As if that was his official title or his trademark or something!"

He loved his sister dearly—but she *could* be exasperating sometimes. After that conversation he remembered thinking, "When Wilhelm performs some splendid heroic act of self-sacrifice some day, *then* she'll feel ashamed of herself!"

Had she felt ashamed of herself? After they took Wilhelm away?

373

Peter saw Kurt Halevy coming towards him across the lounge.

"We're the only ones?" Halevy said. "Do you suppose the others have used their common sense and decided not to show up?"

"Why didn't *you* use your common sense?"

"Me?" Halevy gave his peculiar sharp laugh, which seemed to be scorning everything and everybody, especially himself. "I've always had more curiosity than good sense. That may turn out to be my fatal weakness."

"Nothing fatal is going to happen tonight. This is all going to be as peaceful and bloodless as a tea party."

In the next few minutes the other three arrived—Altdorf and Schlossberg together, then David. That was strange, Peter thought, David was usually ahead of everybody. And he looked strange, too—something in his eyes, a kind of deadness, as if he were deliberately numbing himself. I'll take him aside and say something to him, Peter thought. I'll let him know how sure I am that he won't disgrace himself.

"I'd like to make a suggestion," Altdorf said. "According to the original plan, you'll go into the office, Peter, while the rest of us wait at the entrance to the corridor. You'll take care of Strassvogel by yourself, before you call us to help you with the guns. Well, I've been giving it a lot of thought, and I'm not sure I'm in favor of it anymore. Suppose you don't succeed in overpowering Strassvogel? He could raise the alarm, and that would be the end of everything. So what I think is you shouldn't go to him alone, one of us should go with you."

"By one of us, Franz, do you mean yourself?"

"Well, yes. I think I'd like to be the one—"

"We agreed that Strassvogel's suspicions mustn't be aroused. If he sees two of us there in the middle of the night—"

"He'll be surprised, that's all. But before his surprise wears off—"

Peter asked himself why Franz was making this suggestion. The itch for adventure wasn't one of Franz's traits, he wasn't the type to enjoy hitting someone over the head. He's doing this for me, Peter realized. He sees how nervous I am. He guesses how much I wish that I didn't have to go into that office alone.

Why not accept Franz's offer? There *was* no reason why two of them couldn't go to Strassvogel. The poor slow-witted, good-natured man wasn't likely to be suspicious. And the burden seemed so much lighter now, just at the thought that Franz would be by his side—

"Peter doesn't need any help." It was David speaking up, louder and more determined than usual. "Peter isn't afraid to do this by himself."

Peter isn't afraid? Peter *was* afraid, and that was the truth of it— All right, but was that an excuse to give in to his fears? Was he going to murder Wilhelm all over again?

"We'll stick to the original plan," Peter said. "Don't worry about me, Franz. I'll do this with no strain at all. You'd be surprised at how cold-blooded I can be."

And now it was time to get started. They went up the stairs two by two. Peter, in the lead, put David by his side. "I'm counting on you," he said in a low voice, pressing his hand on David's arm. He realized that he had seen this gesture in a movie once. Still, it worked. David managed to smile and say, "Yes—you can."

They climbed as high as they could, and stopped on the landing outside the door that had "Keep Out" written on it. A dim light filled this landing, and in it Peter could barely see the faces of his friends. Yes, they were his friends. He wished he could stretch out his hand to all of them, tell them he loved them. And to Naomi—to Father.

"Well, I might as well go now," Peter said. He hesitated, then he shook hands with each of them and quietly said each name. "Franz. Kurt. Ernst. David." He turned and went through the door.

He shut it softly behind him. He moved down the corridor at a steady pace—Strassvogel mustn't think there was anything stealthy or nervous about his approach. Sure enough, the door to the office was open, a light was sending a soft glow into the dark corridor. Peter paused at the door, put on a smile, and stepped into the room.

Muller was there. Behind the desk Muller was sitting. His face was yellow and lined with shadows.

"What are you doing here at this time of night?" Muller said. "It's prohibited for you to be here."

"Excuse me—I opened the door by mistake—"

"Did you? That will turn out to be a serious mistake. Children should know better than to play with fire."

Muller reached into a drawer of the desk. His hand came out with a gun. Peter had never been so close to a gun before.

"Are your friends waiting for you outside?" Muller said. "I'm afraid they won't be able to help you much."

"I don't understand—"

"You understand. A smart boy like you. Smarter than all the rest of us, aren't you? Admit it—you think you know all the answers!"

Muller's voice was louder. And his eyes—Peter looked into his eyes, and for the first time panic flared up in him. This was coldness, he thought. Wilhelm hadn't known what he was talking about. This was *real* coldness. This was what it meant to fall in love with violence—

"Please don't move," Muller said. "Don't make any attempt to get your hands on this gun."

"I'm not moving—"

"I warned you, didn't I?"

Muller's finger tightened on the trigger. Peter thought, But he isn't going to— A crash in his ears—flame in front of his eyes—this burning in his stomach— Father, it's all right! I understand! I love—

The boys, huddled close together, heard the shot from the other side of the door. Altdorf reached for the doorknob. Halevy grabbed his arm and whispered fiercely, "Don't be a damned fool!" They struggled with each other briefly until Schlossberg stepped around them, shoved the door open, and rushed through. Halevy and Altdorf followed him down the corridor toward the open office door, and David found himself running along after them.

And all the time there was a shrill whistling noise in his ears, and a voice kept saying to him, "You didn't do anything, it wasn't you, you didn't do anything, it wasn't you—"

*   *   *

The pounding on the door woke Aaron up, and after fumbling for his glasses and his watch he was able to see that it wasn't even one o'clock in the morning. He threw a robe around himself and stumbled to the door. He found David there.

He was about to tell the boy not to make so much noise because Sophie needed her sleep. But then he realized that something was terribly wrong.

"Papa, he's been killed—they killed him, Papa!"

The words came out of him so fast, and he was sobbing

and shaking his head. "David, I can't understand you—go slower!"

Aaron gripped the boy by the shoulders, as if he could stop the hysteria by force. And bit by bit, by coaxing him, reassuring him, making him repeat things several times, Aaron was able to get the story out of him.

"It's crazy," Aaron said, at the end of it. "You were going to take over the ship with guns? My God, you *all* could've been— But why was Muller waiting for you? How did he find out?"

"I don't know, Papa. He was just there—we all ran in, and he was there with that gun in his hand—and Peter—" Then the boy was sobbing, heavy convulsive sobs, while his shoulders heaved under Aaron's grip.

"Did anyone tell his father and his sister yet?"

"They were being sent for when I left."

"I'll go down to the hospital, I'll see what I can do. You wait while I put on some clothes." He started to turn away, then noticed the look on David's face. "What is it, David?"

"Papa, I don't think I want—" The boy broke off, his lips working.

Aaron understood. "It's all right, you don't have to go back there with me. Stay here, try to get some sleep."

He saw the shaky smile of gratitude on David's face, then he went back into his cabin. Sophie was half awake as he put on his shoes and his trousers and hastily buttoned his shirt. She mumbled a question at him, and he told her everything was all right, he was just going out on deck for some air. He left the cabin.

David was still in the corridor. He was leaning against the wall, trembling as if he had a severe chill. "Papa—I want to tell you—"

His voice was high and thin, like the voice of a child who's about to burst into tears. God knows Aaron wanted to comfort him—it was easy to imagine what he was feeling, how much Peter Einhorn meant to him—but there just wasn't time right now, so Aaron patted David quickly on the arm and said, "We'll talk about it later," and hurried down the corridor.

The ship's hospital was two rooms—an outer room in which the doctor examined patients and dispensed prescriptions, an inner room with several beds for the more serious cases. Aaron had been down here once before, the night

377

Ehrlich died. He had met the doctor then, an old man with a gruff professional manner that turned out to conceal a failing memory.

At the door of the outer room Aaron was met by Dietrich, the second officer. His cherubic baby face—one of those faces which would stay young for years and years, then turn old and wizened overnight—was clouded now with distress. "This is a terrible thing, Mr. Peyser. I don't know how to— The boy is in a bad way, his father and sister are with him now."

"He isn't dead?"

"He's unconscious. He's been unconscious ever since— Hardly breathing at all, the doctor doesn't think he can possibly—"

"How did this happen? Why did Muller shoot the boy?"

"He appears to have come to Mr. Muller's office with the intention of laying hands by force on the ship's store of weapons. Technically, you understand, Muller was quite justified. The boy had several accomplices with him, several others who appear to have been involved in the plan."

Stepping aside, Dietrich gave a wave into the room, and Aaron saw the three of them sitting on a bench against the wall. He recognized them as David's friends, Altdorf and Schlossberg and the redheaded one, Kurt Halevy. All three had been up on the deck that night weeks ago.

"We won't be pressing charges against them, of course," Dietrich said. "I've talked to the captain. He agrees that this has gone too far already." Embarrassed, Dietrich excused himself and left the room.

And now for the first time the boys looked up. Their faces were white. There was a kind of exhausted horror in their eyes.

Aaron was thankful that he didn't have to say anything to them. The doctor emerged from the inner room at this moment; he muttered something about shock and loss of blood and told Aaron he could go inside and see the patient.

As Aaron moved past him into the inner room, the smell of carbolic acid filled his nose, making him wince a little. He saw Peter lying on one of the beds. A sheet was pulled up to his chin, and his face was a shade whiter than the pillow behind it. His eyes were shut; the faintest fluttering of breath came from between his blue lips. His father sat by the bed leaning forward, staring down at the boy. Next to him, holding tightly to his arm, was the girl, Naomi.

Aaron went up to them and heard himself murmuring the usual things, the stupid things about how sorry he was that made him sound as if he weren't sorry at all. The rabbi didn't look up at him. He kept his head forward, his eyes fixed on his son's face. Every so often, Aaron noticed, his lips would start moving and continue for a while and then stop. But no sound ever came out, there was no way of knowing what he was trying to say.

Aaron turned and looked at the girl. Her expression wasn't easy to read. Grief was there and pain—but under it a kind of intensity. The urge for revenge might be working in her, Aaron thought. She might be planning to do something crazy, to attack Muller, maybe— But he couldn't really believe that was it. Anger didn't seem to be part of what he saw on her face. Her intensity was turning inward. Was she thinking of killing herself?

"I wonder," he said to her, "if I could stay here with you awhile. You wouldn't think I was intruding?"

She shook her head quickly. She wasn't rejecting his offer, she wasn't accepting it. She was telling him that she just didn't care.

He turned to her father and repeated his question. The rabbi still didn't look up—but a moment later his head gave one slow nod.

Aaron brought a chair up to the bed. He carefully placed it so that he would be sitting farther away from the boy than his father and sister were. . . .

At five o'clock in the morning Peter Einhorn died. The flutter of breath just stopped, there wasn't even a final sigh. Aaron couldn't be sure at first if the rabbi had noticed. His face didn't change. His head didn't move. But then Aaron saw that his lips were moving again, and this time it was just possible to recognize that the words coming out of him were Hebrew.

Aaron got to his feet, put his hand on the girl's shoulder. "I'll send the doctor in," he said. "I'll make the arrangements with him. I'm sure there's some—some regular procedure."

The girl looked up at him and said, "Thank you."

She smiled, a tired smile, and he saw that her eyes had filled with tears. That strange intensity had gone from her face—she was in touch with life again. Whatever it was that had come over her a few hours ago, it had left her now.

Aaron went to the outer room. The boys were no longer

there. He talked to the doctor for a while, then he left the hospital and started up the stairs. The smell of carbolic acid stayed with him. He had to get out on deck.

The fresh air helped a little. He breathed it in, gulping hard. A leaden sky hung above him, a fine gray mist swirled around his head. It was that time just before sunrise when a vague unearthly light, barely distinguishable from darkness, fills the air, sinister and disturbing, because it doesn't seem to be coming from anywhere. In another hour the sun would appear—or as much of it as could force its way through the veils of mist—and the new day would officially begin.

Yes, it's morning now, he thought, and no new ideas have come to me. And no new ideas *will* come to me. There's nothing more I can do—for myself, for my family, for anybody else on this ship. Nothing except to take my place in line with the doomed, to face the horror somehow.

But how? He was filled with curiosity about himself. He wondered if he was about to relapse into his old habits, into whining and wailing. He wondered if the old familiar jellyfish would assert himself now that the Leader of Men had become superfluous. Which of these two would he finally turn out to be?

*   *   *

Just after five o'clock Julia Bender came out on deck. There was hardly any light, and the air was damp and bitter. An absurd hour for civilized human beings to be stirring, she thought.

Other people were on deck, too. Shadowy figures moved in the mist. Lunatics like me, she thought. She saw a familiar figure by the railing, with its back toward her. Wasn't it Aaron Peyser? She couldn't see his face, but from the way his shoulders sagged she knew that he was tired—tired to death. He must be sleeping as badly as I am, she thought. She wondered if anybody on this ship was sleeping much any more. Maybe dear old Monsky, who was no doubt so accustomed to clinging from precipices by his teeth that the experience no longer made him the least bit uneasy.

She thought of greeting Aaron Peyser—but something told her that he didn't want to be disturbed. If ever a man seemed to be lost in his thoughts, huddled behind a wall . . .

So she moved on through the mist, slowly becoming aware of a strange feeling inside of her. What was this feeling that Aaron Peyser had suddenly called up in her? It was more than pity—it was closer to affection. But she barely knew the man. Carl had adopted him as a friend during this voyage, and so she had exchanged polite words with him. All the time she had been conscious of his awkwardness, his constraint in her presence. And from time to time, mostly for the pleasure of annoying Carl, she had teased him about Aaron Peyser, referred to him as "your nearsighted disciple."

She remembered what Carl had said to her one night a week ago as they strolled around the deck, pausing for a moment to look through a window at the inevitable bingo players. "These people are nothing to me," Carl had said. "Sad, foolish people, with their foolish games— Then why does my heart reach out to them? Why do I feel that my own family couldn't mean more to me? Do you ever feel that way, too?"

But before she could answer, he had given his wry little smile and gone on, "Of course you don't. It's different for you, that I quite understand. But for the rest of us— I wonder if it's always this way for people in our position. Miners trapped together in a cave-in—men in the death cell together, awaiting execution—patients in cancer wards together, terminal cases. Do you think there's always this same spirit of camaraderie? Do they all share this special intimacy of dying together?"

Remembering these words, Julia found a strange loneliness welling up in her. She felt like a little girl who's been left out of the party. A most unusual sensation for her—she had never in her life, not even as a child, been the type who gets left out of parties.

She stopped walking and looked around her. This lifeboat here—wasn't it the one Carl and she had passed one night on another of their strolls? Their attention had been attracted by somebody sobbing in the shadows. It had turned out to be Claire Halevy—how long ago was that?

Then Julia saw that somebody was standing in those shadows now. A misty figure— It was Claire again, and soft sobs were coming out of her. The wounded animal always returns to its favorite hole.

Julia started to walk away. She was too late. Claire was calling out her name.

Julia stopped and adjusted a smile on her face as Claire emerged into the light. For a moment Claire's appearance gave Julia a shock. The pallor of her cheeks, the ravaged look in her eyes— And what about me? Am *I* looking any better to *her*?

"Miserable morning, isn't it?" Julia said. "It's reassuring to find that I'm not the only insomniac aboard. I probably ought to be going inside now, however—"

"Don't go," Claire said. Her voice was low, and she was trying a smile. "Are you human or aren't you? Don't you feel a *little* bit curious about why I was making such an idiot of myself just now?"

"If you want to talk about it," Julia said.

She was hoping that Claire wouldn't talk about it. She had a horror of becoming entangled with her friends' troubles. Friendships are supposed to be pleasant and amusing and relaxing. As soon as one of the parties starts belaboring the other party with sighs and groans and gloomy tales, the friendship is bound to collapse from the strain.

But she went to the railing with Claire, and they leaned against it looking out at the mist. When Claire spoke again, her voice was steady, no strain in it. But she kept her eyes straight ahead.

"It's Kurt, of course," Claire said. "When he said good night to me last night— He pulls away if I even look as if I'm going to touch him. As if I had something contagious— leprosy or something. I'm thinking of getting myself a bell." A short laugh came out of her.

"All children are natural little sadists," Julia said. "When Eva gets into one of her snotty moods— Console yourself with the thought that someday your grandchildren will take your revenge for you."

"I'd be easier to console if I could blame him," Claire said. "If I could convince myself that he isn't absolutely right—"

Obviously this was the part she wanted to get off her chest. Julia resigned herself with a good grace, and soon Claire was telling her the story of her marriage. Well, at least she told it briefly and succinctly. A big point in her favor.

"My mother told me I was crazy to marry an artist," Claire said. "She was sure that they all beat their wives—even the Jewish ones. But Stefan was the gentlest man who ever lived. He even won Mother over in the end."

382

Apparently, however, he was never able to earn a decent living from his paintings. "He had a wonderful talent," Claire said. "But he was ahead of his time—he painted abstractions long before they were fashionable—"

Julia could imagine. Blobs and lines and smears of color, nothing looking much like anything. The last refuge of sloppiness, as far as she was concerned. Painting made easy for people who don't know how to draw. Claire had excellent taste, as a rule, but when a woman adores a man, how likely is she to be his most perceptive critic? And so for twenty-three years she had slaved away—a social secretary to dreary, rich monstrosities, could anything be grimmer?

And then she came to the part of the story that made it not too different from everybody else's story. The arrival of the swastikaed hooligans, the money getting shorter and the food scarcer, the succession of dingier and dingier lodgings—though it did seem as if Claire and her Rembrandt didn't have as far down to go as some others.

"But the worst of it was Kurt," Claire said. "It's been terrible all these years, seeing him cut off from more and more of the things he ought to have. He's a brilliant, promising boy, he's got all of his father's talent—"

And just a bit unstable, too, Julia thought. Like every other redhead she had ever met. No surprise at all that he had inherited that red hair from his father.

And then they got their chance to sail on this ship. The desperate attempt to raise the money, the last-minute help from relatives in New York—on Claire's side of the family, of course. And then the sickening truth became clear—there was only enough money for two tickets, two passports, two entrance visas. One of the three of them would have to stay behind.

"I knew it had to be me," Claire said. "It couldn't have been more obvious. Stefan could teach the boy so much more, do so much more for him—they were so much alike. And Kurt always felt so much closer to his father. I told Stefan about my decision—we spent the whole night talking about it, arguing. And the next morning—"

She found him in the bathroom the next morning. He had slit his wrists with a razor blade—very classical, no doubt, very poetic, reminiscent of ancient Rome. But messy. Julia shuddered when she thought of all that blood. She could imagine how Claire had felt. Sloppy to the end, that husband of hers.

Still, it had to be admitted that he had behaved with a certain amount of discretion for once in his life. He had taken the only reasonable course of action. Problems ought to be settled like that—in one quick stroke—saving everyone concerned a lot of fuss. The way Carl was able to settle his problems. But how many men have Carl's kind of courage? How many Carls are there in the world?

Yet here was Claire, an ordinarily sensible person—but instead of being grateful for her luck, she was tormenting herself, loading herself down with guilt. "Why did I let him do it?" she said. "I *knew* that I had to be the one. Why the talk, why the delay? It was up to *me* to do what he did. Why was I such a coward?"

The answer was obvious to Julia. Claire had more to live for than he did. Her instinct for survival was stronger—just as everything else about her was stronger. All three of them were better off. But she couldn't say that to Claire. She had to listen in silence as Claire went on whipping herself. "It was always in the back of my mind that I could put it all on him. That's why I insisted on telling him about my 'decision' —because I knew he would never let me go through with it. I drove him to it—deliberately—"

Then Claire was sobbing again, very softly, her head turned toward the sea. And Julia waited patiently, watching a silvery sheen beginning to appear on the surface of the water.

The sobbing finally stopped, and Claire's voice was steady again. "Kurt understands what happened, of course. He knows that I sacrificed his father to save my own neck. Am I going to blame him for hating me? He *can't* hate me any more than I hate myself."

Claire turned to look at Julia now. A strange, anxious look was on her face. "Listen to me, Julia—nothing is worse than deliberately turning your back on someone you love. No pain is worse than knowing you've done that."

The way Claire was staring into her face— The truth came to Julia in a rush. Claire knows what's been happening. She can see right into my soul. "But what else could you have done?" Julia said. "Killed yourself instead? And *he'd* be feeling the way *you're* feeling now."

Claire just went on staring at her.

"It's ridiculous, perfectly ridiculous," Julia said. "Life isn't

384

some sort of self-sacrifice game. Musical chairs with noble gestures. Now you've brought this idiotic idea up, Claire— I want you to give me an answer. What else could you have *done*?"

Claire smiled, more gently. "Nothing else, maybe. That doesn't help a bit."

"But it *has* to help—"

"I loved him," Claire said, in a very quiet voice. She took Julia's hand, squeezed it quickly, and hurried into the lounge.

Julia stood still, staring after her. Ridiculous, ridiculous, she kept telling herself. Nothing is worse than turning your back on someone you love. All right, but what are those words supposed to mean to *me*? Who loves me? Whom do I love? Don't tell me, please don't tell me—after all these years does it turn out that I've been in love with *Carl*? No, no, not even God's perverted sense of humor would stoop to a joke as rotten as that.

She turned away from the railing and moved into the lounge. It was almost empty. A vacuum cleaner was buzzing at the opposite end. A boy of sixteen, a boy in an apron, was running it over the carpet, over the sofas and chairs, sucking up last night's dirt and debris, making everything clean and neat for today's revelries. Not quite the last day of all—but certainly it was growing closer.

No pain is worse, Julia thought, than knowing you've turned your back . . . It was true. Didn't she know it? For almost a week now this pain had been with her. Since she had gone to Carl and told him . . . I'm not a particularly stoical creature, she told herself. I never let the dentist touch me without giving me novocaine first. I'm not very good at living with pain.

Was it too late to bring an end to this pain? Suppose she went to Carl. Suppose she begged him for forgiveness. She might even abase herself a little. It would be an interesting new experience for her. Wasn't she always looking for new experiences?

And if he turned away from her? If he paid her back as she deserved?

Oh, for Heaven's sake, she told herself with disgust, why on earth are you *crying*?

She opened the door of her cabin with as little noise as she could. She didn't want to wake up Eva.

385

But Eva woke up. She yawned and rubbed her eyes and peered up from the bottom bunk. Maybe it was just as well. Eva had to be prepared for what was going to happen. Better to begin right now, to give her plenty of time to get used to the idea.

Julia sat down on the edge of the bed and took her daughter's hands between her own. Eva looked so small when the sleep was in her eyes, so small and helpless.

"Darling," said Julia, smiling. "Do you remember your grandmother? Your father's mother, I mean?"

"But my father's mother is dead," Eva said. "I never saw her, you know. Only her picture in the album."

"No, no, it's your other grandmother I'm talking about. Your grandmother Von Helmuth—do you remember when we visited her on Christmas Day two years ago?"

Eva began to nod. "Oh yes. And she gave me the Japanese bathrobe with the yellow sash."

"What would you think—if you went and lived with your grandmother for a while?"

Julia turned her eyes away. She couldn't look at Eva's face any more. Whatever she saw there now, happiness or desolation, she knew it would stab her to the heart.

*   *   *

Aaron stood at the railing and looked out at the mist. In those gray and leaden fumes he hoped somehow to satisfy his curiosity about himself. Now that he was face to face with the truth, with the terrible and irrevocable truth, what would he turn out to be? Would he let despair sweep over him now, sweep him back to the state he was in before he came aboard this ship? At the end of this voyage was he going to revert to type?

But surely that wasn't possible. A man couldn't lose—so quickly, so casually almost—everything he had gained with such effort and such pain. You've sailed on the *Franz Joseph*, he told himself. You're strong now, whether you like it or not.

Yes, I'm strong now, he answered himself. And what good has it done? Have I managed to save one single life? Is Peter Einhorn going to live, wave his arms again, make any more of his outrageous Zionist speeches? Are any of these thousand doomed people better off because of my strength than they would be without it? And my wife, my boys—are they any

386

farther away from the horror? Almighty God, why did You bother to make me strong when being weak would have done just as well? Why have You tested me and tested me and brought me triumphantly through each test—only to tell me at the end that none of it makes any difference?

From this moment on, Aaron thought, I give up my strength. You can take it back, God of Israel, with all my thanks. I'll be weak again, weak and confused, scared of what's going to happen to me—just like everyone else.

And already, as he stared into the sinister predawn light, he could feel himself becoming a child again. Already, deep in his heart, he was that pathetic little boy with "delicate health," sipping tea in his bed. He was the jellyfish bowing and scraping and carrying out orders he despised—and telling himself all the time how decent and charitable and humane he was. He was the good father and the good husband and the good employer, who never went out in the rain without his umbrella, who never put up a fight about anything, who passed his life popping pills into his mouth and complaining about his stomach and trudging wearily toward the grave—

A terrible spasm went through him. It shook his whole body for a second or two. When it passed, he was breathing hard and gripping the railing, and his face was stinging with shame. No, I can't do it, he cried out to himself. I can't go back to what I was. Dear God, you can't let me do that— that would be the greatest horror of all.

And a moment later Aaron found himself doing something that he hadn't done in years. He prayed. Even in synagogue it had always made him uncomfortable when the silent prayer came around, but now he really prayed, with his whole heart and his whole mind. Dear God, he prayed, let me have hope. Let me believe that the new life You've given me isn't going to be thrown away before I've even had a chance to use it. Let me believe that a thousand lives, so close to their Promised Land, aren't going to be pulled back to destruction. If You're a just and merciful God, if You've created a world of light, not of darkness, then let me believe that You're listening to this prayer and that You'll save us in the end.

He went on for a while longer, staring into the mist and praying, though he no longer said any words to himself. And finally he spoke out loud, "I believe. Yes, I do."

His words went out into the mist. His voice sounded strange in his ears. Suddenly he felt terribly foolish. He looked around quickly and saw that nobody was near enough to have heard him. With a sigh he turned away from the railing. Time to get back to Sophie, he thought. She'll be worried about me.

THIRTEEN

ON Wednesday morning—at almost the same moment when First Officer Muller was telling Aaron Peyser that the *Franz Joseph* had been ordered back to Germany—the jangling of the telephone dredged Morrie up from his sleep. The sun hadn't risen yet in New York, and the bedroom was dark; Morrie had to fumble for the receiver.

Al's voice exploded in his ears, as sharp and businesslike as if he never made phone calls at any time except five o'clock in the morning. "Put your clothes on! Meet me in the lobby of the Plaza Hotel in one hour!"

"If this is some kind of joke—"

"It's the *Franz Joseph,* something's come up."

Morrie heard the receiver slamming down at the other end. He had wanted to ask Al sarcastically what the *Franz Joseph* had to do with AJDA, the board having turned its attention from European Jews to African Jews—and furthermore, it was none of *his* business, because he had washed his hands of AJDA. But maybe it was just as well he didn't get a chance to say any of these things. If something *had* come up . . .

Ruth was awake now, and she was able in spite of her drowsiness to struggle into a robe and make coffee for him while he dressed.

When he got to the Plaza, Al was already in the lobby, glaring at his watch. "So what kept you?" he said.

"What kept me? I'm five minutes early!"

Al just grunted, then took him by the arm and steered him toward the elevators. "He's waiting for us up in his room, and he can't give us more than half an hour on account of he has to be in Washington by eleven. That's the real reason why he's in America, some kind of confidential mission to the President. We're lucky he's sandwiching us in—"

"Who? Who're you talking about?"

But the elevator came now, and Al shushed him as they stepped into it.

A few minutes later they were standing in front of a door on the tenth floor. Al rang the bell, and the door was opened by a tall young man with a frosty face. "Please come in," he said. "Sir Douglas is expecting you."

The frosty-faced young man ushered them into the sitting room, then disappeared into the connecting bedroom. Sir Douglas Grainger was sitting at a room-service table with a pot of coffee before him and a slice of toast between his fingers. His gray business suit was neatly pressed, his white hair and military mustache were beautifully brushed; he looked distinguished, as he had never failed to look all through the conference in Paris.

"Good morning, so glad you could make it," he said. "Sit down, will you. Have a cup of coffee." He couldn't have been more polite, more affable—with that hard, slippery affability that had reminded Morrie back in Paris of a sheet of unbreakable glass; highly polished, perfectly transparent, absolutely impossible to penetrate.

"I asked you gentlemen to drop in," Sir Douglas said, "so that I might tell you what His Majesty's government have decided to do. The Prime Minister didn't make the final decision till late yesterday, as a matter of fact—just before I caught my plane—and I imagine the Hamburg Line won't be notified till late today. That is, early tomorrow, European time. But I wanted you gentlemen to hear about it as soon as possible, because I rather imagine there are arrangements you'll have to make, people to get in touch with—some of those other fellows who attended the conference and so forth." Sir Douglas took a bite of toast and washed it down with coffee, then went on in the same easy manner. "His Majesty's government have decided to take in a certain number of those people—from that ship, you know—to accept them for immigration into England. Not the whole lot, you understand, just a certain number."

Morrie admired the steadiness of Al's voice as he said, "How many?"

"I believe it's two hundred and some odd. The figure was worked out by Parsons and that crowd on the basis of last year's quota, Jewish population statistics, that sort of thing. Typical bureaucratic hair-splitting. I've got the exact figure somewhere, my secretary'll give it to you before you leave.

At any rate, you may take this as official—and I rather think, once the news gets about, you won't have too much trouble finding places for the rest of your people. It's my experience when England takes the lead, the smaller fry are fairly quick to follow." And he raised his cup again.

And this is it? thought Morrie. All these weeks of sweat and strain, headaches, disappointments, insults and cold shoulders, hoping, praying—and suddenly it all comes to a happy ending like *this,* between bites of toast and sips of coffee?

But Al was making a speech of thanks now, expressing his gratitude to His Majesty's government for its generosity and its humanity, and Morrie thought he'd better join in.

Sir Douglas made no response. He just went on eating his toast. Finally Al said, "I hope you don't mind if I ask you something. It's hard not to wonder—what made the Prime Minister decide to take this step, against Mr. Parsons' recommendation?"

Sir Douglas chewed thoughtfully for a moment. "I can't read the Prime Minister's mind, of course, but I rather think he preferred to listen to *me*."

"It was *your* suggestion that those people should be taken in?"

"Within limits, of course. Just enough to give a prodding to the other fellows." Calmly he went on with his breakfast.

"That was a wonderful thing for you to do," Al said.

"Wonderful?" Sir Douglas looked up at them slowly. "Let me be frank with you. I'm not one bit happy about this, and I doubt if I ever will be. I dislike Jews. Not individually, you understand—individually I've met some very fine ones—but as a group, as a class. They're aggressive, they're vulgar, they don't have the same standards and traditions as Englishmen. Give them half a chance and they'll push their way in anywhere and make room for all their friends and elbow everybody else out. And lately we've been giving them a good deal more than half a chance, haven't we? When I was a young man, there was no 'Jewish problem,' because Jews knew precisely where they belonged. There were places they could go and places they couldn't go, jobs they could have and jobs that were quite out of the question for them. Everybody understood, and nobody raised objections. There was a certain amount of injustice, I suppose—as there is in all human affairs—but on the whole it meant more happiness for all parties concerned, the Jews included. But nowadays—with this passion for 'equality,' with competitive examinations, with the universities opening up to anybody—the truth is that clever Jews are getting in everywhere. I don't like it, and I assure you it gives me no satisfaction to see several hundred more of them swarming into my country."

The words came as a shock to Morrie—all the more because of the calm, almost amiable tone in which they were spoken. Even Al was shocked, it seemed, and couldn't say anything for a second, and when he finally did, his voice wasn't nearly as steady as before. "If you feel that way—why did you help the people on that ship?"

"Why?" Sir Douglas put down his coffee cup and drew himself up slightly. For the first time his face wasn't quite so composed; there was a glow of feeling in his eyes. "The Nazis are beasts. That's all you can say about them, you know. I've seen reports on what's happening in Germany today. I don't much like Jews, but my God— Those beasts can't be appeased any longer, you understand. Somebody has to stand up to them. Some standard of decency has to be maintained."

With this outburst he seemed to have drained himself. The feeling faded from his eyes, and his voice became calm again. "It's a thoroughly impractical point of view, of course. The war will come—sooner than most of us think—and it's going to be a rather unpleasant world afterward. Whoever wins, the beasts will be in the saddle. Everything that has value to a man like me will pass away. With a bit of luck I'll pass away, too—" He was silent for a moment. Then he went on. "In the meantime, though, one can't turn into a beast oneself—can one?"

He gazed at them imperturbably for a while. Then he lowered his head and picked up his toast again. "You'll excuse me now. I'm not making much headway with this breakfast."

*　　*　　*

Morrie went back to the AJDA office with Al, and Dan and Bernie Kramer and several others joined them there shortly. There was a lot of phoning to do. For the next few hours they were all very busy.

All the time, in one part of his mind Morrie was trying to make sense out of what had happened this morning. When he finally thought he had, he felt a strong impulse to come right out and say it to Al and Dan. But then something told him that he shouldn't be hasty; first he'd better find a sounding board for his ideas. There was only one sounding board in his life. He called home and asked Ruth if she'd have lunch with him.

Over a stale chicken sandwich in the cafeteria around the corner from his office he told her about this morning. Her face lighted up. She leaned forward and kissed him. Then she frowned a little. "But you've won, you've been vindicated—why are you looking as if you've lost your best friend?"

"Because I've been asking myself over and over if there's any meaning to this whole damned thing, and I don't much like the answer I've come up with."

"Which is?"

"Decent acts are done by individuals—for completely individual reasons. Not out of any abstract philosophy, not because of some superior political theory, not because of some moral system, not because they belong to a certain type or class or nationality or party or religion—but just because they're individuals, they're alone, they've got this messy, irrational, unpredictable feeling that they ought to behave decently."

"What you're saying is that human nature is corrupted by institutions? We used to believe that in college—"

"No, you don't understand what I'm saying. Of course decency doesn't come from institutions or organizations, or from governments or movements. But it doesn't come from human nature, either. How could it, since human nature *created* those institutions? What I'm saying is it's no use counting on 'people' to be decent. People are just like organizations—shapeless lumps that stand in the way, that keep anything good from happening. They're stupid, selfish, cruel, indifferent, frightened, ignorant—also anti-Semitic—everything that's rotten."

"But people are behaving decently right now. The passengers on the *Franz Joseph* are going to be all right."

"Thanks to one man—one stubborn narrow-minded old man who's riddled with all the prejudices of his class, but who somehow won't quite stay in the pigeonhole. If it wasn't for him, all the governments on earth and all the people in them would've been perfectly happy to see every man, woman, and child on the *Franz Joseph* disappear from sight.

That's my whole point, don't you see? There's nothing 'normal' about decency. It's an accident, a fluke. It pops up out of nowhere. It can't be created, encouraged, or explained." He hesitated, then he brought out the part that was bound to upset her. "Anyway, that's why I'm going to quit my job."

He could see the astonishment in her eyes. "Leave AJDA! But—I don't see *why*—"

"What could be more absurd than giving your time and energy to an organization for the promulgation of decency? AJDA has ideals—principles—that is, it assumes that this is a benign world which is capable of improvement. What use could I be to AJDA when I don't accept that assumption any more?"

She was shaking her head, looking troubled. "It just isn't like you to talk this way. How can you say that decency is nothing but an accident? *You're* decent. Look at the way you've acted ever since you found out about that ship, the way you've been working and fighting, and you wouldn't give up or get discouraged—I don't think that's so accidental or undependable. *I* depend on it—because I know that's the way you are."

For a moment he couldn't look at her. He remembered the feeling of relief that had come to him last night—when he thought that Aaron Peyser and his problems were finally off his back.

"Nobody knows the way he is," Morrie said. "Nobody knows what he might do or think."

He made himself look up at her again. And then he saw that there were tears in her eyes. "Darling—look—you don't have to cry. I'll get another job."

"I don't *want* you to get another job. I want you to keep *this* job. And I know everything you say is logical—and I know I can't think of a single sensible argument—"

So before lunch was over he agreed to give the matter a little more thought. He wouldn't hand in any resignations or take any irrevocable actions for a while. He would wait until the *Franz Joseph* business was settled. And then if he still felt this way—

*   *   *

By the middle of the afternoon six European countries, along with England, had agreed among them to take in all thousand people from the *Franz Joseph*. France would take the largest number, nearly three hundred; she had no intention of being outdone by her ally across the Channel. Sweden would take the smallest number, fifty-five—her trade with Germany had brought in no small portion of her national income last year. The other countries—Holland, Belgium, Denmark, and Norway—would take at least a hundred passengers each.

Some of these countries specified that certain kinds of people, with certain backgrounds and training, must make up a certain percentage of their quota. Other countries were less particular. Holland laid down no specifications at all, except that one of the names on its quota must be Emil Karlweis. And so, through the late afternoon, Dan and Al and Morrie set to work on the complicated task of dividing the passengers into seven groups and drawing up the final lists.

Meanwhile, the Hamburg Line and the German consulate had to be notified. And after this was done, there was an hour of dreadful suspense—would Hitler insist that the ship sail back to Germany anyway? But the word finally came, through the local manager of the Hamburg Line, that the authorities in Berlin were willing to comply. Their intention from the start had been to get rid of those Jews. If other nations wished to take on this burden, that was *their* concern.

The next step was for AJDA to get in touch with Jewish relief organizations in the seven countries where the *Franz Joseph* would be discharging passengers. These people had to be provided for until they could stand on their own feet. But to give them a place to sleep, the bare necessities of life, would be extremely expensive, and so extra financial help had to come from America. Dan retired into his office to spend an evening talking on the phone to members of the board of trustees and other AJDA supporters.

Back in the office after a quick dinner, Al made a call to London and talked for a long time to Abraham Weinstein. It was decided between them that AJDA would set up a temporary headquarters in London, from which information about the passengers could be coordinated and distributed to the proper agencies throughout Europe. Somebody from the New York office ought to be sent over to take charge of this operation.

Al hung up the phone and turned to Morrie. "I'm going

to be busy as hell the next few weeks. Besides, I'm getting sick of airplanes. Suppose you go to London."

After a moment Morrie said, "Aaron Peyser is going to England, isn't he?"

"I'll check the lists," Al said. "Yes—that's right—he and his whole family."

"It'll be interesting to meet him," Morrie said.

Darkness came, but the AJDA staff didn't go home. Lights were switched on, and for many more hours the office bustled with as much activity as if it were the middle of the day. There were a thousand details to take care of, but the main issue really seemed to be settled. Morrie had to be sure of this—he had to be sure that nothing could go wrong—before he did what he had been itching to do all day.

He went to his office and wrote out the radiogram to be sent to Aaron Peyser aboard the *Franz Joseph:*

"HAPPY TO INFORM YOU ARRANGEMENTS MADE FOR DIS-EMBARKATION OF ALL PASSENGERS, ENGLAND, FRANCE, HOLLAND, BELGIUM, DENMARK, NORWAY, SWEDEN OFFER REFUGE. GERMAN GOVERNMENT RAISES NO OBSTACLES. DETAILS OF PROCEDURE, ASSIGNMENT OF NAMES TO EACH QUOTA LIST, ETC. FOLLOW SHORTLY. DON'T WORRY. YOUR ORDEAL IS OVER."

Morrie hesitated, aware of the one big question this message was bound to raise, the big omission staring out from between the lines.

The United States hadn't offered to take in any of the passengers. With all the developments today, the eagerness of one nation after another to jump on the humanitarian band-wagon, not the smallest impression had been made on the Immigration Bureau. Dan called Washington hourly, Congressman Lascoff ran from office to office. Senator Friedkin flew down by a privately hired plane to talk to everyone he used to know, Willie Levy was on the phone to the President —but until late in the afternoon not a single word could be squeezed out of anyone. The United States government was being as silent and inscrutable behind its heavy official doors as any Greek god, enshrined in his temple while the suppli-ants prayed to him outside.

At last one small chink of light filtered through the im-penetrable darkness. A messenger boy appeared in Congressman Lascoff's office with an envelope neatly stamped "From the Desk of Harrison Bliss." Inside, on a sheet of memo paper, was one typewritten sentence: "This department, having formed its earlier opinion in consideration of the national welfare and security, sees no reason in good conscience to modify that opinion now." Beneath this sentence, in a neat, tiny handwriting, were the initials H. B.

And Morrie, when Al told him about this message, had got the point. The key to it was that little phrase "in good conscience." We're all idealists here in America, he thought. The ones who run the country and the ones who knock it, the ones who salute the flag on the Fourth of July and the ones who jeer at them for their naïve patriotism—we're all idealists together. That means we can't perform any act or make any decision out of motives that aren't true and pure and righteous. We can never reverse a decision, we can never regret an action—because that would be admitting that we're capable of error, that we're no better than ordinary human beings after all. In the name of idealism, Morrie thought, there's no saying what crimes we might commit.

But he couldn't explain any of that to Aaron Peyser in this radiogram. He was ashamed. The big question would just have to remain unanswered.

He did add one more line to the message: "GOD WILLING WE'LL SEE EACH OTHER SOON."

At that moment, nearly midnight in New York, it was nearly six o'clock in the morning aboard the *Franz Joseph*. Aaron Peyser was standing at the railing of the main deck, looking out into the mist and praying.

FOURTEEN

ON Thursday morning before breakfast Bender's steward told him the news about the Einhorn boy. Bender knew that everyone in the dining room would be talking about it. He could guess what their feelings would be—the hushed voices, the stunned looks. He was in no mood for other people's despair. So he decided to have no breakfast, and he went up on deck.

He stood on the stern and looked out at the ocean. It was sunnier than usual today. Shafts of light skimmed across the surface of the water like strange unearthly fish. He wished Julia were standing here next to him. The way he felt this morning, a few words from her would help. But Julia and he didn't talk together any more except for the polite remarks they had to make in public.

He returned to the foyer and headed for the stairs. Solitude was doing him no good. If he was going to wallow in gloom, he might as well wash it down with black coffee.

At the top of the stairs he saw Aaron Peyser coming down from the sun deck. A piece of yellow paper was in his hand, and an odd look was on his face. "Carl," he said, as if he wasn't quite sure who Bender was, "you have to read this—"

Bender took the piece of yellow paper from him. He saw that it was a radiogram. He read it. Then he read it again.

Curious, he thought. Very curious. This doesn't make me feel the least bit excited or ecstatic. Not even relieved. My pulse is steady, my heartbeat is no stronger than usual. I don't seem to be feeling anything at all.

"I'm going down to tell my wife," Aaron said. "My family —anybody else I can find along the way. I'll have the purser announce this over the public address system—"

Aaron moved on into the lounge with that same odd stunned look on his face.

Bender didn't continue to the dining room. His appetite

was gone. He felt that he had to find Julia. When he told her this news— But he stopped short before entering the lounge. Julia was no longer somebody he could tell things to. What happened to him no longer happened to her.

He went through the glass doors into the lounge—and the first person he saw was Julia herself. She saw him at the same moment—a kind of light came to her face. She started across to him, talking even before she was close to him. "I've been looking for you—I wanted to talk to you first thing this morning, but you weren't in the dining room at breakfast—"

She put her hand on his arm. He felt himself trembling a little. It seemed like ages since the last time she had touched him. "Can't we talk somewhere in private?" she said.

She was moving him toward the doors, just as she used to do when she wanted him to take a stroll on deck with her. Commandeering him— But he stopped, he wouldn't go any further. "We can talk right here. There's nobody near us."

"All right—whatever you say—let's sit down, at least."

She led him to the nearest sofa and made him sit close to her, close enough so that she could grip his arms and look into his face. She was agitated—more agitated than he had ever seen her. "Carl," she said. "Carl, darling—" Her mouth began to quiver, and then suddenly she burst into tears, started sobbing into his chest. "I've been such a *horror!*" Even between gulps and sobs her words managed to come out quite clearly. "Such an absolute horror—such an absolute *fool!* I've got no right to expect you to forgive me—except of course that I *do,* in fact I'm counting on it—which shows you what an incurably spoiled, egotistical bitch I am!"

Gently he lifted her head and looked into her face. "If you took a few seconds to get hold of yourself, you might give me some sketchy notion of what you're talking about."

"I'm talking about *us,* what else could I be talking about? What else have I been up since before the crack of dawn *thinking* about? Trudging up and down these dreary decks, in this foul foggy weather—I'm sure I'll end up with laryngitis for a week. Do they give you throat lozenges in prison, I wonder?"

"Prison?"

"Oh yes, that isn't what they call it nowadays. Concentration camp—that's the right name, isn't it? Quite hopeless in my case, I'm afraid. I could never concentrate on anything for more than five minutes in my life. But I suppose that's where we'll end up sooner or later. I hope it isn't too much sooner. They'll give us a *little* time together, won't they?"

"Julia, am I to understand—you've changed your mind—"

She smiled into his face, so softly, with such tenderness, and she slowly nodded her head. It was his daydream coming true. The temptation was overwhelming. How easy it would be to let the floodgates burst within him, to let himself be swept away. How easy it would be to pretend that he was an innocent schoolboy again without a brain in his head.

Unfortunately, however, his school days were long behind him. He was innocent about very few things anymore, and especially not about this woman with whom he had lived for nearly eight years. An idea had come into his head while she was speaking, an idea that he couldn't drive away simply by wishing it away.

He smiled at her, knowing that it was one of his soft, ironic smiles. "Julia," he said, "did you happen to run into Aaron Peyser in the last ten minutes or so?"

"Why, no. I don't really see—"

"I was just wondering, that's all. He must have passed through here not long ago. He's been talking to people, telling them a certain piece of news. It occurred to me that he might have told it to you."

"I haven't seen him at all. I haven't heard any news."

He gazed at her a while. Then he found that he was chuckling very softly.

"Carl—please—didn't you understand what I just told you? I want to be with you. No matter what happens. Please, won't you take me back?"

He went on chuckling. Bravo, bravo, he thought. He was on the verge of congratulating her on her beautiful performance, of telling her what a lovely, accomplished, thoroughly entertaining hypocrite she was. One had to admire her boldness, her imagination, the indomitable spirit which could devise, on the spur of the moment, such a daring plan to convert disaster into victory.

Yes, he really thought he was going to say all that, and then somehow he knew that he wasn't. Suddenly he felt tired, quite beaten and battered by fatigue, and the soft chuckle died away in his throat. He got to his feet, still keeping hold of her hand. "Will you wait for me here?" he said. "I want to walk on deck a little. I want to do some thinking."

400

He saw the flash of fear in her eyes. Because she knew that he suspected the truth? Or because she loved him and was afraid to lose him?

"You won't be too long?" she said.

"I won't be long at all."

He went out on deck. He began to walk. With his head bent and his hands clasped behind his back—the classic posture of that most ancient of all butts, the absent-minded professor. He needed this breathing space, these few minutes to himself—but not to make up his mind what to do. He had made up his mind already, before he got up from the sofa. What was the truth about her? Had she really decided of her own accord to return to him—or had she heard the good news from Aaron and decided that the wreck could be salvaged? He had no idea. He knew that he would never know. For the rest of his life this doubt would be in him—it would gnaw at him every time he looked at her. Even so, he was going to take her back. What else could he do? He loved her.

And so they would fall into each other's arms and live happily ever after. Well, anyway, they would live. He would do his best to keep her from guessing what he suspected. Unless, of course, she had guessed it already, in which case *she* would do her best to keep *him* from guessing— And this tricky little game of blindman's buff would keep them interested and amused to a ripe old age. So much for a rational universe.

Yes, he had already made up his mind—but he needed this walk on deck to assume the proper expression with which to reappear before her. Soon it was assumed, and he started back to the lounge. And as he went through the glass doors and saw her sitting on the sofa—and felt the pain and the joy rising up in him—the odd thought came to him that now, for the first time in his life, he was alive.

*   *   *

On Thursday night just before dinner Kurt Halevy went to Peter's funeral. The service, in the main lounge, lasted only ten minutes. Mr. Peyser, David's father, read from the prayer book. The rabbi sat next to Peter's sister; their faces were as white as the prayer shawl around his shoulders. David was there, and so were Altdorf and Schlossberg, but not many other people. Kurt supposed that everybody was sorry about Peter—he had heard people talking about "the terrible irony of it—if only those boys had waited one day more!"— but right now nobody felt much like funerals. When you know you're going to be alive, Kurt thought, it's amazing how easily you can reconcile yourself to somebody else being dead.

When the service ended, they all went up on deck. This was the bad part—sailors lifting the wooden plank to the railing, that long shape under the sheet, then suddenly the sheet going limp. Mr. Peyser read some Hebrew words, and Kurt said, "Good-bye, Peter," under his breath.

He stayed on deck after everybody else had left. He remembered all the times he had argued with Peter, said sarcastic things to him. But he had always known, hadn't he, that Peter was worth a hundred of him? I'm the one who should have gone into that room, Kurt thought. I should have demanded to go. I should have forced Peter to let me go. But I didn't say a word. I kept my mouth shut. For the second time, for the second time . . .

At dinner, Kurt noticed, there seemed to be two kinds of people—those who shoveled in the food and swilled down the wine until they were gasping for breath, and those who could hardly bring themselves to eat a thing. The first group were loud and boisterous, talked steadily, laughed heartily even when nobody had said anything funny; the second group said very little, had glazed looks in their eyes, seemed to be half asleep. It would make a great picture, Kurt thought. An elaborate, detailed, totally disgusting and malevolent caricature in the George Grosz manner.

There was bingo in the main lounge that night. Kurt sat through it just to watch the people. The lounge was packed; every available seat was taken, and some were sitting on the floor and squeezed against the walls. With every number that the chief steward called out, shouts of triumph or groans of disappointment rose from the crowd. When the climactic moment came—when the cry of "Bingo!" finally resounded through the air like a trumpet call—the crowd exploded with hysterical laughter, uncontrollable tears, whistles, catcalls, shrieks. People threw their arms around their relations, their friends, around total strangers; there *were* no total strangers. Somebody flung his bingo card up at the ceiling and all his

402

little counters after it, and in an instant a dozen other people were doing the same thing; geysers of bingo cards erupted all over the room. By ten o'clock, with bingo playing still going strong, the lounge looked as if it had been through an orgy.

The next morning lists were posted, assigning each passenger to his port of disembarkation. For an hour Kurt watched the crowd gathering around these lists, chattering excitedly—"I've got Belgium! What have you got?" Believe it or not, some people muttered complaints about their assignments. Mother and he had been assigned to Holland. It was as good as anyplace else.

After dinner that night a sudden roaring, clattering noise broke into whatever everybody was doing. Kurt recognized it as the sound they had all been waiting for—the anchor was being pulled up. Everybody rushed out on deck and lined the railings. Kurt went with them, though he couldn't imagine what they expected to see. There was no port, no lighthouse, no landmark of any kind to watch slipping away into the distance. Nevertheless, when the throbbing of the engines was heard, people cheered.

At five o'clock the following afternoon the ship sailed into the port of Rotterdam. A little later the public address system announced that customs officials and immigration officers had come aboard and that all those scheduled for disembarkation should report to the main lounge. Kurt was on deck with Mother when this announcement was made, and Mother's friend Mrs. Bender was with them.

"I'm really lucky," Mother said, "settling in a country where so many people speak German. I was rather worried about the United States. I studied English at school for three years, and I can't remember a word of it."

"You'll pick up Dutch in no time at all," Mrs. Bender said. "You've got some brains in your head, that's always a big help. As for me—well, Carl and I are going to Belgium. I gather the university at Ghent wants him to give some lectures, but frankly, I'm positive I'll never learn French if I struggle with it for the rest of my life. It *is* French that the Belgians speak, isn't it? Or is it still that funny old language that nobody else can understand?"

Mrs. Bender seemed to run out of words, and she and Mother looked at each other a moment longer. "Holland isn't so far away from Belgium, you know," Mother said.

"Next-door neighbors really. I'm sure we'll be meeting again very soon."

And then for some reason Mother and Mrs. Bender both laughed.

Mother followed Kurt into the main lounge. Tables had been set up at one end, and several official-looking men were sitting at them. People filed past them, holding out papers and opening little suitcases. It was a very long line; it circled the whole room. Included in this group, Kurt knew, were not only those who would stay in Holland but those who would be taken straight to the airport from the ship, kept overnight in dormitories, and flown to the Scandinavian countries in the morning.

In front of Mother on the line was the conductor Karlweis, his coat thrown over him like a cape. A scowl was on his face, the kind of nasty scowl which had kept people at arm's length from him throughout the voyage. In front of Karlweis was Professor Weissbrod, smiling and chattering away to the people around him. "Denmark is devoted to learning," he was saying. "More universities per capita than any other country in Europe. And many of the lectures, I'm told, are conducted in German. So I'm sure I'll have no trouble finding a position."

Kurt saw Altdorf and Schlossberg coming up to him. He ignored the sudden tightness inside of him. He put on an offhand look.

"You weren't going to leave without saying good-bye?" Altdorf said.

"I didn't know where to find you," Kurt said.

"We're going to Paris—Franz and me," Schlossberg said. "My mother has some family there, and so does Franz's father. It looks as if we'll be living only a few blocks away from each other. That's great luck, isn't it?"

"Yes, that's great luck."

"You'll come to Paris to visit us," Altdorf said. "We'll have fine times together. Maybe David can come over from England, too."

"The French girls are supposed to be beautiful," Schlossberg said.

"Yes, we'll have a grand reunion," Kurt said. "The Four Musketeers. We'll drink a toast to D'Artagnan."

That shut them up pretty well. The line moved forward, so Kurt was able to shake their hands and say good-bye.

Half an hour later the Dutch immigration officer gave Mother and him their passports, and they followed the crowd out to the deck. Here they took their places in the line that was moving slowly toward the gangway.

"Well, it's over," Mother said. "We're alive."

She looked into Kurt's face. She was smiling, and her eyes were wet. He saw her lift her hand and reach out toward his cheek. What was she going to do? Did she actually intend to touch him?

But she caught herself in time, of course. She lowered her hand. He had known that she couldn't bring herself to touch him.

He didn't blame her. She was right to shudder away from him. Everybody shuddered away from him instinctively, even people who didn't know the truth about him. He shuddered away from himself, too. He had committed the most horrible of all crimes. He was the son who had killed his father.

Oh yes, his father had committed suicide. What did that mean? His father had done it to save *him*. He remembered that last night so clearly—lying awake in his bed listening to his father and mother in the next room. They talked in low voices, for hours—occasionally their voices would get louder. He couldn't hear most of the words, but he had known what they were talking about. Which one of them should be sacrificed for *him*. And all the time the real answer was so obvious. Mother and Father ought to leave Germany together. All their lives they had been together—they ought to be allowed to grow old together. *He* was the one who ought to stay behind. But his fear had been so awful. . . . He had gone on lying in bed, cowering between the sheets. He had covered his ears so that he wouldn't hear their voices. . . .

He was a murderer. He knew it, and Mother knew it, too. She never said anything to him about it, but he could see the accusation in her eyes.

He wanted to tell her how sorry he was. He wanted to throw his arms around her and beg her to forgive him—and she would stroke his cheek and say comforting words to him, as she used to do when he was a little boy. But he would never do that, of course. Things would have to go on the way they were going. Until he found the courage—

Mother was starting down the gangway now, and he was by her side. They were heading toward the great black hole

405

of the dock shed. She stumbled slightly, then recovered herself. He was careful not to take her arm.

*　　*　　*

The *Franz Joseph* traveled at top speed all night. Early in the morning, when Naomi woke up and looked out the porthole, she saw houses and trees, cows and people, so close that she had the feeling she could have reached out and touched them. This must be the estuary leading to the port of Antwerp.

A little before ten o'clock the ship put into dock. Then the public address system announced that the customs and immigration officials were coming aboard and would see passengers in the main lounge in fifteen minutes. Naomi heard this announcement in her father's cabin while she was helping with the packing. There wasn't all that much to pack, really, but it seemed important to her that Father shouldn't have to worry about Peter's things. Peter was gone now, but that didn't mean that his possessions could be allowed to disappear. They didn't amount to much—a few pieces of clothing, a razor, a toothbrush—but Father and she were in no position to throw anything away. In Belgium they would need everything they could get, including an extra toothbrush.

One of Peter's possessions was the only book he had brought aboard with him. It wasn't political or Zionist or anything like that. It was his small leather-bound copy of Schiller's *William Tell*. Naomi could hardly bear to look at it. She remembered how Peter used to love to spout speeches from it, waving his arms dramatically, partly in earnest but partly making fun of himself, too.

She closed the suitcase. Then she asked Father again if he wanted her to hold the passports, visas, immigration forms, and other papers they would be needing. He shook his head. It was funny how firm he was being about these forms. He had spoken very few words in these last few days, but he had quietly made it clear that he intended to do this job himself. She was sorry about this. She wanted to help him as much as she could.

She went to the bathroom to check his medicine cabinet again, and while she was there she heard a knock on the cabin door. She hurried out so that Father wouldn't have to get up from the bed where he was lying.

David was standing in the doorway. She had hardly spoken to him in the last few days.

"Naomi—could I talk to you for a minute?"

"We're terribly busy. We have to be in the lounge in fifteen minutes."

"Please—"

The tone of his voice stung her. Hadn't she treated him badly enough already? "Well, just for a minute," she said. She turned to Father. "I'll be right outside in the passageway."

Father looked up at her and squeezed her hand but said nothing.

She followed David out of the cabin. Doors were open all along the passageway, and people could be seen carrying suitcases, putting on coats.

"I just wanted to tell you"—he spoke quickly, in a low voice—"how awful I feel—about Peter."

"You told me that at the funeral."

"That was with a lot of people around. I wanted to tell you—just the two of us—how much Peter meant to me. He was the best friend I ever had."

"You meant a lot to him, too."

He shifted from one foot to another. She wanted to end this, to get back to Father. She wondered how she could do it without hurting David.

"Naomi—there's something else."

She waited.

"I wanted to ask you—if I write to you from England, will you answer my letter?"

For a moment she was almost angry at him. Didn't he understand that he was the one person in the whole world she could never have anything to do with again? After what she had done to him . . .

"I'll write to you if I can," she said. "I don't know what our address will be, though."

"That's all right," he said. "My father will find out. That American organization will know."

He was smiling now. She had made him happy—that small-boy happiness was on his face.

"Well, good-bye," he said. "And good luck—" He hesitated. Then he kissed her quickly on the cheek and hurried away.

She wondered if she had been right to lie to him. The truth would have hurt him, but maybe she should have told it to him, anyway. No, I won't answer your letters, David. I'm finished with romantic dreams now. They turned me into a monster. They made me do things to you— God punished me for it. He killed Peter, that was His way of punishing me.

The loudspeaker voice was announcing that the line was ready to form in the lounge. She went back to Father.

A little later she was up in the lounge with him. They stood in line, and in front of them were Dr. Bender and his wife and their little girl, and Mr. and Mrs. Gottlieb, and Mr. Stieffel with his white hair and mustache. They were all going to Belgium, too.

She remembered saying to Peter once, "Mr. Stieffel is the handsomest man on this ship. Next to Emil Karlweis, of course—" That was at the beginning of this voyage. She had been a child then.

"There's no hardware store waiting for me, of course," Mr. Gottlieb said. "That's a blow—I was beginning to develop quite an interest in the hardware business. But I'll find something else to do. A man with legal training can always talk his way into *something.*"

"At least it's a nice quiet country," Mrs. Gottlieb said. "A nice peace-loving country that nobody wants to hurt."

"It's twenty-five years since I was in Belgium last," Mr. Stieffel said. "That was August, 1914. The country wasn't so quiet then. What we did to those peace-loving people—and now I'm to live in happiness and freedom among my forgiving victims? It's very strange, you know."

"Doesn't it say in the Bible," Mr. Gottlieb said, "that we should forgive our enemies? Or is that in *their* half of the Bible?"

"A noble sentiment," Mr. Stieffel said. "Just the same, one feels that there ought to be some punishment."

The line began to move. Soon Naomi found that Father and she had reached the front of it. Father took out their papers and answered everybody's questions about them. This was more talking than he had done for a long time. He sounded quite calm, quite steady. Nobody besides her, she felt sure, could hear the slight quaver in his voice. And as soon as the officials handed him back his papers and told him to move along, he sank gently into his silence again.

He isn't better yet, Naomi thought. Inside he's still badly

bruised. Maybe he can never be completely all right again. Maybe I'll have to take care of him for the rest of his life.

She was prepared for that. If that turned out to be her duty, she wouldn't turn away from it. She would keep house for him. She would join him in his prayers, though she knew now that she couldn't believe in God. To him she would give all the kindness and pity and love that she had been too blind and selfish to give to anybody before.

And this would keep her busy. She would have no time for daydreams from now on. Whatever else it became, her life would be real. . . .

How troubled she looks, the rabbi thought, watching his daughter intently as they moved closer to the gangway. Something is troubling her, something terrible. It's more than her grief and her shock. And whatever it is, she wants to hide from it. She wants to hide from it in me. She wants to bury her life by devoting herself to mine.

And how pleasant, how sweet it would be to accept the sacrifice from her—

But he couldn't do that. Miriam wouldn't approve. Let the girl have her life, Max—that's what Miriam would say. And Peter would look at him in his sardonic, reproachful way. And even more, it would be an offense against God.

God? He was surprised at himself. For days now he hadn't let himself think about God. Not since that last faint breath had come sighing out of his poor boy's body. Just when I was finally coming back to You, realizing all over again that You exist and that I love You—and how did You show me Your hand? By plunging me into the abyss.

But now he said God's name to himself. Hear O Israel, the Lord our God, the Lord is One. Without anger, without bitterness. If a man believes, he doesn't bargain with his belief. God made life, God has the right to take it away. God made me a man and Jew, and that was good—be thankful for the blessings He gives for as long as He chooses to give them.

Miriam had understood that. "Don't be sad," she had said to him. "You've got your life ahead of you." When did she say that? Yes—in the hospital—almost the last words she ever spoke to him. You've got your life ahead of you.

Peter would understand that, too. Peter believed— He believed what I believe, the rabbi thought. In some way, somehow, we were the same. The homeland he was always dreaming of—that was his way of reaching out to God, to *my* God. How sad that neither of us realized that long ago. How much pain we could have spared each other.

But Peter found it out at the end, the rabbi told himself. He found out the truth, just as I have now, though he never had the chance to tell me so. But I know it just the same. I know I was with him at the end.

And now— The rabbi felt that Peter was closer to him than ever. His son was in him and in the fresh clean air around him—it even *smelled* better, this air of freedom—and in the pressure of Naomi's hand on his arm. His son and his wife—his dead—were still alive. It was time for him to come to life again, too.

"They live in us, you know," he said suddenly, smiling at his daughter, and they moved down the gangway together.

* * *

At midday the *Franz Joseph* reached open sea again and started down the French coast on its overnight trip to Le Havre.

Half the passengers were gone now. The emptiness of the dining room made David feel peculiarly uneasy. His own table remained intact, but all around him were large gaps that somehow filled him with dread. Even though the dining steward had taken people from badly decimated tables and reassigned them to those with only a few empty places, this didn't help to dispel the air of desolation.

David's eyes kept turning to one table in particular. Of the original group there, nobody was left except Mr. Monsky and Mrs. Tannenbaum. Four people he didn't know sat there now, and in the places where Naomi and Peter used to sit were Mrs. Fischel and Mrs. Moritz.

Mrs. Fischel's voice was so loud that David could hear everything she was saying. "So what I said to him was, 'Who on earth made up these lists, a Mongolian idiot? You send someone like poor Rosa Moritz to France when she doesn't speak one word of French—but she *does* speak English, because she worked as a governess for an English family before her marriage, so naturally it would never *occur* to you to send her to England!' Well, he had the nerve to tell me that there wasn't anything he could do. England was willing to take in

410

just so many people, and he couldn't add a single extra one. So I said to him, 'What if someone on the English list agreed to take Rosa's place on the French list?' Well, the bureaucratic mind always has trouble adjusting to a new idea, of course—"

She was talking about Papa, David realized. Papa could hear every word and had to pretend that he couldn't by ducking his head and being very busy with his soup.

". . . so finally he said to me, 'Where will you find someone to make this exchange?' And I said to him, 'Me, of course. I've got plenty of good friends in both countries, since my late husband did business on an international scale. England or France, what's the difference? We'll all be in America a year from now, anyway. So he hemmed and hawed and said that he couldn't make the decision himself because the lists had been drawn up in New York. So I told him to get in *touch* with New York, what did he think this ship had a radio for? And the upshot was—well, I'll give you one guess who's going to France and who's going to England!"

"It was so nice of you, Gertrude," said Mrs. Moritz. "I don't know how I'll ever be able to— I suppose I *could* have managed in France—"

"You were miserable about it," Mrs. Fischel said. "Why be miserable when all you have to do is speak up and demand your rights?"

The meal ended. David wanted to be alone, to get rid of this uneasy feeling. He left the dining room ahead of his family and went out on deck. The twilight was casting a soft haze over everything. Contentment was in the air—and soon it was inside him again. It's all over now, he told himself. She's gone—a hundred miles away by this time. Nobody left to remind him . . .

He had told her he wanted to write to her. He had no intention of doing it, of course. That was just an excuse so that he could see her one last time, take one last look at her red eyes, her face drained of color. She was suffering, that was easy to see. She knew what it was like now.

Papa was on deck, coming up to him. He turned to face Papa, putting on his most serious, respectful look.

"Your mother asked me to find you. She's going to the film with Joshua, she wants to know if you're coming along."

"I don't think so, Papa."

"What are you going to do tonight?"

"I don't know. Read a little. Walk on deck. Maybe listen to some music."

He lowered his eyes. A moment later he felt Papa's hand on his arm. "You miss them, don't you? Both of them."

Papa's voice was so soft and concerned. What a shame it would have been to disappoint him. David nodded his head quickly.

"You'll see her again someday," Papa said. "The world can't go mad forever. It has to turn right side up eventually. For your generation, anyway. With your ideals and principles."

Papa's words annoyed David. What was so wrong with the world? He liked the world the way it was. The trick was to know how to get along in it.

Papa smiled and let go of David's arm. "I'll see you later, son. Good night."

Papa moved away slowly. David had no trouble keeping himself from laughing out loud. Sometimes it was better laughing silently, inside yourself. Poor foolish Papa. As long as David could remember, Papa had been talking, in that earnest tone of voice, about ideals and principles, kindness, decency, justice, that sort of thing. "Help those less fortunate than you—that's the most important part of being a Jew."

That isn't what's important to *me*, David thought. It's power that counts in this world. The power to live life your own way, to do what you want, to sweep away anything that interferes.

It was very late before David got tired of his own thoughts. Then he left the deck and went down to his cabin. Joshua was asleep already in the upper bunk. As he got ready for bed David made no special effort to keep the noise down. Nothing could wake Joshua up, he knew.

Finally David stretched out on the lower bunk and switched off the light over his pillow. The darkness flooded in on him, and suddenly that feeling of uneasiness, of dread, rose up in him again. It was worse than it had been during dinner, a hundred times worse. He began to sweat. It wasn't very warm in the cabin, but his face and neck were wringing wet. And a question was pounding through his head—a fearful question. Had he done enough? Had he proven to their satisfaction that he wasn't contaminated, that he truly belonged among them? Were they ready now to take him back?

It came to him, with a thrill of horror, that they weren't.

More was required of him, even more than he had done already. The Führer wanted more than boldness from his servants. He wanted constancy, too. He wanted to know that he could depend on them not just once but over and over again.

But what did the Führer expect of him next? What could he do—not immediately, maybe, but later, in the near future —to make the Führer sure of him?

A noise broke into his thoughts. It was coming from above his head. Joshua was mumbling in his sleep.

*　*　*

Under a soft gray drizzle the *Franz Joseph* slid into its berth in Le Havre. Eight o'clock in the morning. The loudspeaker announced that disembarkation wouldn't begin till nine thirty.

Monsky ordered every course on the breakfast menu. He had fruit juice and berries, cereal and eggs, toast and sweet rolls, sausage and ham. This could be his last big meal for a long time, so he was going to make the most of it. He washed down the food with plenty of coffee.

While he ate, he talked fast and loud. That was the only way to get a word in edgewise with Gertrude Fischel. He had a lot of stories, a lot of personal reminiscences, which he hadn't told to Betsy yet, and since she wouldn't be getting off the ship with him but was going on to England, he had to squeeze them all in during this breakfast. Some of them he had invented only last night, and they were among his best.

After breakfast he escorted Betsy out of the dining room. On the way they passed Aaron Peyser's table, and Monsky stopped to say a word to those Buberman kids, the newlyweds. They were leaving the ship this morning, too, and this gave Monsky the opportunity to make a friendly little joke about their good luck at landing in France, the center of the world for young lovers. "Do you realize," he said, "that rich people pay a fortune so they can go to Paris for their honeymoon?" Then he caught up with Betsy, and they went out on deck together.

The thin drizzle had stopped and the mist was beginning to lift. The deck was full of people staring at a group of stevedores on the shore who were loading crates into a truck.

From the intense way that everybody watched this you'd think it was one of the famous tourist attractions of France.

"I've still got a little packing to do," Monsky said. "And it's going to be a madhouse around here once we start leaving the ship. So I'm wondering, maybe we should say good-bye right now."

She looked up at him with that smile of hers. A hundred times during this trip he had told himself that there was absolutely nothing special about this smile, about her face. All right, it was a pretty face, but no prettier than a million other plump, blond German faces—and on it you could already read the future, the cheeks that were going to puff out, the chin that was going to double itself and maybe even triple itself. And the mind behind the face had nothing special in it, either. When he had first seen the quota lists the other day, Monsky had wondered if he couldn't get himself transferred to the English list so that he could be with Betsy. He was positive it could be finagled—but then he decided against it. There was no reason on earth why he should go to such trouble for the company of this simple-minded little girl.

"If you think it's time, Mr. Monsky," she said.

"Yes, I think it's time, I think it's high time!" What kind of damned foolishness was this? His farewell scene, and he was losing his temper? He forced his voice down. "So anyway, Betsy—I guess this is good-bye. Let me say what a pleasure it's been sharing this vacation cruise with you. I wish you luck in your new home in England."

"Camden, New Jersey," she said. "Martin will arrange it soon."

"I'm sure he will. I'm positive he will. He's obviously an enterprising fellow, your Martin. It's too bad we won't be meeting someday."

"Why shouldn't you meet? You've got your American quota number. You'll be coming to New Jersey eventually."

"It could be. I've always been something of a world traveler. A rolling stone. A butterfly flitting from flower to flower. But even if I *did* find my way to beautiful, gracious old Camden—what's the guarantee you'd be interested in seeing me? The chances are you won't even remember who I am. You know what they say about shipboard friendships."

"It wouldn't be that way with me, Mr. Monsky." A flush

came over her cheeks. "How could I ever forget you? How could you even *think* such a thing?"

He watched her quietly for a while, and then he said, "So good-bye, Betsy," and started to turn away. But she wouldn't let go of his hand.

"What are you going to do?" she said.

"Go to my cabin, pack my things, face the lackeys of French officialdom, leave this ship—a little older than when I came aboard, but still with a smile on my lips."

"When you get to Paris, I mean. What are you going to do for—for a living? You don't think you'll be—you'll be—" She broke off, her face growing red.

The funny part of it was he was feeling embarrassed, too. On *this* subject? After all these years? "If I'm not mistaking you, Betsy, what you're asking me is am I planning to go back to my Old Life?" He laughed. "You don't have to worry, believe me. Whatever I do, I'll keep myself one step ahead of the jaws of destruction. That's how I managed my life up to now, and it hasn't been such a bad system. I'm still around, right? Which is more than a *lot* of people can say!"

"You've got so much to offer, Mr. Monsky. So much you could do with your life. I *know* what's in you!"

She knew what was in him. Monsky could have burst out laughing. Did she know what he'd been wishing for her all these weeks? Did she know the fate he would have cheerfully condemned her to, just to please his inflated ego?

"You're a nice girl, Betsy," he said, "but about me you don't know a thing—"

The loudspeaker interrupted him. It announced that the French officials had just come aboard, and a line would form immediately in the main lounge.

"So for the fiftieth time, Betsy," he said, "and also for the last time—good-bye. Drop me a line when the baby comes, will you? Otherwise I'll spend the rest of my life wondering if it's a boy or a girl."

"I'll drop you a line, Mr. Monsky."

"And one more thing—" He was all set to tell her that the time had come to call him Leon, maybe they knew each other well enough by now. But then he stopped himself, realizing that she had been right all along. For her he must always be Mr. Monsky. Monsky or Leon to everybody else— but who else called him Mr. Monsky and meant it?

And so he left her and headed down to his cabin. And on the way he asked himself the same question she had asked him. What now? Where are you going, Monsky? What plans have you got for your life?

She wanted him to "do" something with his life, to "offer" all those wonderful things that were in him. She wanted him to turn into a reformed character, a model citizen, a paragon. And he wondered if there was any chance that he could do it. *Would* he give up the Old Life? Had the influence of a good woman made Leon Monsky see the light?

"Why not, why not?" he asked himself. "I've tried everything else, haven't I?"

He was on the landing of B deck now. The door to his right would take him to the passageway where his cabin was located. But a thought struck him, and he went instead through the door to his left. At the end of this passageway he found the cabin he was looking for. He knocked on the door, saying to himself, "If he's in there, I'll do it. If he isn't, I won't bother."

But the door opened. Emma Schwarzkopf was standing in the doorway, and behind her, sitting on the edge of the bed, was Schwarzkopf himself.

Monsky put on his biggest grin and stepped into the room. He felt like an actor moving into the spotlight to play his big scene. "Excuse me for disturbing you, Schwarzkopf—my apologies, Mrs. Schwarzkopf—but I'm leaving the ship in a little while, and I didn't want to go without telling you something."

Schwarzkopf was getting to his feet now. His face was turning gray, positively gray.

"What I want to tell you, Schwarzkopf," and Monsky stuck out his hand and walked right up to the old man, "it's been a pleasure traveling with you. Listening to your opinions on the political situation, taking your money in bridge—only there *was* no money, but you follow my meaning. And all the other interesting experiences we've shared on this trip, you and me. So anyway, before we break up this relationship for good, I want you to know that any little disagreements and misunderstandings we've had are all forgiven and forgotten, as far as I'm concerned. Absolutely and positively forgotten, you follow me? I'll never bring them up again to anybody. That's a promise, Schwarzkopf—and on Monsky's promises you can invest money."

He grabbed hold of Schwarzkopf's hand and shook it up and down as hard as he could and made his exit from the cabin.

He went to his own cabin and packed his bag and carried it up the stairs to the main lounge. A long line was winding around the room already. He stood at the end of it, and pretty soon a dozen or so people were standing behind him. It was going to be slow and boring, he realized. But he had waited in plenty of lines in his day—with good news at the end of some of them, bad news at the end of others—and he could think of much more unpleasant ways to pass the time. The secret of line-waiting was to turn the occasion into a social one—you had to meet congenial people, enliven the hours with conversation, with exchanges of views. Monsky looked around now and couldn't see anyone he knew within calling distance. Even Fischel the Witch would have been welcome at this moment.

Then he noticed the man who was standing in front of him. A small man around his own age with a round chubby face, a thin black mustache, and black hair slicked down and shiny—maybe a wig, Monsky thought. He was wearing a green and brown checked sports jacket, this little man, and instead of a necktie he had a silk scarf, yellow with red polka dots, knotted up to his throat. Monsky couldn't understand why he hadn't noticed him before—he was certainly noticeable.

And there was something in his eyes, a kind of inviting little gleam, which seemed to suggest that he wouldn't be unsympathetic to conversation.

"It's a nice day, isn't it?" Monsky said.

The ice was broken. Monsky held out his hand. "Monsky," he said. "Leon."

The little man shook his hand, gave a quick bow from the waist, and clicked his heels together. Very neatly done. "Winkel," he said. "Ludwig."

He waited a moment, with a smile on his face, as if he expected Monsky to have some kind of reaction.

Not knowing what it was supposed to be, Monsky said, "You're going to France for the first time?"

"Are you joking?" Winkel said, with a laugh. "Paris is like a second home to me!"

"You've done business there maybe?"

"For some it's business. It all depends on your attitude,

how dedicated you are. For me it's an art, a way of life, a religion. To speak plainly, I'm an actor. You've seen me in films, no doubt. That's why my face looked familiar to you and you had a feeling you'd heard my name before. I've been on location in Paris many times. I couldn't even count how many times. I know all the ins and outs there. My French is practically perfect. I'll give you the names of some nice restaurants if you'd like. Cheap but first-rate."

"Thanks, I wouldn't mind. I've been to Paris myself, of course, but it was a long time ago—"

"Think nothing of it, happy to oblige." Winkel gave a wave of his hand.

"Do you expect to find work as an actor in France?" Monsky asked. "Won't it be hard for a German, considering the international situation?"

"The international situation is exactly what's going to make it easy," Winkel said. "German actors will be the most priceless commodities on the market in the next few years. The studios won't be able to get enough of them. The demand there's going to be for Nazis alone! Not to mention concentration camp inmates, underground resistance leaders, Austrian aristocrats, and so on. My God, to be a German actor is the great opportunity of the future. And who says it has to stop with France, either?"

"I don't follow you exactly."

"Hollywood, my friend, Hollywood! Mark my words, in another year or so—especially if the war breaks out—they'll be needing hundreds of Nazis in Hollywood every week. Wait a second—I suddenly got an idea. Yes—absolutely—why not?" He was peering at Monsky, pushing his face close, pulling it back, then nodding firmly. "Why shouldn't you pick up some of this easy money yourself, my friend? There's plenty for everybody, believe me. Not in featured roles like me, of course, but among the bit players."

"But I've never done any acting."

"Is that so? I could've sworn you had some experience in the profession. Something about the way you hold yourself— Well, it doesn't matter. You're a bright fellow, you can learn to say 'Heil Hitler' as good as anybody else. I'll tell you what —tomorrow morning I'll take you along with me and introduce you to some people at the studio."

"You'd really do that for me? That's very kind of you—"

"Think nothing of it, happy to oblige. We sailed together

on the *Franz Joseph,* didn't we? If that isn't a bond, I don't know what is."

Then Winkel began to tell stories about his experiences on the stage and in films, about René and Louis, about Erich and Max and "that bastard Jannings," and Monsky listened with fascination, hardly knowing that the time was passing.

Finally they reached the deck and presented their suitcases and their papers to the officials. Soon the formalities were over, and they stood in another line, and in a little while Monsky and his new friend were strolling down the gangway together, arm in arm. And Monsky, while he was nodding and saying, "You don't mean it, Ludwig!" was telling himself, as he had told himself many times in the past, that Leon Monsky always lands on his feet.

*   *   *

The Channel crossing was rocky. A squall blew up halfway, the ship creaked and shuddered through the jagged waves. Yet this didn't prevent the passengers from going out on deck and leaning on the railing while the wind slashed across their faces. Two hundred and twenty-three of them were left aboard, and few of them felt like spending these last hours indoors.

Under the covered section of the main deck Schwarzkopf strode up and down. What a mood he was in! What a tremendous mood! The whole world was looking good today.

Aaron and the boys were with him. He was making a speech to them about business conditions in the British Isles. The loss of imperial markets once the war broke out. The increasing need for experienced retailers to make the most out of goods in short supply. "According to all my connections," he was saying, "London could use a first-class retail house—fine goods for every pocketbook—the Schwarzkopf quality and stylishness applied to English conditions. A small operation at first—just a couple of floors, a selection of popular items—but the growth possibilities are terrific. Just a little bit of capital, a small initial investment, could get it off the ground."

Sometimes, while he was talking, he noticed that Aaron and the boys weren't next to him anymore. They were lagging behind, or they had stopped to look out at the sea. It was a little annoying. Weren't they interested in their future? But he couldn't stay annoyed at them for long, not on a day like today. So he raised his voice until they caught up with him.

"And the costs wouldn't be prohibitive, either," he said. "An enterprise like the one I'm talking about could be financed in London for about one-third as much as it would cost in New York—"

Already he saw it in his mind. The busy counters, the people swarming in, his office on the top floor—a big mahogany desk like the one he used to have in Berlin. His luck was turning, he felt it in his bones. Look how Monsky had come to him this morning—

He shook his head, felt his face burning a little. With contempt—yes, contempt was what he was feeling. That no-good bum! A big talker like all of his kind, but when it comes to *doing* anything, naturally he gets cold feet. Standing up to a man like Bruno Schwarzkopf—who could believe for one minute that a *schlemiel* like Monsky was capable of such a thing? It was a joke. You had to laugh.

Schwarzkopf heard a laugh breaking out of him. A woman turned from the railing and gave him a surprised look. An elderly woman, she looked as if she'd been crying. On a day like this? When the whole world was opening up, when the future couldn't look brighter, and a man could *be* somebody again?

He laughed again and went on walking. Suddenly he almost liked this ship. He had actually developed a fondness for it. Now that the undesirable elements had been put ashore—

He saw that Aaron and the boys were lagging far behind again. He called out to them, "Why so lazy? Are you afraid of a little exercise?"

He waited till they caught up to him, then he took a boy by each arm. "Now, I was discussing the economic situation in London. Actually, we're a lot better off than we would've been if we'd ended up in New York. In England it isn't strikes, strikes, strikes every time you look around. The English know how to handle their working classes—"

"Bruno! Bruno!"

It was Emma, coming out of the lounge, bustling up to him. "I just can't close my suitcase," she said. "Would you come down to the cabin and help me?"

Suitcases. He was making an important point, a vital point that affected the future of them all, and she interrupts him with suitcases. "God damn it," he felt like shouting at her, "can't you see I'm in the middle of saying something? At your age haven't you learned any manners?"

The words were in his mouth—why didn't he say them? He looked into Emma's face, into her stupid, wrinkled pudding-face, and he thought, Who is she? Nobody! Nobody! But he didn't say a thing to her, and instead he turned away his eyes.

"All right, all right," he said, "let's look at the suitcases— since you're too helpless to do anything for yourself—"

He followed her off the deck and down the stairs. Ashamed, he kept thinking. In front of *her*. Because every time she looked at him, it all came tumbling into his mind again. All over again he was living it—throwing his arms around her so tightly, weeping into her chest. Him—Bruno Schwarzkopf! Shedding tears like a baby, that was bad enough, but letting *her* see him do it— It's all right, Bruno. I'm here, I'm here—

Since it happened, nearly a week ago, she had never mentioned it to him. Not once had she reminded him of it. Could he even be sure that she remembered? But that was the worst of it—it didn't matter if she remembered. *He* remembered. He turned sick inside whenever that memory came to him. And he knew it would keep on coming to him, every day for the rest of his life.

Connections. Initial investments. Fine goods for every pocketbook. Who was he fooling, anyway? "You're an old man, Schwarzkopf," he told himself, "and you'll never be somebody again."

* * *

In Plymouth Harbor the *Franz Joseph* anchored a couple of miles offshore. Aaron stood at the railing and looked out at the land, barely visible in the late afternoon mist. The wind had dropped and the sea was calm again, but there was no sun, only a chalky sky. Off in the distance the hills, shooting abruptly out of the water, were chalky, too. The town, the harbor, the clusters of houses were splashes of color against the background of gray. Who ever would have guessed, Aaron thought, that the Promised Land was made of chalk?

There was still plenty of time, he knew. The ship wouldn't

actually be going into port; in an hour or so the remaining passengers would be taken ashore in a tender and processed officially in the Plymouth customs shed. Aaron was happy just to stand here and look. He felt that he could have gone on doing this forever.

He was looking at the answer to a prayer. That night a week ago he had stood on deck in the mist, knowing that every hope was gone, praying for a miracle. And the miracle had come—God couldn't have delivered it more promptly. How perfectly logical, almost commonplace, it seemed to Aaron now. After everything he had done on this ship, what he had learned, what he had become—obviously God wasn't going to let all that go to waste. The Almighty had to have more sense.

A messenger boy tapped Aaron gently on the arm. "Mr. Muller would like to see you, sir."

For a moment Aaron felt a little weak. Then he realized that the captain *couldn't* have any kind of unpleasant news for him. Probably he just wanted to say good-bye. After that cataclysm of unreason in his office, he wanted to end things on a polite and reasonable note.

Aaron took the familiar route to the top of the ship. He found Muller at his desk. Should he sit down or remain standing? He decided to indulge himself in one final impertinence. He sat down.

"You've got a message from the captain?" he asked.

"You'll get no more messages from the captain. Soon you won't be his passengers—and he concerns himself only with his passengers. This message is from me." Muller paused a moment, without expression. "I like to tie up loose ends, Mr. Peyser. I have an orderly mind. You have that kind of mind yourself, if I'm not mistaken. Now tell me—isn't there one loose end *you've* been worried about, one unanswered question that's been nagging at you?"

"I can't think of any."

"Haven't you asked yourself even once—that night, the night those boys made their absurd attempt to break into our ammunitions store, why was I waiting for them here? Why wasn't the regular guard on duty? How did I know there was going to be trouble?"

Aaron forced his voice to stay casual. He wasn't going to give a thing to Muller, not at this late date. *"Did* you know?"

"Oh yes, I knew, all right. I was informed of the whole

422

scheme, in detail. Aren't you curious to hear who the informer was?"

It was a while before Aaron could speak. "Not particularly."

"But I can't let you leave this ship with that question unanswered. Or have you guessed the answer already? Yes—I really think you have. Your face tells me that you know what I'm about to say."

"No—"

"I'll say it anyway. Then you'll call me a liar. Oh yes, no doubt about it. But later, when you look into the matter more closely, you'll realize that I was telling the truth."

Then Muller leaned forward, and there was a smile on his face. . . .

And ten minutes later Aaron was moving down the corridor, through the door marked "Keep Out," down the stairs. The last time he would ever travel this route, he thought. He remembered the first time. He remembered how his stomach had throbbed. Why should the captain be sending for *him?* And then he read the radiogram—his sponsor, Mr. Gustav Selig, of Selig and Kepler—a short, stout man with a mole on his chin—well-meaning old Mr. Selig, this is where your kindness has brought me. This is why the captain sent for me the first time, so many weeks ago—he hemmed and hawed, he coyly hid his face, and then at last he showed it to me—and the total despair he showed me turned out to be *my* despair all along—

No! No, it wasn't true—Muller had to be lying. Not David, my son. Not my gentle, modest, serious-minded son. And the memories crowded in on Aaron. David as a small boy, holding Papa's hand, walking together in the park on Sunday mornings—those wide, solemn eyes looking up at him with so much trust. David coming home from school on that terrible day, struggling to hold in his tears, finally giving up the struggle—"They hate me, Papa! I'm diseased! I contaminate them!" Holding the boy in his arms then, saying over and over, "It's all right—you don't have to stay there— it'll be all right—" And at the very beginning of this voyage, too—David alone with him in the cabin, telling him about the old man's recklessness, promising to keep quiet, "You can count on me, Papa!" And his eyes still as wide and solemn as when he was a little boy.

No, I don't have to believe such a thing about my son,

Aaron told himself. Not now, not now, with the Promised Land in sight. . . .

Aaron found David and Joshua together in their cabin. "Go to your mother, Joshua," he said. "She may need help with the packing."

"She's been finished for an hour, Papa—" But Joshua stopped himself, looked at Aaron for a moment, then got up quickly and walked out of the cabin.

Aaron locked the door. He turned to face David, who was standing in the center of the room. "I've just come from Muller," Aaron said. He repeated what Muller had told him—and all the time he kept his eyes fixed on David's face.

And before he had finished talking, Aaron knew that Muller had told him the truth.

David tried to smile. "But Papa—that's the craziest thing I ever heard—"

Aaron waited and said nothing.

"You couldn't believe such a thing, Papa," David said. "That Muller—he hates all of us—you especially. There's nothing he wouldn't do to hurt you—"

Aaron waited.

"Papa, how could I do a thing like that? To Peter. He was my best friend. I never *had* such a close friend. Papa, he was like my brother—"

Then David stopped talking, and his face puckered up, it suddenly became the face of a bawling child. "All right, Papa—all right, I did it—all right, all right—"

Aaron came forward. He hit David across the face with the flat of his hand. He saw the red welt springing out on David's cheek, and he felt his hand stinging. That's for Peter, he thought. For Peter Einhorn, who wanted to live, who could have done something *real* with his life.

He hit the boy again, harder than the first time. Deliberately harder. He wanted to hear a loud crack this time, and he heard it. Then whimpering came out of the boy's mouth, and his arms were lifted convulsively as a shield. That's for Peter's father, Aaron thought. For the rabbi, who tried to be kind and decent and serve God and do his best by his children. Who loved his son and didn't want to lose him—any more than I do—

He brushed aside David's arm and hit him again. For Naomi, Aaron thought, who's only a child, who's too young to have her family smashed around her. And with this blow all the rage and the fury was out of him. It had come from nowhere, it disappeared just as quickly. And Aaron felt exhausted, more exhausted than he had ever felt in his life.

"Why?" he said. "Please, David—tell me why."

The boy still had his arms in front of his face. He lowered them slowly. "Papa—I don't know!"

My God, Aaron thought, he's only a baby. He held out his arms, and after one long, frightened stare his son came into them, let them close around him. And a moment later sobs were retching out of him.

"I'm sorry, Papa—I never meant—I'm sorry, I'm sorry—"

Aaron held his son in his arms. "It's all right," he said. "I'll help you. You'll be all right."

Over and over, while they clung together, Aaron said these words. And all the time he was saying them, he was telling the truth to himself in silence. It won't be all right, he told himself. There *is* no making this all right. There *is* no being sorry for this. This boy says something today—but who can know what he'll do tomorrow? He's tasted blood now. What he did once he could do again. At any moment. For any reason. For no reason. He's a time bomb, and nobody can know when he's set to explode.

I'll have to watch him every minute, Aaron thought. That will be my life now. Doing my best with him, trying to help him, trying to make him change—but watching him every minute, hoping to keep the explosion from happening. And never knowing, from one day to the next, if today isn't going to be the day.

The voice began to speak over the loudspeaker. "The tender has tied up on the starboard side. Passengers will gather on the main deck for disembarkation. Disembarkation begins in five minutes."

Aaron let go of his son. He unlocked the cabin door. In a few seconds he was surrounded by his family. David merged with all the others. Suitcases had to be carried, heads had to be counted, passports and papers had to be checked and rechecked. Just the way it had been when they first came aboard.

Up on the main deck the crowd was large. More than two hundred people squeezed together watching that little red boat which bobbed up and down like a cork in a tub of water. And everyone carrying suitcases, wearing coats—the ones who *had* coats—chattering, laughing, some of them crying.

Then the voice came over the loudspeaker. "Passengers will please move by twos through the ropes where the officer is standing—"

In the pushing and scurrying that followed, Aaron was separated from Sophie. He found himself next to the Tannenbaum girl. Her face was flushed, and it seemed to him that her stomach was larger than ever.

"I'm sorry there isn't more light," she said. "Plymouth Harbor is supposed to be beautiful."

It would have been rude for Aaron to say nothing. "You'll be staying in London, I suppose?"

"Until my husband can arrange for me to go to America. It won't be too long, I hope. If it isn't in the next few weeks—" She looked quickly down at her stomach, and he could see the troubled frown cross her face.

"Even if it isn't, you don't have to worry," Aaron said. "The hospitals and the doctors in England are very good, they say."

"Oh, yes—I'm not worried. *Where* you have the baby—that isn't what matters. If it's healthy, and you can be with it—"

A smile appeared on her face. It had so much happiness in it, that smile. So much peace. And no fear at all. People live in different worlds, Aaron thought. Nobody's ever really in the same boat as anybody else.

They had reached the ropes now. Second Officer Dietrich helped Mrs. Tannenbaum across the swaying wooden bridge that led to the tender. Aaron followed her. At last he set foot on the little boat's deck.

And now I'm off the *Franz Joseph,* he thought. Officially I'm no longer on German soil. This was freedom, this was what he'd been yearning for and fighting for. He remembered the crack of his hand against his son's cheek. Why, for God's sake, did he ever have to learn the truth? A fool's paradise is better than a wise man's hell.

But God hadn't meant it to be that way. Oh yes, he understood it all now. The night Peter died—standing on the deck, praying, congratulating himself on his strength. And when the news came a few hours later, telling himself that God had answered his prayer. Nothing must go to waste, he had told himself. God has created a world that makes sense. But God, in His infinite wisdom, didn't want him to go on living with a delusion, no matter how soothing it might be. And so God acted quickly to impress the truth on him, to show him that prayers *don't* get answered, that the world *doesn't* make sense, that what happens to people is a matter of utter indifference to the Almighty. The Promised Land is always in sight, always shimmering on the horizon, but no matter how close you seem to be getting to it, you must always go through one more horror. Otherwise you might find happiness and peace, luxuries that God never intended you to enjoy but only to pine for from the wrong side of the shop window.

Suddenly Sophie was by his side. "Aaron, are you all right? You look so—you look as if you've seen something horrible!"

"I've seen nothing. There's nothing for you to worry about."

"No, there never is. *You* always do the worrying. I'd give so much if I had the strength to help you—"

"You've been helping me all my life. Why, we never would have got married if you hadn't had the strength to stand up to your father."

"My one great triumph," she said. "I've been resting on my laurels ever since."

Suddenly she kissed him on the cheek. Then she took his arm and pulled him close. "We're starting a new life now," she said. "I'll try to start new, too. I'll really try—"

A low humming noise was in his ears. The engines had started on the tender. The wooden bridge had been pulled in, and the ropes were being hauled up the side of the big ship. Slowly the tender was pulling away, then faster and faster, chugging through the black water. Nobody around him, Aaron saw, was looking toward the port. Everybody had turned toward the *Franz Joseph*.

And he realized, as the distance increased, that he had never stood this far away from the ship before. He had never really seen it as he was seeing it now—that great white body spread against the horizon, those smokestacks rising to the sky, that flag flying in the breeze. And the distance grew greater and greater, and the mists began to close around that majestic form. The sea and sky seemed to disappear around it, and it was floating in the mist, riding on air like a ghost ship. Maybe the *Franz Joseph* didn't really exist.

Maybe everything that had happened on it was a bad dream after all.

But then, a few feet away from him, he saw David staring out into emptiness.

Aaron set his jaw and turned his face toward the shore.

FIFTEEN

EARLY one afternoon eight or nine days after the last passengers were disembarked from the *Franz Joseph,* Morrie sat alone in his London office. He was waiting for Aaron Peyser.

His office—"AJDA's London branch," as Al liked to call it—was really just one small, badly lighted room in an old building off Trafalgar Square. The color scheme was bilious, the bell didn't work half the time, and Morrie was glad he wouldn't be here in the winter because the little gas heater in the corner didn't look as if it could keep the mice warm. It was the best place he had been able to find on short notice.

His appointment with Aaron wasn't for five minutes. He knew Aaron would be on time. He was that kind of person—conscientious and polite, occasionally even to the verge of absurdity. In that respect almost a caricature of a German. In some other respects, too. But not in any respect that counted.

Morrie remembered his first sight of Aaron, in the customs shed at Plymouth. He had been struck immediately by how thin and tired he looked, how gray and unimpressive. This *couldn't* be the man he had talked to so many times over the ship's radio. But then they shook hands, and they talked for a while, and Morrie began to see that there *was* something about him. He still couldn't figure out just what it was, though. Aaron said very little, and said it all in such a diffident manner. Whatever was in him, it hardly showed on the surface at all.

The doorbell rang. Right on the dot, Morrie thought, looking at his watch.

He let Aaron in, noticing that he was wearing that same shabby gray suit he had been wearing every day since Plymouth. So far AJDA's resources for the new arrivals had run to food, lodging, and a little bit of carfare money—clothing, except in emergency cases, would just have to wait till later,

429

probably till jobs were found. Morrie wondered if Aaron would be insulted by an offer to stake him to a new suit. He had a feeling that he wouldn't be insulted, that he had already been insulted by experts and such an offer would seem to him like a very small pinprick. He would think it over carefully, Morrie guessed, and then he would suggest a new dress for his wife, instead.

Well, if he gave the right answer to what Morrie was planning to ask him this afternoon, he wouldn't be needing any loans.

"Good afternoon—Morris," Aaron said. They were on a first-name basis—Morrie had suggested it two days after they met—but it obviously didn't come easy to Aaron. He sat down stiffly on the other side of the desk wtith his knees together and his hands neatly folded in his lap. Like a good disciplined schoolboy, Morrie thought. They're a funny people, they really are.

"So how does life in London appeal to you so far?" Morrie asked.

Aaron looked grave. Every question you asked him got the same grave consideration and the same thorough, painstaking answer. In his slow, cautious, almost-accurate English he said, "Life in London is most pleasant and interesting for us all—" Then he explained in detail what they were all doing. His wife's mother and father sat every day in the little park outside their flat and fed the pigeons—unless it rained, of course, in which case they sat in their room and looked out of the window. It was a strange life for his father-in-law, who had always been such an active man; it did seem as if he were beginning to feel his age. His wife, Aaron went on, was keeping quite busy. It wasn't easy to maintain a small flat for six people with no servants and very little money. His sons, he went on, took long walks every day, already they had visited all the principal historical monuments. The oldest intended to find work, and the youngest was anxious to go to school, and so in preparation for this they were attempting to learn the English language from a book; every night Aaron listened to them do their conjugations.

The family chronicle came to a stop. Aaron fell silent but kept his grave expression and didn't take his eyes from Morrie's face.

"Why I asked you to drop in this afternoon," Morrie said. "Our office in New York has come up with an idea,

430

and we'd like to talk to you about it. What it comes down to is this—a lot of refugees have been coming to London lately, and if war breaks out there are going to be even more of them. More than New York will get, considering American immigration policy. So my boss, Al Margolinski, has suggested to the Board of Trustees that AJDA should maintain a permanent London office, a kind of adjunct to our Department of Refugee Affairs. To perform the same function that I'm performing right now, only a lot broader, of course. I mean, you'd have a few assistants and an office that's more than a broom closet—"

"*I* would have, Morris?"

"I'm sorry, didn't I make it clear yet? AJDA wants *you* to take charge of this. The salary won't be exactly princely, I'm afraid—you'll find out the true meaning of working for a non-profit organization—but they won't let you starve, either."

In a low voice Aaron said, "Why this offer to me? What are my qualifications?"

"You've got plenty of qualifications. You're a German, and you know what's going on there. You speak English well. You're a refugee yourself, so you're familiar with the problems. You've had years of management experience in a successful business. But even *those* qualifications aren't the really important ones."

"What then are the important ones?"

"The man who holds this job will be dealing with people who have been uprooted, terrorized, stripped of everything they possess, thrown without preparation into a world where they don't know anybody and can't speak the language. This job will take a man who can win the confidence of people like that, who can give purpose and direction to their lives, who can lead them."

"You think I can lead them?"

"I know you can. I've talked to a lot of people about you. People who were on the *Franz Joseph*."

Aaron was smiling, but it wasn't a very happy smile. "A leader must have a goal, an objective. He cannot lead people in a circle. He cannot lead others unless he knows where he himself is going."

"Everyone I've talked to mentions your firmness—"

"Firmness? Yes, to get off that ship in safety—it wasn't difficult to be firm in *that* ambition. But to tell people the

431

purpose and direction which their lives should take? Morris —I don't know any more the purpose and direction of *my* life. I have seen such things. I have learned what people may become. People dear to me, whose lives are in my keeping— And I myself, I cannot even be sure what *I* have become. I am so—so torn away from myself that I cannot tell you with any conviction who I am."

"Your instincts are basically sound. I'm sure they'll see you through."

"No, no, you make it too easy. My instincts! A man's instincts can change, like any other part of him. They can be bent—they can be crushed if the weight is too heavy. I sailed on the *Franz Joseph,* and this has left me wondering if I believe any more in—in life. You want me to give purpose to other lives when I don't myself believe in life."

"You've been hurt, that's all. You're healthy, and your wounds will heal."

"I would like to feel confident of that, as you do. I would like to accept that my—my unbelief comes from inside of me, from what you call my wounds. But you see, what I fear is that it comes from outside of me. It is not an illness but the natural response, the only response, to the world that I have learned to know. Yes, this is what frightens me—not myself but the world."

"You don't have to think about that world anymore. It's all behind you now."

"Behind me? Morris—my friend—there *is* such a thing as evil. Evil is *real.* The earth has opened up, and the monsters are crawling out. And they will fasten upon us, they will suck the health and the decency out of us. Beginning with the young, the helpless and innocent young— No, this cannot be swept aside with soothing words. No, not even with the fine humanitarian work of organizations such as yours. All of this seems to me most useless, most superfluous, when I remind myself what is coming."

He broke off, then smiled diffidently again. "Well, you have made a most generous offer, and I must consider it. Perhaps these feelings I have are temporary only. Perhaps, as you suggest, once I realize that the worst is over— But there, you see, is the difficulty. I often feel the temptation to say these words, 'The worst is over—nothing more will happen.' If only I could say them and believe them. But you see, I know they cannot be true. I know I have not yet begun to know the worst. This world of mine—of ours is living on—on a time bomb. Somewhere beneath our feet, unheard by us, unseen, this time bomb ticks away. And one day, suddenly, when we expect it least—" He shook his head, then rose to his feet. "But I will consider your offer. How long before I must give you my answer?"

"I don't know—a week, maybe?"

"A week will be ample time." He shook Morrie's hand in his precise solemn way. "Thank you, Morris," he said, and Morrie could see that he was making a point, out of good manners, of using the first name.

Aaron left the office, but Morrie couldn't sit down again. He couldn't understand why Aaron's words had upset him so much. Only a week ago he had said things to Ruth which weren't too different. Just as bitter, just as fearful about the future. Yet when Aaron expressed these fears, they didn't sound the same.

It was part of the peculiar feeling Morrie had had about this man from the moment they finally met. In Aaron's presence Morrie felt like a very young child who didn't know anything at all about life. He felt that Aaron had looked into the face of something and had seen there— He didn't want to see what Aaron had seen. He didn't want to know about it.

It came over him that he had to talk to Ruth. The phone call would cost a fortune, but he had to hear her voice.

He didn't hear it very clearly, when the call finally went through. The connection was lousy, the static cut out half her words. And there was nothing special in what they talked about, either. He didn't say a thing about Aaron. He listened while she told him how the kids were doing in day camp, which of the girls she'd been seeing this week, the plot of a movie that was playing at the Loew's Orpheum. Foolishness, all of it—but as he listened, his anxiety began to melt away.

Then in a hesitant voice she said, "Have you decided anything yet about your job?"

He started to answer that he was still thinking it over, but suddenly he realized that he wouldn't be telling her the truth.

Aaron's words came back to him. "The earth has opened up, and the monsters are crawling out." Just to remember this made his flesh creep. My God, if he believed what Aaron believed, he couldn't go on living. But he *didn't* believe it— whatever he may have told Ruth last week. Aaron Peyser's vision of horror made no sense to him at all. What *had*

433

Aaron looked into the face of, except his own tormented imagination? Life wasn't like that. Life was—life—

All right, life was full of pain and evil. But there was hope, too. And a man could work to make the world better.

He began to laugh. Let's face it, he told himself, you're an optimist. It's an incurable disease.

And into the phone Morrie said, "I guess I'll hang on at AJDA awhile longer. The Army'll get me soon enough, anyway."

*   *   *

Aaron walked through the busy London street. As usual, he had too many impressions, they came thick and fast—the buses swinging dangerously around corners, the shop windows loaded with beautiful things, the policemen in their tall strange hats, the news vendors with cryptic messages scrawled in front of their stands. It was all so confusing, he still wasn't able to sort it out.

He wanted to try, however. He hoped he could be here a long time and finally come to understand. One thing seemed clear to him even now. These people were happy. Oh yes, some of the faces were pinched, mean, angry, discontented—but over it all he saw happiness.

Or maybe the happiness wasn't in the faces but in himself.

How could that possibly be? He remembered what he had just said to Morris Feldman. "The earth has opened up, and the monsters are crawling out." A shocked look had come to Morris Feldman's face. A good man—but so young, such a baby. He found those words melodramatic maybe, exaggerated for effect. He hadn't lived in Germany for these last six years. He didn't see those policemen on the docks ripping open dresses. He never saw the smile on Muller's face. Or Peter Einhorn lying on that bed, his face as white as the pillow, his ruined family by his side. Or David— What could Morris Feldman know of melodrama, of exaggeration?

I know, Aaron thought. I know, God help me, what this world is like. How should happiness be possible for me? Why don't I cry out constantly in revulsion and in despair? Above all, why do I have this strange feeling at the core of me— this feeling of calm?

Maybe this feeling meant that he was blinding himself to reality, escaping from horror into dreams. He remembered what Carl Bender had said to him once—dear Carl, to whom he had hardly had a chance to say good-bye. "The human mind," Carl had said, "contains a mechanism which anesthetizes it against reality. Too much raw reality would destroy us."

Maybe that was happening to him. Yet he didn't think so. This strange unyielding calm—no anesthetic had produced it. For he felt its presence at precisely those moments when the anesthetic was having least effect, when reality had become most raw to him. He felt it not when the *Franz Joseph* was a dream for him, but when he knew most certainly that it existed, that all the dreaming of all the dreamers on earth couldn't wipe it out of existence. He knew then that the voyage had taken place and that the passengers, the crew, the captain were as real as this London pavement under his feet. And the place where the *Franz Joseph* was now, and the people who lived in that place, and the little murdering maniac who ruled that place, and the Jews who would never be able to leave that place—all this was real, inescapably real. And so was the world in which all this could be. And so was the son who waited for him at home. . . .

The calm was in him, he thought, because he *wasn't* going to block out the horror. The ship, the captain, Germany, the world—his son—he knew that he could accept it all, endure it all, *use* it all to arm himself against the future. Yes, life had fearful things in it, and some people were given more of them than their share—and this was unjust and bitter. But this was the way life was. To know this, to master this knowledge, brought the only kind of joy worth having—the joy that was at the heart of pain.

He had reached his street now, his old, heavy, unscrubbed block of flats. There was no elevator. He climbed four flights of stairs and started down the hallway toward his flat. At the door he paused and felt the clutch of fear at his heart that he knew he would never stop feeling till the day he died. Had it happened today? Had the time bomb exploded?

Then he heard Sophie's voice from behind the door. She was humming something—a tune he had heard many times before. Was it "Vienna, City of My Dreams"? The truth was all those old waltzes sounded the same to him.

He found himself smiling and humming along with her. And in this moment, as he opened the door, he decided to take the job that Morris Feldman had offered him. For practical reasons, first of all. With all his fine talk, he couldn't afford to stick up his nose at a steady income. But that wasn't the only reason, it wasn't only the money. To turn away from that job would be like—like telling himself that Sophie wouldn't be humming her waltz tomorrow. It would be like turning his life over to the time bomb. Too many people were doing that already—not so long ago he probably would have been one of them. No more, no more. Life was worth too much to him now. He intended to be happy in the face of the horror. Let God do His worst, he would have his life.

After all, another day had just been given to him. One more day snatched from the flames and presented to him. You don't quit while you're ahead. Not even when you know that the game is fixed. . . .